With A Borrowed Sword

*Book Eight
of the Souls of
the Saintlands*

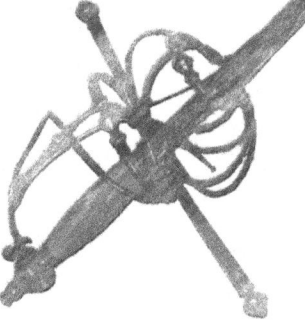

Tonya Adolfson

Published by Fantastic Journeys Publishing,
Boise, Idaho
PUBLISHING HISTORY
E-Book released through Kindle
Soft Cover trial edition June 2018
Mass market edition/ XXXXXX

Cover art: Photo of fabric by John Farmer
Created in Gimp 2.6 by John Farmer
Cover Art copyright by Fantastic Journeys Publishing
Interior Art by Lorraine Barraras, Suzette Urbano, and Erin Leach
Edited by Bri DeMaree, John Farmer, Gwen Bradley
Content copyright ©February 2018 Tonya Adolfson.

Published in the United States of America.

ISBN: 978-1-941276-03-7

The characters and events portrayed in this book are fictitious. Any
similarity to real persons, living or dead, common or deific, is coincidental
and not intended by the author, unless, of course, I know them.
No Augustinians were harmed in the making of this book, though a few
folks were roughed up a bit.

Also by Tonya Adolfson

The Souls of the Saintlands Series
Thine Enemy's Eyes
An Unpolished Gem
An Open Enemy
To Thine Own Self
Full of Sound and Fury
Determined to Be a Villain
All's Fair
With a Borrowed Sword
The Twofold Spirit*

Other Books
Surviving Your Own Creativity
Filling Up on 500 (With Todd Adolfson)

*Coming Soon

Reviews for the Souls of the Saintlands Series

Thine Enemy's Eyes

"I loved it I stayed up late several nights because I had to know what happened! It's a great read with excellent pacing and such entertaining and rich characters. I loved the rich world she created and the details used to make it stand out. I cannot wait to read the second book to learn more about the characters and places mentioned! I highly suggest this book."
Maryanne Durant, Amazon Review

"I cannot wait for the next book, and hopefully, subsequent books to follow."
Steve Nunez, Dragonfleet Studios

"Tonya Adolfson's debut novel is incredible! Full of intrigue, wildly imaginative characters and set in a medieval fantasy world of such authenticity it blew me away. I would heartily recommend this to anyone, and can't wait until the second novel comes out!"
I. J. Smethurst, author of the *E.D.F Chronicles*

"The plot has interesting twists and turns to keep you going straight through the book. When it ends, it leaves you wanting more."
Shelley Wolf, Amazon Review

"…good political intrigue… good action scenes… Not to mention one of the heaviest cliff hangers I've seen in a while."
The William Jones Review

"This is a very well written book, and has more plot twists and turns then I could count, but each one made me all the more eager to keep reading and see where the story would end up."
Durin Boge, Amazon Review

"I've read and reread this book 5 times now, it's easily one of my favorites! The characters are well developed, the twists and turns of the story kept me guessing, and the story line easily kept me wanting more."
Chalyse Padigimus, Amazon Review

"I'm a busy professional without a lot of time to read and this book absorbed my free time quite enjoyably for the past week. It has a touch of the almost magical within an imagined realm akin to medieval Europe. It has romance without focusing overly on the tawdry details as she has better things to do with the plotline. She develops several characters including their background in succinct but inviting storytelling and she juggles all of these characters' knowledge gaps about the current situation of court intrigue quite well. I'm really curious to see what book 2 has in store for me."

Sheila Harmon, Amazon Review

"Some trouble trying to make sense of the geography at first; however, not sticking to a real-world atlas got me over that hurtle. The story itself is very interesting with a nice twist at the end."

Rold DeDog, Amazon Review

"Tonya Adolfson has a way of drawing you in to make you feel like you are right there with the characters. I could not put this book down because I was so in love with the characters, I had to see what was coming next. She keeps you guessing until the very end. At times, I found myself a little sad for a particular character and then later rejoicing with them. I strongly recommend this book and cannot wait to see what happens next in book two."

Kayla, Amazon Review

"This is the first book from Tonya Adolfson I have read and believe me, it won't be the last. She caught my attention for the first page and held it through all the plots and conspiracies. The setting is wonderfully imagined and the characters fully realized, and believable. A brilliantly written fantasy tale filled with exciting intrigue. I'm glad I bought this and the second book together!"

Samuel Sturkie, Amazon Review

"Tonya has definitely found her place on my bookshelf. Now have the first 4 books! Can't wait for the next one!"

Spencer Maschek, Amazon Review

"This is a fantastic beginning to a fantastic series. I could not put it down. An amazing world full of detail."

Adam Wells-Grube, Amazon Review

"Ms. Adolfson has woven a web that will catch you while you're not looking. The characters are dynamic, with relationships we can relate to and an intrigue so deep that I could not put the book down until it was over; and I was begging for more. There are few books that I have found that suck me in the way this one does."
Hannah Therrien, Amazon Review

An Unpolished Gem

"In a perfect follow through to Thine Enemy's Eyes, Ms. Adolfson continues to illustrate just how sticky the politics and personalities of her world really can be. She never lets go of you, even after the book is done. Just when I think I have a character figured out, they surprise me; I can't even tell how many sides to this story there are. I can't wait for book three!"
Julien McBain, author *Ghosts of the Past*

"It is difficult for second books in a series to have the same weight as the first. This is the rarer case of the second book surpassing the first."
Christopher Garcia, editor of *the Drink Tank*

"This book is just as captivating as the first book in the series. Again, I was so enthralled with the characters, plot twists, and story line that I literally couldn't put it down and finished reading it in one day..."
Chalyse Padigimus, Amazon Review

"I love her writing style. She creates this world that becomes real to its readers. Oh, and then there are these great characters with such richness and depth you cannot help but to love and, in some cases, hate them! She has written it in such a way you have no idea where or who, if anyone, the main character will end up with. There is such a depth in the story you just cannot put it down. I read it in a matter of hours. I know these are books I am going to read again and again throughout the years. It has to be a great book for it to have that kind of status on my bookshelf."
Maryanne Durant, Amazon Review

"Love the way the characters grow and mature. Can't wait for the next book!"
Shelley Wolf, Amazon Review

An Open Enemy

"I have flown through these books. I totally love the tangled story with so many twists and turns. These are written by someone who knows how to keep their audience captive and I cannot wait for the 4th book!!! I have been dying to know what happens! This is definitely and awesome read every true fantasy buff should have on their shelf."
Maryanne Durant, Amazon Review

"By the time, I reached this novel I knew I was going to be a lifelong fan. These characters hold pieces of the human experience that filled me with a sense of hope, left me speechless and at times exhausted me. An emotional journey filled with adventure that I will treasure and live over and again every time I read it for the rest of my life."
Anonymous, Amazon Review

To Thine Own Self

The whole series of these books are very cleverly written and very in depth with rich detailing and character development. I absolutely have read these books over and over again. There is a lot of action within the pages along with laughter and pain. The books tend to suck you in and show a world unlike any other.
Maryanne Durant, Amazon Review

Tonya Adolfson will take you further down the rabbit hole with this latest installment. There's only one problem. Nothing can prepare you for hitting the bottom. Riveting and jaw dropping twists that only add to the story are in store for all. Be grateful Book 5 is already out, for the wait would have been unbearable.
Steve "Warky" Nunez, Dragonfleet Studios

This series is 11 stars out of 10!
With some books, it's hard to read them again once you know the plot twists. But with Tonya, she weaves her stories with such sublime brilliance that you want to read them again and again. Whether you're caught up in the beautiful dream like dialogue between two star struck characters or breathlessly page turning during the heart pounding action

scenes, you will love this must-have series! Spoiler Alert: The books just keep getting better and better!

Ethan Shaw

"To Thine Own Self" is a wonderful book full of love, sorrow, adventures, plot twists and turns, and everything you can imagine. Oh, how it ended! After finishing the first thing I said (with a smile) was "I need to go send 'hate mail' to Tonya." In the note, I told her "You're not my favorite Tonya right now." Now I wait patiently… well somewhat patiently, for book 5 to come out.

Stephanie Reese

"To Thine Own Self" is book 4 in the Saintlands series that Tonya Adolfson wrote. This is a wonderful series full of intrigue, adventure, love and magic of the medieval times. This book transports you into the lives of the people and the lands to the point where you don't want to put the book down to go to sleep. I can't wait for the next book to find out what happens next. Tonya has become one of my favorite authors and deserves to have all her books read and reread over and over again. Each book is really that good. Thank you so much Tonya for giving us the Saintlands series

Tish Firmiss

"To Thine Own Self" is a dynamic continuation in the "Souls of the Saintlands" series. A delicate balance of action that moves the story forward without feeling overwhelmed or bogged down. This book in particular adds great detail to both the land and characters that have been introduced. While this is the fourth book, she has not stopped adding new mysteries and plot changes that must only be resolved in the next book. I anxiously await the next release date so I might again join the world that has created and learn how everything is resolved. A truly wonderful book and series.

Krista Wells

I started this series wanting a good story, I'm now fully committed to this universe.

If you're this far along, you already know what a great story you've gotten yourself into. You know these characters are driven as only people can be, not just archetypes. What will stand out in this book is the attention to detail. It isn't just a dance, it's a dance you can visualize. It isn't just clothes, you can feel what the draping of the silk must feel like. Think of what your favorite characters and stories have come to mean to you over time. Now tell them to make room. By the end of this book, you will be hooked. There is no turning back.

Andrea Cortright, Animeland Convention Owner

Full of Sound and Fury

I have never felt such strong emotions from reading a book. I was immersed in this book so much so, that when a certain spoiler happens, I threw my book across the room and cried into my pillow.

After book shaming this title for a while, I had to know how this book was going to end.

Warning! The ending leaves you craving the next book and sobbing into your pillow. People who buy this book should invest in some tissues as well.

All in all, I'm excited to see where all of the relationships are heading, especially Myrgen and Catriona. I want them to be together, but after seeing that the author doesn't rule out ANYTHING from happening, I'm on edge hoping and wondering what fate will allow.

Steve "Warky" Nunez, Dragonfleet Studios

I am already reading it for the 2nd time. I love this book. Tonya Adolfson has done it again, another great book in the series. It starts with where the last book left off so that you are right back into the suspense of it all. She will hold you spell bound by what happens next and, by the end of this book, you will be wanting the next to keep the suspense going. Just when you think you know what will happen next, she throws you a curve and you keep reading to see what will happen. I love her books and can't wait for the next one to come out. I don't care how long it takes her to write it, I want to continue living in this series. What a great place to immerse yourself in. Thank you, Tonya. Please keep writing this series.

Tish Firmiss, Amazon Review

The game is afoot!

We know what to expect from just about everyone, so nothing new on the characters. We've finally settled in to a few less surprises from our friends and focus more on moving the story along. And move it does!

The curtain is pulled back on the pantheons. We're getting A LOT more of the spiritual story than some might be comfortable with, but if people didn't see that writing on the wall by now, they haven't been paying attention. I like that it's ALL of them addressed pretty fairly, not just one or the other. And we're starting to see that no one belief is necessarily right or wrong (they're all right AND wrong), they all have their nuances. They have been part of the story the entire time. I'm happy to finally see them more prominent.

There wasn't the rip-roaring page turner that the previous books have been. I was able to sleep at night reading this one but make no mistake: the blazing fire has only transformed into an intense smolder. The honeymoon is over, but the relationship is only just getting started!

Bring on book 6!!

Andrea Cortright, Animeland Convention Owner

Words can't even begin to justifiably escribe the sheer awesomeicity of this book series. Tonya builds a lore-filled world in a way that few others can achieve with masterful control of her characters. And just when you think you have a handle on things, she throws so many swerves, even Vince Russo would end up with whiplash. But everything that happens keeps you wanting to come back for more. Can't wait to see what she conjures up next.

Richard Englebert

To my fantastic editing team, Gwen, John, and Bri. Thank you for helping make this book worth reading.

Acknowledgments:

First and foremost, I'd like to thank all the people who were inspirations for this book:

Gwen for Gwen, John for Raven, Dartanian for Alexander, Jeff for James, Misha for Emmy, Morgan for Alan and Johannes, Rod for Xeno, Shanna for Fierah, Stephanie for Belladonna, Erik for Dom, Jared for Draethen, Dave for Octavius, Morgan Wolf for Morgan Wolf, Aaron for Duncan, Adam P for Ambroise, John for Myrgen, David for Henri, Jennifer for Ce'Nedra, Daddy for Thessius, Kim for Ysabel, Joe for Nicaise, Jenn for Flora, Aggie for Aggie, Allan Hobbs for Allen Hobbs, Andrea for Aislyn, and all the hundreds of friends and family that have been contributors to this book. Your work has been amazing and your lives inspiring.

A big shout out to the most amazing editors a gal could have: Gwen Bradley has helped with this project for over 15 years and still comments on the initial drafts to this day. Also, thanks to John Farmer for always helping with the read throughs. And Stephanie Reese, you are beyond priceless.

Thanks to Shannon Galarneau for being my agent and helping me fulfill the dream of Fantastic Journeys Publishing. I'd also like to thank Steve "Warky" Nunez for all his enthusiastic support.

And finally, to my wonderful family: Morgan and Misha, for being so tolerant of Mommy's work; to my Daddy, Ray Lamar Manley, for inspiring me to tell stories for the sheer pleasure of my audience; to my Mom, Rosemary Virginia Manley, for reading historical romances; and to the Great and Powerful Todd, for being everything a Prince needs to be.

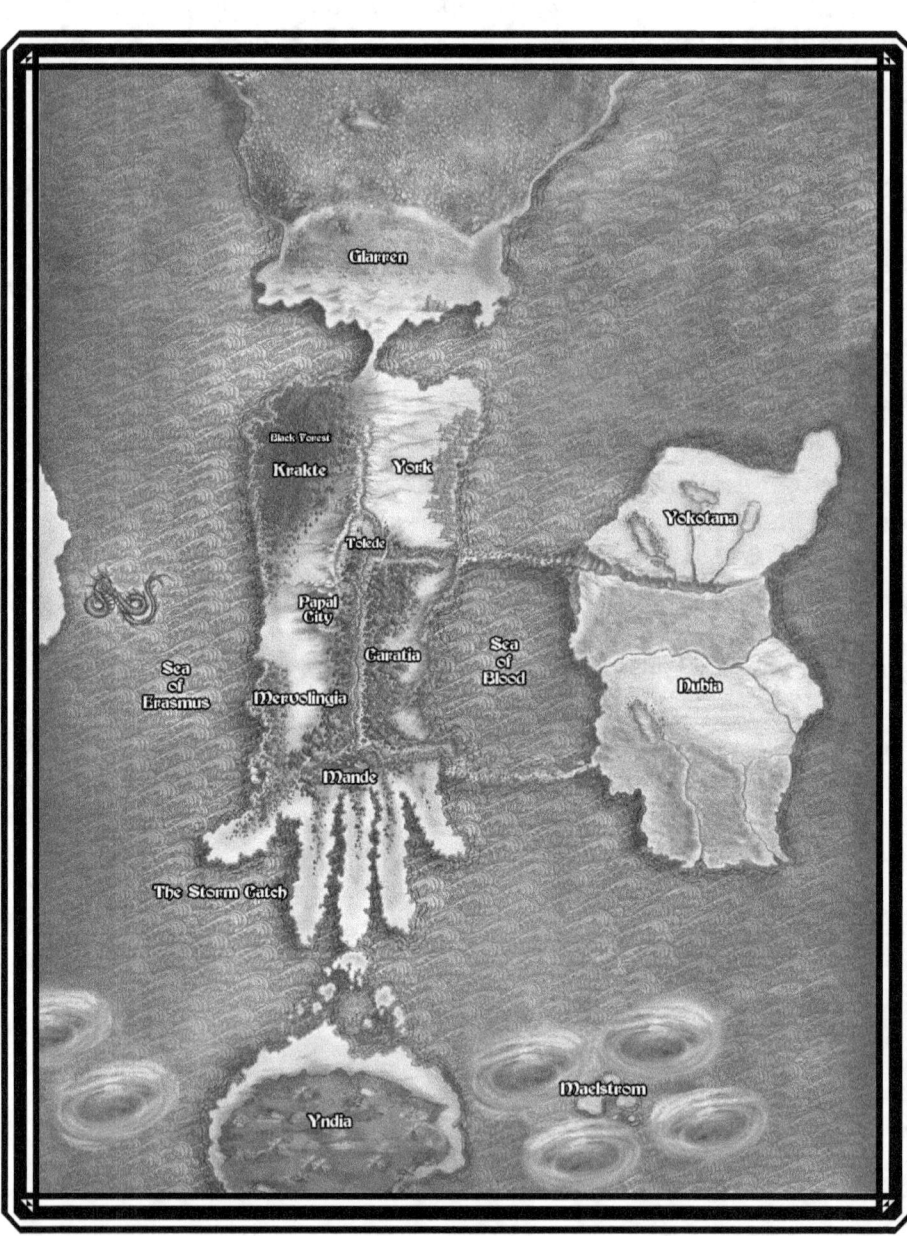

Sovereignlumen

Intro:

The Forty-Five Voices was written by Setsuko Miyako Yamauchi, also known as Snow in the Covenant of Persephone. She left Yokotama in 1207 to travel the world, for in her homeland, language dictated your status. The Empress Wen Kanong Jiang spoke all the languages of the world but one: the tongue of the western mage. As she did not have the Gift, she forbade herself to learn it. Miyako was found to have the Gift and was sent forth to learn it.

While at the Covenant, she also learned of the ways of battle in the Soulless War and returned in 1308, after the death of her half-giant husband Eirdrin. The Empress taught her all the languages she knew in order to complete Miyako's ascension to the throne. Once this knowledge was passed, Miyako escorted her body and spirit to the Air Dragons. There, the Empress Kanong transformed into an air dragon and was welcomed as an advisor to the people of Yokotama.

Miyako wrote several books on life, honor, warfare, and peace while Empress. She died in 1504, having passed her knowledge on to a young transgender woman named Shiang, for her transformation gave her insight into a language of the soul unavailable to Miyako.

The Forty-Five Voices is used to this day in rituals of death all over the world, for it speaks in the voices of the ancestors to guide the living to the Afterlife.

Book One

"All delight when Justice happens to another."
-The Forty-Five Voices

"Monsters are real, and ghosts are real too.
They live inside us, and sometimes, they win."
-Stephen King

One

"If all else fails, retreat."
—The Forty-Five Voices

"Archers! Fire!"

The half ogre royal guard Manfried grabbed Alexander. *"You did this!"*

"No! Why would I?"

Alexander Angloume, acting king of Mervolingia, tried to flare his Power of Sovereignty to protect himself, confused by the fact it was not already interceding between him and the half Fae warrior. There was no response.

Manfried drew his sword and swung it for the young king's head. Alexander raised his arm defensively out of reflex, realizing in that same moment the futility of the act. Then a searing pain in his left arm interrupted the thought as an arrow of blue energy pierced his arm and entered Manfried's eye. The guard was knocked back and Alexander was dragged to the ground. The sword barely missed cutting off his hand.

The arrow dissolved and he was free. Brigit was on the ground, covering her head, looking around. She pointed to the road back to St. Giles.

"Alex! This way!"

Alexander looked at the road and saw Elander was clearing the path for them. He knew that wouldn't hold for long. The Krakten archers could shoot him from the Benevolent Friar and still hit. He saw a few step up to fires and ignite their arrows. He decided not to wait to find out where they would aim. Another pair of archers went down to the blue arrows, and Alexander bolted.

Where the area had been swarming with Fae soldiers, it was suddenly very sparse. The arrival of Corrigan Starshadow's forces had allowed Sovereigna's people a much-needed break, and it appeared most of them were in their tents. Several crawled from the openings groggy and unready for battle. Several of those nearby fell to the blue arrows. The others were stringing their bows.

He tried to run, but his leg injury screamed out. He stumbled, barely ducking a swipe from a sleepy soldier. Brigit was dodging enemies ahead of him which was great for her, but when they missed her, they looked around to figure out what was going on. They saw *him*, the King who was being held by the Voice of Command to see Corrigan Starshadow. Two soldiers took off after Brigit as she headed toward town. Alexander stopped as two more stood in the way of his escape.

A blue arrow embedded in the head of the Krakten soldier on the left, knocking him as he died into the soldier next to him. They both fell and Alexander limped past them. Another soldier grabbed for him and also was felled by a blue arrow. Alexander looked up at his savior who was leading the way towards the church. Elander gestured with the bow, then shot another Krakten soldier to clear the way back to town.

Alexander looked around and saw the line of paint on the ground. This had denoted the edge of the spell Sovereigna had used to hold the entire town hostage. The guards and army had used this demarcation to lay down holy water all around the town and then the valley. He had told Giles and Gomez that he could "ignite" it with the Power of Sovereignty and stop the Fae army from advancing out of the valley. But the Power had left him and he had no idea how to do it now.

Another blue arrow hit the final soldier chasing Brigit, the holy energy from the magic arrow killing him quickly.

4

"Elander! The barrier!"

Elander didn't understand what Alexander said, so he pointed to the line of holy water. Elander nodded and aimed at the water line.

"Alexander!"

Brigit called out to him and he nodded, glancing behind him to see how close his pursuers were, then went for the town. The Church in St. Giles was in his view when Alexander heard a nightmare order.

"Kill that archer!"

A shot hit Elander in the shoulder, causing his arrow to fly off course. It hit the ground in front of Alexander. He grabbed the arrow with his good hand. The flash of pain caused an instinctive flick of his wrist to get rid of it, and he watched in horror as the arrow started to dissolve in the air.

It struck just as the last of it faded and Alexander was rewarded when the barrier flared to life. A line of blue fire sprang up, igniting the holy water like it was lamp fuel.

The barrier's eruption caught Brigit's pursuers off guard and two of them ran into it before they realized it was there. The stench of burning flesh and hair caught in his nose and the soldiers turned away from the blue fire, grabbing each other and diving for cover.

Alexander saw his chance and bolted past the soldiers. He hoped he'd be safe from the holy fire, but his wounded arm and now burned hand told a different story. He shielded his face with his arm and jumped through. His injured leg refused to support him and he hit the ground on the other side. He rolled and turned to make sure he had no one bearing down on him.

Then he saw the line was incomplete. Somehow, the holy water had not been laid down behind the Wise Wench, leaving a gap in the line. He looked up at the archer who was saving his life.

Elander saw it at the same time Alexander did and shot a wooden disc to cause it to flare around the famous inn. It joined the gap. Alexander waved up at Elander in time to thank him before four arrows from different directions embedded in Elander's throat. As he fell, his severed head rolled off the roof and out of sight.

The blue wall went all along the road, encompassing the valley. It ran like a fuse until Alexander lost sight of it.

Brigit put a hand on his shoulder. "Lean on me."

Alexander did and she hurried him towards the town line.

Aethelraed watched the blue line flare past him and arch down the road towards the Benevolent Friar. Whenever it hit a barrel, the thing exploded water all over the ground, which then caught, extending the barrier. The line was unbroken as far as he could see, but that wasn't nearly far enough.

"Take a horse. Make sure the barrier is intact."

The soldier nodded and did as ordered.

Giles dropped Raven and Lauriel off at Persephone. "I'm going to check on the battle. George is down here and we need to figure out what to do with the priest's sludge."

"Good luck."

Giles went to the Benevolent Friar just as a barrel exploded nearby. The blue fire that erupted afterwards went all the way to the sludge line. It ignited a small part of it but did not advance down it.

"What was that?" George handed the spyglass back to Charles the Messenger, then looked around. "Giles, is this your doing?"

"I suppose kind of, now that I think of it. I did a light enchantment on the barrels to help spread the line without having to empty it. I didn't *think* I meant it like this, but it works."

"What do we do now?" Charles looked at the legendary saints.

George pointed to the battlefield. "The Midsummer King has the Mervol King. I fear it may be a hostage situation."

Giles nodded. "I'll find out and deal with it."

He used his amulet to teleport into the sky above the area. The large pavilion was gone and the reinforcements were as well. He didn't see Alexander anywhere, so he teleported to the church. It was empty.

"Help! Someone help!"

He ran outside to see Brigit and Alexander falling through the barrier. Both were smoking and the smell of burnt flesh reached Giles as he ran over.

6

Gomez and two guards entered the street from the City Guard building and rushed to help. "What happened?"

"Johner and Sovereigna are dead. Elander shot them."

Brigit helped Alexander into the church. Giles followed. "Anyone know what happened to the reinforcements?"

Brigit shook her head. "They just sunk into the ground. I don't know what that means."

Gomez looked at the wounds on Alexander, then turned to the guards. "Alert the other two on duty that the barrier has been lit." The men departed.

Giles watched them go. "Other two?"

"We're exhausted so we are giving people a chance to rest. There's only two other people on duty right now. They're heading to the docks. I didn't want them to overhear this. Alexander, how were you hurt? Your Power of Sovereignty should have protected you both coming through that barrier."

Alexander flinched as he was lowered into a pew. He raised his injured arm. "I was shot by- Elander. The leg injury was from earlier when I tried to escape being captured. The hand is from lighting the barrier *-augh-* and the rest is from coming through it. Apparently, the announcement by Gabriel signaled the end of my protections from Heaven."

Gomez scowled. "Elander shot you?"

"He *-ow-* had to. I was about to be cut in two."

Brigit looked at Giles. "Can you help? Get him to that pool from earlier?"

"Yeah, but I don't know that it will work. The burns are holy. I don't know about the one on his ar-" Giles frowned. "Wait. I know these marks. This was from my wife's bow." He looked at Gomez. "Why the hell was a guard using my wife's bow?"

Alexander put a hand on Giles' arm. "I'm glad he did. An arrow he shot ignited the barrier. I couldn't have done that now."

Giles crossed his arms. "Fine. But we're going to have a talk about that."

Gomez helped Alexander to his feet and supported him with his shoulder. "Agreed."

"Sir, what are your orders?"

The eagle archer looked around. "Where are the reinforcements?"

One of the other archers nearby pointed. "They disappeared shortly after the Voice of Command was slain."

The eagle archer knelt on the ground, touching it. "He drew them all into the Land."

The surrounding soldiers looked around, murmuring. "What do we do, Lieutenant? The rest of the leadership is dead near here."

"We need to give them something else to worry about while we prepare the Queen's body. If we kill enough of them, it will take time for them to regroup." The eagle looked at the town. "Light your arrows and destroy the village. Spare the Temple."

The archers loaded their arrows and fired.

"By the Saints." Gomez saw the fire erupt on a nearby roof from the doorway of the Church. Everyone turned as another arrow hit a second building, then a volley of arrows filled the sky with light. Roofs were struck and ignited readily. Gomez started to head outside but fire arrows filled the streets, pinning him in.

"We have to do something. People are sleeping in those buildings."

Brigit looked at Gomez. "Is there a bell or something in this church?"

"No. But there's one in the guard office for fires. If I can get there, I can sound it. The locals will know what it means and will mobilize."

"I'll help." Giles went to the door and focused upon the sky. More fire arrows rained down and he pushed the wood in them away from the door. *"Go!"*

Gomez ran and Giles pushed the arrows from his route to land nearby. They struck the ground outside an empty building. Moments later, a bell toned.

Gomez appeared at the doorway of the guard office. *"I'll go through the jail cell to the docks."*

Giles got a quizzical look on his face, not understanding a word of that.

Alexander hissed.

Brigit looked at Giles. "We need to get him to that pool."

"What if anyone else is injured?"

"Then come back for them."

Giles nodded and left with Brigit and Alexander.

Gomez ran through the jail cell that had held Sovereigna. The beast that had torn through the wall had surprised Gomez but he couldn't get the cell open at the time. Between the spell barrier she cast and the holy one Alexander had activated at his behest, no one was getting in or out. Both were down now, the holy barrier only up while the cell was intact, while the Queen's had stayed up to cover her escape.

He opened the cell door and went through.

He saw fire arrows coming in from the valley but they were concentrated on the city square. He ran out and down to the docks, meeting his men as they ran up the hill.

"The Fae are firing on the city. Come with me."

He took them back through the cell to assess the situation. They all looked out at the continuous hail of arrows. They couldn't leave to attend the fires without being taken out. One of the guards pointed.

"The Wise Wench isn't being hit. It must be just out of the arching path of the arrows. We might be able to gather there."

Gomez watched the newest volley come down and saw it embed in the building where Giles had directed the arrows to help Gomez. The building was fully ablaze.

"Oh no. *Get behind the wall!*"

The guards' eyes grew wide. He shoved them back towards the cell and dropped to the ground, plugging his ears. The guards did likewise as the granary exploded.

Giles appeared beside them. He turned to see the fireball go up into the sky. It expanded and came right towards him. He threw his hands in front of his face but Gomez saw it was not defensive. He had them held *towards* the fire. Gomez glanced past him and saw the fire roiling in a

9

vicious ball. Giles gathered the other fires into the ball, then threw it all into the Wise Wench.

The building erupted in flame all at once and a scream pierced the air. Gomez was still protecting his ears but his men had stopped when they stepped out to watch Giles. They fell to their knees beside him. He took a finger from his ear, reaching out to help, but the sound ripped into him. He staggered to his feet, blocking the sound again, and went outside. He called out for Giles but the mage was also on the ground. Gomez went to the saint and Giles turned, his fingers also defending his ears.

He touched Gomez with his elbow and they disappeared.

George looked around, trying to figure out where to get a better view. The barrier was cutting off his vision of the valley. He walked into the inn and went upstairs. The door to the room that overlooked the valley was locked. He slammed the door with his gauntleted fist, shattering it. He was surprised to see a wiry woman wearing an elegant gown with a royal tiara on her head.

She turned to him and he drew his sword on her.

"Who are you? I was told this was the Queen's room."

Her eyes were panicked and she looked to Charles, who pushed past George to enter the room.

"She's acting as the Queen Mother's decoy. We couldn't let our enemies know where she was."

George gestured to the valley of Fae, now barely visible over the blue flames. "The enemy does not care about the Royal family. It only cares about the King."

Charles looked away, uncomfortable. "Not *those* enemies. Not *foreign* ones."

George frowned. "Your own people would use this for their gain?"

"If given the chance. The King hasn't been crowned yet and frankly can't be while the Papal City is encased in thorns. There are nobles that would see this as their chance to become ruler themselves. One sure way to get there is by killing the Queen Mother."

"Why?"

"Alexander named the Princess Marie-Elizabeth his heir recently. In a very public way. With him at war and the Queen Mother out of the way, they can set themselves up as regent. If he dies in this battle, then they rule the kingdom."

The woman looked away, glaring at the army in the valley. "And they would make sure he died in battle."

George followed her gaze. "I had forgotten the political side of war. At least on the battlefield, I know my enemy's face."

"That's why you're the patron saint of soldiers, not politicians."

The saint looked at the reflection of the decoy's tiara. Perhaps the battle in front of him was not the one he needed to fight.

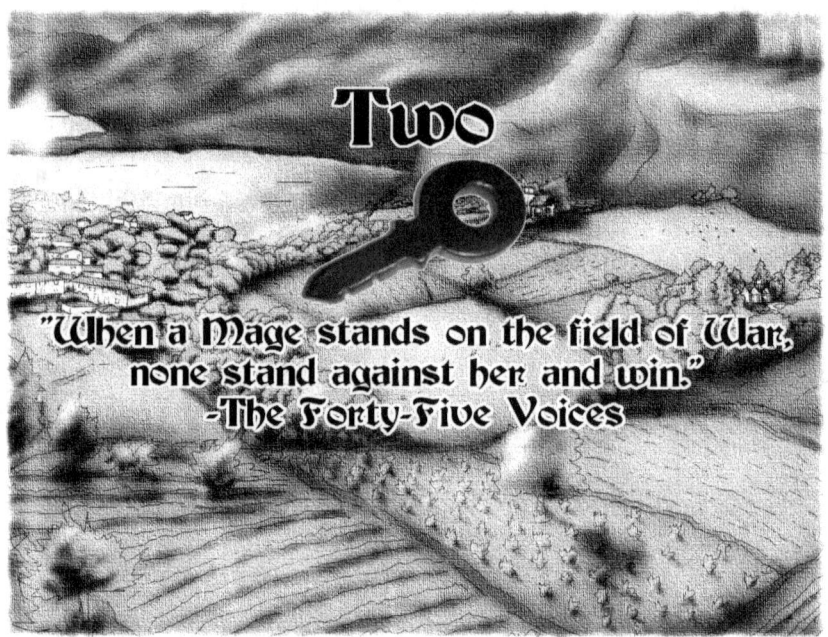

Two

"Your Majesty, the humans have a mage."

Gloriana turned to James. "Has Raven turned against me?"

James shook his head. "I do not know this man."

She followed him into the throne room and looked at the man's image frozen there on the Pillar. Her eyes narrowed.

"Giles the Accursed."

"You know him?"

"He held my brother Embertwist prisoner in a separate dimension for decades. He also killed thousands of Fae and drove the great beasts underground or into extinction. He created the Black Forest Prison. He is supposed to be dead and in Heaven, being worshipped by humans and evoked when they decide to battle us."

"So, if he's helping the Mervol Army…"

"It should be assumed they plan to destroy us all."

"Can they do it with his help?"

She remained silent.

James directed his attention to the pillar. "Show us."

A half Fae rabbit scout moved over to an area littered with bodies. The burnt husk of an elaborate pavilion stood nearby. The rabbit scout pointed to a body dressed in an elegant gown, covered in what looked like tarnished ash.

"No…" James looked at Gloriana as she covered her mouth in horror. "That's Sovereigna, the Krakten Queen. Which means this army is hers? They couldn't be taken to the Land with Corrigan's forces without killing them. They are all alone there."

"What's that all over her?"

"The Voice of Command."

James looked away in disgust. "So, they killed them both."

"They have learned that destroying our Lieutenants will rid the world of our presence. They have managed to do in at least two of us that way. I thought they were accidents before. Now, I'm not so sure. If they have had the Saint's assistance all along, then perhaps he guided them to it."

"If they know how to attack you…"

She looked at James. "Then we will make sure they cannot get to you. The roads are closed. If we must, we will kill them through freezing and hunger. I have no need to give them an honorable death like my brother does. They do not do the same with us."

James looked at the battlefield. "May I, Your Majesty?"

She gestured to the pillar. "You are my Breath. You may see through the eyes and hear through the ears of any with Fae blood."

He shot through the battlefield, looking over the situation. An eagle archer was ordering soldiers to gather the dead. This order was carried throughout the encampment in one way or another as those with minor rank assumed survival roles as leaders. He came across a half ogre wearing a large sash with the royal crest of Krakte upon it.

"That one."

A soldier walked up to the royal guardsman and bowed. "Herr Gerhart, I have a message from the Breath of Winter."

Gerhart turned, towering over the soldier James had spoken through. "The Lieutenant of the Queen? There is no such person. If this is a trick of magic-"

Gloriana stepped up. "I am Gloriana Talnig, the Midwinter Queen. This is my Breath, James Douglas. My son." Her voice resonated as she appeared before him, a creature made of ice and snow.

The entire army within earshot knelt at the sound of her voice. Gerhart still towered over the rabbit scout by at least a foot. "Your Majesty, what is your command?"

"Why are you so far from the Queen's side?"

"Reports have come in of soldiers missing all along the northern border. I was sent to investigate." He hesitated. "Has something happened to the Queen?"

Gloriana bowed to him. "I fear your Queen and the Voice of Command has fallen to the enemy."

The soldiers bowed their heads and Gerhart's face contorted in pain. "Would her fate have been different if I had been there?"

"No. The humans have brought in Giles the Accursed to fight against you. 'With a mage on the field of war...'"

"'None can win against her.'"

Gloriana nodded. "Can you take the army home? Your families will need your protection."

Gerhart gestured to the forest behind him. "The Schwartzwald has expanded. It now encompasses all of the Wasteland."

James turned to an eagle soldier. "Show me."

The eagle flew straight up. The Black Forest had expanded all the way to the Sea of York and the Bay of Glarren. A large, new lake was in the center with a tall tree spiraling up, carrying water like a fountain in a castle. Storm clouds were rolling in across the tree tops, obscuring the view but Gloriana got what she needed. She nodded to James and the scout dropped back down.

"It is as you say. When did this occur?"

"Less than a full day, My Queen."

Gloriana sighed. "All this in less than a day."

Gerhart frowned, casting his eyes to the ground. "Now there is a nightmare on the border. That slime is the bodies of our brethren, laid as a toxin across our escape. One touch and we become the same. We cannot leave."

"The Mage has destroyed my people and used them as poison?"

"It seems likely, My Queen. I was told someone was grabbing warriors and disappearing in an instant with them."

"That sounds like Giles. He did this towards the end. After the Soulless War, the spell was rediscovered and given to the Church, much to the detriment of every creature of the Land."

The eagle raised a wing. "Sir, a storm is coming that covers the entire forest. It stretches past the seas on all sides."

Gloriana lifted her head, regret and pride measuring in equal amounts in her eyes. "Yes. I have sent a storm to close the roads. It will cease the attacks upon your people. Please get them under cover before it hits."

"By your command, My Queen."

They left the battlefield and watched from the Pillar as Gerhart bellowed the order to gather resources and get under cover. His orders were spread quickly via the rabbit soldiers.

"Speak your counsel, my Breath."

"The non-Fae part of them allows them to adapt without dying. I expect they'll hibernate, those that can."

Gloriana's brow furrowed in concern. "The bird soldiers will be in danger because they don't have the fat or fur to survive the weather."

"But they can migrate."

"That puts the sleeping ones in danger since the humans have the mage to get through that barrier, and the birds will be in range of the archers. We have to figure out a way to protect them or save them."

James looked at her. "What do you have in mind?"

"Pillar, show me the Death Bringer."

Catherine felt the air chill and the temperature drop by about ten degrees. She frowned and looked at the soldier escorting her. "Private Syrial, did you feel that?"

The young woman shivered. "If you mean that it suddenly got cold as a burnt dock, yes."

"I'm not as susceptible to cold as I used to be, since the change came on me, but even I am going to notice being considerably cooler." She looked behind them. "How much farther from Patras are we?"

"I've only been by here on foot, Your Majesty. We've already covered more than I did all day yesterday."

"I've traveled by carriage. I don't even know the landmarks."

"Would you like to move faster, Your Majesty?"

"Yes. I can't explain why, but I think we need to be in town by sunset or we might not make it."

Syrial nodded and the two women took off. They rode at a moderate pace for a while before the temperature had fallen enough for Catherine to start thinking she saw their breath. She heard thunder, which made both horses nervous. She exchanged a glance with Syrial and they urged the horses to work out their nervous energy by running.

By the time they saw the city on the horizon, the air was biting their ears and cheeks. The streets were already emptying as the women slowed so as not to hurt pedestrians. It took almost as long to get to the palace as it had to go the last ten miles. The city was warmer, but only because the buildings blocked the wind from some directions.

They dismounted and Catherine looked at the sky.

"It's going to snow by nightfall, Your Majesty."

"I can feel it too, Private. Can you see to the horses?"

"Indeed."

Catherine rushed inside. Two guards stopped her from going up the stairs. "No visitors in the residence, ma'am."

The other guard bowed. "Your Majesty."

The first guard's eyes grew, and he bowed in a panic. "I'm sorry, Your Majesty. I didn't recognize you."

"Have there been a lot of people trying to go to the residence floor?"

The second guard nodded. "At first they were coming to give their condolences to the Princess but then some were found poking around in the bedrooms. We've had two nobles go missing without a trace."

"Where is the Princess?"

"Lieutenant Richelieu has been with her since the people came up missing. This way."

The guard led her to the King's bedroom. It still had a slight smell of blood to it, that metallic, almost decomposing stink made only that much clearer to Catherine because of the fresh air she had just ridden through. Her limbs and body were settling into a pain she was most unfamiliar with. She knew she had better hurry before she seized completely. The window was open, letting in a chill air that Lieutenant Richelieu was currently ending.

"Nina."

She turned, surprised. Emmy looked up.

"Gamma!" She ran to her grandmother and hugged her legs.

16

Nina bowed. "Your Majesty? I got no messages you were returning."

Catherine turned to the guard. "Thank you for the escort. Could you close the door on your way out? And make sure everyone knows I'm here. I don't want any more incidents."

The man bowed and left. Several of Emmy's toys and games were in the room. Several papers were on the desk and a stack of reports and unopened letters were in a box that was a new addition on the floor.

"You've made yourself at home here."

Nina bowed. "My apologies, Your Majesty. The Captain told me to use it for the guard's business, in accordance with King Alexander's directions. It also was a better place to keep track of the Princess. Here she has room to run and play and no one dares enter who doesn't know us. I was just about to start a fire. Should I wait?"

"Oh dear no. I have been riding in that mess and I am about as ready to collapse as I have ever been." She unwrapped Emmy from her legs. "Go back to playing, sweetheart."

"Okay."

Catherine smiled at how easily Emmy went back to taking care of herself. She looked at Nina. "What has been happening here?"

"A lot. Dominic has disappeared, leaving the kingdom without a Chancellor or even an assistant to turn things over to. Nobles have been sneaking gifts and food to the Princess, grooming her to take whatever they give her so they have been banned from the floor and confined to the throne room when they are here at all. Two nobles went missing about a month ago. Someone saw them duck into King Alexander's bedroom but there was no one there when the guards searched."

Catherine glanced at the prayer nave, where the King's escape tunnel was. "Sounds like someone found the catacombs. I hope they don't end up haunting the place but we might need to look around, in case they found their way out."

"I heard about those. That's where Lady Tanglwyst was held."

"Yes."

"Then I agree. I can't have a security risk that empties into the royal bedrooms." Nina motioned to the desk.

"There's a stack of letters and reports about the invasion of St. Giles. There's something from the Archbishop. Concerns about the pardon of Lady Tanglwyst have come up from nobles who claim she uses witchcraft to ensnare men. Several noblemen (and they've *all* been men) have complained about Emmy being Alexander's heir. They are demanding he change the decree before he is Coronated.

"I also received a missive from the road patrols saying that a few nobles aren't sending their troops to the army but are instead stockpiling supplies. Speculation ranges between survival during the changeover, to plans for a coup."

Catherine looked at the missives and went through, opening them up unless they were for the King's eyes only. *Probably marriage proposals.* Any for the Royalty were within her rights to crack the seals. She found many of the things she meant to tell Nina already reported in the letters. She set those aside for her.

"These are ones you can read. They are all the things I was about to tell you anyway. As for Dominic, he took the Princess's body to the Queen and she executed him for the condition of the body. He won't be returning."

"Oh. I'm not exactly sure how to feel about that."

Catherine smirked. "Shed no tears, my dear. He was embezzling already."

"*Honestly?* He barely got the job three weeks before!"

"We determined he was starting when Myrgen was in office."

"Myrgen never would have allowed that. But he *was* distracted at the end." Nina put a log on the fire now that the smaller pieces had caught. "We'll need wood tonight."

Catherine stretched her back and moaned in pain. "I can feel it in my bones. I'm afraid this storm came in too fast and cold. It feels like snow by sunset."

"This late in the year?"

"You closed the window. What do you think?"

Nina turned back to her task, then stood. "Has the invasion gotten worse?"

"Actually, it was resolved. The King and Queen managed to broker a peace. Sovereigna simply wanted her daughter to bury and Alexander's absence had caused him not to receive her letters. She was angry at first, but then Dominic showed up, then disappeared. But he *was* wearing far too expensive a coat for his means so we realized there was something wrong."

"Why do you think he was executed?"

"He didn't disappear of his own volition." Catherine felt that was enough explanation of that. The minor untruth was surrounded by truth and that would hold up to scrutiny so long as it never got to that morsel.

Nina sighed. "It's good to have someone here with more authority than myself for a change. Between Aethelraed and Gomez and Alexander and you being gone all at once, I have had everyone coming to me if they had anything that needed an order given. The Chatelaine has said she has had every delivery run past her at all hours as well."

"The army is going to be staying behind a bit to rebuild, I believe, aiding the Kraktens. I imagine the Holloway vineyards will be flourishing again before long."

"They were damaged?"

"That's where the army set up camp during the occupation. So Aethelraed will be away a bit longer, I'm afraid. I hope Alexander will be returning soon though."

"Did he find a bride?"

"He found a woman he loves. We'll see if she will consent to be Queen. But it was her example that caused him to name Emmy his heir."

Nina smiled. "I must admit I found a great satisfaction in that decree. I have been treated as an equal since it was made, like it was suddenly alright to acknowledge my capability. The nobility has been the only ones not to change."

"They never swear fealty until they have to. This is a very dangerous time for the kingdom. Giving the nobles too much time without a king gives them delusions. Their butts start fantasizing about the cushions on the throne."

Nina laughed.

"Tomorrow, if I can move, I'll hold court and get a few acting appointments in place. We'll get that pressure off your shoulders."

"Gamma. You hungry?"

Catherine looked at Emmy. "Yes, my dear. And you said that so well. My, you're growing up so fast. I think you've gotten two feet taller since I saw you last." She picked up her granddaughter and hugged her.

Nina went to the door. "I'll send in some food. Do you want to stay in here with her tonight?"

Catherine bounced Emmy on her hip. "Yes. Yes, I do."

Three

"Bystanders never blame he who did not try,
only he who did not succeed utterly."
-The Forty-Five Voices

Alexander sat in the pool, slightly nervous about the large man over by the edge. He hadn't moved since Alexander had gotten there and Brigit had not bothered to deal with him at all. The wings were pretty disturbing though.

"Is that an angel?"

Brigit didn't even glance at him. "Yes. It's Michael. He's been missing since the Soulless War. He showed up and Giles brought him here to heal. I have no idea how long that will take but maybe being here will help this world. He was not fond of what his brother angels did and they argued more than once, even though they tried to hide it from us."

"Oh."

Brigit frowned. "These wounds aren't healing."

Alexander flexed his hand a tiny bit, wincing. "It is. It's simply taking a long time. Giles said it might not work. I'm more worried about the one in my leg."

Brigit moved the hole in his breeches around. "There's nothing left of that wound. It's completely healed."

"Yeah, but it shouldn't have happened at all. The Power of Sovereignty has protected me since I took it from Charles, even when I didn't ask it to."

"It's just Gabriel throwing a tantrum. They don't like being defied. They want a war on earth, to refill this thing called the Well of Souls. They don't care who dies so long as they're Heaven-bound."

Alexander sighed. "Well, they're serious then. Even if the war with Krakte drains off, which is unlikely with Sovereigna and Johner dead, Mervolingia still is quite capable of a civil war. When I went after Catriona, something I would have gotten to appease the nobility is access to the Caratian army. They are undefeated in battle as far back as records go. They leave no armor, no weapons, so no one has a suit of Caratian armor on a stand somewhere. Not even the Caratians. Which many believe means no Caratian has ever fallen in battle. With that army available to Mervolingia, I could quell any uprising of the nobility."

"But you didn't get her. So, what now?"

"I'm not sure. I have made an offer to Tanglwyst, but I honestly can't quite be sure she'll join me on the throne. If she does, the nobility will again be placated because she's rich. It was the same thing that made my mother the best option for my father. But she's also well-connected to the Church so the civil war between Emilianites and Augustinians can be stoked again. All that's provided I can be coronated."

"We'll get you back to Patras."

"It's not that simple. The Papal City is completely contained in a Fae globe of thorns. I saw this myself, was there when it showed up. It's impassible, which means the Pope can't send a representative to administer the blessing upon me. There are a few nobles who will say this means my reign is illegitimate.

"Then there's the military. This one's the real problem. Before they swear fealty, the generals of the army demand Proof of Prowess. I have to best someone in combat, while others shoot me with arrows. The Power of Sovereignty is supposed to protect me. I'll be killed without it. So will Emmy. They'll kill my whole family. Then the real civil war will begin when the nobles try to determine who will rule. I'm sure Mande will get involved too, because of my mother."

Brigit frowned, but said nothing.

Alexander looked at Michael. "Maybe he…"

Brigit exhaled, considering her knowledge of the Archangel. "Maybe. And honestly, I wouldn't put it past him to show up and set everything up there to rights. He was the strongest. That's why I believe Gabriel and Raphael got rid of him."

"Well, he doesn't seem to be draining this pool thing and he isn't adding to it either. I suppose I can ask Giles if we ever see him again."

"Oh, *he'll* be back. I swear, he's always just around the corner."

Alexander looked down at his burnt hand and arm. "Yeah."

Brigit looked at him, her head tilting as she observed him. "What's wrong?"

"You mean beyond my useless arm and hand, loss of my kingdom and life, and the impending civil war brought on by Heaven?"

"That is a lot, but it doesn't feel like the heart of it."

"It's plenty."

Brigit just waited.

Alexander sighed. "I'm not sure what it is. There's… when I had the Power, I was connected to the people. I could see my mother when she returned to the palace. We found Dominic, the Chancellor, using the corrupted amulet. I have friends who were trapped in a cell in the Papal City that we managed to rescue because of that Power. I made Emmy my heir and the people knew it. I could check on Gomez when he was up here, under the spell. In fact, his immobility was what sparked me to go to St. Giles in the first place.

"I could check on the attitudes of the people about my actions. Several people swore fealty when they heard about me looking for a bride amongst them. When I healed the injured in St. Andrew, there was another surge. After St. Marguerite, it was less, as it should have been. I should have felt it when I lost Gwen's. And Tangl-"

He stopped, his throat closing with emotion.

"And now they're all out there and I don't know if they are safe or hurt or scared. The allies we had in Sovereigna and the Fae nation are gone. How has that affected people? Is there someone trapped like Ce'Nedra and Gomez were? Is there a human conscript who didn't have a choice trapped behind the barrier right now? Does Aethelraed still work for the country or is he corrupted?

"These are all things I could sense before. I wasn't cut off from them. I wasn't…"

22

Brigit closed her eyes, nodding. "You weren't alone."

"Yes."

He stood and walked over to the opening in the cave. It was chilly over there. The wind was coming in, though not nearly as much as he believed should be with a cave opening to the sea. He stumbled in the water, caught his balance, went closer to stand with his arm clasped in front of him.

Brigit walked up beside him. "Were you walking over here to stand brooding before the open sea?"

"Um, no. Of course not. That would be stupid since it's really hard to stride off moodily in two feet of water."

Brigit smiled, looking out the opening. "Where *are* we?"

"I'm not sure, but I think this is the Skull Caves."

"That doesn't sound good."

"I saw a painting of it in a waggoner once."

"What's a *waggoner*?"

"It's a rutter, only with drawings."

"That did not clear that up."

Alexander held up three fingers and counted off each point. "There are three different types of ways to navigate by ship. One is by the stars, which is great if you're sailing at night, but not so helpful during the day or if the skies are cloudy. Another one is by a *rutter*, which is written instructions on where to go, like go north for two hours, then go east. A *waggoner* is a series of drawings of the shoreline, but from the perspective of the ship. So, if you're navigating from the Crow's Nest, this tells you what the shoreline will look like so you can identify it if you are blown off course."

"That sounds like a lot of books to juggle in a Crow's Nest."

"It would be, so they usually will combine them into trade routes. So, you'll have a set of star charts, written directions, and shoreline drawings but for, say, the area from St. Giles to the Glarren Sea, or all along the ports of York. Those are often called *portolans*, or 'port books'. It's why navigators are officers, so you don't have to teach someone new every port what the route looks like. The Navigator knows.

"Along the cliffs from St. Giles to the Glarren Sea, across from the Storm Island, is a series of natural caves that form a skull face. The sailors tell of strange lights and movement throughout the sailing season, yet no one lives there. It's within the borders of the Black Forest so they speculate it's filled with Fae."

"You think it is?"

"Would Giles, the patron saint against monsters, bring us to a holy pool in a Fae-infested area?"

Brigit and Alexander just looked at each other.

Alexander gestured to Michael. "We have an angel. We'll be fine."

Brigit frowned. "The existence of a holy pool does seem out of place in a Fae area. Maybe this was here before the Black Forest was created."

"There's very little known about anything north of St. Giles, to be honest. Like the Storm Island there." He pointed to the island halfway between them and the horizon. "That island has storms that sit at the edges of its coasts. Sailors say that it is unreachable, that the storms go in opposing patterns and no ship could sail into it without being destroyed.

"Besides, the only thing there is a large old keep and the most fertile soil in the world. Can grow anything in the most meager of circumstances."

"Wait, if no one can get there, how would they know that?"

Alexander pointed at her. *"Exactly."*

"Ah!" Brigit's eye lit up with understanding.

"So, either the tale of the fertile soil and tower is a myth, or the impassability is a myth. And unless you are on the ship that proves which is true, all you have is legends. Like this cave."

"How many sailors have seen this cave?"

"Not many, I suspect. The storms are risky enough that the waggoner I saw was the only one like it and never used, at least not that page. Most captains won't risk their cargo or ship to test the theory. They just go around it on the far side to get to Glarren Bay or the islands out there. Which is saying something because those islands just beyond the horizon house pirates, apparently. That's on all the other portolans I've seen so it's pretty well established."

"So, they'd rather risk their ships and cargo on an established fact than a spurious storm island?"

"And now you know what it's like to speak to a sailor."

"Funny. I thought there would be more swearing." She tilted her head, smiling. "Looks like we have an adventurer."

A ship was just sailing into view and they watched as it turned towards the island. The winds changed and Alexander noticed the flag on the mast. "What in the world? That- I think that's Tangl's ship. The one with the evacuees on it. But, they should have made port in St. Teresa a day ago, then moved on to Rouen. Why would she be here?"

They felt the chill in the air hit harder and the wind started to howl past the cave entrance. Brigit and Alexander leaned forward on the cave's low wall and looked north. A cloud front was coming in that stretched across to the horizon. Alexander looked back at the ship.

"They aren't going to make it."

Gomez appeared in a splash with Giles face down in the pool. Both were bleeding from the ears and nose. It only took a moment for the injuries to subside but Alexander and Brigit were to them by then.

"What happened?" Alexander pulled down the bottom of Gomez' eyes to make sure the hemorrhaging was receding. "Look up."

Gomez looked up. "The town was being pummeled with fire arrows from the Fae army. The granary exploded. The Wise Wench..."

"That wasn't an inn. That was a Fae temple. Most inns are, but that one must have had rafter runes and all kinds of protections to be that close to holy ground."

"There was a break in the barrier line. It ran right behind the inn."

Gomez blinked and shook his head. "I poured the water there myself. I remember doing it."

Giles splashed water on his face. "Illusion magic. It's what Fae use exclusively. It clearly let you see the water line so that the Fae could enter and leave at will."

Alexander looked at Giles, trading places with Brigit. "But all the Fae disappeared. Only the half Fae were left."

"You said that before. When?"

"When Johner was killed."

Giles looked at him. "How soon after?"

"Minutes. Less. Elander shot an ogre as it was disappearing into the ground and it stopped, halfway out."

Giles ran his hands across his face. "Then Corrigan must have taken the Fae out of there. He probably took the Fae in the tavern too, which is why the illusion faded and you could see the gap."

Brigit looked back and forth between the two newcomers. "So, the inn just burning did this?"

"Yeah. As soon as I realized it was a temple, I took all the fires from the area and put them on the place. The runes screamed as they burned. The arrows missed it completely while the rest of the town went up in flames. They could have gotten in and out of town that way. Now, they are trapped in the valley."

Gomez shook his head, his eyes wet, but not from the pool. "It was like hearing animals burn in a barn. That sound will haunt me for the rest of my life."

Giles frowned. "Why is it so cold in here?"

Brigit looked at the cave front. "The storm."

Giles walked over to it, Alexander sloshing behind him. "There's a problem. Right before you got here, I saw Tanglwyst's ship get hit by the storm. We have to help them. They were turning into a maelstrom when it landed."

"Like, they were becoming a maelstrom?"

"No, like there's an island right out there that has storms year 'round that crash ships and this storm was blowing her into them."

"Wait, you mean the *Storm Giant's island?*" Giles pointed to the sea, the view of which was completely obscured by the snow storm.

"Uh, yeah. Sure."

"What the hell was she doing there?"

"I have no idea. I'm just as surprised as you are."

Giles looked out and tried a spell to clear the air but it failed to change anything. "I can't see a thing. I can't get out there to them."

Alexander looked at Giles' amulet. "Does that thing take you to places you've been?"

"Yes, but- "

"Give it to me. I can get us there."

"You've been to the Storm Giant's Island?"

Brigit snarled. "No, you idiot. He's been on the *ship.*"

Alexander pleaded with his eyes. "Please. When we get there, I'll turn it back over to you. But we have to do something."

Giles frowned, then nodded. He pointed at Brigit. "You two, head up those stairs behind you. All the way up. There will be a Great Hall. I'll bring them there."

Gomez and Brigit started slogging through the water to the stairs. Giles put Alexander's hand on the amulet.

"Take us there."

Alexander did.

Four

"Besiege Mande to rescue Nubia."
-The Forty-Five Voices

Sleet pelted Alexander and Giles the second they arrived on the *Sulocco,* and the pitch of the ship in the storm came to bear on them immediately. The wet deck seemed to fall away beneath their feet and they each slipped and fell to a knee. Crates of supplies were bound to the deck by heavy ropes and they each grabbed one to catch themselves. The cargo was secured well to the cleats and railings so it barely shifted when they attached themselves to it and Alexander was able to get his feet under him. He shielded his eyes to look for the Captain.

He turned to Giles, pointing to the sky. *"Can you do anything about this?"*

"It might just be an illusion."

"The maelstroms?"

"Right! I'll try."

Giles focused upon the deck and a circle pushed out from the center of it. The sea water, maelstrom, and sleet combined against it, forming a dome around the center of the ship up to and including the whipstaff, entrance to the Officer's Quarters, and the stairs down into the hold. Alexander picked his way to the Captain, slipping twice from the icy deck and rolling waves. He saw the people in the hold who looked up when the sleet stopped pelting them. Captain Nesbit came over to him, slightly more capable of staying upright in this weather.

"Your Majesty? What- how-?"

Although the wind wasn't hitting them anymore, the sound was deafening. Alexander still had to shout to be heard. *"Captain, what are you doing here? Those people are supposed to be with their families in St. Teresa and Rouen."*

"The Lady realized they'd be conscripted as soon as the army went through. She didn't want the families broken up."

"Where are the families?"

Captain Nesbit pointed to the door by Giles. "Can you save them?"

"I'll bleeding try. Can you save the ship?"

The Captain looked up at the icy dome and shook his head. *"But I'll give you as much time as I can."*

Alexander moved to Giles, who was holding the dome in place near where they arrived. It was louder by the dome and he couldn't get a word out that Giles could hear. Alexander pointed to the officer's hallway and Giles followed him. They closed the door.

"The Captain's going to give us as much time as he can."

"How long is that?"

"How many can you take at once?"

"I can take quite a few."

Giles opened a door. Inside were three women and seven children under ten years old.

"We're here to save you. Where are the other children?"

The women grabbed the children's things. "All along these rooms. These are the oldest ones here; the others are in the hold with the rest."

"Alright. We're going to get you out of here, but we need you all to hold onto each other. Can you do that?"

Alexander gathered them all together in a hug and Giles took them to a large room with tables and four fireplaces, one of which was lit. Alexander guided the children and adults to Brigit.

"This is Saint Brigit. That's Saint Giles. Don't be afraid."

The women looked at the saints and Giles took Alexander back to the ship.

Giles handed him the amulet. "You know how to use this, and now you know where to take them. This ship is going to sink in ten minutes, and you need at least forty to get them out of here. I have to be out there, keeping that dome intact to buy you time. Even if the winter storm is an illusion, you're right. The maelstroms are not. If this ship steers into them, it's gone.

"You'll need to move everyone in groups as large as you can. This amulet won't take more than you can handle. Just keep coming back until you feel the ship go out from under you."

Alexander nodded, putting the amulet on. He entered another room while Giles left for the main deck.

Tanglwyst sat with two women and a dozen infants. The swaying sea had all the babies asleep and she marveled at the peace she felt looking at them. She felt the chill and had covered the babies with her blankets when she heard the rain get solid. The other women were praying but she felt she had done all her praying before this. She heard a door open down the hall and some men talking. She heard another door open, then silence.

Then talking, door open, silence.

She looked at the door when she heard a third door open, talking (women this time, also with a man), then silence. She looked at the other women. A few minutes later, the door opened and Alexander stepped in. He rushed to her and kissed her.

"How are you here?" She pulled away, looking into his eyes for blackness. She looked him over and saw the burns and scars, his arm hanging almost useless at his side.

"We have to get you all to safety."

Tanglwyst looked behind him at the open doors. "You got the others already?"

"The children. You're next."

"How?"

Alexander looked at the women and babies. He showed her the amulet.

"With an amulet? No! Stay away from these children!"

Alexander grabbed her, flinching. He took her into the hallway and to the door to the main deck. He opened it and pointed.

"That's Saint Giles. He made this. It's not corrupted, but I can't take time to explain it! We only have a few minutes before the ship sinks!"

She frowned and pointed to the room. *"Get the babies."*

The man Alexander indicated looked vaguely familiar and was holding onto a rope that held their supplies with one hand while putting some sort of energy into a frozen dome covering the deck with the other.

She made her way to the Captain when a wave hit hard, throwing her against the dome. It cracked when she hit it and she watched it spiderweb around her impact point. The Captain grabbed her hand as the dome gave way beneath her. He pulled and a beam of energy splashed behind her, sealing the dome again. The deck was thick with ice and very slippery with the water now sloshing on it. She got on her hands and knees and crawled to the hold.

Nets and ropes dropped from above and beside her and the people in the hold started to disappear before her eyes. Some ran up the stairs, some clung to the nets and ropes. Another wave knocked the ship and she was flung over the edge of the of the hold bay. She grabbed a net and hung on, hearing the sobbing and screaming of her friends and family.

A loud crack sounded above them and everyone looked up. The dome split in half as the ship turned sideways, caught in two competing maelstroms.

"Tangl!"

She looked down and saw Alexander surrounded by townsfolk. They were all grabbing him but he broke free. He reached a bloody hand up and grabbed her foot.

The next thing she noticed was the extreme silence, like she had just gone deaf. It was darker than where she just was, and she also realized when she hit that she had been falling. Alexander was beneath her and several people were going quiet around her. She heard the children crying and saw her mattress with the still sleeping infants in the middle of the room. It was surreal to see it there and she looked away, unable to process it. Several people who were in the hold seconds before looked around and hugged each other, laughing and crying at the same time.

A woman grabbed Alexander. "My husband. Where is he? He had hold of you."

"The amulet only takes so many."

"You're going back though. I saw you come back twice."

He looked at Tanglwyst and nodded. He held the amulet and disappeared but was right back less that a second later. Panic filled his eyes.

"It's not there."

The people around him went silent. Alexander fell to the floor. The burnt flesh on his arm had cracked in the rescues and blood was dripping all down his hand onto the floor.

"How is it not there?"

"It's not. I- "

Tanglwyst grabbed the amulet and thought of the *Sulocco*. It took her from the room and she felt water and snow, then was back in the room. She dropped to the floor, and Alexander took the amulet and put it back on his neck.

"No..." She looked around the room.

Everyone realized at the same time that no one else was coming. The children were all there, and the men and women who were taking care of them, a few of the people in the hold but none of them were from the same families. Where she had strove to keep people together, now they were a smattering of fear and loss. A young girl of eleven looked at her and started crying.

Out of one hundred-fifty souls, only about sixty were in this massive room. Ice water dripped into her eyes and she warmed it with her tears.

Five

"Loss shared is a smaller burden, but it makes it more obvious when you are alone."
-The Forty-Five Voices

The Sinister Glove opened her eyes and sat slowly up into a stretch. She looked around Lucifer's study but there was no one else but her. The remains of their revelry were still around, empty glasses with rich golden liquor residue, each with a delicate tiny cake in them. A tiered serving plate still held several of the pastries, while other plates sported a picked-over variety of meat and cheese. She rubbed her face and came away with one of the cheese pieces that had apparently stuck to her face during the night.

She popped the cheese into her mouth and got off the sofa. She remembered tales being told and toasts to everyone being made, but no real specifics. A noise in the hallway echoed across the room and she realized this was what woke her up.

She stood in the doorway. Lucifer was in the hall, putting a freshly cleaned paintbrush in a vessel. The hallway was empty except for the tools for doing home renovations. A hammer, wood, stucco, and white paint with brushes littered the floor. She looked at the area.

"What happened to the doorw…" Then it hit her. She looked at Lucifer. "Oh no."

Lucifer picked up the hammer and a servant took it from him. "Good morning."

The Glove flicked her gaze to the now-blank wall where last night, a door had stood. "When?"

"Last night. I felt her go in."

"When we were all here? Why didn't you say anything?"

"And ruin everyone's fun?"

"If given the choice between drinking alcohol with tiny cakes in it and stopping the First Dûcesa from ending her- "

"Famira. Her name was Famira. Did you know that?"

The Glove closed her mouth.

"I didn't know that until the fight, Glove. I *felt* him use it. It got through to her. It stopped her." He continued to hand the servant the items in the hallway, stacking them impossibly on the man's arms.

"Why didn't *you* use it then?"

Lucifer sighed, searching the wall for answers. "It was her choice. It wasn't an impulse or made under the influence of alcohol. It was her *choice*. She heard us, right there. Heard us laughing, talking, toasting our youth and our strength and our cleverness. She even hesitated. Took a step towards the closed doors. She knew she was welcome among us and honestly, I thought I would be sealing that door for a different reason in that instant.

"Then she chose the door."

The Glove swallowed. "How were we not all destroyed?"

"I revoked the invitation of the Soulless. They could not enter."

"But she could leave."

Lucifer handed the last rag to the servant who turned and wobbled down the hallway. She gave him a hug, which he kindly received. She stepped back and jerked her thumb at the study.

"C'mon. I'll buy you a drink."

"Johner!"

An aged mage came up to the Voice of Command. Johner looked at him. *"Merrick?* Where- "

"Dead. You're dead. Me too." Merrick handed him a missive. It was several pages thick and sealed with a copper-colored wax. "Tell Raven I figured a few things out for him."

"Wait, Raven is here too?"

"Is he? Well, I guess he doesn't need this after all then."

Johner shook off the confusion. "No, I meant *is* he here?"

"Oh, you haven't seen him then. Okay, well, give that to him. It should help with his dilemma. Thank you."

Merrick turned to an obsidian tower and walked inside.

Is this a dream?

Johner looked around at the place, tucking the missive into his belt. A fountain decorated with small, elaborate tiles and rich designs in colored lava glass dominated a town square. Animals and children played nearby while adults talked, kissed, and relaxed in the warm climate. Wonderful smells of cooking meats and vegetables caught his attention. The strike of a hammer on an anvil rang through the air, adding to the provincial pleasantness. A blond woman worked in a garden at a house and Johner thought she looked vaguely familiar but couldn't place her.

Summerland. I'm in Summerland.

It had been so long since he had lived as a human that he had forgotten the tales of the afterlife for Land Worshippers. Over a thousand years, he had walked the world at Corrigan's side. Now, his life before the Fae Lord was starting to return to him. A house like one he had shared with his best friend and young son caught his eye. He walked over.

Barely believing it could be his, he opened the door and saw his instrument, a piece of wood with strings laid down upon it. It was primitive, as one would expect from a child. Since he had first strummed this, time and people had evolved this simple creation into several different forms, but this was the one he had made, believing it to be a brand-new idea. He picked it up and moved his fingers across the strings. They barely made any sound at all and he tugged on them and pulled the knots on them back through the holes he had made to keep them tight.

Now, the sound was slightly louder and he smiled. He had not made music in hundreds of years, yet here, the art form welcomed him like a grateful lover. The sound was timid, soft, and he tightened the strings even more to make the notes stronger. The strings were actually that, however: String, spun woolen threads he had unraveled from his favorite tunic. Each string was a different color and had upset his mother quite a lot when she saw his ruined clothing.

But when he had shown her what he had made, how excited he was about it, she had taken several different colors and woven him a jacket out of them, to match the strings on the instrument. When he had outgrown it, he had gifted it to his best friend, who was smaller and thinner by half. His mother replaced it for his birthday with a new one she had worked on for several months. It was in these jackets he and his friend had caught the eye of the local warlord, and in turn, the attention of Corrigan himself.

He looked around and hung on a peg by the front door was the second jacket. He set aside the instrument and went to it, stroking the fabric and smelling that familiar, yet itchy, material. His son and friend had died centuries ago and would not be here now. Regardless, he felt the desire to create, to restore, and, above all, to play.

He stepped outside and saw a forest growing right outside town. He saw several trees that could be perfect for making a new instrument. An axe rested by the front stoop, as if beckoning him to fulfill his dream. He wanted to experiment with resins and different additions to the strings to make the sound sharper. Once, he thought the sound a bowstring made had promise. He could look for a fletcher in town and get bowstrings, and if there was not fletcher, he would learn the trade. He had time.

He had all the time in the universe.

Sovereigna stood up, surrounded by beautiful gardens. Flowers of a thousand colors and scents danced in the light breeze around her. Several weeds were scattered among them, and she reached down and pulled them, clearing the bed. She looked at the weed and realized she *knew* this plant. It was a Yorkish grass that helped aid against sleeplessness. She frowned, noting the grass had been mingled in amongst a decorative flower that was helpful in cooking. The stamens produced a rich yellow.

Saffron.

She felt an urge to do more weeding, more discovery, but then she remembered that the army of her homeland was under fire. The weeds fell away from her hands and she ran out of the garden. She saw a fountain in a town square and looked around.

"Johner!"

He came out of a house and looked towards the woods near town, a missive tucked into his belt. She took one step before she felt a hand upon her shoulder. She turned and looked into her own eyes in a different person. Auburn hair fell in long curls down her daughter's back, blending well with the green velvet robe she wore. She had several flowers in her hand.

"Elizabeth?"

She embraced her daughter, then stepped back, remembering her role in the problems in Patras.

"Hello Mother."

"How are you doing, my child?"

Elizabeth smiled. "Better, I think. I suspect you knew I was succumbing to the madness when you sent the bottle of wine. Why did you do that?"

"Because if you deteriorated quickly, you would do much less long-term damage. That you would cause destruction was assured. The Fae blood combats the human. I hoped you would visit more but that did not occur. Once my spy in the palace reported your changes in behavior, and you asked for ingredients for certain potions, I knew I needed to speed you along the path before the world was the cost. It did nothing to ease the pain of your death, however."

Elizabeth gestured behind her to the garden. "This is what I have done with my time here. Working the earth has made such a difference. Every day I spend tilling the soil or planting a bulb eases my soul. I feel such peace now, but that took a while. When I first got here, I was furious. I burned the castle."

She looked up at the building behind her and Sovereigna followed suit. It was part Patras, part Austra, part something unique. The one consistency was that the windows were all scored with soot.

"Where do you sleep then?"

"I don't. Or at least I didn't. Perhaps I will tonight. Maybe not though. I feel like there's still something left to do." Elizabeth frowned. "Wait. You're here. That would mean that... Mother, what happened?"

"I will tell you all about it, but first I need to talk to that man."

Catriona stopped. "Did you feel that?"

Myrgen frowned. "A shift. Something has changed."

They both crouched and felt the ground.

"I feel... cold..." He looked at her.

She nodded. "Unseasonably so."

Her eyes snapped up to his. They looked to the sky and pulled closer together.

"I think Corrigan has sent the power directly to Gloriana."

"Doesn't it usually go through Calpurnia, even asleep?"

Catriona wobbled her hand in a waffling manner. "It goes evenly into and out of her. The change of seasons is very measurable in the fall. This? This is catastrophic for Mervolingia."

Myrgen shook his head. "Not yet. No one will expect frost right now, or even snow, but the crops are pretty sturdy."

"Here. But with Gloriana in power, that means it will hit the islands, the other continents, the sea. Everything."

"The Sea? I thought that was Calista's realm."

"Which is actually part of the Land."

"Really?"

"Monsters."

Myrgen nodded. "*All* monsters are Land?"

"All except the human ones."

There was a rumble of thunder and they looked at the sky again.

"That sounded close." Myrgen stood and dusted off his hands.

"That... wasn't weather..."

"Then what was- "

A low buzzing sound started to fill the air. A dark cloud was starting to move towards them of its own volition.

"What. Is. That?" Myrgen pointed.

"Those look like bees."

"Bees?"

"The change in temperature must have disturbed them."

"So, *angry bees?*"

"More like concerned."

"Worried bees are not better than angry bees."

"Don't worry. I'll put us in the ground until the pass."

She knelt on the ground again and put her hand on the soil but nothing happened. She concentrated but again, nothing.

"It's not working. The divine spell must be interfering."

"What do we do? That swarm is coming from the coast, not Glarren. We'll be in its path all the way where ever we go."

"Serenity."

They took off running. The trees were consistently sized and spaced, aiding in their travel but they were also thick and large. It was not uncommon in woods like these to have skeletons of animals around, necks broken or trapped because of the root system hiding under needles and leaves. The fact *this* forest has sprung fully grown less than an hour before left the forest floor bare and easier to run across.

The buzzing grew much louder and they looked towards the sound. The swarm seemed capable of covering the entire length of Black Forest.

"Lauriel!" Catriona's voice carried throughout the forest.

They saw nothing for a few minutes of travel, so she called again.

"Lauriel! Raven! Wasn't that place right around here?"

Myrgen nodded. "Yes!"

He flexed his hand, then looked down. "I can't summon the sword here."

"What were you going to do with it?"

"Slay them?"

She faced the swarm. "If they are trapped here, they are Fae and I can connect with them. If they are not, they won't be trapped here- "

"And we'll still be full of bees."

"Good point."

Myrgen grabbed her and covered her head with his arms. They crouched down behind a tree as the swarm caught them. Catriona reached out to the bees and felt a presence.

She looked up at him. *"They're monsters!"*

"That shouldn't make anyone this happy."

She reached out to them and felt an intelligence. "They are a hive, many talking as one. They are afraid. The weather is not good for their eggs. They need a place to go that will protect them."

"Send them to Persephone."

She looked at the bees and they flew off. "They said the snow is coming. It will be here by nightfall."

"Can they get there in time?"

"I hope so. Come on. We need to move. If we get to the war front, we can meet with the army there and find out what happened."

The two got up and started moving as fast as they could for the southern border.

Raven and Lauriel looked around. "Hey! We didn't die, boy! Now I just have to remember why I wanted to go here."

Lauriel shook, dust flying off his fur like water after a swim.

"Right! The Trap! Thank you. I need to study it proper, though. Can you go through to Sovereignlumin and get me some supplies? Merrick's books should all be blank sadly. It's enough to make me just hide out in Serenity and become the greatest mage in the world. Since I'll never die, I can just write it all down and it will last for future generations."

Lauriel snorted and looked at Raven sideways.

"Oh. Good point. I kind of felt Brigit turning our way. Maybe she could record it for me?"

Lauriel blinked.

"Well, there *has* to be a way to… to… oh. I guess Giles *is* the only hope."

Lauriel's ears twitched and he sniffed the air.

"You're right. It *is* colder. We'll need a fire tonight. I think my bed is salvageable."

Lauriel shifted.

"No, I don't mean burn the bed. But there was a fireplace or something, wasn't there? I mean Wilge was human. She wouldn't have wanted to be cold."

Lauriel nodded and went to the storeroom.

Raven went into his bedroom. It was a mess, covered in roots and vines that were used to set all his bones when Lucifer killed him, or *didn't* kill him. Healing sap had pooled and dried on the bedding.

In the larger room was a door to the south of his. He went to it, hoping to find the giant bath room the Covenant had. It was below the chamber where the store room and his sanctuary were housed.

The stairs terminated in a hole where a giant boulder engraved with Giles' symbols blocked all passage. He couldn't see the path it went through to get here because of all the overgrowth in the courtyard. He knew from experience that his *terra* magic could not move these and once again became angry with Giles for being who he was.

I can't do it. I can't risk Giles raising mages like him, that serve the Church. He may be rejected by Heaven but his legacy tells a different story down here. If he did *tell Alexander about Corrigan's weakness...*

Raven only assumed he knew their weakness because he had studied Fae creatures. But now he realized there was no good way to ask about it. If Giles *didn't* know, he would learn through Raven's inquiry. And it wasn't like the Fae Lords told people anything about their lieutenants. No, the idea that Giles knew this secret was very unlikely.

Then who is killing the lieutenants?

He heard a noise, a low humming and went back up the stairs. The humming was louder and seemed to come from everywhere. Raven remembered that he was looking for wood or warmth or a place to sleep for the night since the forest would rob him of any Land-based magic. The humming became a buzzing and he started looking around for a disturbed beehive in the tree in his room.

Then an onslaught of bees rushed out of the trees to the west. The sky went black with them. They flowed into the main chamber and started to gather. A presence in his head tried to take control of him. He felt it drive in, stinging and attempting to penetrate his mind. He lost control of his limbs and laid down on the floor of the chamber.

Several bees landed on him and started walking across him. He tried to fight against them but the force was overwhelming. There were millions of them. In minutes, he was covered. He couldn't breathe and he stopped being cold and started overheating. He knew he couldn't die but that never stopped him from experiencing the death anyway. He was suffocating and his greatest fear wasn't enduring the madness of being almost dead.

It was that Lauriel would come back any second.

Raven grabbed a part of his mental magics and divided his mind, leaving the part that was being controlled to continue doing the hive's bidding. He felt bones crack under the weight of the bees. With the free part of his mind, he went through his options and realized the reason the bees were here.

The cold.

The cold!

He summoned power from the oncoming storm and gave it a push in this direction. He felt the cold responding but there was no change in his situation. Instead, he reached out to Lauriel, hoping to catch him when he entered the Covenant again.

Lauriel stuck his head into the store room and Raven touched his mind.

Leave. Now. Come back at dawn.

Lauriel went away and Raven waited for the snow to come.

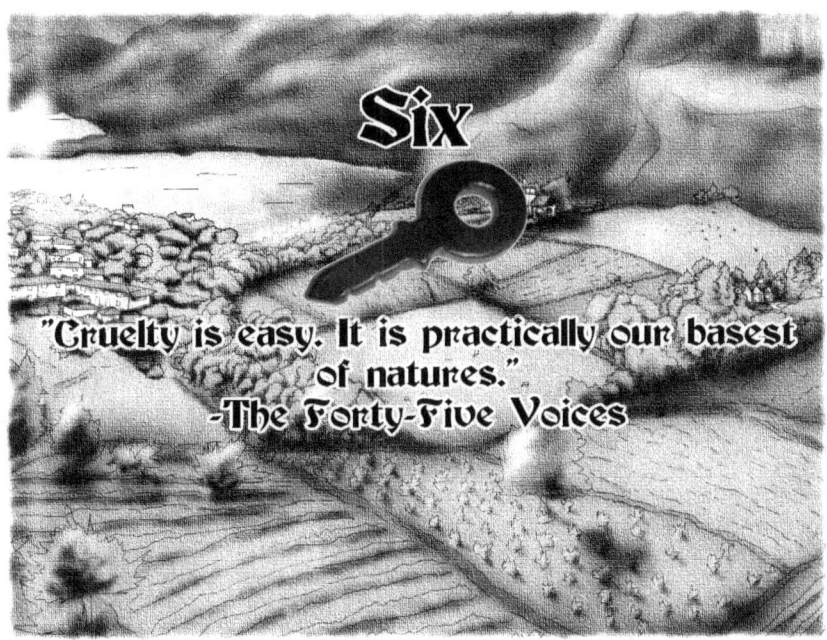

Six

"Cruelty is easy. It is practically our basest of natures."
-The Forty-Five Voices

"Wh-where are the others?"

Alexander turned to the man addressing him. Tanglwyst looked up at him.

"Martin… they… aren't coming."

Several people came over. Alexander helped Tanglwyst to her feet. A woman looked back and forth between the two. "What do you mean they aren't coming?"

Alexander swallowed and sat heavily on a bench, holding his arm. Tanglwyst took his arm to examine his wounds.

"He means the ship is gone, Madeline. We can't get back."

Disbelief rippled through the survivors who had come over.

Madeline looked at the others who came in the last group. "Where were all of you?"

The little girl looked at her. "The hold."

Another man stood up from the floor, helping others to their feet and looking around. "Where *are* we? How did we get here?"

Alexander looked at him. "I have an amulet made by Saint Giles. He was the man protecting the ship while we evacuated."

Martin looked at the others. "I didn't see anything like that and I was on the Main Deck."

Tanglwyst gestured to the page-aged children. "Were you checking on Alice?"

"I-" He looked at the kids. "Wait. Yes. I came here with her."

Alexander winced as Tanglwyst touched the damaged flesh. "I brought him to the ship. He bought us time to get people out by stopping the storm."

"How did you *find* us?" Tanglwyst touched his face.

"I was on it, when we loaded everyone on."

"Kidnapped us, you mean."

Tanglwyst stood, turning to the woman. "Madeline?"

"We were *safe* in St. Teresa! We were with *family*. But you put us back on that Saint Bleeding ship with *nothing*. Told us only *after* we set sail you were going to maroon us on some storm-ridden island!"

"I'm sure she had a good reason." Alexander started to stand but winced and sat back down.

"Why did you do it? Why would you rip us from our homes, only to throw us around the ocean to *die?*"

Madeline had a knife in her hand and suddenly, it was in Tanglwyst's chest up to the hilt.

Tanglwyst crumpled. Martin grabbed Madeline too late and pulled her back. Alexander watched Tanglwyst drop and slide onto the floor, trying to get his wounded arm to respond to catch her. She hit and the knife jostled.

Blood splashed on Alexander's face and he threw his injured arm across her. The next instant, they were in the healing pool.

Blood wandered out of her body into the water as he held her stab wound under it.

It can't heal with the knife in. That's what's wrong. I have to get the knife out.

He pulled the knife from her chest. The water grew even more red and warmer. He thought he felt her twitch or breathe. He stroked her hair.

"Come on... Come on, my love. I'm here. Don't leave me. By the Saints, *please don't leave me.*"

44

After a minute, he held her to his chest, then let her back down into the water. The blood soaked his shirt from the contact, but there was nothing pumping out anymore. He stood and looked up at the ceiling, then disappeared.

Giles stepped into the Great Hall.

"Here you are. Everyone, get warm. There are bedrooms available for you and your families. I'll get the kitchens going."

Captain Nesbit looked around as he entered the Great Hall from the stairs. He saw a group of people standing together near the end of the hall. They were shouting and he thought he saw Tanglwyst for an instant. He turned to his first mate.

"Let's get the deck unloaded in the morning. I'll go see if I can find the King and Lady."

"Aye Captain."

His first mate started gesturing to the townsfolk to move from the hold into the room, echoing the saint's comments. A little girl near the clot of people looked at them.

"Daddy!" She ran past Nesbit to a man just coming in the doorway.

The people at the end of the hall turned to see their friends starting to file down the stairs from the Inn above. Several cried out as they were reunited with their loved ones. He saw his Bosun standing, holding onto a woman who was looking very distraught as her eyes fixed on something behind Nesbit.

"Madeline?" A man pushed past Nesbit and ran to the woman. "Why are you holding my wife? Where did this blood come from?"

Nesbit moved through the bystanders. There was a spurt of blood on the woman's dress and on the floor, there were smears like someone fell and was moved.

"Martin, what happened here?"

Martin and the rest of the crowd were in stunned silence, staring at the people coming into the hall. *"Captain?"*

One of the young children hugged the man asking questions. "Mommy lost her food knife. That lady took it."

The Captain and the child's father looked at the young boy, then at the woman.

"I was… I thought everyone was dead." Madeline looked at the people around her. "They were saying everyone was dead."

Nesbit gestured to the stairs he had come down. "The man, the one creating the dome, he, just as the ship started to crack, he took everyone in the dome, the whole center of the ship straight down to the keel, just away. It's outside."

He looked at Martin. "Martin, who did she stab?"

"Why did we leave St. Teresa? *Why?*"

Nesbit looked at the woman. "Because they had received a bird saying the Mervol Army was on its way. All wood and personnel were to be made ready for their use. Your families would have been torn apart. They weren't even allowed to build sturdy temporary shelters for you because they couldn't damage the harvested wood."

The child's father picked up his son. "Where were we going, exactly? I couldn't understand what we were being told."

"There's an island that has food, shelter, and fresh water. We sail there a couple times a year. It's protected by maelstroms so pirates and thieves don't go there. You would have been safe if that winter storm hadn't shown up out of nowhere."

Nesbit looked at the others. "I've answered your questions. I've protected your families. I have helped you. Now someone tell me *what happened here*."

Alexander appeared in front of Madeline, dripping water on the floor where the blood had been smeared. It ran away from him in pink eddies. He looked at the woman, dropping her knife on the floor at her feet.

"She'd dead. You killed her."

Nesbit looked at Alexander. "Who's dead?"

"Tanglwyst." Alexander blinked. "Captain? I thought you were lost."

The First Mate walked up, smiling. "Oh, that fella with the dome just snatched the whole center of the ship, keel to Crow's Nest and plopped it outside. Everyone was gathered together in the hold trying to get to you, Your Majesty. That mage just got everyone at once. Isn't that remarkable?"

Nesbit put a hand on Alexander's shoulder. "Are you sure?"

"Wait. Giles was with you. Where is he now?"

Gomez and Brigit walked into the Hall from a hallway nearby. Gomez rushed over to the group. "Alexander! You made it!"

Giles walked out of another hallway and Alexander ran over to him. He grabbed the mage's robe.

"Help… she's…"

Brigit put her hand on his shoulder. "Alexander, what's wrong?"

All three of them were standing in the pool in a breath.

Tanglwyst's body floated, her face just under the surface in a translucent red cloud. Brigit and Giles slogged over to her as Alexander watched, unmoving.

"Giles, lift her up."

Giles did so and Brigit looked at her wound, desperate for some sign of hope.

"Can you save her?"

Giles and Brigit looked at the King, then each other. They both shook their heads.

"But you have magic. You made this pool."

"That's not an area we're allowed to work. Once the soul leaves, then it isn't healing. It's necromancy."

Alexander looked at his beloved again, then returned to the Great Hall. The knife was still on the floor and Alexander picked it up. Madeline was in her husband's arms nearby and he looked at her and the small boy.

"I brought your mother's knife back."

The boy's father pushed himself between the child and Alexander. He reached out and carefully took the knife from the King.

"It worked, by the way. You killed her. You killed the woman I loved, your future queen. Your *friend.*"

The room got very quiet and people stepped back a little from the frighteningly calm royal.

"Why? Why did you kill a woman who did everything, sacrificed *everything* to save you?"

Madeline dropped to her knees, her face contorting in fear and distress. "I'm sorry, Your Majesty! I was frightened, cold, tired…"

"You said she kidnapped you!"

"I wanted to be *home*! Safe with my family!"

"You wanted to be home, or safe?"

"I- "

"Let's take you home then."

Alexander grabbed her and took her to the center of St. Giles.

Burnt arrows littered the ground by the hundreds. Two soldiers were drawing water at town well, shirtless as their clothes were torn to make bandages. Every building in town was a smoking ruin or currently on fire. The Wise Wench was engulfed. The whole area was lit by the blue fire of the barrier. A freezing wind was flowing through the town, causing the men to shiver at the well. Their arms and backs were bruised and red, streaked with soot. The wrinkles in their faces were filled with pain and smoke, while their necks sported angry S-patterns from where their armored coifs had gotten too hot and burned them. They picked up the bandages and went into the City Guard office to tend to three more people with burns.

Snow joined the wind as he pulled her to her feet. The smell of burning flesh was in the air for a minute and screams of pain came from the guard office.

"Look carefully. See anything at all that you recognize?"

The Wise Wench collapsed, causing her to yelp in fear. Down the street, Elander's head rocked back and forth as the wind stroked it. His burnt body lay beside it in the street as a single guard fetched the head and returned to the body. An arrow whipped through the holy barrier between the buildings and buried into the guard, piercing his heart and dropping him to the ground. Elander's head remained gripped in the man's hand as he hit the street.

Alexander was unfazed by the incident. He moved her towards the well where they would have the partial cover of the remaining structures. He wanted to hurt her, to kill her and leave her body for the crows and the Fae monsters. He wanted to throw her into the barrier and let the Krakten army deal with her. He wanted to push her ungrateful face into Elander's burnt body and force her to smell it. She *deserved* to suffer.

Madeline.

Her name is Madeline.

Not *"her"*. Madeline. He knew her name because Tanglwyst had used it.

Because she *knew her.*

Alexander watched her-

Madeline.

-watched *Madeline* a moment longer, then put his hand upon her shoulder. He brought her back to her family, who rushed to her.

Her husband looked at her, inspecting her for injury. Finding none, he turned to Alexander. "What did you do?"

He looked at Madeline, on her knees hugging her son. "I'll let her tell it."

Gomez put a hand on his shoulder. "You okay?"

"I'm cold. And I don't want to use this thing again." Alexander gripped the amulet.

"C'mon. Let's walk back."

Gomez turned Alexander towards the hall he had entered from with Brigit and they left the villagers.

Seven

"Bring forth your compassion and do what
you can to heal the injured."
-The Forty-Five Voices

Catriona and Myrgen got to the edge of the forest at sunset and the wind blew through them like rapiers. They were too cold at this point to even speak, the shivering and teeth chattering making communication next to impossible. Hand signals and body language was all that was left.

Myrgen was about to step out of the forest, his eyes set on the campfire in a tent when Catriona grabbed his shoulder. She looked down.

His foot was suspended over a thick line of black sludge, barely touched by the snow. They looked down the line in both directions, then Catriona closed her eyes. The earth opened up and hot steam and magma set the entire thing on fire. The immediate stench was almost vomit inducing, but it lasted only a moment. Afterwards, the line was simply a warm, steaming fissure, then nothing.

The action got the attention of hundreds of Kraktens. Several ran up, gathering weapons, but then a shimmering figure appeared before them.

"Death Bringer."

Catriona didn't risk speaking and just bowed.

The nearby soldiers stopped, looking at each other. A snowy rabbit scout ran up to them.

"Follow the white rabbit. We'll speak inside."

They nodded and stumbled behind the soldier into a large tent. Several others were in here as well, and they stood as the pair entered, drawing their weapons on the humans.

The snow rabbit raised a hand. "The Midwinter Queen sent them. They destroyed the poison on the border."

Relief and wonder rippled through the tent and two soldiers went to check it out. They came back almost immediately, nodding.

One rabbit was larger than the others and she bowed to the newcomers.

"Please, sit by the fire. We don't have many blankets but you are welcome to them for ridding us of the poison trapping us here."

Catriona and Myrgen waved off the blankets being offered by the soldiers. Instead, she put her hand on the ground and vents of gentle steam spider-webbed out from her touch. Warmth and light eased the tense atmosphere in the tent, helping her and Myrgen breathe easier. Some of the fur-bearing soldiers became more alert and the feathered ones cozied up to the vents and nested.

Gloriana bowed. "Thank you, Death Bringer."

Myrgen looked beyond the encampment. "What's that blue fire?"

An eagle soldier ruffled the air from his feathers. "A divine barrier that encompasses the entire valley. It went up in minutes after the Midsummer King left."

Catriona met the soldiers' eyes. "We determined something must have happened to turn the season. Can anyone tell us about it?"

Roast venison was offered to the pair. They took the food, mindful of the number of people who needed to partake.

"My Breath spoke with several soldiers. Only two survived who witnessed the incident with the Voice. He was felled with an arrow, the same kind that now lights that barrier. It was fired from a bow made by Giles the Accursed himself and was responsible for thousands of lives lost in the past."

The rabbit commander gestured to another rabbit. "Scout Albrecht here was tending to the Midsummer King when the attack came. He heard the guards protecting the King and his final words before they were forced underground. The Breath communicated the information to the

Nachricht Hase who helped spread the word about the season change and the storm."

Myrgen gestured to the barrier. "And that thing stops them from coming in here?"

"It stops us from leaving. I do not know if it affects them as well. But arrows do penetrate it. We have lost a few border soldiers to arrows fired blindly through and a dozen tents were destroyed before fires were contained. About half an hour before sunset, the attacks stopped happening. We imagine either they ran out of ammunition or the cold got to them."

"Or both."

The Commander nodded. "Most likely. But unlike us, they can harvest wood to make more arrows."

Catriona lifted her head, her eyes jade with anger. "They'll find no steel or stone to tip them. They'll take nothing more from the Land to use against you."

The earth rumbled around them and then settled.

Myrgen took Catriona's hand and she blinked and exhaled, her eyes returning to normal. The effect was not lost on any of the soldiers in the tent.

"Your Majesty, we would like a word with you." Myrgen motioned to the open air.

Gloriana nodded. Catriona and Myrgen stood and stepped outside. He noticed the ears twitch of several rabbit soldiers, or *Nachricht Hase,* and looked at Catriona with his *read me* expression. She did.

"Your Majesty, follow us."

Catriona took his hand and moved them into the Land and out again at a cliffside cabin. He looked around, not quite sure where they were. She opened the door and entered.

Gloriana appeared outside the threshold. Myrgen bowed. "Please come in, Your Majesty."

"That is not yet your right to grant, good Hunter."

He looked at the door and tried to enter but the doorway was impenetrable. Catriona was inside, looking around and frowning.

"Uh, Catriona?"

She looked at him, then shook her head. "Oh, forgive me, please come in, both of you."

The entrance gave way and he and the illusion of the Winter Queen entered, Myrgen closing the door behind them. "You wished to speak to me in private, Bringer?"

"Yes. Your Majesty, we believe the lieutenants are being targeted."

Gloriana sighed. "We have figured that out as well. If they did not know it before, slaying the Voice of Command would have confirmed the idea. Do you have any suggestions?"

"Outside of 'Don't expose your Lieutenant'? I do not."

"But that army in the Mervol Valley…"

Myrgen looked at Catriona. "We're here now. We'll get them out. The northern border is clear. They can get home."

"I tried all day to reach you, Bringer. The forest prohibited it. If they enter it, I cannot help nor protect them. I cannot even watch them from my home. Tooele is closing the roads so that should impede the enemy from invading. But nothing stops the humans from entering or leaving. They can follow and hunt the Fae down now."

Myrgen snorted. "Oh, the Fae can handle themselves just fine, thank you. We ran into a massive swarm of intelligent bees in the forest. Any human who enters that place will learn the hard way that the inhabitants aren't defenseless."

Catriona spread her hands. "And the summer Fae would be at risk, which is why your brother took them into the earth. The Kraktens are half human. They can get back or continue to fight, should their leaders make that decision."

"According to my Breath's investigations, before the assassination, the Krakten Queen had brokered a peace, but the treaty had not yet been inked before it was shattered. According to the Army, they are in need of leadership to determine their course. Several of their officers were slain in the aftermath."

Catriona looked at Myrgen. "I understand. We will look into giving them a leader to follow. For now, they will not freeze, but the humans will find they will get no aid from our purview."

"My thanks, Bringer."

"So, the peace was brokered. Where is the Krakten Queen now? I assume she must be captured or she would have appointed new leaders."

"The Krakten Queen was also slain. The arrow that killed Johner, killed her as well."

Myrgen sat back. "Uh, that's extremely problematic. The rulership of Krakte goes through the women. No man has the authority to appoint or elevate. There's no King to take over."

Catriona sighed. "And her daughter was likewise killed."

Myrgen held up a finger, tapping it on the table. "But her *granddaughter* still lives. Elizabeth's father was a Fae. It's why she went mad. If she's gone from the Fae-adjacent lands for more than a year, she suffers from a sickness. I remember Sovereigna begging Elizabeth to return home but she was never able to leave."

Gloriana scowled. "They held her prisoner?"

"No. It's just she would need an escort and the Prince was constantly gone from the palace during the summer. With Catherine in the Papal City and Alexander leaving unexpectedly all the time, Charles couldn't risk leaving the kingdom in, well, *my* hands. To be honest, that was probably the right choice. But he had enemies everywhere so any vacancy of the throne would spark a coup."

Catriona studied her hands. "So, this was my fault."

Myrgen looked at her, then reached out for her hands. "No, *Llaldeen.* This was Catherine's fault. Her travesty on Saint Michael's Day caused a bloody wound that has never healed. All of it stems from that day. The nobles knew nothing of you or Alexander's pursuit of you. They focused upon what they could see: The Church. You were invisible."

"That doesn't make me innocent. But that is not important right now. With the Queen gone, will the Army be forced to go to Patras for the Princess?"

"That would explain what we saw in the encampment. I'll bet they have no idea what to do."

Gloriana glanced to her left. "James says the army won't take orders from a man, possibly not even Corrigan. Their laws preclude it. So even if Alexander offered to be her guardian and rule both places, they couldn't allow it."

"Catherine could. Or you, Your Majesty."

Gloriana shook her head. "Not now that the forest covers it. She could live with me in Glarren but that would not help her govern her people."

Myrgen looked at Catriona. "You could do it."

"Live in Krakte?"

"We're immortal beings. We go between life and death to visit our friends and family. We can leave a battlefield in Mervolingia and end up at a cabin in- "

"Mervolingia. St. Giles is half a mile that way."

"-In Mervolingia in seconds. We can be in Krakte and sleep in Caratia."

"Except the forest stops my abilities."

Myrgen stopped and closed his mouth as he thought. "So? Still immortal. We live in Krakte and visit Caratia a lot. Or we move the capital of Krakte to Persephone. Make it closer to Caratia."

"Move a major capital? They'll never go for that."

Myrgen sat back. "Wait. Sovereigna was *outside* the Black Forest."

Gloriana folded her hands together solemnly. "We saw her body ourselves."

"Sovereigna was half Fae."

Catriona and Gloriana looked at each other and then at Myrgen.

He leaned forward. "So, Tangl told me that she saw a bottle on Sovereigna's vanity once when she visited Elizabeth for a summer, before Elizabeth was married to Charles. Tangl thought it was a perfume and used it. She said her appearance changed but she seemed uncomfortable with the result. Anyway, it was the Queen's *distilled Fae essence*. She had a way to remove it to enter and then leave the forest. That's how she got here."

"Which means the Princess could leave and come back to Patras regularly."

Gloriana looked between them. "But the queen had the formulae and she's dead."

Myrgen grinned. "Exactly. She's just *dead.*"

Catriona put her hand on Myrgen's arm. "But she'd still need a guardian with her in Austra until she was of age."

Myrgen, Catriona, and Gloriana stared at the table for a few minutes.

Myrgen shrugged. "This sounds like a much longer conversation. And possibly a summit between rulers."

Gloriana nodded. "What do I need to do, Bringer?"

Catriona looked at her. "Keep the army safe and the roads closed, please. We need to sort out this succession before we make another decision."

"I'll listen for your call."

"Please tell James hello for us."

"I shall." Gloriana faded from view.

Myrgen scratched his arm. "That did not go as I expected."

"Same here."

"I'm going to start a fire."

"Thank you."

Myrgen looked at the fireplace. "Um, dear? Do you see what I see?"

She looked at the fireplace. "*That* was what I noticed."

She walked into the bedroom, the bathing room and privy, and looped back into the main room and kitchen. She inspected the items for making tea on the counter. She shook her head.

"He brought a woman here."

"Any particular 'he'?"

"Alexander. This was the place where we finally made love after seven years of mourning."

"Oh. Is this a good place for you to be then?"

She looked at him, the emerald in her eyes clear. "It is my cherished home. I brought him here because it is special, not the other way around."

Myrgen examined the subtle cues that this was hers and not a shared place. "Is anything missing or broken?"

"It looks like nothing untoward happened here and she left in the middle of making tea. Not even in the middle. At the start." She frowned. "I think it was Tanglwyst."

Myrgen arched an eyebrow. "Alright, I long ago admitted your powers of observation were astounding, but I think you just jumped a line there."

She smiled. "That tea is grown exclusively in Zara, so she would never have seen it. She knows her craft, which is trade. So, when she found tea she's never seen, she would have figured out its origin. And the fact that the only person still alive who has been here is Alexander, I think he and she are traveling together. Or at least they were before she left."

"What makes you think she left?"

"Nothing is broken or out of place. She simply stopped making the tea. If she were interrupted, there would be something completed. Cups on the drying board or on the table. More wood burnt instead of a single log that was stoked and not tended. See how it is burnt on the bottom and still untouched on top? They got in late enough that they didn't eat or get water, just got the fire going, then banked it for the night.

"She woke up ahead of him, was going to do something nice, then stopped and left. The bed was slept in by two people, but only one was under the covers. Your sister is notorious for being cold so nothing sexual happened between them here, yet they were comfortable enough with each other that the shared bed prompted her to make him tea to be nice."

"Maybe he ordered her to do it?"

"And then let her leave without finishing the task? If he was in here and not asleep, why did he let her leave? If they were disturbed or attacked, they would have to let the attacker in because they can't get in otherwise. And this cabin is not visible from the road or sea. The only way to find it is to know it's here so they weren't pursued here or discovered. No, all the things I see here point to her leaving while he slept after discovering he brought her to my home, one we shared for three nights when we cared for each other."

"Were they just here the one night?"

She looked around. "I don't see any indicators otherwise. Not enough has been disturbed to speak to a longer visit."

Myrgen sat on a chair. "Well, if anyone can say the wrong thing, or the right one, it's Alexander. Sometimes he's capable of doing both at once."

She put her hand on his, crouching beside him. "Are you okay here?"

"Oh yes. *Llaldeen,* Alexander was not here long enough to leave a trace. Everything you just read was my sister. He didn't leave so much as a footprint in the dust. I do not feel threatened by him at all. Are you alright having my sister despoil your bed?"

She smiled. "Strangely enough, I am happy knowing that she left him for his dishonesty. She might be good for him. So, you handle the fire, I'll handle the tea?"

"Done."

Eight

"A priest or wine can achieve the same intelligence."
-The Forty-Five Voices

General Aethelraed stood, putting his hands on the table. "Okay, what happened?"

The guard from St. Giles set down the cup of warm wine he had been given. His shivering was under control now. "I noticed a bow had been removed from the guard armory. I had put it there myself not long before and had wanted to try it out on the practice range.

"I saw Elander on the roof of a house on the watch route, near the Wise Wench. I saw he had the bow."

"Did you say anything to your superior?"

"Yes, I think I said, 'Damn. I was too slow.'"

The other officers in the tent snickered. Aethelraed nodded. "Continue."

"Yes. So, he sees something and then he drew the bow and a blue arrow just *appeared* in it. He shot it and the place went crazy. Screams from the Fae encampment go up and there's a bunch of movement. We see the enemy scrambling for weapons. The Captain and I drew our swords and he shouts up at Elander, 'What is happening?' He shouts down that they are attacking the King. The Captain shouts something up but the place gets really loud and chaotic. The Captain runs to the edge of the town between the two buildings and suddenly, the barrier just erupts.

"The captain was caught in it and stumbled back, on fire. I see he has a flaming arrow in his chest. I dive behind the building and get out of range. Next thing I know, Elander's head hit the street near me. It's been ripped off. I hear a clatter a few seconds later and shoot a quick look down the alley. There's that bow, right there on the ground. I can't see through the blue barrier so I risk it. I ran for it and grabbed the bow.

"I ducked back under cover and tried it. It drew a blue fiery arrow for me too. But I couldn't see anything. There was a window in the building I was hiding behind so I ran inside and up the stairs. I opened the window looking out over the valley. All of a sudden, I saw every other soldier out there just get sucked into the earth, like they were going under water. Gone. The ones left behind are looking around and running. Then, they started firing fire arrows on the town. I shot a few arrows at the army until they shot the building I was in. I ran outside and saw that the granary was on fire.

"I ran. After I was out of town, I knew I needed to get this to you. So, I came directly here."

"Do you know what that screaming sound was?"

The guard looked at the officers around him. "Uh, no. No."

Aethelraed narrowed his eyes. "Are you sure?"

The guard shook his head. "I just came here."

"You didn't try to take out more of the enemy?"

"Sir, I'm a guard in a town that caters to sailors and trade. I can break up a street brawl with a single punch. But I'm no archer. I don't have bird eyes, like they do. I figured the army would have archers. The bow needed to be here."

Aethelraed looked at the others. "Very well. Head outside and get under cover. That storm is hitting us pretty hard."

The guard opened the tent flap, then turned back. "Sir. I need you to understand I'm not a coward or a deserter, like those folks that left on the ships. I am great up close in a fight. I just ain't no archer."

Aethelraed accepted the man's admission with a nod and he left. The General arched an eyebrow at the officers assembled. He gestured to the table and they all leaned in.

"Speak your counsel."

The woman in the group, Captain Carolina DeGroot, spoke up first. "He was lying for certain. He saw something in town when that screaming occurred."

Aethelraed nodded. "I saw that too, Carolina. You have an archer in your regiment that can put this to good use?"

Carolina smirked, her dark brown hair, sleeked back into a tight braid, causing her eyes to have an elongated appearance. It gave the smirk a sharper look than normal. "I have someone that could drop the Pope from here."

"Get them this bow and set them a watch for any more Fae arrivals. Josephus, what have your scouts heard?"

"Someone went along the entire northern edge of the valley and, overnight, poisoned it so that the Fae will die if they touch it. It happened before the Black Forest expanded. I heard from another scout, up by the Benevolent Friar, that there's a foreign warrior here to fight on the side of the Mervol forces."

The third man turned to him. "How are you getting the messages from the other side of the valley?"

"Remember that line of barrels Saint Giles set up with three men at each? They essentially hand it to each other down the line. Messages can travel pretty fast when they just have to be handed to someone nearby to get to us. So, I am getting intel regularly from the whole line."

Dietmar shook his head. "The enemy is encamped practically right in town? How is that possible? Villages don't grow in just one direction. They spread out. How can the enemy be putting up tents *next to* the homes of the citizens?"

"They destroyed them to intimidate the townspeople. The queen just drew the whole area into the ground, promising to return their homes when their King returned her daughter. The army did destroy the vineyards outside in the valley, out of vengeance against the Lady Tanglwyst de Holloway."

Aethelraed nodded. "Did any of your operatives see what happened to make the reinforcements leave?"

"No. But I have new information to bring into it: A blue arrow. That should spark anyone who might have seen something and didn't realize it."

"Good. And have someone on that guard. He's afraid to talk, but confession is good for the soul. He might seek a priest or campfire to share the tale."

"A priest or wine..."

"Exactly."

The Intelligence Officer bowed and left.

The final officer looked at Aethelraed. "What do you think, sir?"

"I don't know. You were born in Krakte, Dietmar. What do *you* think?"

"I think this storm means the Midwinter Queen is now in power. Summer, or any other season will be months away. We may get a Fall, but then back to Winter."

"So, we need to solve this now."

"I'm afraid so. Sir, I'm the ambassador's aide. I can go and find out what is happening with the Krakten army."

"No. I need someone who understands the Fae *here*. I am trying to handle an invasion where, even with the reinforcements gone, the enemy outnumbers us two-to-one. War is a summertime activity and the only reason young men and women join up is because their family fields don't need tending in the summer. The promise of returning for the winter months is why we have an army at all."

He waved at the billowing door flap that occasionally coughed snow into the tent. "That will be a detriment to recruitment, meaning we'll need to conscript to swell out numbers and that has long-term consequences to the country. If that bow can end all this in a single shot, then we need to seek that choice."

A soldier tapped on the tent flap. "General Aethelraed? I have a missive from St. Giles."

"Come in."

The soldier handed him the missive. He opened it and read a report dated yesterday, stating the King and Krakten Queen had made peace and would be drafting a treaty in the morning. He set it aside. *A lot can happen in a day apparently.*

Gomez and Alexander entered the Healing Pool cavern. Brigit had pulled Tanglwyst's body up onto the edge. Alexander took off the amulet and dropped it in the pool.

Brigit walked over to him. "Where did you go?"

"St. Giles. I showed the woman what Tangl saved her from."

"And?"

"It worked. For both of us. Any change?"

She looked at Tanglwyst. "I believe the pool is drained. It's had to heal a lot of people with no time to recharge. The only reason it was able to do as much as it has is because it had millennia to build up. But we've surpassed its regeneration. We have to wait for it now."

"How long will that take?"

"Let's see how it looks in the morning."

Gomez patted Alexander on the back. "Giles said there are a lot of beds. We should get you in one. It's been a very long day."

"I can't just leave her."

Gomez looked at Brigit but spoke to Alexander. "Okay then, what do you want to do?"

"I don't know."

He walked over to her. "She's... she isn't... deteriorating."

Brigit looked at Gomez then at Alexander. "No. I think the pool may have inherent preservative properties. It at least keeps wounds from getting infected or going septic. Your arm should have shown signs of inflammation but it doesn't. It might be able to recover a little faster but it has to preserve him too. I can't imagine having him in the pool is having a positive effect."

She gestured to Michael's unresponsive form.

"Then maybe it's time he wasn't."

Alexander walked over to the archangel and tried to pull him from the pool. His arm was still all but limp beside him and had no strength. Gomez started to come over but Alexander cried out in frustration. He jumped into the water, retrieved the amulet, and teleported them both to the church in St. Giles.

He dropped the angel on the altar, holy water splashing everywhere. Several people were sitting in the pews, wrapped in bandages. Their eyes grew in astonishment as the figure dripped water from his large white wings. They looked up at the King and the angel, stunned, before scrambling away in panic.

Alexander saw the questions in their eyes but he was just too exhausted to answer them. He closed his eyes and returned to the pool.

"That should help."

"Sire..."

"I'll stay here, Gomez. You and Brigit rest. I'll watch over her."

As he lay beside her, the two sighed and went back upstairs.

"General, wake up."

Aethelraed opened his eyes, struggling to get out of the deep sleep. He waved off Captain Manglebottom. "Yes, yes. I'm up. What is it, Josephus?"

"A rider from St. Giles just got here. He says there's an angel in the church."

Aethelraed frowned and started putting on his boots. "Where is he?"

"In the medic's tent. He's badly frozen."

Aethelraed stood, threw on his cloak, and strode out to the medic's tent. They had set up alongside the main road for a quarter of a mile, out of range of the Kraktens' arrows. The "medic's tent" was a string of three tents together, though they had not endured many casualties yet from battle. Thus, he was surprised to find it actually quite full. Several soldiers had hands or feet wrapped in bandages.

"That's him."

The General started for the ginger-haired man in the City Guard uniform. The Medic got up and intercepted him.

"General, what do you need?"

"That man just rode all the way from St. Giles in a blinding snowstorm to get information to us. Did he say anything to anyone?"

The Medic nodded. "He was incoherent. The ice had taken hold of his blood, and he was confused and slurring his words. He was exposed for at least three hours to the storm. Fell off the horse when he got here. The only thing keeping him up was that animal's warmth and it is in equally bad shape."

Josephus looked at the man, then tapped on Aethelraed's shoulder. "Sir."

A soldier next to the man was waving at them. The officers went over to the woman.

"Yes, soldier?"

"I heard him. What he said. He was hard to understand, yes, but he kept repeating himself and trying not to lie down. Said he had to get to you."

"What did he say, Private?"

"He said, 'The queen is dead. Johner and the queen killed.' And, 'The king appears and vanishes'. Just before he went to sleep, he said the king killed an angel on the altar of the church."

Josephus and Aethelraed looked at each other, then at the guardsman. "Thank you, Private."

Aethelraed nodded them towards the tent flap and away from the resting soldiers. Josephus looked at the sick, keeping his voice low.

"I know that name, General. Johner. A few of the townsfolk who escaped told us about them at an inn near here. He is the Lieutenant of the Midsummer King. He was keeping the Queen in check. If he's dead, that actually answers the question of what happened to the Fae. An observer saw the blue arrows flying, then shortly after, all of the Fae disappeared. If the Queen and this Lieutenant were killed by that bow…"

"Then we know how to destroy the Fae Lords." Aethelraed glanced at the guard. "We need to get up there right now. Get my horse."

Josephus put a hand on his shoulder. "Sir. The cold."

"I know. We'll bundle up. Luckily, it's snowing, so the ice won't hit my blood as deep. And that man didn't have gloves or a hat. He left before the storm hit. I know what I'm getting into. Have a unit join me in the morning."

Josephus patted him on the shoulder. "Alright. Be careful."

Aethelraed returned the gesture and left.

Nine

"Live life. There is plenty of time to be dead."
—The Forty-Five Voices

"You ready?"

Myrgen stood, securing his coat around him. "Yeah. Hey, did you hear a horse go by right before dawn?"

Catriona frowned, adjusting her scarf over her ears. "No. You heard a horse go by *here*?"

"No, I thought, on the road?"

"The road is as far from here as town is."

Myrgen shrugged, discovering gloves in his pockets. "Where did you find winter clothing?"

"Under the bed. It was put there in case I ever wanted to stay the winter here."

"How long ago was that?"

She squinted at the ceiling. "Three years? I'm hoping the waterproofing held. I'm glad it fits."

"What's it made of?"

"Fae cat furs. They molt their skins each spring for mating. They are just lying around the forest. Still dangerous to collect them, but you don't have to kill the cats to gather a bunch."

"Oh. Interesting." He clapped his hands together and nodded at the door.

They steeled themselves for the blast of cold air and were not disappointed. The cold consumed his breath and energy.

"Let's- just- s-s-send a l-letttttterrr."

She scolded him with her eyes and they closed up the cabin and moved through the woods to St. Giles. It took almost an hour but by the time it was mid-morning, it was starting to feel warmer. The valley's temperature change had also put the town above freezing, and they both noticed.

They came into town between some houses that were snow-covered charred messes. Catriona pulled her scarf down, horror in her eyes as she surveyed the devastation. Nearly every building around the well was damaged or destroyed and the entire eastern side of the town was just not there, cut off by the blue barrier.

"Oh no. Not the Wise Wench." Catriona's voice spoke of thousands of hours in merriment lost.

"The one from the book?"

She nodded. They saw only one set of tracks in the snow and it came from out of town. Closer inspection revealed hoofprints. Near the City Guard office was a horse that looked tired and cold but covered in cold weather trappings. They saw a few more tracks going into the Church.

"I'm going to check over here. You check the Church?"

Catriona went towards the Tanglwyst Trading Company office. He went to the church and opened the door. The cold wind blew in but the room was fairly warm and sheltered. A large cloth covered something on the altar, and Myrgen wondered if it was a half Fae soldier from the size of it.

A man in a coat, with bandages on his head covering his ears, looked at Myrgen. "Can I help you?"

Several men with soldier's armbands sat in prayer. Four turned to face him.

"I um, I'm looking for Al- the King. I have a message for him from Caratia."

One of the soldiers squinted at him. "You look familiar."

66

"I used to travel years ago with the Lady Tanglwyst."

The soldier nodded. "She left, I heard. Helped evacuate the town. They went to St. Teresa."

"Wait, she was here?"

"A couple days ago, I think. Someone saw His Majesty here last night. Follow me."

The soldier took Myrgen past the Guard office to the Guards Barracks. "Gomez will know where he is if he isn't here."

The name made Myrgen's blood run cold as he realized the last time he had talked with Gomez was in Patras.

The soldier opened the door and stepped in. "Ah, General. I have a messenger."

Aethelraed turned to the door and locked eyes with Myrgen. Myrgen swallowed as the General recognized him.

"Seize that traitor!"

Myrgen stepped back and fell in the snow. The soldier grabbed him and hauled him to his feet.

Aethelraed stepped into the street. "You have a lot of gall walking into a Guards' Barracks."

"To be honest, I kind of forgot I was wanted."

"Killing *one* king wasn't enough for you? You came back for a second one?"

"No. I have a message for him from the Dûcesa of Caratia."

"The hell you do. The Dûcesa would never be this far from home and would hardly send a *traitor* as a messenger."

"You can ask her. She's here, looking for the King."

Aethelraed drew his sword.

"By the power vested in me by the Crown of Mervolingia, I sentence you to *Death.*"

He put his sword through Myrgen's chest.

Myrgen looked at the sword, then stuck out his tongue at Aethelraed.

The General raised his sword and beheaded the former chancellor.

Alexander awoke, extremely stiff and sore. Tanglwyst lay beside him and for a second, he forgot about her circumstances. Then the hole in her doublet reminded him and he felt that loss all over again. He slipped into the water and the stiffness eased.

Good. It's recovering.

His arm was better too. He watched it repair, slower than the instant healing of his leg wound, but still fast enough to see. He could flex his hand now and it didn't hurt. It slowed and he got out, not wanting to drain the pool again. Its restorative properties were still keeping Tanglwyst preserved.

That's sick, you know. You're preserving a corpse. You slept next to a corpse, Alexander. You banished an archangel that could restore your friends to Heaven so you could wake up next to a dead woman.

Alexander closed his eyes. His inner voice was right, and he realized he heard the admonishment in Tanglwyst's voice.

"It appears you're still with me, my Love."

He needed to go get Michael. He had probably scared the souls right out of the people in the church last night and he hoped there would not be a chanting mass touching it when he returned. He might be able to go quick enough that no one would see it leave and they would just assume a miracle happened or something.

He looked at the amulet and put it on. Then, he willed himself to the church.

Aethelraed rubbed the toe of a boot into some snow, leaving a small, bloody stain. "Check his pockets for any messages."

"You think he was telling the truth?"

"No, but I want to make sure."

The soldier rifled through Myrgen's clothes but came up empty. He looked at the General and shook his head.

"I knew he was lying. Throw that piece of offal in the harbor."

Aethelraed looked up as a woman in black came up the road. He gestured to her.

"Who is that girl? What's she doing in the street?"

The soldier stood. "She's not familiar. No one here has black hair."

The soldier grabbed the body by the feet and started to pull, but the snow made that difficult. He walked to get a different grip and accidentally kicked the head. It rolled and came to rest at the woman's feet.

She blinked slowly and lifted emerald eyes to the General. The soldier scurried over.

"My apologies, Miss."

Catriona looked at the General's sword.

Aethelraed wiped the blood off on the snow and then dried it on Myrgen's coat. He noticed the style was definitely *not* Mervolingian, and as he let his eyes walk up the woman's attire, saw the distinct features adorned hers as well.

"What are you doing with my messenger?"

Aethelraed stood slowly, deciding not to put his sword away just yet after all.

"I beg your pardon, My Lady. I do not know you."

"And the means of our introduction has just been kicked at me by a bystander. So, allow me to provide another."

She opened her hand and the White Granite Sword of Caratia rose from the ground to meet it.

The soldier stepped back, moving towards the barracks and almost stumbling in the red snow. Aethelraed understood the impulse. Like all soldiers, he had read of the legendary sword of the Caratian rulers but had never considered them more than inspirational fiction. Now the sight of the fairy tale felt unreal.

The woman lifted the Sword and leveled it at Aethelraed. "Your sword is still bloody."

The General bowed without taking his eyes off her. "My apologies, My Lady, but that man was a traitor to this country. He could not be trusted. I undoubtedly saved your life by doing away with him."

The Dûcesa made no expressions of anger or gratitude. "What were you doing with my messenger's body?"

"Disposing of it."

She shifted her head the slightest bit. "Allow me."

She did not take her eyes off him, but the ground opened up beneath the body and consumed it, blood and all. The soldier fell on his bottom, scrambling away into the barracks. He got to his feet and started to draw his sword, but Aethelraed raised his hand.

"Ho there, son. No need for that. We're all friends here."

The soldier looked at Aethelraed and eased his sword back in the sheath.

"Are we?" She started at the top of his head and took a long walk down to his boots. He felt almost violated by her scrutiny, it was so intense. When she took her gaze past his face, he finally looked at the Sword. Then, an idea came to him.

Caratia's army is rumored to be undefeated. If the Sword is true, perhaps that is as well. And Mervolingia will be saved without sacrificing a single soldier to this waste of a war.

Caratia was on the other side of that cliff to the east. They could be here in a week.

Unless they are already on their way.

Aethelraed's eyes returned to hers.

Well, if they are coming to assist the Fae, then having their ruler as ransom would end that alliance. All paths lead to her army under my control.

Aethelraed got the smallest of smiles on his lips and waited for her to finish her inspection.

"My Lady, inside the Church is a bedroom with a fireplace. Let's get out of this cold and get you set up in there. I'm sure His Majesty would want you warm, dry, and safe. As soon as you're settled, I'll find him and bring you two together. This way, please."

He turned away from her, an act of confidence and trust. She let him get ahead of her before she lowered her sword and let it sink back into the ground.

Good. Let's get you onto holy ground, young lady. Once there, you won't be using your Land magic against me.

Ten

"When the time arrives, the prey becomes the hunter."
-The Forty-Five Voices

Myrgen awoke in their home in Summerland and felt his neck. "That was so weird."

He got up from the chair, fully dressed this time. He noted that his preferences were maintained in the afterlife regarding how he wanted to be dressed upon his return. Although, he imagined that was a very unique situation. Most visitors did not have repeated trips into Summerland.

He stepped out, noting the new tower. An old man was entering it, which was surprising.

An old man? Someone that comfortable with how their life ended should just-

Oh, nope. The tower is fading away. Guess he had only one thing to do before moving on. Wonder who he was?

He looked around.

While I'm here, I can talk to Sovereigna about the essence potion.

He saw a man stepping out of a new house near Myrgen's own. He wore a woolen jacket of multiple colors and had a letter in his belt. He picked up an axe by his doorway and slung it over his shoulder.

"Johner!"

Myrgen turned to see the Queen of Krakte. He had seen her at Elizabeth's wedding but had not officially met her. He looked at the man and walked over to them.

"Your Majesty. Lord Johner."

They turned to Myrgen. Sovereigna frowned. "I know you. You were at my daughter's wedding. Her friend's brother"

Myrgen bowed. "I am honored you remember me."

"You seem to have done alright for yourself."

"I have your daughter to thank for it all, to be honest."

"He was always destined for more, Mother."

Myrgen turned and saw Elizabeth standing nearby. The encounter threw him completely off guard.

"Elizabeth?"

"Surprised I'm here? I wasn't allowed to interact with others at first. I needed to shed some anger before I could touch other people's dreams. People come here to achieve peace and move on. That can't happen if they are assailed with unrest."

Myrgen tore his eyes away from her. "Yeah. I just noticed someone move on. There was a tower there a few seconds ago. It looked a lot like the towers in ruin at Persephone."

"Hi Myrgen. Back again?" The Sinister Glove walked up. "Johner?"

Johner smiled. "Glove! You're alright!"

He hugged her, which she responded to like this had never happened before. "Okay, that's never happened before. And as for 'alright', you know we're dead, right?"

Johner gestured. "Yes, Merrick told me… Oh. That's the tower you were just talking about moving on."

"What? Merrick moved on?"

Elizabeth put a hand on the Glove's shoulder. "Don't get too upset. You'll be isolated."

"No, this is *bad*. I was just up at the mansion. The First Dûcesa is gone."

Myrgen's brow furrowed. "Gone? Like kidnapped?"

"No. Kinda… worse. She… Let's go to her house and talk about it. I don't want to put this out here in the open."

Gwen walked out of a house not her own and bowed to Myrgen, then gestured inside.

Myrgen nodded to the group. "Go on. I'll be right there."

He walked to Gwen and stepped inside. Then he realized the house was Drake and Anika's.

And it was empty.

He ran back outside and looked around but did not hear or see the things he sought. He closed his eyes and turned back to Gwen.

"When?"

"Shortly after you two left last time."

"Tib too?"

"He said he was fine and didn't need to grow up. There was nothing he had needed to accomplish that he had not already done. They left this."

She handed him a letter addressed to him and Catriona. He tucked it into his doublet. "I'll read this when I see her again."

The house behind Gwen dissolved into nothing and a lovely tree grew in its place.

"The First Dûcesa moved on last night. I was about to get the details. We're meeting in her house, if you want to join us."

Gwen smiled. "I'll see you there."

He started to walk to his house to put the missive in there when he realized Elizabeth was still standing nearby.

"Do you want to join us too?" Myrgen gestured to the house everyone was going into.

"In a moment, if you can spare it." She walked over to him.

"Sure." He looked at her. The time here had restored her to her original splendor.

She glanced at her hands. "I'm sorry for what happened. I didn't… I don't…"

"I understand."

"My mother said once it got to the toxicity it was, there was no cure. At that point, my death was inevitable. The only question was how much I would destroy in the process."

Myrgen blinked, understanding. "The Fae Essence. That's how your mother handled it."

She nodded. "She would draw it out each season. She used it to travel into the Black Forest and help Fae who were in distress. It was also a healing remedy for the soldiers."

"I need to find out how to do that. For Emmy."

"I'm sure she'll be happy to teach it. But you'll need to hurry. Her third birthday is coming up and she'll need it done then, or it will turn to poison."

"Don't worry. I'll make sure it happens."

She smiled. "You really can, can't you? You'll make sure my daughter is safe."

"It is uppermost in my mind. Emmy being taken care of is essential to the kingdoms carrying on. My beloved and I are working to that end."

"Who are you with now?"

"Catriona Morstadora."

"The Stâpâna of Caratia?"

"Sort of. *I* am the Stâpâna of Caratia now. Well, Stâpân. I think she's probably the Dûcesa now. We've been quite busy of late."

Elizabeth sighed. "Well, that's over now if you're here."

Myrgen smiled. "That's a story for another time. How do you know Catriona?"

"She was at my Coronation, briefly. She told me in Private to reach out to Caratia if Mervolingia needed aid. Then she saw the Prince and left."

"Yeah. Their relationship has gone through some changes."

"You *stole* her from him?"

Myrgen scoffed. "No. Her decisions are her own. He burned a village to the ground out of spite and destroyed her ship. There was no recovery from that."

"He loved her. To the exclusion of all others."

"I'm pretty sure that's where the trouble started." He stopped himself and gave his head a scratch, then ran his fingers through his hair. "You know, that's not true, really. He loved a lot of people. He was even kind to me after Arnold was killed. He considered every servant in the palace, every messenger, every cook and guard to be his true family. It's why he so despised the nobility, always sniffing around for favors.

"*That* man was worthy of her love, and he had it. It was he who burned it."

"And it appears you have become worthy of it yourself."

74

She touched his face and he smiled. He took her hand and kissed it.

"I need to get to this meeting."

"You look happy. Fulfilled."

"Yes."

"I'm very glad. Go. You'll need what my mother can teach. Tell her my garden will have what she needs."

"You're not coming?"

"I… don't think I need to…"

She thinned and faded before his eyes.

George looked out over the valley. The innkeeper and his wife had let him stay in the Queen's room, especially since the door was destroyed. He had watched the enemy movements until the snow hit.

Their immediate incursion of arrows at his command had driven the enemy back along the border but now, they weren't in range and the barrier was a two-way impediment. Humans could not go through without burning. The end result was him staring over the valley as it went more and more obscured until the night and the snow covered it all.

He had discovered he didn't sleep so instead, watched the valley all night. At a certain point, the snow around the Inn was lighter, fluffier, and he could see the valley looked a little different, but he wasn't quite sure what was going on there. Now at full day, the situation was no better.

He went downstairs and walked up to one of the soldiers on duty. He was sitting on a chair by the hearth, trimming branches. A pile of them lay beside him. An unstrung bow leaned against the wall.

"I need you to fire an arrow into the air."

"That's gonna be difficult, since we ran out of arrows during the assault."

"That was a day ago. Why haven't you gotten more?"

The soldier looked at him. "No feathers. No tips. I can fire a *stick* into the air but it won't fly true."

"Very well."

The soldier blinked, then picked up his bow, restrung it, and pulled a shaft from the pile. He walked outside, followed by the Saint. Charles was handing missive after missive to the men who handed it to the next person, all along the perimeter of the valley.

The archer put a stick against the bow string and pointed it at the sky. George put his hand on the soldier's shoulder and concentrated on the projectile. The man glanced at the Saint's hand, then fired the bow. The shaft jumped up about twenty feet and then came back down to embed in the snow.

George frowned. "I don't understand. I should have been able to imbue you with my skill."

"Um, yeah. You know, any other tenday and that would have been a weird statement. It's not a matter of *skill*, sir. I know how to fire an arrow. I'm a hunter by trade. But a blunt stick isn't an arrow."

Another soldier stood in the doorway. "What were you hoping for, Sir?"

"To ride the arrow and survey the situation with the enemy."

The soldier in the doorway exchanged looks with the hunter. "Is that something you usually do?"

George sighed, his breath forming clouds in the cold. "No. But I've never been down here since becoming a Saint and I thought, maybe..."

"That being the patron saint of soldiers gave you magic like your friend has?"

George sighed and they walked back to the Inn. "Exactly. I feel the need to get to the other side and my companion has not returned."

The soldier in the doorway stopped him from entering. He glanced around at the others. "So, you don't need an arrow. You need this."

The soldier opened up his hand and unfolded a cloth.

Inside was the priest's amulet.

Alexander appeared in the Church and looked at the altar. Someone had covered the angel with a large cloth. Four soldiers stood in the room and Aethelraed was walking a woman past the pews. They all looked up at the King.

Blue eyes met familiar emerald and she stopped.

Aethelraed bowed. "There he is, my lady. As promised. Your Majesty, this woman has a message for you."

Alexander didn't look at him. "Everybody out."

The soldiers glanced at Aethelraed, who nodded to them.

"You too, General."

"Your Majesty, we don't know who this woman is. She was with the traitor Myrgen de Sablonierres. She *claims* to be the Dûcesa of Caratia, one I do find to be quite credible, of course."

"*I* know her. Go."

Aethelraed frowned but bowed and started to leave.

"General, where is Myrgen? I need to tell him something."

"He- he was executed this morning, Your Majesty."

Alexander closed his eyes. Aethelraed did not push the issue and left.

"I'm sorry to hear that. Are you alright?"

"I am, thank you." Catriona tilted her head, glancing him over. "You have suffered a loss as well."

Alexander was barely holding himself together. Having her here made things more acute. "I thought you couldn't read me."

She remained silent and came up to him, staying on the other side of the altar. "What did you need to tell Myrgen?"

"It's not like it matters now. I just lost Tanglwyst. A confused villager stabbed her. She died almost instantly." He leaned on the figure under the cloth.

She watched him struggle a moment with admitting the news. "You had truly committed to her."

"Yes. I don't think I'll be able... to... do this without her. I haven't really accepted it yet. I will, but I'm still denying it."

She touched his hand. "You think she kept your soul clean."

"I *know* she did. She destroyed the poisoned amulet I had in Zara."

She glanced at his chest, withdrawing her touch. "And yet you have found another."

Alexander lifted it to look. "Yeah. Turns out the ones from before were made with an infernal component. This one was made by the Saint who invented the things, before the Church corrupted the process. We only have the one though."

"Your eyes are clear and you do not stink of rotten eggs."

He smirked. "Thank Heaven for small miracles. If I stink, it's my own eating habits now."

She let a pained smile grace her lips. She looked at the cloth covering the angel. "And what is this?"

"Oh, this is the salvation of the world, my Lady." His bitter tone was not lost on either of them.

He pulled the cloth from the angel and she looked upon the creature. Alexander studied the face. "I never noticed before. You know who he looks like?"

Tears rolled from her eyes. "Michael."

The creature on the altar opened its eyes. The color was light brown, and she *knew* them. She had seen those eyes as they threw her into a pit over and over. She knew them from the knife he burned her Hunter with and cut his flesh to drain his blood for their wall paintings. She knew him from stab wounds and losing herself again and again to their *refusal* for *years* to let her release a suffering child.

A child that became a part of the First Dûcesa's soul, and now hers.

Catriona felt the wrath of the Land below them and connected with the stone that ran throughout the cliffs, untouched by Heaven. She called to Calista in Her watery domain and the sea answered her summons. It rushed through the channels in the cliffs and drove through the caverns beneath the village.

She drew her rage from within and the White Granite Sword was in her hand. She screamed in anger as the monster on the slab before her turned to her and recognized her.

She brought the sword down upon him but it was blocked by another. The Archangel rose, pushing her blade aside. He flapped and she was tossed back into the pews.

"Catriona!"

Her eyes shifted to jade and armor covered her, black stone shot through with lava. The wooden pews beside her started smoking.

Michael pulled the sword in his hand into a spear and leveled it at Catriona. Lightning scored the white blade, making the room glow. She crouched, waiting. The lightning flew at her and she jumped over it. It caught her leg and she felt it go numb. She cried out and brought the Granite Sword down on the Angel.

It scored down his left arm, embedding in the altar and shattering it down the middle. Chunks of marble flew up and Alexander ducked around the corner to the hallway where Aethelraed had been leading her. Catriona pushed the stones at Michael and slammed him in the chest. The effort pushed them apart, both landing on the opposite ends of the church.

She hit a candelabra, knocking it down, the candles melting in the intense heat of her armor. She flung the lava in her armor across the room. The cold air solidified them and they pelted him, burning his skin. He shot the lightning at her and it hit the metal in the candelabra, which aided in sending it through her. Her foot slid in the melted wax just before it evaporated.

The lead in the stained glass behind her liquified and the panes fell to the stones, shattering. The snow was pulled from outside and filled the room with precipitation. The heat and snow made the air wet and she realized this played directly into his hands.

"Alexander! Get out now!"

Michael drove the tip of his spear into the floor and sent the lightning everywhere. It lashed out at her and she dropped to the ground, burying her hands into the stone. The water pooled around her and conducted his attack all through her. She channeled it into the ground, but still felt her muscles seize.

She couldn't breathe. Her heart stopped.

He waited for her attack but she couldn't move. She felt the call of Summerland on the edge of her mind. She could see Myrgen talking to a woman. He kissed her hand and she smiled and a moment later, she faded away.

Then Michael was towering above her. He kicked her, sending her sprawling along the wall. He raised his spear, lightning cackling.

She looked into his eyes and allowed an inner voice to rise.

"Uncle?"

Michael wavered, recognizing his niece's voice.

Catriona pushed the Granite Sword into the stone and it thrust straight up into his crotch, through his torso. She pushed harder, penetrating his heart. He thrust the spear down into her body right before she scattered the Granite Sword to reform beside her.

The sword ripped through him, large chunks now missing from his chest and lower body. A chunk went through his head and cleaved it open. He slumped to the floor.

She reached out to his exposed heart.

"You do not deserve what you stole. I return it to her now."

The heart exploded at her touch.

The roof came down upon her and she was grateful for the arms of Summerland.

Eleven

"Wait at leisure while the enemy labors."
-The Forty-Five Voices

"General, there's been a development."

Aethelraed looked at the guard, then at the church. He motioned them away from the doors as the soldiers watched through the windows. "Watch her. Be ready if she attacks the King."

The soldiers nodded.

He stepped away from them and looked to the Guard. "Report."

The guard glanced at the barrier. "I was just in the woods getting a deer and I saw the valley nearby. It's completely free of snow. They are even walking around without coats. I used a spyglass to get a better look and I saw them preparing the Queen's body. They were making something to carry her. I think they plan to return her to Austra."

"Into the forest? Won't that stop them from returning to the battle?"

The guard shrugged. "I think so."

"When did you see this?"

"About a quarter hour ago. I snuck back down and came right here."

He looked at the barrier, which ran right up to the forest. "Thank you."

He saw riders coming up the road. *Josephus. Good. This will be some good news for hi-*

Light screamed through the windows and the soldiers cried out. *"General!"*

He rushed over and opened the door. The Angel was charging a large spear. He saw Alexander in the hallway.

The woman yelled something and then the entire church was blasted with electricity. Aethelraed was knocked back into the snow, his ears stinging. The guard knelt down beside him.

"… the King… help… the King…"

The roof caved in on the church, and he passed out.

He came to as people were carrying him through the barracks doorway. He looked up and saw Josephus and several other skilled personnel.

"Did you bring the whole… damned unit… Josephus?"

Captain Manglebottom looked down and smiled. "Seemed smarter that camping in the snow."

He pointed to the scout. "Make sure you… talk… to him… about the… King…"

Then he drifted back to unconsciousness.

There was a flash of light and Catriona came out of their home. She saw Myrgen standing alone and he smiled and met her halfway. They exchanged a kiss.

"*Llaldeen,* I wasn't sure you'd join me."

"I… I wasn't about to leave you to your own devices."

Myrgen noted the changed in direction from heavy to light hearted. "Is everything- "

"Catriona!"

Catriona turned to the Sinister Glove waving from the First Dûcesa's door.

She turned to him. "We'll talk later."

He nodded and they went to the cottage. He gestured to the new faces. "This is Her Majesty of Krakte and the Voice of Command. This is my beloved, Catriona Morstadora, the Embodiment of the Land, and the Death Bringer."

They rose and bowed.

Everyone was introduced and it was quickly established who knew whom.

"You are with the Stâpâna of Caratia, young man?"

Catriona smiled. "Technically, he has become Stâpân. The Duce and Dûcesa are actually here."

Myrgen caught her eye and he shook his head in the smallest of negatives. She let her sadness almost show to him, then she gave the tiniest nod.

"I stand corrected."

The Glove glanced at her hands and fidgeted with the seams on her gloves. "Apparently there's a rash of that. Merrick has moved on as well. And the First Dûcesa."

"And Elizabeth, just now."

Sovereigna snapped her eyes to Myrgen's, then looked past him to the window. When she did not see her daughter, she settled back into her chair.

"I fear there is a lot to talk about. We should get started." Catriona looked at Myrgen. "Who should go first?"

George landed on the destroyed roof of the Church in St. Giles and vomited. Black icor ran from his eyes and nose, the sludge in his stomach spreading across the stones and snow. He realized it looked like the foul atrocity that had been smeared across the top of the valley by the corrupted priest and vomited again. He threw the cursed amulet away from him and it *tinked* against stone and fell into the snow.

He sat back on his heels and inhaled, letting the cool air ease the burning in his lungs. He grabbed some clean snow and rubbed it across his face, cleansing himself of the retching residue. He realized there were chunks of rubble in the snow when they scraped his cheek.

He looked around for the first time. The only thing still standing was the back wall of the church, where the Combined Holy Symbol included his own. When he had used the amulet, it was focusing upon this window and Giles that brought him to it. He expected to see Giles here and was surprised he wasn't.

He gave himself a couple more moments before getting to his feet and stumbling across the rubble. The building had been brought down very recently, smoke still billowing from beneath the stone roof tiles and broken walls. The doors were hanging off the hinges, but the ceiling collapse made it impossible to go through them. He climbed slowly down to a shattered stained-glass window and worked out that he could get through if he bent the glass and lead.

He punched through with his gauntlet, then shoved the metal and glass aside with his shoulder. He fell through unexpectedly and cut a long gash across his cheek, nose, and forehead in the only unprotected areas on his head. The angle of the cut had barely missed his eyes.

The blue fire barrier was directly in front of him and he turned away from it. He went around the building and saw several horse prints and a few booted ones leading away from it all. A lot of prints also went into two buildings near the Church. He saw a well in the middle of the square and went to it. He drew up the water and splashed it on his face to help clean off the blood. The cold air made his face hurt but it still felt better than the sludge.

He waited on the edge of the well until he saw movement in one of the windows. He looked at the sign that said *City Guard Office* and went inside. A man in a guard's uniform looked up from a bench.

"Can I help you, Sir?"

"What happened to the church?"

"Some foreign woman fought an angel to the death."

"Which Angel?"

"I don't know. The King brought him here last night. I watched the whole thing. She said she was from Caratia.

"More than that, she was in the company of a traitor to Mervolingia. The General executed him in front of her. I personally think she was coming to declare war on us. Why else travel with him?"

"Where is this General? Is he still in the area?"

"He is but he's unconscious. The Angel shot him with lightning."

"Lightning from a *spear?*"

84

"Yeah, how did you know?"

"I have met the wielder. I am Saint George of Canterbury."

"The Patron Saint of soldiers?"

"The same."

The guard looked him up and down. "This way."

He walked to the next building over and went inside. The room was lit with a fire and a few soldiers were shivering near it. Socks and padded armor steamed on armor racks, drying out, while the men, with shaking hands and blistered fingers, ate stew from bowls. Another man sat beside a bed with a figure still in his padded armor lying upon it. The sleeping man's armor showed signs of electric scoring.

George nodded to the companion. "General?"

The companion looked up and stood. "Me? No. The General is that one. General Aethelraed Rhydderch. I'm Josephus Manglebottom, his Commander of Intel."

"Saint George of Canterbury."

Josephus arched an eyebrow, then shrugged. "Of course you are. What can I do for you?"

"I was sent down from Heaven to assist in the war."

"Great. We need you to destroy all the Fae in the valley and then kill the Queen of Winter. Or at least her lieutenant."

George frowned. "I'm not sure I can do that."

"Then you can't really help us. That army threatens our country and as long as it's here, these soldiers can't return to protect their homes from bandits, which are going to start attacking homesteads as the food runs low. Since the fields are going dormant under this snow, we won't have food come harvest. This town's granary blew and the ships are all gone. Others aren't bringing supplies because groups that usually sell off their excess, like *this* place, won't be doing that. We need that valley because right now, it's the only place capable of growing food."

George glanced at the pile of reports the man was reading. "What is different about this valley?"

"Come on. I'll show you."

Josephus left and went between the buildings to the forest. Once within, the canopy filtered much of the snow and they could move without leaving tracks. The forest floor here had pine needles and fallen branches and a blind was set up that hid the pair as they came up. The blind was well established, obviously part of the town's means of acquiring wild game throughout the year.

Josephus put a finger to his lips and pointed to a spyglass.

George picked it up and got into place to peer through the blind.

The valley was devoid of snow and there was even a regimen of soldiers moving tents and others digging rows in the soil. Bird soldiers would jump into the air and snatch birds that flew by, saving their arrows for other duties. Although they stayed away from the edges of the valley, they weren't cautious of it, as if they knew the Mervol army was out of arrows.

Josephus tapped him on the shoulder and pointed to another area near town. George looked and saw that the Krakten Queen's body was being prepped for transport. The larger members of the army had green sashes that denoted them as special and only they were moving her corpse. The rig they were creating was designed to be carried by four, and it looked like a dozen were packing up. Packs of food and supplies were being amassed and extra blankets were being sewn into coats as he watched.

He looked at Josephus and nodded and the two returned to the village. They went into the guard office via the jail cell, something George found curious, and didn't speak until they were fully inside.

"Any suggestions from Heaven?"

"Some. First off, your soldiers must stop wearing the armor all the time. The loss of feeling in their extremities is causing them to turn black. They are wearing their armor because it's the only coverage they have. The Krakten army is settling in for the long haul. Your army needs to return its soldiers to their homes before they desert or die."

Josephus blinked, his arms crossing as he listened to this reprimand.

"Second, your king appearing and disappearing means he has my friend Saint Giles' amulet. I need to confirm he has it with Giles' consent, so we need to find him. Then we need to explain the seriousness of this situation so he stops treating it like a toy to frighten people."

Josephus shifted, eyes casting down as the truth of this rebuke landed.

"Third, the army is devoid of arrows and the enemy knows it. They are tilling the soil to grow food. We need to get every arrow in the neighboring areas to the army. I saw your message system at work earlier. Get the word to your soldiers. Those that want to return to help their families, go. Those that wish to continue to serve, get them winter clothing until we can get this sorted."

"Yes sir."

One final thing. I am looking for Saint Clara, the Patron Saint of Barren Women. Has she come here?"

"That I can't tell you. I only got here an hour ago at most."

"Alright then. Hopefully, Saint Giles will show up here soon to check in and I can talk to him about this. I'll set up in this building. Let me know when the General wakes up."

Josephus gritted his teeth, but bowed, and left.

Alexander reappeared in the healing pool. Gomez was standing next to Tanglwyst and looked over at the splash. The King nodded to the woman whose hand still dangled in the pool.

"Any change?"

Gomez shook his head. "Where did you go?"

"St. Giles. I was going to get Michael but he woke up and fought… Catriona was there."

"Wait, *your* Catriona, the one you were pursuing?"

"She was never mine, but yes. She- Gomez, I've watched her fight before. This was different. This was *brutal*. She's not like she was. And Michael was throwing lightning around with no regard to humans. I guess the entirety of Heaven's host consider us insignificant.

"But she *hated* him Gomez. *Hated* him like she *knew him*. He wronged her personally. She distracted him and told me to leave when he would have killed me. I have no idea if she's even alive or dead right now. She saved my life."

"What do you want to do?"

Alexander looked down at his arm. He could move it and the scarring was lessening. "The pool is regenerating fast."

"That's probably best. We need it ready if people get hurt. The townsfolk are bringing in the supplies for the ship but they can only stand the cold for so long."

"I'll see about helping once we…" He looked at Tanglwyst's body.

"Regarding the Lady, Sir, Brigit is looking for Giles. We need to figure out what to do with her. I'm sorry, Your Majesty, but she can't stay here."

Alexander sighed. "Alright. I'll be here. I won't leave her alone. She might…"

Gomez nodded. "Yeah, of course."

He cast a glance back at his King and left the room.

Twelve

"Create something from nothing."
–The Forty-Five Voices

Gomez made his way up the stairs. The floor immediately above the pool had dozens of bedrooms, with desks and bookshelves, that many of the single people or couples had set up in. Gomez had heard of other rooms for families elsewhere in the Covenant but he didn't know where yet. Regardless, everyone was settling in.

He went to the end of the hallway and up the stairs at the end to the Great Hall. Several people were gathered at tables, some eating, some talking. People were carrying supplies from the ship down the stairs that came from outside. Others directed them to different areas by content, marking things down on empty log books.

Brigit and Giles stood by a hearth in low conversation. Gomez waved and turned so he could join them.

Giles gestured to the room. "The kitchen is up and running so there's plenty of food. I went through and got the privies and bathing areas active. The bedding has been freshened. People seem comfortable, at least so far. Better for sure than back in Cliffport."

"Was that the name of the village before? Cliffport?"

Giles nodded.

Gomez glanced at the people. "I think I might recommend it. Less confusing."

"Well, no one knows about this place so it won't become a target. These people are safe until all this blows over." Brigit turned worried eyes on Gomez. "How is he?"

"He wasn't there when I got there. I thought maybe he went to the privy or maybe even found a room to sleep in, but then he reappeared in the pool."

"Where did he go?"

"Cliffport. He went to go fetch Michael back. It apparently didn't work. However, he might be ready to inter the Lady."

Giles sighed. "Well, let's get this taken care of, then."

They started walking back and Brigit indicated a woman at a table. "That's the one who stabbed her. She's told everyone here how the town has been ravaged by the war. She has stated Tanglwyst probably saved all their lives. After that, everyone decided things would be best if examined in the morning and went off to find beds to sleep in."

Giles lowered his voice. "The families don't seem to care that they've set up in the apartments for the servants. Students never brought their families to study at the Estate, so we didn't build larger rooms for them."

Brigit rolled her eyes. "*Anyway,* everyone settled down and there was peace for a few hours. It seems to have worked. People are less stressed and there are lots of volunteers to help bring in the supplies. The place is bonding through the adversity."

Gomez stopped them right before heading down to the Healing Pool. "Giles, *can* you... is there anything you can do for *preserving* her or possibly... I don't know..."

"No, I can't bring her back. Only the Giver has that power and, well, she's indisposed right now."

"Well, apparently, Michael got into a battle with Catriona and was throwing lightning around just now."

"The woman he pursued?" Brigit frowned. "Why would Michael fight her?"

"Alexander said she seemed to know him. He said she hated him and was going for the throat."

Giles acted wistful. "Ah, for her to take out an angel. If she succeeds, maybe we can take her up to Heaven and have her do in the rest. Free the Giver."

Gomez started heading down the stairs. "Wouldn't that just cause a total mess in Heaven?"

Giles shrugged. "It might restore the Giver's power. Then she could free herself."

Brigit stopped. "You think so?"

He looked at her. "Yeah. They spent hundreds of years keeping her weak. If she got her strength back, she would likely break out and return to the world."

"And what exactly would that look like, do you think?"

Giles furrowed his brow in thought, then his eyes grew wide. "She'd *create!* The Black Forest! It now covers an entire wasteland, and it grew overnight."

They ran down the stairs to Alexander.

"Alexander, do you still have my amulet?"

Alexander lifted it from his neck and held it out. "Why?" He stood, suddenly hopeful. "Did… Is there something you can do?"

Giles looked at Tanglwyst, then crouched down and took her hand. He reached out with his other hand and it glowed. "Her heart was cut. I can repair that so she's whole again. I can repair everything right now, just in case."

"Please."

Giles concentrated and the glow got brighter, then dimmed. He stood. "There."

"Then she's fixed?"

Giles put a hand on Alexander's shoulder. "Do you want an ugly truth, or a pretty lie?"

"Tell me the lie and I'll know the truth."

"Very well. When a person's soul leaves their body, it goes to a great table where it either moves to sin or salvation. While it is on this table, a person can still be revived. It's how people who fall or drown but come back do it. That's a real truth.

"She might be rolling around on that table, her soul's fate not yet decided, thanks to that pool or your love for her or whatever. People come back for any number of reasons. But that is usually only temporary. If she's actually dead, the table will judge her. If she was more sinful

91

than saintly, she goes to hell to be purified. If she's more saint than sinner, she'll go to Heaven."

"Heaven. Where you were betrayed and cast out."

"Yes."

"That's not a very pretty lie."

"We haven't gotten to the lie yet."

Alexander folded his arms and waited.

"I'm going right now to find the Giver. Perhaps if I can bring her back here, she might choose to bring your friend back. I don't know for sure but she might.

"Until then, we need your friend not to deteriorate. I'll put her in a state of repose and we'll seal her in a place where she will come to no harm. Will that work?"

Alexander's eyes filled with the hope the mage just promised, then, after a moment, he looked in Giles' eyes and exhaled.

"That was the lie."

Giles said nothing.

"Where should I put her?"

Giles motioned to a door. "This way."

Thirteen

"In order to capture, one must let loose."
-The Forty-Five Voices

Catriona looked at Sovereigna. "Are you alright?"

The Queen sighed. "I suppose the point of this place is to achieve peace and move on. It's… a *good* thing, in the end. I just feel like I have so much to do at this point. I left in the middle of things."

The group was up and walking around, digesting all the information that was just shared. Sovereigna was looking at the carved wooden desk in the cottage of the First Dûcesa.

"This piece is magnificent."

Gwen headed to the kitchen to start cooking. "She was here a very long time. Over three hundred years. You can learn a lot when you have a reason to just stick around."

"She lingered here for three hundred years? Why?"

Catriona crossed her arms. "I never wanted to read her, but her pain was so obvious. She loved someone that was taken by the Soulless. He was her Hunter, her other half. She remained here in the hopes that perhaps things would work out and he would be restored to the world, leaving his soul to join her in Summerland. She always believed there would be this beautiful, blissful reunion and they would embrace, leaving all this behind. But it sounds like she finally went to him instead."

"To be so connected to someone that they hold you back for three hundred years..." Sovereigna shook her head.

"I can understand the appeal. Myrgen felt like part of me, even though we didn't meet face to face under the best of circumstances."

"How did you meet?"

Gwen leaned back from the stove to look at them. "He kidnapped her and tried to extort her into murdering Charles."

"So, a fairy tale beginning, I see." Sovereigna smiled.

Catriona echoed the smile. "Indeed. But there was so much more to him than I was led to believe. Together, we healed and grew. I know he will always be with me now."

"I wish I had known him in life, then."

"You know, he was in love with your daughter. You should talk to him about her. You did not get to see her in her final years."

"You would want your beloved to recall his love of another?"

"She tried to poison him at the end. I'm not worried he'll start pining for her. And that ordeal brought him and I together. I cannot look upon it as an event I would avoid."

"I'll speak to him then. But first, Merrick gave Johner something and told him to take it to someone. Can we do that? Send actual letters to people beyond?"

"It must be possible. Our clothes don't disappear when we leave unless we go through the fire."

"There's more than one way out of here?"

"Yes, though it is not an option for everyone."

Sovereigna tapped her finger on her lip. "Would there be parchment here?"

Catriona turned to Gwen.

Gwen, her hands full with cooking, waved an elbow towards the desk. "Check the drawers."

Sovereigna did so and found what she needed. Catriona smiled and left her to it.

She walked outside. Johner was sitting on a chair in front of his house, playing a stringed instrument. The Sinister Glove was perched on a log under an eave, enjoying the shade and music. Myrgen came out of their home with several cups of mead.

Johner stopped, grinning. "Ah, there's a hero if ever I met one!"

Myrgen handed him the outermost mug and the Glove came over and grabbed another one. He offered Catriona her choice of the four remaining.

"The Queen and Gwen?"

"She's writing something. I recommend against bringing something wet and sticky to her right now. Gwen would appreciate it though."

Myrgen went into the cottage and came back out a minute later.

Catriona looked at the place where Merrick's tower had been. "It seems so strange. A Lieutenant comes to Summerland and leaves after writing a single missive?"

The Glove shrugged. "I don't know why he bothered. He said that everything he wrote was gone now that he was dead. Magical texts don't remain after a mage's life force fades. That missive is likely to be blank now that he's moved on."

Johner looked at it. "I hope not. He was quite agitated when he handed it to me. It didn't seem to register that I was unlikely to be able to hand it to Raven myself. And Raven being here rendered it unnecessary so I really don't know what he intended."

Catriona eyed the magical seal on the letter. "It's not for any of us so we can't check. We'll leave through the mansion instead of the fire, then. That seems to preserve what we have on us."

"If we leave through Sovereignlumin, we can come out by Persephone." Myrgen took a sip of the mead.

Johner set aside his instrument. "You can get to Sovereignlumin from here?"

The Glove gave him a hesitant look. "Well, yes, but only as a ghost. And you need permission to use the door."

Johner cocked his head. "This sounds like a bad idea to you?"

"Of course. First of all, we are three lieutenants down and I prefer not to be beholden to Heaven at this point. We have no idea if they're behind this."

Catriona shrugged. "I managed to return Michael's stolen energy to the Giver. I hope it aids her."

The Glove smiled. "Then that's three of theirs as well. Lucifer sent Raphael and Gabriel to the Soulless yesterday. That leaves Uriel and Gloriana. Uriel is on our side though so that helps."

Myrgen arched an eyebrow. "He is?"

"He and Ember were rivals for a thousand years. Then something happened in Heaven and Uriel came down and stayed down. Ember noticed he wasn't leaving at the end of the season and they became friends. Uriel walked the world the rest of the year, helping people, then would prank with Ember in the Spring. It was Uriel who got his brother Michael to help with the Soulless war."

Johner looked hopeful. "If the Angels are gone, then whichever one was killing us is no longer doing so."

Catriona shook her head. "There are still two up on their side, and I'm not entirely sure Lucifer isn't the one behind all that."

The Glove narrowed her eyes at Catriona. "Did you see something?"

"I see two Angels, one Fae Lord, and two entities of the beginning and end of life."

"And Karma." Myrgen pointed to them.

"Right. So, that's still a lot of very powerful beings toying with all of humanity. Perhaps they are balancing things, but my concern is more that we are being picked off."

"And now we have two mages, one Land and one Heaven, both conveniently immortal." The Glove frowned. "This is sounding more and more like Karma."

"Except Heaven made them both immortal."

"Did it? Raven has been around for centuries, always unchanging."

Myrgen shrugged. "He's half Fae. Isn't that inherent?"

Catriona shook her head. "So was Gwen, and James is also, yet they aged. Out of sequence and at different rates, but they aged. No, he must have something."

"Well, it wasn't Ember." The Glove took a drink.

Johner looked at the others. "It wasn't Corrigan either. I know his allegiances. They reported to me."

Myrgen furrowed his brow in thought. "Every Lord has a human lieutenant. That's their connection to the world."

Johner straightened. "What makes you think they are human?"

Everyone looked at him.

Myrgen gestured to the town around them. "You're here."

"Sorry. Reflex. Go on."

"Right, but do they *have* to be *all* human?"

The Glove and Johner looked at each other. "I think so."

"So, it isn't that he's a lieutenant since Raven's only half human."

Catriona steepled her fingers, tapping them together. "James can't actually be one either then. Gloriana's his mother."

The Glove blinked, then looked at Johner. "Maybe half is enough?"

Johner arched an eyebrow. "Or maybe she is setting him as bait to draw out the assassin."

"Then they will not survive the encounter."

Everyone turned to Gwen.

"Food's ready, by the way."

Everyone filed in and sat at the table. Mead accompanied a meal seasoned by gratitude. When they were finished, Sovereigna handed Myrgen two letters.

"These are my wishes for Emmy. They need to get to Austra, and Catherine. Can you arrange that?"

"Of course."

Catriona folded her hands together and leaned on her elbows. "So, we came to the conclusion outside that James might be bait to draw out the killer of the Lieutenants. Does that really sound like something she would do?"

The Glove tore a piece of bread. "Wouldn't you?"

Johner rubbed his chin. "If she has no Lieutenant, the killer has to take her out personally. James sounds like he could thwart that."

"Unless they used magic." Sovereigna drank from her cup.

"Magic is inherent to the Land. She should be able to protect him."

"Not against *divine* magic."

Johner shook his head. "There hasn't been a divine mage in a couple hundred years. The Church put to death even their own."

The Glove rolled her eyes. "No, there's one out there. Giles, the one Brigit and Raven were traveling with. He's a divine mage."

Johner sat back in his chair. "I remember that one. Foul beast to be sure."

Catriona turned to Sovereigna. "With you gone, Myrgen says your granddaughter inherits."

"Yes."

Myrgen leaned forward. "Elizabeth said her garden held everything necessary to make the Fae Essence Extraction you used but that we needed to get it to Emmy soon."

Sovereigna closed her eyes. "Oh, of course. Yes. She is turning an age soon. Her blood is diluted through her father, but she can still suffer the effects. I'll write down the recipe. I also have a bottle in my vanity at Austra. You need to get it to her by the end of the season."

"It is my primary mission at this time."

"Thank you. Catherine is with her and I don't want anything to happen to either of them. I hope she will escort my granddaughter to Austra and be her regent."

"Well, for that to happen, Alexander needs to be coronated and in Patras. As long as he is gone, Catherine will be pinned down handling his business. And Emmy's kingdom just expanded to overtake what has widely been seen as York's abandoned wastes. There might be wars over the land."

"Until they learn the truth of the Black Forest. It cannot be harvested. Krakte has a much larger problem in that the small number of farms we had no longer can produce."

Catriona cocked her head. "Who can she have as a Consort? Is a marriage to someone possible?"

"Anyone she chooses. But her offspring will only come from…"

The Glove looked at her askance. "A Fae Lord?"

Sovereigna nodded.

"I knew it. It was Ember, wasn't it?"

Sovereigna furrowed her brow. "No. Corrigan. Why did you think the *Fae Army* came to my aid?"

The others just blinked.

"Johner knew, of course."

Johner patted the Queen's hand. "He loves and mourns every human wife he's had."

Catriona looked at him. "Who was Estelle's mother?"

"A tree, I think."

Myrgen and Catriona paused considering this, then nodded. "Yeah, that tracks."

Myrgen leaned forward. "Wait, is Raven *your* son?"

Sovereigna shook her head. "No, no. He's my ancestor's son."

Myrgen started counting on his fingers. "Wait... Corrigan breeds with..."

Johner leaned forward. "I think we're getting off topic. Corrigan and Embertwist are in Torpor. There are no Fae Lords to sire a half-human child to secede her. Sovereignlumen died horribly millennia ago from being scarred. His children found him and built an effigy illusion to hide it."

"I thought he was killed by the Church. There's a children's story I used to read to my son that told of it. 'Holy Warriors from the Sky stabbed the Fae King in the eye. They made his heart the magic keep to grant all children blessed sleep.'"

Gwen swallowed, disgust clear on her face. "That was a *children's* story?"

"The Church is not very nurturing."

Catriona turned the phrase over in her mind. "'Made his heart the magic keep... Myrgen, I think it's talking about the trap."

The pair told them all they knew of the trap.

Sovereigna's eyes were wet from the tale. "So, he lured her there to power a spell?"

The Glove looked away. "It sounds like it cost him his life. Whoever did that spell stabbed him and ruined his appearance, changing him. But he was already corrupted by then. He was going to die anyway."

Sovereigna looked at Catriona. "It released *her* to take in *you*. That would change the nature of the spell, possibly weaken it."

"We think so too. After it grabbed me, it has not held on to anyone else for long. And I felt a connection to something within it. I have requested Raven get the Giver in it. Perhaps between us, we can get some insight into what it is and how to end it."

The Glove tapped her fingers on the table. "Unfortunately, that's what Merrick was working on when the Incident happened. He was so panicked when he came here. Which is understandable. If he had figured things out and written them down, the findings he was handing Raven would be blank afterwards."

Sovereigna now was deep in thought. "The spell needs a constant power to draw from?"

"It appears so, yes."

"Then what you need is something that will disrupt it."

"For how long?"

"For a spell like that, it has a power source that can run dry. That means *any* time without quintessence would end it."

Catriona lifted her cup, nodding. "So, if we free the captive, we can end the spell. But it will grab whomever is nearby to not be without a source. How do we interrupt it without letting someone die?"

"We give it another, larger source."

Everyone looked at Gwen. She returned the look. "We give it Fae essence, and cast a Fae spell to make the source appear bigger than what it already has. It releases the source, grabs the new one. We get their victim out of there and then the source drains away because- "

Everyone said it with her.

"-it's an *illusion!*"

Sovereigna exchanged a glance with Catriona, then turned to Myrgen. "Would you mind helping me gather the things I need? If we are going to do something like this, we will need a lot."

Myrgen glanced at Catriona. "Sure. Elizabeth said to tell you her garden would have what you need. Catriona?"

"I'm gonna stay here and clean up, alright?"

Gwen nodded. "I'll help."

Myrgen offered his arm to the Queen and they went to Elizabeth's garden. Myrgen looked around at the diversity of the plants.

"I'm glad she left this to you. She must have known what we would be up against."

"I think, as we get closer to the point of peace, we can see farther around us."

"I'm glad I was able to speak to her again."

Sovereigna smiled. "She might have been holding out for you."

Myrgen smiled, shaking his head. "When she knew me, I was an Augustinian. She never would have expected to see me here. But you? She might have known you'd be here eventually."

She smiled, but the sadness lingered on her lips. "That bears a true sound. The Stâpâna tells me you knew her the years that I did not. She suggested you might be willing to tell me about her from the point of view of someone who loved her."

"Did she, now? Well, I must admit that seeing her was a surprise. The Land doesn't have a Hell or punishment village, does it?"

"No. Apparently, it merely keeps you locked away from others until you work out your personal monsters." She pointed to the ramparts and windows of the castle beside the garden.

Myrgen looked up and saw the signs of scarring around the window. "Well, I'm glad she could do it and move on."

He saw a bushel basket and picked it up. "Now, you tell me what we need to pick and I'll tell you everything from the moment I met Elizabeth."

Sovereigna put her arm in his and led him to the flowers.

Johner and the Sinister Glove stopped by his house. "Which one of these is yours, Glove?"

"I didn't make one. That wasn't something I needed to feel safe or comfortable. For me, having *no* home means I'm safe, free to leave or stay."

He looked at his home. "I haven't had one of these for over a thousand years. I didn't realize how much I missed it."

"Yeah, hey, so I think I'm going to go to Sovereignlumin. Stay by Ember's side."

Johner looked at her. "You can do that?"

"I've been there before. I'm just a ghost there, but I feel a hole in my heart being away from him. He's just been there so long."

"I understand. For me, it's almost the opposite. Corrigan took me from my home and family to fight at his side and the thing I never knew was missing is sitting right here again. I feel like I have given plenty to the Midsummer King. I should like time of my own again. However, I should like to walk you to your entry point. I would like to see the Fae Resting Place in case I wish to visit my Lord."

The Sinister Glove looked up at the mansion, then back at Johner. "You know what? This is a *Land* afterlife. There's got to be a way to get to another *Land* afterlife from here."

Johner looked at his instrument and smirked. "I remember hearing of a wood that would play like a flute when the wind blew. They said that the sap would stop an instrument from ever going out of tune. It's called Perfect Pitch. I think I'd like to find this wood."

She smiled. "Sounds like a fairy tale."

He nodded. "It does indeed."

"Well, get your necessities together. We'll leave when you're ready. I'll meet you back here in a bit."

Fourteen

"The dead have no need for sorrow. That is
the realm of the living."
-The Forty-Five Voices

Alexander arranged Tanglwyst's hair around her head like it had been on the pillow the last time he lay beside her. The moss around her glowed a soft gold, like the light of a candle, making her look peaceful and relaxed. He stepped back, glancing at the other shelves coated in the glowing moss. One or possibly two had mounds on them, completely covered in it.

"So, how long do we have before she…" He gestured to the lumps.

Giles picked up some from a lump. "This is called *corpse moss*. It serves several functions here. First, it's a preservative. It will keep her looking like this for a tenday, like she's just sleeping. After that, it will start to absorb her, turning her into *čaro*, it's second function. Third, it prevents her from becoming a ghost."

"And where do I put her if I *do* want her to become a ghost?"

Giles pointed to a door. "In there."

Alexander looked at the door. "Is that part of the lie?"

Giles said nothing.

Alexander closed his eyes. "Thank you."

Giles looked him over, concerned. "You can find your way to your room?"

"I don't really have one yet."

"Can you find your way to *a* room?"

Alexander furrowed his brow and looked at Giles again. "Yes?"

Giles smiled. "There are rooms for visiting dignitaries on the Great Hall floor. Try there."

"Again, thank you."

Giles bowed and left him to his mourning.

Alexander went back into the Pool Room, which was adjacent to the tombs. Brigit looked past him to the soft glow illuminating the King.

"How did he take it?"

Giles glanced back. "About as well as one could expect. I'm heading out. Did you want to come with me?"

"I'm needed here."

"Try to get some rest then. Do you know where the amulet is?"

"I think he still has it. Do you need it?"

Giles scoffed. "No. By the time I could make it, I could move a house. Give me a circle and I can take, well, at least a hundred people, apparently."

"Why do you want it then?"

"In case someone here needs to find me. I'm heading to Raymond's. I'm gonna see if they have seen any sign of the Giver specifically being down here."

Brigit leaned in. "You mean what you told him is true?"

"I don't want to say. But can you think of someone else who could resurrect? Get him a bath and some food if you really want to help him. He needs to be functioning."

"I'll try. We should have a few hours before the next insurmountable crisis."

She turned and walked to the tombs.

Giles envisioned Raymond's shack and willed himself there.

He appeared outside the door and knocked. It was dark, with the Black Forest now blocking direct sunlight most of the day. Light snow filtered down from the trees. He had forgotten to wear a coat, and realized he needed to stop doing that.

"Come in!"

Giles opened the door to see a donkey in the living area. Clara was on the bed, leg still magically splinted by Raven, while Raymond puttered with cooking. The place was warm and smelly.

Raymond turned to him. "Giles! This is unexpected!"

Giles motioned to the donkey. "So is this."

"Oh, during the winter months I often have to bring him inside. He usually knows before I do. Last night, he practically kicked down the door in a frenzy. Had the forest not been there to break the storm, we would have been frozen solid."

"Where were you when it hit?"

"Looking for food, to be honest. My stores rarely had meat to them and I thought I could catch a rabbit or something. It worked too, though it did take all day."

Raymond turned to Clara and gave her a bowl with stew in it. He looked at Giles. "Would you like some?"

Giles nodded, surprised at how hungry he was. "When I was a young mage, fresh out of the Estate, I would eat every chance I got. Then, as I learned more, I always got distracted when I was working on a spell or item. It was quite common, so the wizards at the Estate long ago had a treatment we could drink that stopped us from needing food until we slept again. We also had a concoction that let us go without sleep for a tenday. Little did we all know that all you had to do to achieve both those things was die, go to Heaven, then get kicked out!"

He set the bowl Raymond handed him on the table that had been shoved to the wall by the window.

Clara blew on her stew. "What did you need here?"

"Well, I went up recently to see that the Forest here has *vastly* expanded. Now, it goes all the way from where I had it before to as far north as I could see and as far east as I could see. I think you also have a few rivers nearby too."

Raymond perked up. "Really? How exciting! I get to learn to fish! What a time to be alive!"

Clara smiled. "I can teach you how to make a trap, Raymond! It's easy and you just stake it in the river and come back when you want to start dinner."

Raymond bowed. "Thank you, Clara. I have not had fish since... I can't remember! I hope I like it."

Giles held up his hand. "Friends, friends, you're missing the point. My *forest* spread *overnight* to encompass *the entire wasteland.*"

They blinked, silent. They exchanged a look and shrugged.

Giles pointed to himself. *"I didn't do it."*

"Oohh!"

Clara's eyes got bright and she sat up. "Wait! You think maybe she..."

"More than that, I think she may have killed an archangel or two to do it. Where else would she get that power? They wouldn't have let her stay gone if she hadn't done them in. I think she's here."

"What about our friends? If a fight happened in Heaven, are our friends alright?"

"Well, George is fine. He came down before the Forest expanded."

Clara threw a slice of carrot at him. "Why didn't you tell me he was here?"

"I literally just did!"

"Was he cast out too?"

Giles waved her off. "No no. He was sent here. To fight the battle."

"So he's *fighting?!* Where?"

Giles pointed with his spoon. "Finish your breakfast. I'll take you to him. Glad to see your leg is better though."

She looked at her leg, still completely encased in the blossoming foliage Raven gave her. "I didn't even realize I moved it."

Giles smiled and continued to chew.

Gwen picked up a dish and dried it, then put it in a cupboard. "So, James is serving Gloriana, huh?"

"Yes. He found out the truth about your conception and sought her out."

"That's gotta be a tough conversation to have."

"He had a substantial scar on his face when I saw him."

Gwen looked stunned. "She *scarred* him?"

Catriona focused on the dishes. "Yes. But she also healed it. He just must have stopped her from healing it all the way, so it would scar."

"Why?"

Catriona looked at her friend. "So he wouldn't look like Alistair anymore."

Gwen opened her mouth a little, then, the tension flowed out again. "That makes sense, actually."

"Did you know about Alistair?"

"That's… a tricky question. I learned about him after I came here. Of course, by then it didn't matter. But I'm glad James and Gloriana are having some connection. Even though she cut him, she also healed it so there's healing on both sides now."

Catriona looked at her ward. She had grown so much in the past few months. It was hard to believe that Catriona had stayed with Tib at Gwen's house outside Patras the last time snow was on the ground. She herself had been deeply in love with Alexander at that time, fantasizing about him leaving his responsibilities and her leaving hers.

What a difference a near apocalypse made.

"Are you okay?"

Gwen took a deep breath, letting it out slowly. "You're leaving through Sovereignlumin, right? I'd like to go with you."

"Back to the living?"

Gwen shook her head. "Just to the tower. It *is* an actual tower, right?"

Catriona smiled. "Yes. And it's beautiful. You can go anywhere from there too."

"I want to see it before I go."

Catriona felt her throat close. "Are… Is that soon?"

"I don't know. But I'd rather see it first. Just in case." She put the last dish in the cupboard and looked around. "This place will likely be gone once we step out that door."

"I know."

"Is there anything you want of hers?"

Catriona smiled. "She gave me a legacy. I couldn't ask for more."

They linked hands and left the cottage. Outside, the building that had been a staple for three centuries faded away. Behind it on the ground was a gold stone with black flecks in it.

Catriona used her shirt to pick it up and held it to the sunlight. It was so thick with gold, it could have been an ore sample.

"Wow. That's a lot of gold."

Catriona put the stone in a pouch. "Get your things. We'll leave when Myrgen gets back."

"Where do we take these now?" Myrgen lifted the bushel basket filled with flowers and components.

Sovereigna looked at the castle. "If she grew these, she must have an apothecary's table inside. Let's see if we can find it."

They went in the open archway and found a flight of stairs going up. Across from the stairs was a door.

"Would you check that door, Myrgen? I'll look up here."

He nodded and went to the door. Sovereigna went upstairs and noticed a lot of scoring all the way up the tower. At the top, it looked like her daughter had extracted her demons, made them manifest, then went about fighting them with fireplace implements. Blackness smeared everything and all the furnishings, bed, desk, bookshelf, wardrobe, all were charred. There was no mattress anymore and on the floor under the bed, a log had burned through the rug to the stone beneath.

Nothing had escaped her wrath and it looked like her daughter might have left here to work the garden and never returned.

She heard footsteps behind her and Myrgen walked in.

"Hey, I think I found… Wow."

He looked around at the extensive damage to what was obviously fine furnishings. "Is this what the Land's Hell looks like?"

Sovereigna shrugged. "I imagine so. She was so angry when she came here, she just lashed out."

"Did this place give her fire control or is this all natural?"

Sovereigna pointed to the log on the floor under the bed. "It looks like she set fire to it herself. It burned straight through."

Myrgen was impressed. "You have to admire the sheer level of contempt she felt. I wonder how long she spent like this?"

"It looks like she left and one day just didn't return. Maybe that day was today or yesterday."

Myrgen looked at her. "I'm glad she found peace."

Sovereigna's eyes were wet. "So am I. Now, you said you found something?"

"Yes."

He led her to the other door. This looked much more solid and sane. A bed, dresser, and desk occupied the edge of this room, with the apothecary station dominating one wall. There was a book open whose pages were thick and uneven. They walked over and Sovereigna leafed through it.

She smiled. "She's brilliant!"

"What?"

"When magic is written down, it dies with the author. She made a scrap book of recipes!"

She flipped to a page. "See. Two roses, two tarragons, one dragon tongue. The spill here shows the color and consistency of the potion."

"Can you tell what the potion is?"

"No, not from the ingredients. But look." She pointed to the desk. "She has a dozen of them."

Myrgen put his hands on his hips and looked down at something in his belt. "Do you need anything else, Your Majesty? I need to be going."

"Of course. Thank you for talking to me about her."

"My pleasure. Good day, Your Majesty. We'll return soon."

He bowed and left. Sovereigna looked around the room and then sat at the table and started sorting ingredients.

Catriona looked up at Myrgen when he got home.

"Is she settling in?"

Myrgen nodded, going over to the kettle by the fire and pulling a mug from the shelf nearby. "She is. We went over Elizabeth's castle and I got to see what the aftermath of dealing with a personal demon looks like. You said the Land is purveyor of monsters? Well, they might actually be *real* demons then."

"That wouldn't surprise me."

Myrgen looked at the gold nugget on the table as he tapped some tea into a tea cloth. "What's that?"

"It was left behind after the Dûcesa's cottage faded."

He blinked. "Is that her…?"

She looked back at it. "I think so."

He set the mug down and walked over. "May I?"

She waved to it.

He picked it up. "That is a *lot* of gold."

"I know."

He put the stone back down and finished making his tea. She set her hands on the table and rested her chin on them, staring at the stone.

"You gonna touch it?"

"No."

"Why not?"

She glanced away, not lifting her head. "Reasons."

He narrowed his eyes. "Should I carry it then?"

She closed her eyes. "Yes, please."

He put it in a pocket. His hand brushed across the missive Gwen gave him and he glanced down, then pulled it out.

"What's that?"

He looked at Catriona and waited.

She frowned, then looked at the note. "That's Anika's handwriting."

"Yeah."

She sat back in her chair and looked out the window, brushing her hair behind her ear. He leaned his elbows on the table and listened as well. After a moment, she untucked her hair.

"Who gave it to you?"

"Gwen."

She stroked her lip for a moment. Her eyes were already wet. "It's why they come here, you know. To move on."

He started to say something but realized the lump in his throat wouldn't allow it anyway. They sat still for a long minute. Then she blinked slowly and glanced at the letter. Her eyes drifted up him.

"What are the others?"

Myrgen glanced down. "These two are the missives for Sovereigna's seneschal and Catherine. The other one is the message for Raven."

"You're going to need a satchel."

"I have no doubt one will be by the door when next we leave."

She smiled. "That it should."

When Gwen came to the door, Catriona stood and put their empty cups in a basin. "We have work to do, Myrgen."

Myrgen nodded, went to the door, and shouldered the satchel on the peg next to it.

Fifteen

"Remove the ladder when your enemy has
ascended the roof."
-The Forty-Five Voices

Myrgen and Catriona stepped out of the house bedecked for winter.
Gwen was not, but that didn't really matter. She would be alright in the
Fae Lands. The Sinister Glove and Johner were also dressed for an
expedition but they were saddling horses. The beasts were beautiful in
cascading colors of blue, lavender, and silver. Johner's was spotted with
sapphires on the flank while the Glove's mane shimmered with
diamonds.

"You're not going through the mansion?"

The Glove shook her head, climbing onto the back of the Fae horse.
"We decided that being beholden to Heaven didn't make sense. For all
we know, they're behind all this. There's gotta be a way into the Fae
afterlife from this part, so we are going in search of it."

Catriona patted her horse. "Good luck."

Myrgen exchanged a wrist embrace with Johner. "Pleasure to have
met you, Sir."

"The honor was mine." Johner checked the saddlebags and secured his instrument inside. He climbed onto the Fae horse and breathed deep. "It has been too long since I felt the call to adventure."

Catriona patted the horse's neck. "Fair winds, my friends."

The pair turned from their companions and rode off to the south. Myrgen, Gwen, and Catriona watched as long as they could before turning to the mansion. They went up the hill and Catriona swung her legs over the short wall.

"I'll be right back."

She went into the hallway and saw the study door was open. She peeked inside and saw Lucifer staring at the fire. A brandy in his hand was untouched and he swirled it absently.

"Lucifer?"

He turned to her. "Ah, Catriona, so good to see you." He set his brandy next to a small letter on the hearth table and rose to greet her properly.

"I have a friend for you to meet. She would like permission to enter your home."

Lucifer gestured to the note. "It appears I have room. That arrived about an hour ago."

She picked it up.

Lucifer,
I feel the time has come to decline your hospitality. Thank you for your warmth and kindness.
The Sinister Glove of Embertwist

She looked at him. "I'm so sorry."

He took it from her. "The invitations have always been a choice for both parties. I do regret losing people at every turn, though."

"I understand. My family has moved on. I suspect the Lieutenants are about to. Even Myrgen's ex-lover has gone. Merrick too."

He hugged her and she returned it.

"You have a place here should you need it."

She bowed, wiping her eyes. "I appreciate that. May I?" She motioned to the brandy.

He offered her his glass. "I haven't touched it."

She smiled. "I know."

She drank some and then gestured to the hallway. "Shall we?"

"Should I get lunch ready?"

"I would leave that as *her* choice."

Lucifer grinned at the acknowledgment and they went to the garden. Myrgen was leaning against the wall, arms crossed, and he stood when they emerged. Catriona gestured to Gwen.

"This is my dear friend Gwen. She wants to visit Sovereignlumen. I imagine there's a way to get there from Summerland but I don't know it. I do know this path."

Lucifer was staring at Gwen and Catriona exchanged a glance with Myrgen.

Lucifer started, then reached across the wall. "My lady, you are most welcome in my home."

Gwen stepped back at the sudden appearance of the place. She took his hand and he raised it in salute. He reached into his coat and pulled out a small card. She took it and he stepped aside, assisting her in climbing over the low wall.

"This place is amazing."

"I try to keep it presentable for company. Excuse me but have we met?"

Gwen looked at him, not yet retrieving her hand. "I don't believe we have. But I swear…"

Lucifer bowed. "Well, thank you for introducing us, Catriona."

He released her hand almost reluctantly. "Is anyone hungry?"

Gwen shook her head, her long hair glittering in the sunlight. "I cooked lunch just a little while ago. Had I known you were here, I'd have saved you some."

She reached into a pouch at her side. "I do have this though. Please take it."

"What is it?"

"Shortbread. It's a travel cake."

He tasted it. "This is a delight! Your recipe?"

She smiled, nodding.

"I would love to trade recipes sometime. Perhaps a mutual dinner where we both cook?"

She glanced at the Mansion. "You do your own cooking?"

"It, like everything with me, is a choice. But why are you going to Sovereignlumen?"

"I have family there."

He put his hand to his heart. "Well, I shan't keep you. Please, hold onto that invitation. If you ever wish to no longer visit, simply return it. No explanation necessary."

Gwen bowed. "My many thanks."

They group went down the hallway and into the other viewing area. Gwen stopped a moment and marveled at the sight. She turned to Catriona. "That's it? That's where we're going?"

She nodded, smiling. Gwen's youth was restored in her delight. Myrgen took Catriona's hand and squeezed it, also smiling. Gwen went to the gate and Lucifer opened it for her.

"Can you come with us?"

"I fear that is not my realm to tread."

"Well, thank you for this opportunity." She took his hand and squeezed it.

Lucifer held her hand a moment. "I know we've met... Are you... the Giver?"

"Me? By the Fae, no! I'm dead and in the afterlife of the Land's followers. I'm no more the Giver than you are the Bringer."

Lucifer blinked, then smiled. "Of course. How... Of course. Please, enjoy your visit."

She bowed and walked away from the patio. Myrgen and Catriona patted Lucifer's shoulder on the way by. They met up and went to the tower.

Lucifer waited until they had all entered the tower before opening his hand. Within it was a single hair from the lady. He looked towards the tower, then back at the hair.

Did she give it to me?

No. Long-haired people shed like cats. More likely it was accidental. In the afterlife? She sheds in the afterlife?

That thought gave him pause.

He walked to the stairs and went down to Hell. The throne was a ruse, like the entire fiery motif here. He used it to put his brother Angels off from coming down here. The more arrogant and insufferable he was at the beginning, the happier they were to leave him alone.

Not that it matters anymore.

He waved his hand and dismissed the throne room. The mountain of purified souls towered behind it. He grabbed a handful and laid the hair across them.

It blended right in, but even so, caught the dim light that the souls gave off.

Caught the light?

Gathered the light. Stimulated it.

He lay the hair on the mountain of souls and noted that it stood out against the marbles of white light. Even stepping back, he could still see it. He turned when he bumped into the staircase leading to the mansion, then turned back to discover he could still find it if he looked for it, even at that distance.

I'm no more the Giver than you are the Bringer.

He glanced down at the lava rock beneath his feet, the bedrock gifted to him by the Death Bringer after she destroyed his corrupted village. He had felt a kinship to her at that moment. He knew he could connect those afterlives but he looked over *what* he had connected. Sovereignlumen to Summerland, where he lingered instead of rebuilding Heaven now that his family was gone.

No. Not his family. He had divorced them long ago. And they weren't "gone". They were *dead*. He had killed them. He had brought Death to Heaven.

He harvested souls like he had the *right*.

He ran up the stairs and continued up to Karma's door. He hammered on it until it opened. Alistair stood in a purple silk robe with matching loose bottoms, barefoot and bare chested.

Alistair frowned. "Luci?"

"I'm interrupting something?"

Alistair glanced at a Yantap woman in brilliant pink with a silver chain from her nose to her ear sat playing a board game with a Yokotaman man in blue printed silk. A Nubian woman with a beautiful poof of black hair wore an orange top and skirt. She drank wine and watched the match, contemplating their moves. Everyone was barefoot and relaxed, engaged in the activity.

"We were just discussing belief systems. There's a Glarren woman and a Caratian man using the bedroom right now so we're on a break. Would you like to come in?"

"Would you like to come out?"

Alistair blinked at the direction change, the called over his shoulder. "I'll be right back."

He closed the door behind him, assuming his regular clothes.

He followed Lucifer, pausing at the main floor before realizing the Angel was continuing down.

"Oh, we're going all the -okay."

Lucifer pointed to the mountain of souls. "Tell me what you see."

Alistair looked around. "You've redecorated. I don't quite remember that feature."

"I only bring it out for the holidays."

"What's that?" Alistair frowned, walking to the pile. He reached out and pulled the hair from it.

Lucifer exhaled. "So, it wasn't just me."

Alistair turned to Lucifer. "What do you mean?"

Lucifer gestured to the hair. "That's from your daughter, Gwen."

Alistair's eyes sharpened. "She was *here*?"

"No. The mansion. She left."

Alistair closed his eyes. "Where did she go?"

Lucifer felt the hair rise on his neck. Suddenly, he wasn't sure he wanted to share his new theory with his friend. "She went to visit family, I think. I thought you might want to witness the reunion."

"Really? Then why bring me here?" He cast around. "You even dismissed your Pillar."

Lucifer moved his hand and the Viewing Pillar arose beside him. "That's easy to restore. See?"

"Did you give her anything?"

"I…"

Alistair shook his head, running his hand through his hair. "Of course you did. No one is here without your express, *written* consent. I gotta admit, I never would have suspected *you* for her hidden thread. And Gwen is the other one. Good to know."

"I'm unaware of any thread, Alistair. Maybe we need to go upstairs and have a brandy. Talk about this."

Lucifer's fight or flight instinct was mounting and he felt adrenaline, which he should not have been able to feel. He realized right then that he was suddenly human and that the man across from him was not.

"Yeah, if I could *talk* about it, we wouldn't be here right now."

Lucifer realized what Alistair meant. "You know about the trap, don't you?"

"When I became Karma. Remember that bout of depression I went through? This here is exactly why. I had a secret that no one alive understood. No one alive *could* have understood. That is a burden no one person should have to bear."

"Then don't. Share that burden."

"*I can't.* Don't you understand? It will *die* with me!"

Lucifer swallowed as Alistair brought a scimitar from behind his back. "I'm sorry, Lucifer."

"Don't do anything stupid, Alistair. Don't hurt yourself."

"You already know this blade isn't for me. I'm not ready to condemn the world to utter destruction. And now that I know who the threads are, I can sever those and stop this madness."

Lucifer opened his hand. A sword was in it and he looked down. It was a white granite sword. He looked back up in time to see Alistair slicing at him. He brought the stone sword up to block it. The swords clashed and Alistair's eyes grew wide.

He stepped back. "I suppose this proves it. The White Granite Sword answers your call."

Lucifer did not take his eyes from Alistair. "Apparently."

Alistair threw an attack and pressed it. The sword could handle the blows but Lucifer had not fought in thousands of years and Alistair had used his weapon within the last year. Lucifer felt himself losing ground fast.

"This is ridiculous, Alistair. We are evenly matched and immortal. We won't tire or let the other win. Let's go upstairs and drink. You can tell me about this thread issue."

"You don't seem evenly matched to me."

Alistair got the drop on Lucifer with a feint and cut him across the arm. Lucifer almost dropped the Sword. There was no blood but Lucifer started leaking the soul stuff that rested in a pile behind Alistair. He covered the wound with his hand, and barely got the Sword up to block the next blow. Alistair was winning and they both knew it.

118

I have to get upstairs. It's the only way.

Lucifer flung his fingers at Alistair and liquid soul splashed his eyes. Alistair flung his arm up to wipe it away and Lucifer ran. He got up the stairs and thought he was out of range when a searing pain slashed his calf. He limped the rest of the way into the main floor, but Alistair was right behind him. Lucifer glanced at the wall where the Soulless door had been and suddenly remembered that he had sealed it.

"This is *wrong!* I really liked you!"

Alistair advanced. "I know. I liked you too."

A blue arrow struck Alistair in the shoulder, spinning him away from Lucifer.

"Gwen?" Alistair's voice sounded betrayed.

The blond Glarren woman drew the elaborate bow again, another blue arrow forming from nothing.

Lucifer glanced at Alistair's coat and saw a black note sticking out. He plucked it out and ripped it up.

Alistair glared at him and disappeared.

Gwen ran over to Lucifer and put her shoulder under his. She half-carried him to the study and set him on the couch.

"Where did your bow go?"

"Where did your sword go?"

Lucifer looked at his hand as if just discovering he had one.

Gwen got a cloth and some water. "I was walking back here and heard the clanging of the fight. I heard you scream in pain and ran up here. When I entered the garden gate, the bow appeared in my hand."

"That's almost exactly what happened to me. I felt like something was amiss and then the sword was in my hand. I was surprised that Alistair knew what it was. He said it proved I was 'her hidden thread'. I have no idea what he meant."

He looked at his leg, then his arm. "I'm getting really tired of metaphysical entities trying to kill me."

Gwen smiled. "Yeah, I imagine that's pretty annoying. So, what happened?"

"There's a spell that traps people, in Persephone."

"The one that captured Catriona and killed her the first time? I was told about that."

"Well, it held Magic at the beginning and I'm pretty sure Karma built the thing. And I think my brother Raphael helped."

"And Sovereignlumen."

Gwen and Lucifer looked at Catriona as she and Myrgen came through the study doorway.

"We felt the White Granite Sword go to you. Are you alright?"

Gwen looked at her. "Wait, they were married, weren't they? Sovereignlumen and Magic?"

"Yes. I already tried to reach him when I realized my place as the Bringer of Death, but he was beyond my reach."

Lucifer lifted his injured leg onto the low table in front of the couch, wincing. *"- Eesh-* What about your role as the Land?"

"Part of why he was beyond my reach is that his soul is not part of the Land, at least not so far as I have control over. It became the Tower of Sovereignlumin."

"Why didn't he go to Summerland like the rest of the Land followers?"

"We don't know. Maybe it didn't exist yet."

Lucifer moved his pant leg to look at the damage.

Gwen put a wet cloth to it. "Should I sew this up for you?"

"Sure. But in the meantime, I need to show you guys something."

"So, you haven't seen the Giver or any sign of her?" Giles put the spoon in the now-empty stew bowl.

Clara shook her head. "I haven't, but I've been unable to go outside."

"I didn't see anything when I was out hunting, outside of there being a forest here now." Raymond put the bowls in the hollowed-out stone he used for a basin.

Giles stood up. "Alright, you ready to go?"

Clara pointed to her leg cast. "What do we do about this thing?"

Giles stroked his chin. "I can take you to the pool at the Haunted Covenant. Make sure your leg is healed. Then I can remove the vines."

She nodded and he put a hand on her shoulder. "I'll check in periodically to see if there's been any sign of her."

"I'll take note of anything unusual."

Giles and Clara disappeared.

120

Raymond turned to the donkey and gave him a carrot. "I probably need to let you outside for a few minutes to take care of your morning constitutionals."

The donkey just munched his carrot. Raymond let him finish, then led the donkey outside to the water trough. He broke the thin ice on the top and the donkey drank his fill. He waited until the donkey did his business and wanted to be back inside before finally letting him in again. He cleaned the dishes and set them to dry on the shelf.

"I never thought I'd have to wash *two* dishes, Fenn, much less *three*! What an exciting day indeed. And now I have to find sticks to make that trap Clara described. I've never had to find sticks before."

A knock on the door caused him and Fenn to just look at it. He walked over and opened it. A pale, almost translucent woman stood all but nude in the snowy forest. A man stood with her at the door.

"Hello, I'm Saint Jude. This is the Life Giver. Can we come in?"

Sixteen

"Let the enemy's own spy sow discord in the enemy camp."
-The Forty-Five Voices

Catriona, Gwen, and Myrgen looked over the destruction in Heaven.

Lucifer pointed as the Pillar before them showed the different areas. "That's where the Saints would add souls to newborns. That pillar is intact, but this one over here was shattered."

"The demolition, it's so… *complete*." Catriona looked at Lucifer. "The Giver did this?"

Lucifer nodded. "I figured I'd show you since you couldn't see it yourself. This one only shows Giver properties and humans."

Gwen went back to prepping Lucifer's wounds.

"Mine will only show Land holdings and affiliations. That's why this mansion is so unique." Catriona studied the wreckage.

Myrgen sat down in a chair. "So, no one is up there right now?"

"The Saints were all over the place before. That shattered Pillar was where they heard prayers. This is the first chance I've had to look the place over since it happened."

Catriona sat as well. "The Glove told us about the Soulless."

"Yeah well, I was about to do the same thing to Alistair but I had walled up the place."

"You would have destroyed Karma? What would keep the balance?"

"The long arm of history arcs towards justice, they say. Maybe 'balance' is just keeping it even, fighting the inevitable."

Myrgen leaned forward. "You can view *Giver* properties. Can you view *her*?"

Lucifer arched an eyebrow. "The Giver herself? Yeah, yeah, I think I can. Hang on."

He concentrated and she appeared in the Pillar. A donkey and an older man with a beard stood next to a younger man with a beard. An almost translucent woman with long, silver hair turned to the viewers.

"Hello Lucifer, my friend! I see you finally sought me out. I have so much to show you."

"That's great! I have some friends of yours here." He motioned to the others in the study and gestured to his nurse. "This is Gwen."

"Ah Gwen. So nice to finally meet face to face."

"You *know* me?"

"You were my only hope. I was devastated when you died."

Gwen glanced at her friends. "Why? How was I hope for *you*?"

"I had a way to escape thanks to you. If a Glarren woman has her first bleed in a pool of my making, that life blood connects us. All she has to do at that point is give birth to a girl child and I would re-enter the world!"

Gwen frowned. "That is *really* specific."

"Hence why I was so devastated. You were one of three in all the time I was captive."

"My first bleed was in Glarren."

"In a pool that was formed before the Soulless War, yes."

"My brother…"

Catriona sensed something was disturbing about the memory. "What happened to the others?"

"One fell through the ice after hurting a Fae fish. The other froze in a cave after chasing her betrothed's lover into it and getting trapped. And Gwen here gave her life to protect a corrupted king."

Lucifer's lip twitched in a sneer. "That all sounds like Karma to me."

They all looked at him.

Catriona sat back pondering. "So, Alistair…

Lucifer raised a finger. "Not Alistair. That was the previous Karma. Alistair *killed* Karma for hurting his daughter."

Myrgen tilted his head. "But once he killed it, he inherited its entire domain."

Lucifer turned to Gwen. "It didn't click with me before. You're the woman from the village, his daughter. I have seen you from the garden. He would look for you whenever he came over. I think he was worried you might move on and he'd lose even that connection to you."

Catriona looked at Lucifer's wounds. "How did he hurt you?"

"Scimitar."

She just kept looking at him.

"Okay, okay. Look, I was just as surprised as you are that he attacked. Whatever this thread is, he seemed intent on severing it. Once he realized Gwen was the other thread, it… I think he was sad, because he knew he had to kill her too. Whatever this is, it's pretty important. I think he wants to die. Like really die, disappear. I remember Karma telling me she would be here forever because there was no one else to take up the mantle. When Alistair showed up, she was scared. She hid it well, but we were together for a very long time. I knew she was scared because she had never been scared before and she didn't understand it.

"I think she knew he would take the mantle. And I don't think she knew she could trust him with the secret. Seeing the toll it has taken on him as we fought, I can now get behind her sentiment. She made the trap, I'm almost sure of it now. Which means there's a balance that has to be there. Hence the Land and Heaven components that were *not* the actual Bringer and Giver entities."

Catriona frowned, thinking. "Karma is balance, above all else. For every helpful interference, it must be unhelpful to the same degree."

Lucifer rubbed his slashed calf. "This is definitely unhelpful."

Gwen slapped his hand. "Don't rub it while I'm trying to fix it."

The Giver pointed to Lucifer. "Hand her the pearls in your pocket, Lucifer."

Lucifer reached into his pocket and handed Gwen a couple of small glowing orbs.

She took one and touched it to the wound. It was absorbed like a raindrop on turned soil. When the glow faded, the cut was healed.

"What was *that*?"

"Souls. Or rather, pure Giver essence. They get all of their humanity burned from them when they come to Hell. They revert back to that."

Catriona looked at the Giver. "So, what's happening now to souls that *don't* go to Hell? Are you getting them back?"

The Giver shook her head. "I don't think so, but I don't know."

Gwen touched another orb to Lucifer's wounded arm and healed that wound as well.

Catriona leaned over to Myrgen. "I need to talk to you about something Alexander told me. It's pertinent to this discussion. I was going to tell you on the way to Persephone but we didn't get the chance."

Myrgen turned to her. "Okay. Speak."

She took his hand. "Tanglwyst was killed by confused villager. Alexander was very shaken by the loss."

Gwen closed her eyes and sank against the sofa. Lucifer put a hand on her shoulder in comfort. "You knew her?"

"Alexander put a spell on her that forced her to chase him, at the cost of her life. It took a lot to convince her to remove her fealty to him but once she let go of it, she was free of the spell."

Lucifer grew angry. "He put a spell on someone whose fealty he held and forced her to do something that would kill her? Oh, I may go get him myself." Lucifer started to rise from the sofa but Gwen pulled him back down.

"She was going to the Papal City to report him to the Pope. She intended to have him removed as King, or at least not endorsed. I guess I just hoped she did it and was safe there."

Catriona shook her head. "No. Apparently, he committed to her and was with her when she was killed. He said she kept him sane and focused. He wasn't sure how he would do without her."

Myrgen snarled. "If he needs someone *else* to keep him from doing evil, then he's already a villain."

"A villain in control of thousands of lives. And in control of Emmy's fate. He seemed repentant. Maybe her influence mattered."

Gwen looked at Lucifer. "Is it possible her soul is up there among the debris, or in the forest below Heaven?"

The Giver furrowed her brow. "You wish to retrieve it? To what end?"

"Resurrection." The younger bearded man spoke up, looking at the Giver and Lucifer.

Myrgen looked at him. "Sorry, I didn't catch your name?"

"Jude. I am the patron Saint of Hopeless Cases, so I heard stuff like this all the time. The souls that come up there are a little different than the ones Lucifer has. They still have their humanity, their personalities. Essentially, they are still the people they were before. If she could be located and not liquified, she could be resurrected."

"Liquified?"

"When souls returned before, they went right into the Well and were liquified into the homogenous mass. But with the Well gone, they are likely just lying around as beads, like the ones in his pocket. They don't liquify automatically. It has to be done to them."

Lucifer crossed his arms. "I won't endorse putting anyone in a relationship with someone who abuses them. He took away her choice. How do we know he wasn't doing it when she was killed?"

"Maybe she could be given a protection then? Something that stops him from controlling her? I doubt she wanted to be slain by a confused villager. It wasn't her choice to die." Jude's eyes flicked to meet everyone's in both rooms.

The older man by the Giver raised his hand to get the group's attention. "A few minutes ago, before everyone arrived, Giles came and took Clara to Saint George. He is fighting a battle in a valley south of here. He may be able to apply that protection you speak of. He is invoked against monsters."

Lucifer arched an eyebrow. "Human ones?"

Jude shrugged. "That was more often my realm. But I heard a lot of prayers requesting Alexander after he healed all those people in St. Andrew. Humans are very complex, capable of great good and great evil in the same body."

Myrgen crossed his arms over his chest. "Yeah, after St. Andrew, he shot at a fleeing ship, endangering the woman he loved and her entire crew, whom he knew, while he let the city burn. I think he might be in the running for the next Karma."

There was silence while the weight of the matter settled fully upon the assembled. Catriona finally broke it. "He needs to know about Emmy, regardless. Perhaps now, while he's still vulnerable and contemplative, he'll be receptive to a solution. I'll speak to him."

Myrgen looked at her. "Are you sure?"

"I can read him now. If he tries to betray me, I'll know. Can anyone else say likewise?"

Lucifer rubbed his chin. "I don't like it. This feels a lot more like we need everyone to sit down in the same room and have a summit. I don't like this division. He needs to know what's needed from him, we need to know what everyone's doing. This piecemeal and hearsay is counterproductive. You can still read him, my Lady, and keep him honest. Does he know you can do it?"

Catriona nodded.

"Then he'll know not to lie or be evasive. It's better that way."

They all agreed. "Where do we meet and how?"

Raymond raised his hand again. "Giles said he would return here. If someone goes to the battle, we can let him know."

Catriona glanced at the other Land people. "We know where this battle is happening. Gwen, can you reach out to Gloriana and see if we can get her input on this? We may need her to stop the weather assault to get people moving in the right directions."

"I can try but as a ghost, I don't know how helpful I'll be."

Myrgen looked at her. "I'll go with you. Giver, can you find another Pillar and contact Lucifer from there?"

"Maybe."

Myrgen snapped his fingers. "What about Serenity? It has that inn and is sheltered from the weather."

Catriona waved him off. "Entering a pocket dimension under the control of a mage? Isn't that how the Soulless were defeated?"

Lucifer spread his hands. "Here?"

"Same power principle. We need neutral ground. Besides, some of the attendees would be mortal."

"I made a tree."

Everyone looked at the Giver. Jude nodded in agreement.

Catriona thought about it. "We'd need protection from the weather though."

Raymond pointed at himself and Jude. "We can help her construct something."

Jude smiled. "I *am* all about hopeless cases. This has *all* the earmarks."

Catriona stood. "Thank you, all of you. Giver, I look forward to seeing you in person."

The Giver bowed. "Same to you, Bringer."
The Pillar faded to darkness.

Myrgen and Catriona stepped into the hallway.

He handed her the missive from Anika. "I want you to take this with you."

She looked at it, taking it slowly.

He squeezed her shoulder. "I know we wanted to read it together. But we haven't gotten the chance and I don't think we're going to. We're going in different directions. Again. I have no idea when we'll meet up again."

"We've taken life and death so lightly since we learned we can't die. I know Summerland has always been a place of peace to help souls move on, but it still hurts to know I'll never see them again."

He stroked her hair, then lifted her chin. "Hey, it's leaning into afternoon. We can go somewhere, like the cabin from last night. Spend the night there, then head out tomorrow. We might need some time before all this happens."

"And put the world in the limbo of uncertainty? Every day it feels like a week passes. It leaves no time for grief. Even here, it seems like we need to always be running. Last night, when I was watching my tea steep, I realized it was only a few *months* ago that I was in Rouen, fighting Nicolai in the street. Not years or decades. *Months*."

He took her hand. "I know. I almost said I will miss Drake and Anika so much, Tib too. But then I realized that, as welcoming as they were to me, I had *not* lived with them for ten years. And yet, I have a puppy at home to take care of, and a bow of legendary proportions that I just realized I've blocked out because of its role in Gwen's death. I have a better relationship with Gwen than I do... *did*... with Dominic, her fiancé. I have no idea if he's mourning her or what. And Michael..."

His throat became clogged with sorrow and she wrapped her arms around him in comfort.

"Why isn't he here, Catriona? Why isn't he right here with us?"

"I…" Her own eyes were filling. She couldn't tell him what she saw in the Archangel's face. "I think he didn't have time to choose a path that would converge with ours."

He nodded. "You know, I don't know if Michael chose his fate either. If… if they can find *Tangl's* soul…"

"Maybe…" She stepped back as his hug loosened. "We'll get through this and stop somewhere. I promise." She handed back the note. "When we're together, we'll read this."

He put it in his satchel, then settled himself with several deep breaths. "Okay. Let's get this done."

He opened the doors and went back in the study. Lucifer gestured to two drinks.

"Figured you were gonna need these. Hey, I took the liberty of tracking down Alexander."

He indicated the Pillar. Alexander was in a dark cave with Tanglwyst on a bed of glowing moss. He turned away from her and left.

Lucifer glanced at the assembled crowd. "Anyone know where that is?"

Catriona frowned. "Underground. Maybe I can find him?"

"This is divine attuned. If I can see him, he is unlikely to show up on your Pillar. He'd be blocked from Land sight."

"Then what do we do?"

Lucifer dismissed the vision. "Tell you what. *I'll* go to Alexander. Myrgen, you and Gwen talk to the Fae. You, Catriona, need to talk to Alistair and find out what we don't know. Specifically, that thread business."

Gwen motioned to Catriona. "But I thought you wanted her to keep them honest?"

"They're a bunch of Heaven worshippers and I'm an Archangel that governs Hell. If I want to, I can make a demon come with me and have them shaking in their snow boots."

They all looked at him.

"I have a supply of all the darkness that takes a person down to Hell when they die."

The others glanced around the room.

"Not here though. It's in a very specific place."

The group exchanged a look.

Lucifer slapped his knees. "Okay then! I guess we should all be going. Let's make some headway on this group gathering."

Seventeen

"Trust people who are kind to animals."
—The Forty-Five Voices

Raymond turned to Jude and the Giver. "That went well."

Jude clapped his hands and rubbed them together in anticipation. "So, what do we need to do to make this place?"

"First off, where is it?"

Jude motioned to the west. "She built the lake about half a day that way. We just came from there."

"Hm." Raymond looked at his donkey. "My friend here needs some time to acclimate to the weather change. I can't leave him here without supervision. He'll eat all my crops."

The Giver smiled and petted the donkey. "I can help him grow his coat, but he will still need shelter. The forest will not bear food for him."

Jude's face showed his concern. "Is there anything you can do about that?"

She looked out the window. "Maybe. There's an essence that connects to me, but there's a purpose interwoven into the nature of it. If I make this part of the forest capable of being harvested and the ground tilled, it will unravel the integrity of the purpose, possibly destroying it. I'd need to understand why it is the way it is before I tamper with it."

"What would that take?"

She shrugged. "Speaking to the person who made it, most likely."

Raymond thought for a moment. "I think Giles did it. I remember him saying something about it when we were in Heaven together."

Jude snapped his fingers, smiling. "*Yes.* The story about the necromancer and the *marpies.*"

The Giver folded her hands and sat down. "What was this story?"

Raymond waved a hand. "It's been years since I heard it. Do you remember it, Jude?"

"Something about a mage who wasn't as gifted as he needed to be for training, so he gathered creatures and surrounded himself with their stolen power, enslaving them. The forest was built to house those creatures and stop them from being able to return to his summons. Once he couldn't drain them for a year, they were free. I don't remember the details, because in the middle of the story, he always got very technical. He was quite proud of that part of the tale, but since I don't understand magic, he always lost me."

Raymond rubbed his forehead, then back into his hair. "That's what I remember too. Once the actual *how* part of the discussion came up, I lost track of it."

The Giver touched both men's arms. "Well, you said you could help me make a hall for the gathering. How, if the forest can't be harvested?"

Jude waved his hands around. "Like you did with the tree and the lake."

She laughed. "I fear all that has burnt off. That was the tainted essence I consumed. Without that experience and diversity, I can only make what is natural. That tree is glorious to me, but I cannot create like that now. I can encourage things that already *are*, but I can't make anything *new*."

"What about the Pillar thing?"

She shrugged. "Those have always been available to me to summon. I just need a place I'm safe and that is all mine."

"Like the tree?"

She nodded. "I must admit that felt so good to accomplish. I've never done something like that before. That's never been my purview. I know the Bringer is capable of showing creativity, but I never could. I felt a kinship to the things that were familiar, comfortable, things that people experienced every day. There was enough wonder in those things for me."

Raymond looked around his home. "If you can't do that, then we can't make a safe place for the meeting. They can't all come *here*."

"There's a place near here where I used to rest. We can meet up there. It will still be subject to the weather though. And I can summon a Pillar from there."

"Well, it would be better than here. Do you want some soup or something before you go?"

Jude shook his head. "Won't be joining us then?"

Raymond scratched Fenn's head. "I can't leave him. It wouldn't be right. Especially with him no longer having food to eat. I have to get him somewhere he'll be okay. Too bad too. Raven had made a lovely swath of healthy grass for him."

Catriona knocked on the door at the top of the stairs in the mansion. She couldn't hear anything inside but she didn't know if that was the fault of the mansion or Karma.

"Alistair, it's me. Please open the door. Lucifer has released the mansion's hold on it. I can come in if you open the door."

Nothing.

She turned and looked at Myrgen and Gwen at the bottom of the stairs. They shrugged.

She came back down and looked around. "What do we do now then?"

Myrgen looked at Catriona. "I think it's a sign. One more night."

Catriona looked at Gwen. "What about you?"

"I'll head back to Sovereignlumin. See if the Glove and Johner have made it there yet."

"We'll head through tomorrow on our way to Persephone. Will you be alright?"

Gwen smiled. "Don't worry. I have a few more things to handle before I move on. I'll still be around."

Myrgen and Catriona walked towards home, waving goodbye as Gwen turned and crossed the patio to the Fae afterlife.

The Giver and Jude made their way through the light snows now covering the forest floor. Neither seemed to feel the cold, and this gave Jude pause. He wasn't hungry, didn't feel exactly tired.

Am I immune to these things?

Raymond ate food, slept apparently, even relieved himself. Jude couldn't remember doing that anymore. He wasn't sure he'd remember how. Clearly, time in the world took away the things they had as saints. He didn't realize how much it was taken for granted on his part. He imagined all the Saints down here now understood that.

"George is in the valley south of here, right? That's what they said."

The Giver nodded.

"He came down here on his own. I wonder if he's feeling the effects of being in the world again."

"Do you want to go find him and ask?"

"I do. Is it alright if I go with you to your safe place first? I need to know where it is if I'm to guide people to it."

She smiled and bowed. "Of course. Let's do this the easier way then."

She put her hand on him and grew to her huge height again, carrying him in her hand. This time, though, she made herself ethereal so as not to cause any damage. It took only a few strides to get to the area she remembered. She diminished again, this time into a grotto with an overhang and a small stream babbling through it. A large tree grew on one side of the grotto.

Jude looked around. "Is that a bed?"

"Are you tired?"

Jude suddenly realized he *was* and worried the world was catching up to him. "I might ask to take a small nap."

"Well, this *is* a resting place. Please do. I'll prepare the place for company."

Jude stumbled over to the bed and as he drifted off, realized this might not be the best idea for a meeting place after all.

The Giver waited until Jude was asleep, then grew again. She wanted to find more of the souls because she wanted to be creative again. Making that art earlier had felt better than anything. She recognized that the years of captivity might have made that more acute, but nonetheless, her heart wanted more. Now, she had a reason to do it that would benefit the world.

Again, she became ethereal so she could remain unnoticed and preserve where she trod. She felt the pull of the souls on the forest floor to the west, and moved in that direction. When she grew close to them, she became human-sized again but remained transparent. She didn't exactly *fear* being caught again, but she no longer trusted anyone to have her best interests in mind.

She found the beads of people's souls glowing under the snow. They didn't melt it, but instead, they were preserved there. She carefully brushed the snow away and found about a dozen souls. She looked at them in her hand, various shades of gray. She put one on her tongue and it melted like the snow. She felt a slight tingle of that person's life experiences, but it was gone too quick. She put two in her mouth and the combined flavor lingered longer.

She then put the rest in her mouth at once. The differences of lives lived gave her insight into the human condition. Sorrow, joy, love, hate, betrayal, all infused into her being. She started to get ideas of things to build. She leaned against a nearby tree and it shook, dislodging several more beads to fall in the snow. She picked them up and put them on her tongue. One was a man who hunted demons. One was a woman merchant.

They melted and became part of her, giving her a chance at this happiness she craved. Visions of the great meeting hall started to come to her and she shook all the trees around her to catch any other souls. Three more entered her mouth and consciousness.

When it was clear there was nothing more here, she closed her eyes and focused upon finding more. Then she heard… *something.* It sounded like a clear, silver bell to the east. It was far from her, on the other side of Raymond's house now, but she grew to overcome that. As she walked farther eastward, she heard the sound getting louder. Finally, she saw an area in the forest that was overgrown with weeds, vines, and fruit trees.

On the ground nearby three towers, two demolished entirely but still lying in identifiable chunks. One was still partially intact. The upper part of the tower was broken and lie on its side in front of its base. The sound was coming from within the base.

She diminished again, and found strange pebbles all over the ground. When she stepped on them, they crunched under foot. Some had spikes and they stabbed into her feet. She avoided them after being stuck a few times. She went through an open door to an area with a larger crack in the ceiling, exposing her to the sky. The sharp pebbles were *everywhere* here, and a large pile of them sat to one side before a door with vines growing out of it.

The vines went along the floor, through the pile of pebbles, and into a room across from the first room. She followed them, the silver bell sounds growing louder still. She entered a tunnel and followed it down. She saw a light at the end and recognized it as her own life energy. The tunnel opened up and the Archangel Uriel was hanging suspended in an X above the ground in a smooth cavern. A man with green hair stood near him, and looked up when she came to the opening.

"Oh, hello. Can I help you?"

"What are you doing with my friend?" She looked down but the drop was several feet to enter the room.

"Your friend? I was trying to figure out how to get him down from there. I have an idea but I can't do it alone."

"Can I help?"

The man turned to her. "Let's find out."

She sat and was about to drop down but suddenly, she was grabbed from behind under her arms and pulled back. A handsome man with interesting lines of experience in his face turned her to look at him.

"Forgive me, my lady. I could not let you suffer the same fate as the Death Bringer."

The green-haired man stepped forward. "Alistair. What are you doing?"

Alistair put her behind him. "I'm stopping you from catching her in this trap, Raven."

"Trap?" The Giver stepped back. Images of the cage imprisoned her mind in fear.

136

"I'm afraid so, my lady. The Bringer escaped but as you can see, another has taken her place."

Raven shook his head. "Please. Don't leave. Don't you want to help your friend?"

"Don't you use her loyalty against her, Mage."

Raven stepped back and bumped Uriel. The angel jostled and came loose from a manacle, which instantly attached to Raven. It grappled him, dropping Uriel altogether. The Archangel fell to the floor and the mage was raised into his place.

"No! No!"

Once he was in the air, the manacle chains pulled taught. Raven struggled against them but with no positive results.

Alistair turned to the Giver. "Wait here. Do not go in there."

She nodded and Alistair slipped into the room. The manacles jiggled for a moment, but then settled again. Alistair grabbed Uriel's leg and pulled him as Raven strained against his bonds. Alistair looked up and smiled, then gathered Uriel up and brought him to the edge.

A growl came from the tunnel and the Giver looked back. Alistair tossed Uriel up and jumped, grabbing onto the Giver's leg. She stumbled as a massive, grass-covered wolf leapt at her. Then she was in a room of pillows and silk. Alistair picked up Uriel and took him into a room with a bed. He laid him down and the Giver came over to him. She touched Uriel's hair.

She exhaled in relief. "He's still alive."

"Yes, but very drained. Can you help him?"

The Giver shook her head. "I don't think so. What I gave him already is gone. It would possibly change him. I don't want him to…"

Alistair touched her hand. "To become like those who captured you."

She looked at him. "You know about that?"

"Lucifer told me."

"You know him?"

"Who do you think sent me to help you?"

She smiled and hugged him. "Thank you, sir."

"Please, call me Alistair. Would you like to rest a bit? I have other rooms."

"That might be a good idea. I feel a bit weak right now."

Alistair showed her to a room and she smiled at him. He started to close the door and she stopped him.

"Please don't. I am uncomfortable in enclosed spaces."

He dismissed the door entirely. "Is that better?"

She relaxed. "Yes. Thank you."

"You rest. We'll talk when you wake up."

The Giver laid back on the bed and fell asleep.

Gloriana felt her energy dip suddenly. She looked at the snow elf reporting before her but its features and words were muddled. She waited until it finished, then inclined her head.

"I want to consult with my Breath on our next course of action. Thank you, my friend."

The snow elf beamed a smile and bowed. Gloriana looked at James and raised her hand for him to escort her. He took it and she leaned on him as they left the throne room. She maintained her composure until she was in her chambers and the doors closed. Then she stumbled and lost all strength. James caught her and lowered her onto the bed.

"What is it?"

"I can't tell. I just suddenly felt a drain on my energy. It was a huge reserve suddenly gone."

"Can you tell from what?"

"No. It… it feels almost like a promise of service that's unfulfilled. The service uses a bit of my essence to maintain the person at peak efficiency. This feels like I just conscripted a dozen at once."

"How long does that usually take to recover?"

"A few hours."

James covered her with a fur. "Okay then. You rest for the night. We'll revisit this in the morning."

He got up and sat in an adjacent chair and pulled a fur over his legs.

She closed her eyes and let rest take her.

Lucifer stepped into Heaven. It was still wrecked from the fight days later. Tiny soul beads were everywhere.

The Judgement Table still believes this is a viable place to send them. I guess that's good.

Still, no Saints had attempted to clean the place. Had there been a revolt? A mass eviction? Just an exodus right before the Giver got free? Or just as it was happening? Had the Giver been a distraction to cover the Saints abandoning Heaven?

The Giver had looked re-energized but he knew that energy had not come from Raphael or Gabriel. Their stolen essence was lost to the Soulless. Uriel was being evasive, so that left Michael. Lucifer couldn't sense him anywhere. There always used to be this small, Michael *hum* in the world that was now gone. Where he went was-

Lucifer felt a slam to his energy and he fell to a knee. Something was draining him. He looked at the main room's Pillar, but there were dozens of souls scattered across the floor between here and there. If he tried to get there and call for help, he would crush them or lose souls down the holes in the floor. If he used his wings, that was assured.

He reached into his pocket and pulled out the last soul he had grabbed from the pile in Hell. He ate it and got enough energy back to stand, though his stance was very shaky. Several beads fell to the floor of Heaven suddenly, no doubt from the Judgement Table, bouncing at least one into a hole. He glanced down and saw there were more than a few around his feet.

What was I thinking? That this woman's soul would be just sitting here with a beacon on it? It could be any of these.

He glanced behind him at the shaft where the cage had hung, and took a single, careful step back. The souls weren't disturbed by the motion and didn't roll. He managed another step back and then the platform got several more souls scattered on it. At least three rolled off the platform into Hell. He closed his eyes and steadied himself with a breath.

She wasn't one of those. She died yesterday, not this second.

He needed a way to find her, for Myrgen, and for more than that. More than anything, he didn't want Alexander to get his hands on this poor woman's soul. But this sudden energy drain was a threat and he couldn't risk losing consciousness and doing more harm than good.

He felt his heel come down on nothing and he fell backwards off the platform. He got out of range of the souls, then unfurled his wings and let them take him out of the fall to land on his feet. He summoned the throne from his furniture storage and rested on it for a moment. He consumed some souls and recovered. He held a few more in his hand and studied them.

We made all of Heaven out of this stuff. It wasn't this. It was that liquid Jude spoke of. Maybe I can...

He looked at the pile and sighed.

Might as well get to work.

Eighteen

"Find your way home."
—The Forty-Five Voices

"Do you want to be in here, or in the world?"

Catriona glanced at the garden at the mansion. "Going into the world means going through Persephone. It's a long walk to the Cabin on the Cliffs, which is where I would prefer to be."

"I thought you said that place was a Land center, like an island in the area."

Her eyes glittered emerald. "You're right. I didn't realize that at the time but you're right! But we can't go through the fire regardless. It destroys everything."

Myrgen ran his hand through his hair. "Can we get there through Sovereignlumin?"

She gave it some thought. "Maybe? You know, the Glove is right. There *has* to be a way to access these from the Land side. Let's see if we can find it."

They went over the wall and looked around.

"So, the Cabin is on a cliff, in a dense wooded area. It's really difficult to see from land."

She closed her eyes and listened. They were quiet and still for a long time as she reached out to the Land to find the sea. Finally, she felt it.

"There."

She pointed to the other side of the town from the mansion to a wooded area that formed the western border. It was denser than the ones on the opposite side near the southern end of the valley. They walked past their home and across the area where Merrick's Tower had been.

Catriona smiled as she entered the forest. "This is it! I recognize the smell."

Myrgen breathed deep. "The woods mixed with the sea. Yes."

They pushed past trees almost growing upon each other, roots embracing like lovers, until they saw a small light. They moved closer and smelled wood smoke from a hearth fire. A few trees closer and they came into a clearing with her cabin overlooking the ocean. She ran to it and opened the door, breathing deep the scents and sentiments.

"This is it. Better, this is *mine*. No one else has ever been here."

Myrgen walked up, smiling, hands resting on the satchel on his hip. "You sure you want company here?"

She turned to him and grabbed his collar, drawing him close. "Get in the house, Hunter."

"Ooh."

He walked in with her and she started peeling accoutrements off him. He barely got the door kicked closed before they were kissing. He bumped his hip on the table as he tugged his boot off with his other foot, which resulted in a howl of inconvenient pain. She started laughing and he frowned, rubbing his hip.

"That's gonna bruise."

"We're still in the afterlife."

"Then why did it *hurt*?"

Catriona knelt down and kissed his hip.

"Okay, that feels better."

Then she kissed across his groin and he forgot about his hip.

Catriona flopped back on the bed, sweaty and satisfied. Myrgen lay panting beside her in the same state.

"Is this why the Bringer was so insistent on having her Hunter?"

She wanted to speak but her throat was dry and a little hoarse from the vocal workout part of their coupling. She pointed to him, then to her nose. She waited a moment before getting to her feet and wandering into the bathing room. A white fluid ran down her slick inner thigh and she frowned.

I guess we are *in the real world.*

She washed up and used the facilities, then grabbed a robe from a peg by the door, and put it on. The bucket by the sink was full and she poured wine into the bowl at the end of the counter to feed the hearth Fae to thank them for it. She pulled a cup from the cupboard and filled it from the bucket. The water was cool and she drank deep, then dipped another cup to bring back to Myrgen. She turned and her foot caused the discarded satchel to skitter across the floor.

The lid lifted and she saw the letters inside slide to the top. The one from Anika was on the bottom and she could just see the darker parchment her foster mother had used. She stopped, then set the cup on the table. She picked up the satchel and opened it, pulling the letter out. It was thicker than she thought it would be. She sat down and looked at it, afraid to open it.

Myrgen stepped out of the bedroom and stumbled to the bathing room. He came out a minute later, likewise in a robe. He saw what she was looking at and filled a cup with water as well before sitting down across from her.

"I don't want to open it."

He touched her hand. "Why?"

"Because then they're really gone."

He looked at the note. "I know what you mean."

She closed her eyes. "But they are just as gone with it sealed as they are with it open."

Myrgen said nothing.

A pair of tears escaped her eyes. She looked at the letter and opened it. Her voice cracked as she read it to him.

Our beloved daughter,
Drake and I woke today and realized we would be gone by sunset. I'm writing this while he talks to Tib.

143

Catriona, Myrgen, because I know you're together, we are so proud of you. You have become the Land's Protectors, for all its children, and we know you will do well by them.

Oh, the tears are coming now! But I'm not sad. I'm at peace and so is Drake. We don't know when you'll be back again but we didn't want to leave without saying goodbye.

We love you both. Catriona, sail. Myrgen, paint. Protect and love each other.

And know we love you.
Drake and Anika

He got up and walked over to her. He held her as she cried.

Another page was behind the first and he picked it up.

"It's from Tib."

"By the stones. I can't..."

He kissed her forehead. "Do you want me to?"

She nodded.

He cleared his throat.

Mom,

Drake told me they were leaving today and I went to talk to my friends. But they weren't here and I realized I don't really have anything I need to do. I protected Ashstone and our family from the invaders. I got my name. I won't sail on the Enigma because it's gone.

I don't need to stay behind because I'll get lonely and you aren't here. You are off helping people and saving the world. I can't help, so I'm going to leave with them.

I love you though. I really do. Go make great stories! And make Myrgen paint them!

Love,
Tib

A third page was behind it and the lump in his throat strangled his voice for a moment.

Myrgen,

144

Thank you for coming into my family. I never got to spend the time I wanted with you, but my dog really likes you so that means you're a very good person. Dogs don't like bad people.

Thank you for him. And thank you for making Mom laugh. Tell Drake the Dog I'm okay and hug him for me. He's still my dog, but you can take care of him, if you want.

Sincerely,
Victor Tiberius Morstadora (Tib)

The letter fell from Myrgen's hand and he leaned on the table, tears staining the parchment of Anika's letter. Catriona stood and grasped him from behind until he was able to turn around and hold her. They spent their grief into each other's shoulders until the hearth was just coals. Then, wordlessly, they went to bed and slept.

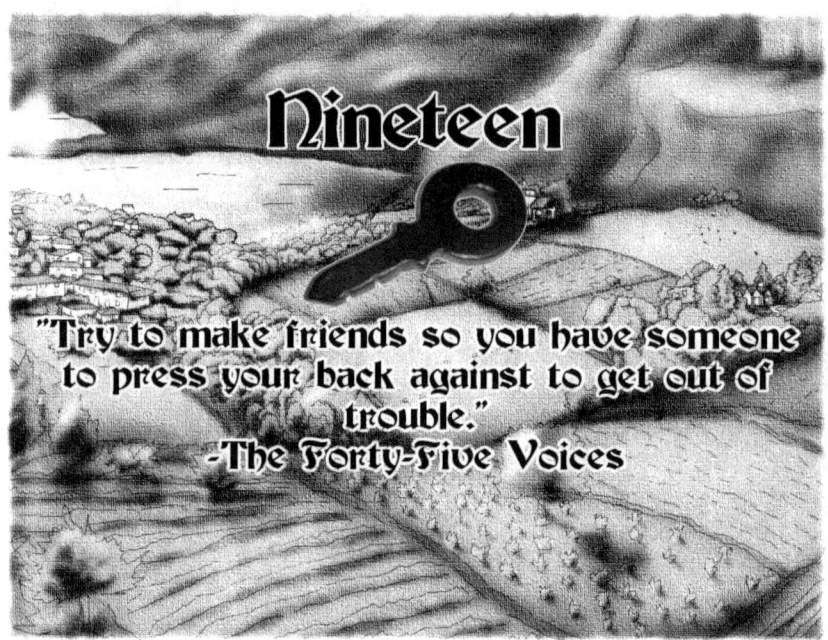

Nineteen

"Try to make friends so you have someone to press your back against to get out of trouble."
-The Forty-Five Voices

Giles and Clara popped into the wreckage of the Church in St. Giles and both stumbled and fell on the debris. Clara landed on her injured leg and cried out. She put her hand down on the rubble and hissed in pain. Giles landed hand first in a puddle of black sludge and screamed as it burned him. Snow covered everything.

They heard the sound of boots running in the snow around the walls of the building and a couple of faces showed in the windows.

"Clara!"

She looked at the face in the single remaining stained-glass window. "George!"

He showed up in another window and started climbing through. Giles was holding his hand, trying to concentrate and then a gush of water flowed across his body. It washed the sludge from his hand. He looked at Clara and then at George.

"Clara, don't move."

George looked at Giles, then at Clara. She turned her head and looked behind her. Her hand was at the very edge of the black sludge like Giles had landed in. A few snowflakes were the only barrier separating her hands from it. George came over to her and carefully lifted her from the ground.

"What happened to you?"

"My leg mended wrong after falling from Heaven. We had to re-break it and set it so it healed right."

"George, I need to get to the healing pool. Can you come with us?"

George nodded and Giles moved them elsewhere. They came down in a splash. Giles plunged his burnt hand into the water and sighed in relief. He brought it out a moment later, healed. George set Clara in the water and she felt her bones do their last bit of knitting together.

Giles went over to her. "I'm not good at plant magic, but I think I can move these branches apart."

He concentrated on the brace and it separated, loosening its grip on her.

"George, can you pull that off of her?"

Clara pointed her toe and George pulled the brace off her. She bent her knee and it creaked, stretching the muscles. She flexed her toes. Her feet were bare and she was cold and started shivering.

George turned to Giles as he helped Clara to her feet. "She isn't dressed for this weather."

Clara squeezed his hand. "None of us were. We didn't have temperature in Heaven."

"It might be shock. She shouldn't be feeling the weather either yet."

"I don't feel it at all. I'm still able to return there."

Clara looked at Giles. "What *was* that stuff?"

George bowed his head. "Corruption. Please. We need to get you out of this water and before a fire."

Giles walked to some stairs. "This way."

They followed him to a dorm area where many people were settling in for the night, then up more stairs to a Great Hall with four fireplaces. George moved them to the nearest one, and Clara sat, stretching her leg and spreading out her wet dress to dry it out.

"I'll go find her some dry clothes."

George looked at Giles who excused himself and left them alone. Clara looked at George.

"So, what was that really?"

"A bad decision on my part. There was an amulet that could take me to the other side of the battlefield in a single thought. The previous user was destroyed by it. I thought I could use it just once and be alright. I threw it away after I arrived in the village."

"So, it's just lying in the snow where someone could stumble upon it?"

"I wasn't thinking. I was muddled, sick. I just wanted it away from me. Clara, it burned my soul. I can still feel it inside me. I'm... unclean."

"George..."

"Throw it in the fire."

George and Clara looked at Giles, who had a pile of blankets.

"George, you still have it, right? That amulet the priest had?"

"No. I threw it away from me. I don't know where it is."

Giles rolled his eyes to stare at the ceiling. "If anyone finds that thing, if they realize what it can do... George, the humans can enter the forest and go into the valley. That stuff will kill the army."

"Won't that bring victory to the forces of Heaven?"

Giles shook his head. "Is that how you want to win?"

"I don't... know. The darkness inside screams for more."

Giles set the blankets down, and unfolded one, handing it to Clara. "How are you feeling?"

"Better. Thank you. People are settling in for the night. Where should we go?"

"There are bedrooms up here. As many as necessary. You can have rooms near one another that suit your needs."

George cast his eyes around the area. "Do you know where the King is? Apparently, he fought someone, a woman, who destroyed the Archangel Michael."

"He's here, somewhere. He interred his lady earlier today in the tombs. George, I figured out that the forest's growth means the Giver is down here somewhere. I was going to ask if you can return to Heaven."

"I believe so. I left at their behest, not cast out, like you were. I believe I can get back. I still feel the connection."

"Take me with you."

Everyone looked at the man who spoke, who stepped into the firelight.

George frowned. "Who are you?"

"A man who has lost someone dear to him, and just wants to see about saving her."

Giles sat down and gestured to the bench across from him. "Alexander, these are Saints George and Clara. This is King Alexander of Mervolingia."

George straightened. "The Heavenly Champion."

Alexander nodded. "The same. Good to meet you in person, Clara. Raven spoke well of you."

Giles rubbed his eyes. "Your Majesty, are you truly thinking of going to Heaven to find her soul? How would you even do that?"

"I hope a solution will present itself once I'm there."

Clara patted Alexander's hand. "Alexander, Heaven is an afterlife. You will die."

"Then we'll be together. I designated my heir a while ago. But I've been cut off from Heaven. Gabriel severed my Power to rule Mervolingia and I need to re-establish it or I'm dead anyway. So, I truly have nothing to lose."

He looked at the Saints. "Besides, you all were received in Heaven at the edge of death, subsumed before she touched you. If you could walk around up there, I should be able to as well."

Giles looked at Clara and George. George shrugged. "He might be right."

Clara wasn't convinced.

George tried to be supportive. "Your Power of Sovereignty is from Heaven. It might protect you, maybe think you belong there."

Alexander sighed. "I'm hoping the proximity to Heaven will restore it, maybe recharge it if it's just a matter of being drained. The essence came from there to begin with."

Clara folded her arms. "It came from an *angel*. Not *exactly* the same thing."

Alexander shrugged. "I've got to try."

Giles pointed to Alexander. "If this fails, you let this go."

Clara looked at them. "If she's up there, she's in the Well, liquid. She's already dissolved."

Giles shook his head. "Not necessarily. Look, the Black Forest has spread across the entire country of York in less than a night. She got that energy from something. Either the Well, the Angels, or both. If the Well is intact, yes, Tanglwyst's soul is gone. But if the Giver destroyed the

Well her captors were trying to get her to replenish, the souls wouldn't be in it."

Clara frowned. "What makes you think she would have destroyed it?"

Giles looked at her. "I would have."

George thought about it. "If that's the case, then the souls will just be all over the floor."

Clara's face became lined in concern. "Where anyone can step on them and destroy them. That's if the other Saints haven't already put them in some other container."

George shook his head. "The other Saints are locked in cells, unable to leave. Only one Saint was allowed on the Ensoulment Floor at a time because the Well was so low. They can't even interact. It was a preventative measure after your revolt."

"*Revolt?* Is that what they are calling it?"

"You were trying to stop their War. Speaking of which, where is Brigit?"

Alexander steepled his fingers. "She's sleeping."

Clara sighed. "Your Majesty, I understand you're in pain. But death and life are a part of us."

"It feels inappropriate for a person who can't die to speak of life and death like that."

Clara blinked, nodding. "That was insensitive of me. I'm sorry. But the souls belong to the next person who gets them. The person your friend was is done with her life. She has bequeathed it to the next generation."

"She didn't *donate* her soul. She was *murdered.* This wasn't justice, or sickness. This was a *crime.* And if I can save the life of someone taken too soon, I shall try."

Giles crossed his arms on the table. "You may have a large number of souls to look through. This storm has shown up out of nowhere. People weren't prepared for it."

George exhaled. "True. We were in full summer or Corrigan couldn't have marched."

Clara's worried face did not diminish. "So, the people were in full planting? There will be no food come harvest. More will die. And with no one dispatching souls to newborns, they are being born dead too."

150

Alexander took her hand. "Then it's imperative we get up there as soon as possible. Perhaps we can free the Saints and get Heaven working again. And the only thing I ask is that I be able to *look* for her soul." Alexander turned to George. "If it was someone *you* loved, would you do less?"

George swallowed, his eyes drifting towards Clara but stopping short of actually looking at her. "We need to hurry then. Aethelraed has a plan to kill the Fae Lord of Winter to end the weather onslaught. If he succeeds, the deaths will slow down, but the births will increase."

Clara's gaze met each man at their table. Then she closed her eyes and nodded. "Go. Be quick about it."

George and Alexander rose. George kissed Clara on the forehead. He walked to Alexander and put his hands on his and Giles' shoulders. A moment later, they both disappeared.

Twenty

"He who serves two masters has to lie to one."
-The Forty-Five Voices

George and Alexander arrived near an open door in a hallway of closed ones. Each door had a name on it.

Alexander read the names on the ones nearby. "These are those cells you mentioned?"

George nodded. "It's also the furthest from the Ensoulment Floor, so there are far fewer chances of any souls being under foot when we arrived."

Alexander checked out the floor. "So far, you're right. Giles isn't here though."

"Not really a surprise. How do you feel?"

"I felt a small surge in the Power. It seems to be protecting me and possibly drawing strength from the area. But it feels *really* thin, like I'm wearing a veil as a disguise. Unfortunately, I can also feel it burning off. But I don't feel that connection from within like I need."

"What do you want to do?"

"First, see if the Well is intact. If it is, we know not to stay and risk it."

George nodded. "Stay here."

George walked to the hallway that went to the Ensoulment Floor and saw the wreckage that was Heaven now. The floor near him was clear but he could see a mild gray tint to the floor further in. He slid his feet forward, not lifting them to move. He checked the cage room, the door to which was no longer present. The Well was in shards. He focused on the floor and saw among the holes were hundreds of small pearls of various shades of dinge.

He returned to Alexander. "There's no one out there. No sign of the Archangels at all though there was obviously *something* that happened here. Giles was right. The Well has been destroyed, which is good news for you. Your lady friend isn't just liquid soul stuff."

Alexander ran a hand through his hair, not looking as relieved as George expected. "What do we do?"

"I don't know." He looked at the doors. "But we'll need help."

George tried the doors. He heard voices on the other side but they were too muffled to understand,

"What are you doing up here?"

George turned to Lucifer. "I'm a Saint."

"I meant him."

Alexander swallowed. "I lost someone. I'm here to find her."

"Wait. I know you. You're Alexander."

Alexander exchanged a look with George. "Yeeess?"

"The one who used a woman's fealty to risk her own life."

Alexander closed his eyes in shame. "It is that lady I have come to save."

"Why? So you can betray her trust again?"

"Actually, she no longer gives me her fealty. I gave her the power to rule the kingdom and now, she has no such obligation."

"So, *she's* the ruler of Mervolingia?"

"That depends upon if I can rescue her from this place or not."

Lucifer looked him over, then offered a smile. "Fine. But I'm aware of you now. I don't have to let you ever leave here. Remember that. By the way, Catriona asked me to speak to you."

George frowned, suspicious. "Why would the Death Bringer send *Lucifer* to speak to him?"

Alexander's eyes went wide. "Lu...*Lucifer?*"

"Because she's busy and couldn't come herself."

"How is she? Is she okay? Did she get hurt?"

"She died from the wounds but that's not as fatal as it sounds. She is currently trying to save your kingdom as well as the invading one, so I don't want to make her job harder. Regardless, she never could have come here to see you. She's not allowed here."

Alexander settled back. "I feel like I'm talking to Raven all of a sudden..."

Lucifer looked away, contemplating something clearly unpleasant. "I heard about your friend, the one you're up here to fix apparently."

"You did?"

"Yeah. Sorry for your loss."

"I... thank you..."

George looked at Alexander. "There's more though. Tell him about the rest."

Alexander told Lucifer about the Power of Sovereignty and the Trials to become king.

Lucifer listened, nodding. "That is a problem but I might be able to help with it. Believe it or not, I'm still an Archangel. Why does this Lady inspire going into the possibly lethal afterlife?"

"She has been where I have and seen what I've seen. She has held the Power herself and saw fit to return it to me. She's wiser than me and I need her. We have a bond that I hope I can use to find her after I've recovered the Power."

"And if I required you to give that Power up after you find her?"

"I will hand the Crown to my heir. Gladly. They won't require Emmy's death to prove her worthy. She's not even three years old."

"That's a lot to give up."

"If I'm unworthy, I'm unworthy. As long as Tanglwyst is restored, I'll be satisfied."

"What if she doesn't want to be restored?"

"Then she will read me out and slap me, Sir."

"And leave?"

"Possibly. As is her right."

Lucifer cocked his head at the King. "And you won't stop her?"

"I don't want her to be where she's not comfortable. It's her choice to stay or go."

154

Lucifer arched an eyebrow, then glanced at George. "Did you coach him?"

George glanced around. "Uh, I only know you because I don't know who you are. I've seen the other Archangels. You're up here, so you must be Lucifer."

"Smart. So, Alexander, the Power of Sovereignty is granted by Heaven?"

"I believe so. I mean, I had it until Gabriel declared I was the enemy of Krakte. After that, the protection afforded me was gone. I've been shot with an arrow and burned, without so much as a flash of the protection I had before. Plus, I'm rather frightened at the moment and there's no barrier between us, just the one keeping me alive up here."

Lucifer got a look of mock injury on his face. "Frightened? Of me?"

"No. Of the reputation you have."

Lucifer's brow flashed slight confusion and he glanced at the floor for a moment. Then he smiled. "*By Heaven,* you're good! Wow. Okay, yeah, I can see what she saw in you. I'm feeling it myself.

"So, you were cut off during the Holy Tantrum. That's when your Saint friends were locked away and the others were thrown to the world. Well, the bad news is that, if they granted it to you at all, they can't do it now. They were devoured by the Soulless."

"Then their energy was *not* returned to the Giver?"

"No. Only the Bringer managed that. I failed."

George got a worried look. "And Uriel?"

Lucifer sobered. "I don't know. I can't feel him anymore."

Alexander saw the exchange between them. "We need to restore the order up here. People are dying and we suspect infants aren't surviving birth."

Lucifer looked in Alexander's eyes. "That is not truly a concern. Look, before all this happened, people were born with souls regularly. Birth is a primal thing, an essential to everything. You think dogs aren't having puppies because Heaven is in disarray? People are still being born. In fact, they are better off because the Giver is in the world again. Heaven was *never* essential until the Giver was stolen and held prisoner. The babies are fine."

George felt a relief, and Alexander seemed to breathe easier as well.

"But you are right about the souls up here. We could send them all to Hell, I suppose. And in fact, that's truly the best choice. I just hate losing all that creativity."

Alexander swallowed. "But my friend. Please."

Lucifer leaned against a door and pulled something from his pocket. He popped it in his mouth, then looked at the other one in his hand. He handed it to Alexander.

"Try that. See if it reconnects your Power."

Alexander put it in his mouth and closed his eyes. A second later, a barrier surrounded him. "There it is. And I feel the internal connection again. I know where she is. This way."

He went into the main room and looked at the floor. He turned back to the other. "What is the choice here? Can I go get her?"

Lucifer folded his arms, his distrust still heavy in his stance. "Try not to destroy the other souls."

"Walk without lifting your feet." George demonstrated and Alexander nodded.

He walked forward towards a broken shard of the Well. Lucifer stretched, trying to locate the wayward soul. "George, do you see it?"

"Is he going for that liquid?"

"No. If it was liquid, it couldn't call out to him. It would be just stuff."

Alexander carefully took a knee and gently brushed some souls away from his path. George and Lucifer exchanged glances as the King picked his way forward.

"I'm glad we never made carpets. This would be impossible."

George smirked.

Alexander put his hand on the floor in a clean spot and carefully balanced to clear the floor so he could crawl. He picked the beads apart in groups, moving them to make a path. Finally, almost spread out to his full height, he reached out and picked up a single bead.

"Help."

George and Lucifer ran up to him, and reached out for his ankles, then pulled him carefully away from the spot. A few souls scattered but none were lost or crushed. He stood up and inspected his clothes. He plucked a couple souls off of him and handed them to Lucifer.

"Thank you. The Power faded right before I touched the soul but I was able to find her."

Lucifer handed him another pearl. "Make sure."

Alexander ate it and smiled, nodding. "Yes. She's here." He looked at the path he cut. "Did we lose any?"

George shook his head. "I don't think so. What happened here though?"

"I was downstairs in Hell when I heard a commotion. Screaming, destruction, a real war zone. I flew up and saw her cage ripped apart and everything as you see it here. Well, destroyed, walls taken out, holes in the floor. Uriel was lying on the ground, Gabriel and Raphael nearby. They were blacked by fire and their wings had been burnt off. She was gone."

Alexander thought a moment. "Burned off?"

"Yeah. Removed completely. Stank like burnt chicken up here."

"But yours were intact?"

"Yeah."

"Any idea why?"

"I'm gonna say either she didn't include me because I kept her alive, or because I was in Hell, which is partitioned away from here. It's still part of the pantheon, but not the place."

"How did you keep her alive?"

"I was feeding her purified souls, like those I gave you, to keep her strength up. The ones in the Well were barely more salvation than corruption. It looks like she broke free of the cage, consumed the rest of them, then shattered the thing."

"What makes you think she consumed it?"

Lucifer gestured to the area. "There's no pool of souls. If there were, your friend would be gone, and so would all those people. I think she reclaimed as much of her power as possible."

Alexander looked at the small beads all over the ground. "These souls are *not* what you just gave me?"

"No. These are still people. When they come to me... Well, let's just say that is no longer true."

"So, they are purified through suffering?"

"Suffering never purifies anything."

"How long does it take?"

"Not long."

George frowned. "So, you were lying this whole time?"

"So were you."

A long pause stretched between them all. Alexander gestured to the souls. "What can we do for these people here?"

Lucifer nodded to the far side of the room. "I noticed the shard over there has liquid in it. Once we clear a path to it, which you have kindly started, then we'll do a few experiments."

"Experiments?"

"One pure bead, one impure one, two souls. Creativity remains but we won't be having as much evil in the world."

Alexander smiled. "I would like that."

George visibly relaxed. "Me too. Can you open the doors for the Saints?"

"Yeah, but we might want to get you back down first. Too many folks might have an issue with you being here."

"I promised I'd earn her release by helping up here."

Lucifer leaned against a piece of rubble and took out a pearl to eat.

Alexander looked him over. "There's something wrong. You're fighting weakness."

"I'm being drained. Someone with a connection to me is in a trap, I suspect, and it's draining me. I'll be alright but I need to stop consuming so much energy. Look, I'll release the Saints but I need to head down with you. The Giver and Bringer and a bunch of folks are looking to have a summit and share recipes and braid each other's hair. We need to be there. The fate of your kingdom and your heir's kingdom are in the balance. Take him down, George. I'll start the process up here."

George nodded. Lucifer staggered to the place where the cage had been and fell off.

Alexander and George left.

The Saint and the King returned to the Great Hall. It was empty, except for Clara and Giles.

She smiled at them. "You're back, how was it?"

"It's pretty scary."

Alexander started to leave and George put a hand on his shoulder.

"Are you sure you want to do that?"

"Seems like an odd thing to ask at this point."

"What did you learn up there?" Giles looked at Alexander.

The King sighed. "I learned that Heaven isn't necessary. In fact, it caused a problem it then had to solve. And I have a summit to determine the fate of at least two countries and that politics now seems so petty. Above that, I learned that no one is a good person, and that makes dealing with other people a lot harder."

George shook his head. "That wasn't the lesson here. It's not that no one is a good person. It means that everyone here is more good than bad or they wouldn't *be* here. And that for every person damning their soul to Hell, there's another person doing more good than harm who will get another chance when they go. The important thing is that now, you'll know the difference."

He looked around the Hall, remembering the people who helped others, who kept track of the goods coming from the ship so Tanglwyst would know what was being utilized. He remembered people tending to the children and keeping them calm while the maelstroms attacked the ship. He remembered people lifting others onto the nets so they could get out of the hold when he was rescuing them.

The Hall was empty now, but hours before, it had been filled with people erasing gray from their souls. Even the woman, Madeline, had been trying to redeem herself from the black that had tainted her. If he could bring Tanglwyst back, then Madeline would no longer be a murderer. That would help her soul as well.

Alexander smiled, nodding. "You're right."

Giles propped his chin in his hand. "You should go. George, tell us what you found out."

Alexander bowed to the Saints and George sat down to regale them.

Twenty-One

"Be present."
—The Forty-Five Voices

Lucifer released the locks on the Saints' doors. He heard murmurs and discussion and eventually, he saw them coming into the hallway.

"Hello everyone. As you can see, there's been a development."

He took a moment to answer questions and give directions. Then he went back down to Hell. He grabbed a handful of glowing beads and put them in a pouch, tucking them in to a spot in his coat. Then he grabbed a handful and put them in his pocket. He swallowed a couple of beads to get his energy up, then went up to Heaven.

Several Saints had cleared the way to the Pillar. He went over to the hole where Raphael had been hovering and looked down. It was only visible at a very specific angle, but he saw Raven in energy manacles, motionless.

He glanced behind him and waited for the Saints to be looking the other way, then he dropped down into the tunnel that led to the trap. He walked to the opening to the trap room and watched Raven. He started to drop down into the trap room when Raven spoke.

"Don't."

Lucifer looked up. "You can talk? What happened?"

"The Bringer needed the Giver in here to learn something important."

"Can you tell me what?"

"Some connection. I think I see it."

"You're drawing energy from me. I keep having to replenish to stay functioning."

"Really? So, it isn't just drawing on my life energy? That might be problematic for Gloriana then."

"What? You have more than one source of your immortality?"

"Well, you don't stay this pretty by accident."

Lucifer pulled a pair of soul pearls from his pocket and replenished. One fell into the room and he watched it, sure it would be sucked up.

It wasn't.

He looked at Raven, then dropped into the room. The spell surged, then settled, remaining on Raven.

"I thought so."

"You aren't enough."

Lucifer nodded. "Yes. With you in there, it draws from me and Gloriana. I'm not valuable to it and I won't be as long as you're there. I'll die before you will."

"Well, please don't do that." He started to drift off.

Lucifer smiled. "I won't. Now, hey, pay attention, can you?"

Raven strained to follow Lucifer's movements.

"Raven, I need you to find out for sure what Catriona needed you to learn. Do that, and I'll keep you alive."

Raven's head lolled again and drifted to unconsciousness.

Alexander stood before Tanglwyst's body, her soul in his hand. Images of her these past few months filled his head.

Her laugh.

Her smile.

Her anger at him for all he'd done to her and his friends.

When they had truly met, he had been a different person. He was a nicer person, helpful, loving. Becoming King had changed him.

Hurt him.

Grayed him.

Suffering has never purified anything.

Was he ending her suffering, or continuing it for his own selfish purposes?

What would she *want?*

He leaned against the wall by her crypt shelf, hugging the bead to his chest. He was frozen, unable to decide if this would be her wish or not.

His eyes settled upon the door Giles had told him was where he would put her to make her a ghost. That felt like a final decision, that putting her body in there would end her ability to be restored.

But what if you just took her soul *in there?*

If *he* went in, that would not make him a ghost. Giles hadn't told him the living couldn't go in that room. Obviously, the living *could* because Giles knew what was in there.

But the bead was pure soul energy. What would stop it from becoming a ghost immediately?

He looked around and saw the glowing moss.

Giving her a body.

He took some moss and made a little hollow, then put the bead inside. He covered the hole with more moss, then held the little ball of *čaro* to his chest and opened the door.

He had expected a dark place, with random spirits floating around, oblivious and marred by the instruments of their deaths. He was confused when he saw houses and streets. He turned to look behind him and saw the door open, the tombs still there where he left them.

A woman walked by, pushing a fish cart. She glanced at him and stopped.

"Hello. You look lost."

"I… I wanted to talk to my friend."

"Do you know their name?"

"Tanglwyst."

The ghost shook her head. "There's no one here by that name. It's a pretty small village and we know each other."

"She's… I have her here." He lifted his hand away from his chest.

162

"In the moss? That's a strange place for a friend. Is it a snail?"

"No. It's her soul. I have a decision to make and I need her help."

"You went and fetched her soul from the Afterlife?"

Alexander nodded, feeling very much like a child before this woman.

She crossed her arms. "You must have loved this friend very much. How did she die?"

"She was stabbed by a woman who thought her whole family was dead."

"That's terrible. Are you to blame for your friend's death?"

Alexander swallowed. "Yes. Ultimately, none of them would have been in this situation without my bad judgement. I took a wrong step and it led down a path that has caused untold suffering and death. I can't fix everything, but I think I can fix this."

"Why this one?"

"Because with this one, I think I can fix a lot more. Without her, I think I will continue to make the wrong steps and I can't see the way clear anymore."

"And you believe *she* can?" The woman gestured to the moss.

"She sees things almost as clear as the Death Bringer can."

The ghost woman looked forlorn. "I never met the Death Bringer. Our village was destroyed by a man who just wanted our *čaro*. The Covenant gave us back our homes and lives, so to speak."

He frowned. "Do you *want* to meet the Death Bringer? Because I might be able to arrange that."

The woman smirked. "What would I say to her? 'Hello, I've always wanted to be dead'?"

"If you have always wanted to be, she might be able to help you."

She looked wistfully at the sky. "Maybe."

"Wait... Would... would you like others to be here? Maybe make the village bigger?"

She cocked her head, confused. "Grow the village? Imprison people here?"

"Is this a prison?"

She stopped to contemplate that. "I'm not sure. I don't think so. But I don't think we move on here. That might just be because we don't think to try to."

"And if you could?"

"Some of us would, I'm sure."

He looked at his hand. "Is that what souls ultimately want? To just move on?"

"I think we want the choice to."

"That's what I want for her. To be able to choose. She didn't choose to die and she has so much more that is needed of her. But if she prefers to move on, I worry I would be preventing that."

"What happens if she is restored and she doesn't want to be? Can she die again?"

Alexander thought about it. "Yes. Dying once won't make her immortal."

"Well then, I think you have your answer."

He smiled. "Thank you. Thank you, My Lady…um…"

She shook her head. "I don't remember my name. I haven't used it in years."

"Then simply thank you." He bowed and backed out the door.

He closed it and turned to Tanglwyst's body.

"There's a lot to say. But I don't want to say it to the dark. Had you gone to a paradise, I would not have brought you out. But you were nowhere, and I think you can do more as yourself, than as someone else."

He put her soul bead in her mouth and watched it liquify on her tongue. He closed her mouth and stepped back, his hands on the edge of the crypt.

She's gone now. Either she awakens or she doesn't. The die is cast.

She swallowed.

Alexander dropped to his knees in joy.

It took a minute for her to start breathing again. Once she was, he took her from the shelf and returned her to the pool. He wasn't sure if there was any damage to her body since her interment, but just in case, he wanted her complete. Her color returned and her eyes opened.

She looked around at the water.

"Hey there."

She turned her gaze to Alexander. "What happened?"

"You want the truth or a pretty lie?"

She blinked. "Truth."

"You were stabbed and I was unable to get you here before you died. I had the chance to go up to Heaven and find you. I did. I brought you back down here. I have something to ask you, and you don't have to

164

answer it right away. Take your time and I'll just keep asking periodically."

"Ok. Ask."

"Is it okay that I brought you back? Do you want to return to Heaven?"

She cocked her head. "I was not expecting that."

"What were you expecting?"

"Marriage proposal."

"Oh, I can do that too. I can do that right now."

She laughed, waving him off. "As for the other part, I don't feel as though I am missing a part of myself for having been in Heaven."

"Can I show you where I'd rather go when I die?"

"Sure."

They went through the door across from the crypts.

Twenty-Two

"The hardest part about 'everything happens for a reason' is waiting for the reason to come along."
-The Forty-Five Voices

Alexander and Tanglwyst walked down the hallway of dorms.

"Do you know how Madeline is?"

"Right after she... Her husband walked in with Giles. Apparently, he moved the entire center of the ship. I haven't been upstairs to look at it."

"Oh. That is horrible and great at the same time. That poor woman."

"I wasn't exactly kind about it when I found out."

She stopped. "What did you do?"

"I took her to St. Giles and showed her the town."

"In the middle of a war?"

"I'm not proud of it. I thought she needed to see why we took them out of there."

She frowned. "And?"

"And it worked."

Tanglwyst shook her head. "You were angry and you took it out on her. And now she will be traumatized by that."

"I'll not deny that was the impetus. But it was worse than I knew. The granary had exploded. Everything near it was scorched. The Wise Wench is gone. Burned to the ground. I should have returned there before then, to check on everyone."

"Was anyone left?"

"When Madeline and I went there, we didn't stay long enough to see. Some soldiers were tearing their shirts into bandages. They had the blisters and burns from the fires. An arrow came through the barrier and killed another guard on patrol. I got us both out of there. When I returned, I didn't see the rest of the town."

"Perhaps we should go there now."

He searched her eyes. "It's dangerous. That man was shot down without warning."

Her eyes flared. "You put *her* in danger to show her how precarious the situation was. If she's traumatized by this, it's *your* fault."

"She killed you."

"I know."

He shook his head. "No. I won't do it."

She closed her eyes and snorted in anger. Then she grabbed the amulet on his neck and disappeared.

"Tangl!"

His first instinct was to run, to find Giles and have him take them both to the village. His mind flashed images of her being shot by an arrow, burnt by a column of fire, or crushed by a collapsing building. He was panicking. Had he really gone all the way to Heaven just for her to die in the streets?

He stopped himself. Several deep breaths later, he was under control again. He had told Lucifer it was her choice if she left. She had left. It was up to her if she returned.

It was her life.

A door opened and Madeline looked out into the dim hallway. "Your Majesty?"

"Madeline. I'm sorry, I didn't mean to wake you."

She gathered the robe tight up to her neck. "I thought... My mind was playing tricks on me. I thought I heard the Lady's voice, saying my name."

"You did. She was here."

Madeline glanced behind her, then scuttled out, gently closing the door behind her. "You mean like a ghost?"

"No. I... I had the opportunity to go to Heaven and retrieve her. I spoke to an Archangel and promised him I would take care of the war down here in exchange for her returning with me. He allowed it."

"Where did she go?"

"To St. Giles. To the village. She wanted to see it for herself."

Madeline bit her lip. "I see."

"My lady, I want to apologize for my behavior. My grief got the better of me and I put you in danger. I'm sorry."

Madeline looked at his eyes. "Sire, I would rather know than not know. The same with the other folks from there. People aren't turnips. They don't grow when kept in the dark, and you don't need to carry us. We can handle being told what's going on. My family and friends are grateful you didn't execute me for it. I undoubtedly deserve it."

"She's back again and although my instinct is to say she's fine and forgiving, I know better than to speak on her behalf."

Madeline patted his arm. "Good luck, Your Majesty. I hope she returns."

"Thank you." He bowed and she returned to her room.

Alexander went on to the Great Hall and looked around. Giles, George, Clara, and Brigit were sitting at the table by the fireplace. Brigit was standing and sat as Alexander joined them.

"I was just coming to check on you. How did it go?"

"She came back and is very much her old self. None the worse for wear."

Giles glanced behind Alexander. "Where is she?"

"Cliffport. Is that wine?"

Clara frowned. "The place with the broken church?"

George joined her in frowning. "How did she do that?"

Alexander tapped his chest. "Amulet. She grabbed it and went."

"Is she okay?" Brigit's worry was as obvious as the others.

Alexander shrugged. "I don't know. But I promised Lucifer that if she left, I'd let her go."

"'Her choice.'" George shook his head. "I don't know that I could be this calm in the same situation."

"I am doing my best not to beg Giles to take me to her. She is scared of those amulets too, yet this is the second time she's used it to see things for herself. She's no turnip, that's for sure." Alexander took a drink and drained the cup.

They all watched him, confused.

"Giles, I'm tired and really need to sleep."

"Oh! Yes. Um…" He pointed across from the stairs. "That way. I'll take you." Giles and Alexander stood and Giles tapped on a door once. He waited a second, then opened it. The room beyond was surprising.

"This is Tanglwyst's room, in St. Giles."

"It is? Interesting. It sets itself up to be whatever the person finds most comfortable."

"You mean it's an illusion?"

"Not exactly. The cosmetics of it is illusion. It has everything you see here. Bed, dressers, etc. The Covenant has several configurations available."

"There's a bath in its own room?"

"Mhm. Must mean you desire a bath. The stuff only has what the guest wants."

"That is very handy. Well, the wine is starting to hit me so, good night Giles."

"Should I send the Lady in if she returns?"

"If she were returning, she would have done so by now. Also, there's supposed to be a meeting of several entities tomorrow, I think. Is there a room we can meet in if it ends up happening here?"

"Yes. There's a meeting room at the foot of the Hall."

"Thank you, sir. Good night."

"Good night, Your Majesty."

Alexander closed the door behind him and sat in the hearth chair to take off his soaked boots. He was surprised to find they were not coming apart. Leather was weak while wet, and he had not gone easy on his shoes. Then again, the way he had been traveling, it wasn't like his soles were wearing out. He set them by the hearth. There was a large basket near the dresser. He opened the dresser and found clean, dry day wear and night clothes.

He took off his doublet and shirt and tossed them into the basket. In a second, the basket was empty and a flash of light went off in the drawer beneath the open one. He closed it and opened the other drawer. His shirt was cleaned and folded neatly within.

He smiled and disrobed. Each item disappeared and was in the drawer moments later. He even tossed in his boots and caught a flash in the wardrobe.

Nude, he walked to the bathroom to look for a chamber pot. He found a privy instead, to his relief. When he finished, the bath was full and the water the perfect temperature. He climbed in and soaped up, suddenly aware that he had not done any grooming since Tanglwyst's bedroom. His teeth felt slimy and sour from the wine, and he looked around for something to clean his mouth with. There was a tooth cleaning stick with bristles on one end and when he put it in his mouth, it tasted of clove oil.

After a half hour, he felt relaxed, destressed, and smelling better than before. He got out and grabbed a towel. By the time he had dried off completely, the tub was drained, clean, and the utensils sparkling.

Okay, that's going to be problematic when I return to Patras. I'm going to never be satisfied with a normal bath again.

He pulled on the sleeping pants and crawled onto the bed. He wasn't sure he was actually tired anymore and didn't want to get under the covers.

That was the last thing he thought before sleep overtook him.

Tanglwyst looked out at the road from her south-facing window. She could see the edge of the valley and the quiet from the Krakten army. She could also see the Mervol army all but blocking the road from Patras. They looked to be lining the valley so the Fae could not leave. The cold bit her cheeks but she didn't feel it. The cold in her heart matched it.

She was angry that her home had been destroyed by the Fae, but at least she understood it. She knew why Sovereigna blamed her. She didn't accept that guilt, but she understood it.

The damage to the town was overwhelming. The Church, the Tavern, all the stores and homes. The granary. That would be a starvation issue, something Alexander had no doubt realized and, if not, she was certain Uncle Aethelraed had discussed it. The fields in the valley were fertile enough to grow miles of grapes for the winery. But they were planting crops in there, not going home. And why?

Because they could never leave if they do.

And with Sovereigna and Elizabeth dead, Emmy would inherit the throne of Krakte.

So, there they were, at an impasse. The blue barrier kept humans out and Fae in and nothing would change. She would never get her land back. The town would stay in ruins and become abandoned. It broke her heart because she loved this place above all her other homes. The estate in Patras was nice, but it was also gruesome. She built it so she could overlook the alley where her abusive first husband was murdered. It didn't hold joy. It held revenge.

Her flagship was dead, leaving her its twin, the *Nostromo*. But the twin had its own routes and trade contracts. It could not take on the role of the *Sulocco*. The captain knew nothing of navigating the maelstroms, and she needed to get to that island before Walpurgisnacht to trade with the hidden cove. They depended upon it.

She stepped away from the window and noticed the blood on her feet. She sighed and went to the washing station. She waited in the tub, naked, for the miscarriage to fully release, then poured the water over her to clean away the blood. The drain emptied into a hole that fed the caverns under the town, she did not worry it would become some part of a spell by the Fae.

She was sadly grateful for this side effect of being dead. It had ended the pregnancy with Nicolai's child. This sudden winter was problematic all by itself and she had not been looking forward to raising that child on her own, even without the seasonal complication. She had not told Alexander about the pregnancy because, when he had refused to lie with her before, she had lost the window where she could have claimed it his.

It was better this way though. To have him raise the child of the man who ruined his life would have been the height of cruelty. Hence her sad but grateful stance on the subject. She did not know if she would tell him, but it didn't matter. It was over now.

She put on her undergarments and attached the bleed cloth to them. She felt drained from the miscarriage but also recognized the aftereffects of the event. She knew the path it would take and how long. If she rested now, with the proper preparations, she would be alright here soon.

She opened a jar of willow bark and took out a small piece, then resealed the jar. She then made a strong tea of a miscarriage herbal mix she bought from the village in the hidden cove. The remedy sold well to midwives across her trade routes and they would need their annual supplies replenished, even more so with this weather. She chewed the willow bark while the tea steeped and relaxed by the fire until she finished the tea.

Her mind was blissfully blank as she watched the flames. She felt herself slipping into sleep and prepared for bed. She set the cup by the amulet, on the counter in the bathing area. She had not known she would be bleeding when she took it, but she was more than grateful for the privacy. She did not fear Alexander would suddenly appear beside her and she would have to explain why she left. Giles could bring him of course, but he had never been here in her room. Her door was locked. She had time to relax, time to heal.

Time to mourn.

Gwen stepped into the Doorway of Winter and tried to call out. The wind blew hard at her, throwing sharp snowflakes at her face to no avail. She stepped back, frowning.

This isn't working at all.

It was late, but that didn't matter to her. She didn't sleep. She looked beside her at the stairs that went upwards into the tower. She glanced one more time at the snow and walked up. At the top was a kind of bedroom and laboratory in one. There was a large bier in the center, complete with a glass covering, like Calpurnia and the others. The difference was that this one was open.

An enormous and varied medicinal herb garden dominated the wall across from the window, flanking the door. Sunlight streamed through the window to the plants, even though she knew the storm was blocking the sky from sight. The rest of the room was lined with bottle after bottle of potions.

She looked around and got an idea.

Worst case, nothing happens.
She climbed up onto the bier and lay down.
The lid closed and she fell asleep.

Book Two

"There's no such thing as a small evil and there's no such thing as a small good."
-The Forty-Five Voices

Twenty-Three

"No one is actually dead until the ripples they cause fade away."
-The Forty-Five Voices

Myrgen opened his eyes and saw Catriona open hers. Her eyes were still a little red and puffy, but considerably better than when they finally passed out. "Did you sleep at all?"

She shook her head. "I just laid here and watched you sleep."

Myrgen shifted away. "Really?"

She laughed. "Of course not, but it feels unsettling to have someone say that to you, doesn't it?"

"Well, yeah, I guess so."

"Then why do men think we won't feel like that when they do it?"

Myrgen opened his mouth, then shut it again and kissed her. "I'm taking a bath and ignoring that question."

She smiled. "Tea?"

"Yes, please."

She got up and put the water kettle on the hearth hook, then got dressed. "So, I was thinking about this gathering."

"What about it?"

"Tanglwyst has passed and Alexander blames himself. Are you going to be able to handle being around him? Especially given how you two parted company in Zara."

"I must admit that I was horrified and angry when Gwen took that Granite Arrow for him. But now I know she is fine and capable of still doing what she desires. I know now that death isn't a thing to be feared and moving on isn't a bad thing. I know that our people return to us as bit and pieces of others. So that's why we see our mother's eyes in our children or hear my friend's laugh in another person's mouth. I also know that Death has cold feet and needs to trim her toenails periodically, so I'm not afraid of her."

"Ouch! Fine, I'll do that next time I'm in the bath myself."

"But Tanglwyst isn't a Land follower. She didn't join us in Summerland. Instead, she's a bead on a floor in the sky, awaiting the honor of being erased completely. In the end though, the Well and Summerland do the same thing: They take the things that make someone unique and distribute them among a wealth of others. I'll never see her again as my sister, but I will see her again. And that means I can accept her death easier.

"So, I guess, the end result is that Alexander feels guilty about her death, which will make him treat me nicer, possibly. I can't be upset because I know how this stuff works now."

She dipped hot water into a cup and put the cloth square holding the tea inside the cup. She walked it into the bath room.

He turned to her. "Thank you. So how about you?"

"Well, the reason I asked was because I think I might try to reach Alistair again today instead of joining you. You know everything *I* do."

"Are you sure? He might throw you in the trap."

"He might. But I refuse to treat him like an enemy until I have more information."

"And if he truly *has* turned against us?"

She glanced down at the tea. "Then you'll need that essence from Sovereigna even more. And if it drains me to death again, I'll simply choose not to return from Summerland, ending the spell. No power source, no spell."

"And consequences be damned?"

"And consequences be damned."

Catriona left out the front door. Myrgen got dressed, banked the coals in the fireplace, and left as well. He turned towards the village, hoping he would be able to see Alexander before he saw Aethelraed. He didn't fear him as much as he found the prospect of the death sidetrack to be a time waster. He slipped past a house in the woods with a mark on several trees and stopped when he got near the edge of the town. There was a line on the ground he had not noticed the first time, but he had been coming at it from a different angle.

He looked down the street and caught movement in an upstairs window. He looked and saw *Tanglwyst* dumping water out of it. He looked around and didn't see anyone. He whistled and caught her attention. She looked in his direction and he stood. She smiled and waved him over, pointing at the door to the office.

He ran over, mindful of how open the area was. He got the door open and slipped inside, then locked it behind him. He went for the stairs and met her at the landing with a hug.

"I was told you were dead!" He looked her over.

"I was. Alexander fetched me from the afterlife."

"I'll need to thank him then. We saw the shape Heaven is in. I'm glad he got you out of there okay. Is he here?" Myrgen looked past her up the stairs.

"No. I came here alone. I needed some time."

Myrgen looked at her. "What's wrong?"

That's when he noticed the blood on her skirt hem, diluted with water that crept up to her knees.

She shook her head. "I'm fine. But being a dead body gets rid of certain… *conditions*."

He frowned. "Alex?"

"Nicolai. Alex and I haven't gone that direction."

"Oh. I was kind of hoping he was around. I have a meeting with him and whoever else I can from the Heaven side of things. We have to compare notes on the current situation."

"I'm almost done with things upstairs. Come on up."

They went up to her room. On a counter, she had a basin covered with a cloth, pink with washed out blood. He looked around and saw the floor by the window was wet.

"Are you alright?"

She nodded. "I'm weak. I won't be up for long today so we'd better get you to Alexander so you can talk. Just let me change clothes."

Myrgen let her go and stepped out of the room.

Catriona stepped over the wall at the mansion and walked down the hallway, checking the study for Lucifer. He was laying on the couch asleep, so she went up the stairs to Alistair's door. She knocked and waited but he didn't answer.

Guess I do have to bother him.

She went back down the stairs and knocked on the open door to the study. Lucifer started awake, grabbing the sofa. He calmed when he saw it was her.

"I'm sorry to bother you, but I need to use your Pillar."

"Oh, sure." He waved his hand and the Pillar rose on the low table by the sofa. "I'll give you some privacy. I'll be downstairs if you need me."

"Thank you."

He closed the doors on the way out. She looked at the Pillar and concentrated.

"Alistair."

Her friend's face appeared in the Pillar. "Catriona?"

"I tried to see you yesterday. You weren't home."

He folded his arms across his chest and looked at the study. "Judging from your surroundings, I'm pretty sure you have a good idea why I didn't open the door."

"Do you want to tell me your side?"

"Well, yes and no. There are a few things I can't adequately explain."

Catriona leaned forward, crossing her arms on her lap and letting her hands dangle. "Try me."

Alistair ran his fingers through his hair, assessing the situation. "Fine. But not from there."

"Ashstone then?"

Alistair nodded. "I can do that. I'll listen for your call."

She let the Pillar go black and opened the study door. Lucifer was coming up the stairs.

"Finished already?"

"It didn't take long to convince him to tell his side. I'll head back to Ashstone and we'll meet there. I'll have an advantage in my power base."

"Well, don't underestimate him. I think he's captured the Giver."

He explained the situation with Raven.

"So, as one part of his immortality, I'm worth more to the trap alive than in it. But it means Gloriana's being drained too, and she doesn't have a three-thousand-year supply of souls to see her through it."

"Was Giver the reason babies were born with souls while she was in Heaven? I have a memory of her walking and helping life renew and restore on its own, like I only came for people if they could not get to death on their own. But most people lived and died, crops sprouted, animals gave birth, all without our direct supervision. I don't know if she needed to walk the world in order for souls to exist though."

"To be honest, I don't know. But I think her being free matters. The souls aren't automatically going into infants from Heaven. The Saints are trying stuff though."

"Is it working?"

"Yeah. There's a couple shards of the Well and we're mixing purified souls with gray ones so we don't lose the creativity. It seems to be working but it's much slower because there are only two shards big enough."

"If I see her, I'll see if she'll give me some way to hold them. I'd offer something of mine but I don't know that it would have the right effect."

"We'll figure something out. Don't worry. You be careful with Alistair."

She put her hand on his shoulder and then hugged him.

"I'm sorry for your loss."

Lucifer stepped back. "He's not lost, My Lady. He thinks he's right. He has a moral imperative to do what he's doing. He's captured the Giver, which, if she *is* the source of normal births and can't trigger that while she's locked away, it won't be but a few years before all that worship Heaven are gone."

"Could that be his goal?"

"That might be. If it is, we'll talk."

"And if it's just a way to keep the spell going?"

Lucifer sighed. "Then there will be those that oppose him."

She hugged him again, then left for Ashstone.

Lucifer turned his attention to the Pillar and sought out George. He was leaving a room and smiling at a dark haired young woman who was exiting a room across from him.

Doesn't that guy ever *get out of that armor?*

"George."

George looked around.

"It's me, Lucifer. I figured, since you were still connected to Heaven, I could reach you. Where are you?"

"A haunted Covenant somewhere. I haven't seen the outside."

The woman turned to him. "What?"

"Lucifer is talking to me."

"Oh. Take the discussion in your room. I doubt the villagers will take kindly to overhearing that."

George stepped back in his room.

Lucifer frowned. "I don't really have a connection to that place. How can I find it?"

"Does that mean we're meeting here?"

"Well, we wanted to keep it neutral ground but I think Karma has the Giver so that isn't important anymore. Who do we have that can give me some sort of direction to you?"

"You can't just follow this connection?"

"No. I thought about that already. The divine isn't that significant there and I feel like there's something obscuring it."

"Maybe Giles can help. He knows how to get here. Or Alexander."

"Ask Giles."

George left his room and went to Giles.

"Hey, where *exactly* are we? I have someone trying to come to that meeting I mentioned."

"We are in a set of caves north of Cliffport... er, St. Giles, facing the sea. The caves look like a skull."

Lucifer thought for a second. "There's a church in this Cliffport?"

George nodded. "Yes, sort of. It might be wrecked."

"It's still holy ground, right?"

"Yeah. Hey Giles, can you get to Cliffport and meet him at the church?"

"Sure. Be right there."

Lucifer smiled. "Thank you."

He turned the focus of the Pillar on the St. Giles/Cliffport church and it came up. It had definitely seen better days.

This is that place Catriona mentioned, where she fought Michael.

He braced himself and willed himself to the location.

A moment later, Giles arrived and took him to the Great Hall.

Twenty-Four

"Always behave as if this is the day you'll be
remember for."
-The Forty-Five Voices

Catriona opened the door to Gloriana's tower in Sovereignlumin and saw Gwen asleep in the bier. She rushed to it and tried to lift the lid but it wouldn't budge.

"What are you doing?"

She turned to see James coming in the door, dusting snow off his shoulders. He was adorned all in furs now, blue to match his eyes.

"I am going to Caratia and wanted to catch Gwen up on what has happened since she left. I found her like this."

"Yeah. She was reaching out to us. She didn't have any other way to get our attention." He lifted the lid and Gwen looked at her twin brother.

Gwen smiled. "It worked."

"Yup."

Catriona looked between them. "You can see her?"

James nodded. "I died for a few minutes when we were children. Drowned in a pool. There was so much blood in the water, I thought I had gotten my throat cut but it was a head wound that bled so much. I saw ghosts for a few years after that."

Catriona nodded. "And now you can see her. Good. Well, I'm glad you're here. There have been some developments to tell you about. Do you want to sit?"

James motioned to a small table with benches around it and the three of them sat.

"The Giver has been taken by Alistair. We don't know why."

Gwen's brow furrowed. "He attacked Lucifer out of the blue. Something about how he and I were 'hidden threads'."

James sat back, rubbing his palm with his thumb. "Anyone know what that means?"

Both women shook their heads.

Catriona leaned on the table. "Also, when they left, she was at the trap in Persephone. Raven was trying to get her into it."

"Why?"

"I asked him to. When I was in there, I felt a connection to something deeper. I needed her to do so as well."

"Could this have been that thread thing that Alistair mentioned?"

"Possibly. It felt thin and almost invisible. I guess Gwen and Lucifer have something similar. Alistair tried to kill him."

"Over this thread thing?" James looked away in disgust and anger.

Catriona waited a moment before continuing. "How is Gloriana?"

"She's fighting something right now. Something weakened her recently."

"That was Raven going into the trap. Moreover, Lucifer was able to go in the room and not be seized."

"And that's that manacled thing in the bowels of Persephone, right? I remember Michael and I went there to rescue you but that golden woman was in that thing. After that, we just left. Michael went with you to Caratia…"

"No, he didn't. He was being drawn west by a dream."

"Of a lion. He was the thing that exploded near the standing stones. Wasn't he?"

Catriona felt her heart wrench in her chest at the memory of the blinding flash that took her friend. "…yes…"

James was silent and stood up, walking to a small table with a bottle of liquid and four glasses. "Drink?"

"Thank you." It was all her throat could manage past the lump. He took his time, which enabled her to get herself through the wave of loss. When he returned, he had a glass for Gwen as well.

"I wasn't sure if you could or not but I wasn't about to leave you out."

Gwen smiled and gave it a try. It didn't work. "I appreciate the gesture."

He smiled.

Catriona took a swallow and smiled at the quality of the drink.

James returned to his seat. "So, the reason Gloriana is feeling weak is because Raven is in this trap?"

"Yes. It drains your life force until you die. His immortality comes from two sources so both of those are being drained. Gloriana needs to stop the winter onslaught and save her strength. Unless she can go into torpor voluntarily."

"That would be a tough sell. With her siblings in torpor, that leaves the seasons unregulated."

"But if she enters under her own power, she might be able to leave the same way."

"If Raven is being drained, her going into torpor will cut him off. But I think I can convince her to limit her actions. The roads are closed. That is enough right now. What will happen with Alistair?"

"I'll talk to him, see if we can find out what is going on."

Gwen looked at the glass. "Don't trust him."

"Gwen…"

She looked at Catriona with deep, sharp concern. *"Don't.* He raped our mother. He's killed his friends. Don't trust him."

Catriona glanced at her ward, knowing she was right. "What will you do?"

Gwen looked at James. "I can go with you and take messages back and forth to Summerland."

James nodded. "I would like that."

Catriona drained her glass and James drained Gwen's. They both stood. "Myrgen is with Alexander. Tanglwyst was killed recently so we aren't certain he'll be rational with his power. Hopefully, we can keep him from simply ending the world by attacking the Fae. If Gloriana will pull her storms back, then the crops can be saved, possibly. Humanity may not fall to starvation."

186

"I'll speak with her. Be careful with Alistair. I realize now I never knew him."

"I do. He's in an impossible situation. I just need to figure out how to help him."

They all realized there was nothing else to say, so they passed out hugs and parted company.

Alexander left his room and saw Tanglwyst and Myrgen arrive in the hall. Lucifer greeted Myrgen and the lady, to whom he was introduced. Alexander smoothed his hair and checked his breath. The clove oil was still active. He walked into the hall and over to the gathering.

"Myrgen."

"Alexander."

"May I speak with you in private a moment?"

Myrgen glanced at the others, then nodded. They stepped away from the others to an empty table.

"I wanted to apologize for… well… all of this. The beating in Patras, the incident in Zara. I feel I have done so much evil and I cannot undo it. But I want to make sure I make amends where I can."

"Oh, Gwen's fine. I saw her yesterday."

Alexander frowned. "What?"

Myrgen laughed. "Land afterlife is very different from the Heaven one. Catriona and I saw that horrible place yesterday, thanks to Lucifer."

"Yeah, it's not where I want to go. What's it like where you went?"

"We have a house there. The Land encourages you to work out your darkness or finish anything you want to, so there's a village, forest, lake, etc. I saw Elizabeth there, right before she moved on."

"Moved on?"

"Went on to be reborn in others."

"They work out their darkness there? Is it a violent place?"

"No. It turns out they isolate you until you are capable of being around others."

"I suppose that's better than lying around on the floor, waiting to get too gray to be reborn."

Myrgen glanced at the floor, then at Lucifer. "Lucifer indicated things were getting cleaned up."

"I'm glad. But that isn't important to me anymore."

"Now that you pulled her out of it?" Myrgen looked at Tanglwyst.

"I am not requesting she stay. She left last night in fact. Did she say anything?"

"Just that she needed to work some things out on her own."

"I see she's wearing clothes she wasn't wearing before. She went to her room in the village, then?"

"Yes. I think it was important for her to be alone."

She sat down at a table and seemed a little stiff. Myrgen looked at Alexander again.

"Any chance we can get things moving?"

Alexander nodded. "Yes, of course."

He went to the others and they all started moving to the meeting room at the foot of the hall. The room was large enough to accommodate everyone. Large maps hung on the walls and the huge round table itself was a carved *bas relief* of what the maps showed. The chairs showed a series of events that led to the next one and Alexander deliberately looked at each one.

His eye fell upon Tanglwyst and he glanced at her subtly as he examined the chairs. He realized what he was doing and chuckled to himself. Then he actually looked at the chairs and saw they told a story of the necromancer that imprisoned the ghosts that existed next to the crypts, as well as other remarkable creatures. Harpies, but with male upper halves instead of female. Lion centaurs. Griffins. Bees that mesmerized a whole village. A troll building things.

Each chair back showed a different group of mages assisting too. Sometimes, it was clearly Giles, but there were a group of others that likewise showed up regularly, in various configurations. One woman rode a zephyr and fought in glorious manner against many foes. He even saw Anna, Giles' wife, wielding her bow. He looked at Giles and gestured to him and the chair. Giles smiled and nodded.

He continued around the table until he had seen every chair scene, then looked around to see what seats were left. The table was full.

"Your Majesty?"

He turned to see Tanglwyst gesturing to an empty chair. It was next to hers.

"Do you mind?"

She smiled. "Not at all."

Giles gestured to a panel and a section of the wall dropped down. Several platters of cheese, bread, meat, fish, fruit, and vegetables were on sideboards, and periodically amongst them were decanters of various colored liquids.

"For anyone who has yet to break their fast, please help yourselves."

Everyone got a plate and at least one goblet. The portions were moderate and Alexander had just set his plate at his seat when he realized Myrgen was speaking to Lucifer.

"Do we have any way to check on her?"

Lucifer shook his head. "Not here. This isn't a seat of power."

"What should we do?"

"I have an idea. Get things started and I'll get something that can help."

Lucifer put his plate at his spot and then left the room.

Alexander looked at Myrgen. "Is everything alright?"

"Yeah. We just have a few extra people we need to include and Lucifer thinks he has a way to do it."

Catriona stepped out of the pool of lava in the Meditation Chamber and summoned the Pillar to her. She closed her eyes.

"Alistair."

Her friend's face appeared in the Pillar's surface.

"You ready?"

She could tell he had something planned but she refused to read him. She needed her responses to be pure.

"Yes."

Alistair appeared beside her and then they were gone.

The room they entered was colorful and lavish with silk pillows and drapes everywhere.

She smiled. "I remember this place. The incense house in Yantap."

"It is one of my better memories. Would you like a robe?"

She glanced down and remembered why she preferred to go through the mansion instead of the fire. "If you have one to spare."

He gestured to the wall behind her. She took a bright orange one and put it on.

"You even recreated the servers we had?"

"I liked them. They remembered us, our orders, even our drink preferences with what entrees."

The servers brought over a tray of coffees and pastries, setting the small cups beside trays of candied fruits and nuts. A musician played music for them while a cook filled the air with intoxicating, familiar smells.

"So, what happened?"

Alistair picked up a fruit. "You know I can't tell you that."

"You have me captive. I can't leave unless you release me."

"Yeah, about that. Why? Why did you let me bring you here? You had to know this was a trap."

She took his hand. "Because you wouldn't tell me unless you felt entirely safe."

"What about you?"

"I likewise feel entirely safe. So, we should be able to talk. I want *my friend* to talk to me."

Alistair sighed. "Your friend is barely here anymore, my love. I cannot see him in a mirror these days. Being Karma is being a betrayer. Too much kindness leads to balancing the scales with cruelty. I don't want to be a bad person just so good can exist. That's what killed the spirit of my predecessor. She became... evil, to balance the good. She saved the world, only to make it a world no one would want to live in."

She squeezed his hand. "The role of Karma is to give a little nudge towards justice."

"Ah, but history arcs towards justice already. Karma has no purpose on that level. The little, *personal* nudges are the ones that stack up."

"What do you need from me?"

"I need you to stop me."

He closed his eyes and the room changed. They were naked in a lush bed with purple and orange silk draped above it. She was lying on her side, looking at him. He stroked her face and kissed her hand.

Then his eyes and smile turned cruel. "Luci, I was just thinking about you."

She turned her head and Karma's Pillar was at the foot of the bed. Lucifer turned and looked at them.

"Catriona?"

She rolled her eyes at the Archangel, like she had just caught their child in a blatant lie. Lucifer caught the look and turned to Alistair.

Alistair kept his eyes on his former lover. "My friend, can you put Myrgen on the line?"

"Hardly. He's off with some auburn-haired beauty right now, no doubt engaging in some tawdry misstep."

She let her surprise show to Lucifer and read that Tanglwyst was alive and well.

"But enough about him. Are you doing alright, Alistair?"

"Well, a good romp in the silks with a beautiful woman will always brighten one's day."

"Sounds like I should join you then. I could use some day brightening."

Alistair swallowed and Catriona read honest regret in his face. "I wish you could, my friend. I would like that a lot."

Alistair turned to look at the Pillar.

Lucifer glanced at Catriona, who gave the barest of nods. "Let's do it, then. We can put yesterday behind us. What's a little attempted murder between friends?"

Alistair stroked Catriona's bare shoulder. "I can't say the lady is ready for that level of debauchery."

Alistair's eyes cleared and turned serious. "Lucifer, I didn't want to attack you. What you discovered could be deadly to the world. It's something I need to protect and I don't want to. That's why I brought them here. With them here *and not in the trap*, I don't have to do anything to balance things. Understand?"

Lucifer looked at Catriona and she turned her gaze on Alistair. He was so wide open, she almost couldn't help but read him. He looked at her, pleading.

Read me. Please.

She turned away, her eyes going to Lucifer's. He saw what was happening and was gripping the Pillar on his end, as if ready to leap through and stop Alistair if he tried to hurt her. She shook her head.

"I will not read you, Alistair. I cannot steal your secret."

"No, you really can right now. I won't even report it missing to the authorities."

"At what cost? If I know it, and I learned it from you, your actions will still need to be the same. Right?"

Alistair closed his eyes and screamed in frustration and rage. He disappeared from the bed, leaving her alone in the room, save for Lucifer in the Pillar.

She sighed.

"Do you know what's going on yet?"

She shook her head. "No. But Raven will. Maybe not yet, but he will."

"What will you do?"

"I have to get it out in small pieces. That way, the consequences to me finding out will cause minimal ripples. Expect a lot of minor annoyances."

Lucifer leaned on the pillar. "Be careful. He doesn't want to hurt you."

"I know. But he has to. I know what's coming, so I'll be alright. Take care of things out there and I'll do likewise in here."

They said goodbye and the Pillar went dark.

Twenty-Five

"Life is a balance of holding on and letting go,
and knowing when to do which."
-The Forty-Five Voices

Lucifer walked into the meeting room with a few arm-length pieces of a black crystal. He set one on the table.

"This is a piece of the Pillar from the Saint's Prayer room. It was shattered but I can see everyone here knows what it was. Which is why you are in this room. Nearly everyone here has used one."

He looked at Alexander and Tanglwyst. "This will be new to you folks. I figured there are people who we need to talk to that are unavailable. I just spoke with Catriona. She's with Alistair, but she is captive there. I tried right after I finished with her to reach out to the Giver but to no avail. I didn't get the impression she had found the Giver yet so he must be keeping them apart."

Myrgen frowned. "Do you think they are in danger with him? What does he want with them?"

"Catriona didn't say, but she was able to speak to me because Alistair used his Pillar to contact me, then let her speak when he left. She believes he can't tell us everything at once but she can get it out of him in little pieces. Unfortunately, that means bad luck for each of us. I suspect she'll get him to direct it at *us*, specifically, because we can prepare ourselves for it."

Giles exhaled. "Right. Does his retaliation have to *succeed* to work? Actually, never mind. It only makes sense that it has to work in order to balance the scales. Any idea what we'll deal with?"

"No. But just remember that every inconvenience is a bit of information extracted."

Brigit looked worried. "What if he tells her something and she doesn't understand it?"

Tanglwyst shook her head. "She can see things others can't."

Myrgen rested his index finger alongside his temple. "And Alistair knows it."

Lucifer pointed to Myrgen. "That's what I'm counting on. He was *begging* her to read him and she told him it would be the same as if he told her outright because he knew she could read him. Then he left the bedroom and we were able to talk."

Alexander twitched. "Bedroom?"

"Yeah. He was hoping Myrgen would see it."

Myrgen nodded, mulling it over but didn't appear to be taking it personally. "Thanks for letting me know. Hopefully she'll be able to get something now."

"Sure. You know I'm here to help."

Clara looked between the two. "Was… was that just one of them? The attempts to cause problems?"

Myrgen glanced at Alexander, then back to Clara. "Undoubtedly. Alistair believes Catriona and I belong together. He actually tricked us into the same bed before we finally took that step ourselves. He would not try to damage our relationship."

"When was that?" Alexander folded his hands on the table.

"St. Andrew."

Alexander's jaw set, but he forcibly relaxed it. "Good. Hopefully she'll get even more from him now."

Myrgen looked at Alexander. "Nothing happened."

"It still hurts. And I'm going to let that soak in. It may only free up a single word, but that's one more word than she would have gotten otherwise."

George glanced at Clara, then stood. "What else do we have? This meeting was called for a reason. Who has that information?"

Myrgen raised his hand. "I have part of it. Lucifer, this Pillar, it's attuned to Heaven, right?"

"Oh. Yes. I think, even smashed, it's still attuned to Heaven."

"Can they be realigned?"

Lucifer shrugged.

"I'll see about getting something from home then. I want there to be a way to communicate between us all."

Lucifer handed him a small shard. "I got this one for you, and one for you too, Your Majesty." He slid another one across the table. "Myrgen, I don't know if you'll be able to operate it to reach out to anyone, but I can reach you through it. So can anyone attuned to the Heaven Pillar."

Alexander handed his to Tanglwyst. "Now we need something from the Land, and someone to operate it. Myrgen, who do you have?"

Myrgen took a deep breath, glancing at Brigit. "I'm not sure. I don't know who is a Land worshipper here."

Brigit swallowed. "Give it to me."

The group looked at her. Myrgen slid it across the table and she took it and concentrated. Nothing happened.

Myrgen smiled. "Looks like it can't be changed just yet."

George shrugged. "Or it's the fact she's a Saint and isn't of the Land."

"I think she just revealed otherwise."

George looked at her, his brow furrowed. "Brigit?"

"You *had* to know I was never going back to that place. The Angels built it on deceit and has done nothing but torture us and the world."

"That might be because of that whole Karma thing though!"

"It might be. No, you're right. It most likely is. Which is another reason. When I actually die, I don't want to be reduced to some opulent liquid where my creativity is lost forever. I want to go to a place I can be with friends."

Myrgen leaned forward on his elbows. "Johner, Corrigan's right hand, used to be a musician. He's got the opportunity to play again and he's taking it. You can make your art there, whenever you like."

Brigit's eyes grew wet. "Without pain?"

"Without pain."

Giles was sitting with his arms crossed, staring at the goblet in front of him. "The Tavern owner. In town."

Tanglwyst frowned. "Monique?"

"When we get a shard or two that works, she can operate it. That place was a Fae temple. That's why it screamed when it burned."

Myrgen looked at him, his eyes fighting between displaying his shock and horror. *"It screamed when you burned it?"*

Gomez nodded. "Killed half the guards."

Tanglwyst shook her head. "Monique has been a very upstanding citizen, a good taxpayer, and a world-renowned author. If you are accusing her of murdering the guards – "

Giles held up his hand. "No, nothing like that. I'm stating that the owner of that tavern is a Land worshipper. If she's here, she can operate the Pillar shard."

Myrgen looked skeptical. "How? Unless she's part Fae herself."

Giles looked at Tanglwyst. "Ever see her in Church?"

"No. She just opened the door and windows of the Wise Wench so her customers could hear services. But she was always busy in there so she never…"

Gomez interrupted the silence. "I haven't seen her in here. She stayed behind. She didn't go on the ships."

"What about Rowena?" Alexander looked at Gomez. "She stayed behind to help with putting together silver amulets to protect the men. I didn't see her after the incident with Father Robert."

"Father Robert?" Tanglwyst's face revealed her fresh horror.

Gomez looked nervous and sad simultaneously. "He… We believe… Giles showed us an Angel talking to him and giving him the plans and impetus to craft one of those corrupting amulets."

"No… by the Saints, please no…"

Gomez tried to go on but her tears interfered.

Alexander spared him. "He used the amulet to draw a line of that Fae-killing sludge all across the top of the valley, so if any of the Krakten army tried to leave, they would be trapped, and killed."

Myrgen leaned forward, scowling. "Wait. *An angel* passed out those plans?"

Giles couldn't meet Brigit's eyes, so he met Myrgen's. "Yes. I'm afraid so. More of Karma's balancing act."

"Cipriano, King of Mande, *invaded* Zara and killed Catriona's family using a fleet of those amulets."

Tanglwyst looked at her brother, her expression overwhelmed by the atrocities being exposed. "Did he take it? Has Zara fallen?"

Myrgen snorted. "It was a trap. The Land destroyed the entire army and fleet, including Cipriano, with fire. But several people still died as a result, including myself."

Gomez blinked. "Um... so... exactly how many times have you died?"

"Just the two times, I think."

"You think?"

"There's a lot that goes on there. I go back and forth these days."

Gomez raised his hands. "Alright, who all here has died?"

Brigit, Giles, Clara, George, Myrgen, and Tanglwyst all raised their hands.

Gomez pointed at Lucifer. "You never have?"

"Nope. I found a jar and touched the contents. Straight to Angel." He opened his wings, just for emphasis.

Myrgen leaned forward, using the curve of the table to stay out of the way of their sudden appearance. George leaned back and was knocked over by them, slamming his chair onto the floor. His armor pinched the chair between him and the floor and scarred the inside of the wooden back.

Myrgen watched a feather drift down in front of him and alight on the table. He looked at his friend. "Put those away."

Lucifer did. Clara and Giles helped George back to his feet.

"Warn a guy next time, will ya?" George picked up the chair and looked at Giles. "Sorry about the damage."

"It'll repair itself."

"Really?"

Lucifer frowned. "Do you wear that stuff all the time?" He looked at Clara. "Does he wear that stuff *all* the time?"

Clara shrugged. "I've never seen him without it."

"Doesn't that *pinch*?"

She spread her hands. "Where?"

Lucifer gestured to his thighs, then his chest, his mouth open as if to try and explain. Then he looked at her confused expression and turned to George. "You *can* take it off, right?"

George sat down. "I don't know. I've never tried."

"You've been a Saint for a thousand years. You've never tried to remove your armor?"

George blinked, then looked at Giles and Brigit. "Have I?"

Giles scratched his chin and Brigit shook her head with confidence.

George frowned at himself. "I guess it never occurred to me. I haven't had a reason to remove it."

Lucifer raised a finger and his mouth hung open, then gyrated through a few options before settling on closing again. "I hope you do. Good luck with that."

Alexander cleared his throat. "Let me see if I understand this. Cipriano is dead, so his daughter Gillian is now sitting the throne. Caratia has no ruler. Krakte has no ruler, and I have to survive a trial by crossbow to become coronated."

Myrgen shook his head. "Krakte has a ruler. It's your niece, Marie-Elizabeth."

"Emmy?" Tanglwyst frowned.

"Yes. More than that, she's coming up on her third birthday and she needs to be in Krakte when that happens, or at least in the company of Fae."

Alexander rolled his eyes. "Of course. The *Einberufung der Strähnen*, the *Summons of the Wisp*. It's what drove Elizabeth mad."

"Sovereigna says Emmy needs to be there soon. Have you been to Austra?"

Tanglwyst nodded. "I have. I can take her."

Alexander looked at her. "We'll both go. We'll need to take Mother as well."

"You need to prepare for being coronated."

"This will be how I prepare."

Myrgen furrowed his brow. "Is that the usual process? I remember you being at Charles' coronation."

"I'll need to negotiate peace with Krakte before I'll be able to try. Right now, I can easily be overthrown because the Papal City can't be reached to send a delegation. We have to prove I have the right to rule or there will be civil war."

"The roads are closed, thanks to Gloriana. At least you won't have them marching on Patras while you're here. Are you sure Catherine will be willing to leave you at this time? I know you don't care for her but–"

Alexander raised his hand. "Actually, I've made up with my mother. She helped save me and your sister. Believe me, she'll be willing to help Emmy. Going to Austra will be a dream come true for her. And she speaks the language."

"That's a huge help. We were very worried about broaching the subject. Asking a guardian to part with a young child…"

"I understand the risk. I know about the Wisp Summons. We saw what it did to Elizabeth. You endured the worst at her hands."

Tanglwyst shuddered. "I can't even imagine what it would be like to see or hear that for a small child."

"Well, she turns three at the end of this month so she needs to be there soon."

Alexander looked at Tanglwyst, then back to Myrgen. "Does that need to be our mission?"

"I'm afraid so. Having Emmy succumb to the Summons will be a problem since no man can hold the throne of Krakte. The Army won't obey him. If legend holds, the only reason the army is in the valley and not storming the area in a berserker rage is that there is a female of the ruling line in the world. But they'll be getting more agitated as the days pass. Within a week, I suspect they'll either crash through the blue barrier in an attempt to break it down, or worse."

Tanglwyst looked at the people at the table. "I saw them from my window last night. They were planting crops. The ones I saw looked peaceful."

"Well, there will be no more stone or ore available to the Mervol army while they lay siege to the Krakten one."

George frowned. "The Mervol army is already out of arrows. They expended them all. I met a fletcher that said there were no stones or iron for making arrowheads."

Myrgen looked at George. "Catriona denied them the resources."

Giles leaned forward. "She can do that?"

"Yes."

"How?"

Myrgen looked at Lucifer, who shrugged. He looked back at Giles. "Because she's more than just the Death Bringer. She's the embodiment of the Land. Every monster, every stone, every part of the world is hers to command. It's why she doesn't want to go to war, Alexander. If she is forced to, the opposing army will be destroyed."

George crossed his arms. "That *hardly* seems possible. I'll be – "

"Crushed. Or swallowed by the ground. Or burned in a stream of lava, like the Mandians were. She opened the ground to allow vents of heat and steam to transform the valley so the Kraktens wouldn't freeze. Trust me. This will not end well if she is forced to take the field."

Alexander watched the exchange. "What about the Caratian army? Can they be deployed?"

"To what end?"

"Stopping the Kraktens from attacking the Mervols."

"The Caratians will not stand *against* other Land worshippers. This isn't meant to be a challenge, my friends. This is a precaution."

Gomez turned to Alexander. "When Aethelraed asks these questions of you, you'll need these answers."

"I'll need them for the nobles as well."

George got a thoughtful expression on his face. "Maybe not. Do you think you'll encounter resistance from the nobles who wish to overthrow you when you say you do not want to fight the army?"

"Yes. I'll be seen a weak."

"And if you press the attack and the army is slaughtered, you'll be called unwise."

"Yes. Frankly, when it comes to my detractors, I can do nothing right."

"So, they believe they can do better."

Alexander narrowed his eyes. "Interesting thought. That could work. But at a huge loss of life."

Tanglwyst leaned in, her eyes sparkling in conspiracy. "Only if they actually attack. Let them deal with the stalemate. Then you can get the Princess to her new home and when you return, you can take command and settle the dispute. And if anyone dies under their command, you execute them."

"That's very cutthroat."

She looked at him. "Explain that in advance. Let them know they are responsible for any victory or defeat on this field. Myrgen, do you have access to the Caratian army?"

"Yes."

"How long would it take to deploy them?"

"I don't know. One, maybe two..."

"Weeks?"

"Hours. I'm almost sure it's hours. Maybe minutes. In fact, I think I can have them ready to deploy suddenly the instant your new commander takes charge. That will be my next task. I also need to visit Gloriana. Let her know what's happened here."

"Oh!" Lucifer pointed to Myrgen. "Catriona came back through, before she went to Karma's Hand. She said Gwen is available to take messages back and forth to Gloriana. James can see her or something."

"That's handy! Can you see her, through the Pillar?"

"I cannot. She's not available to me."

"That's an expedition for me then."

Gomez got up and refilled his glass, offering more to his companions. "What else is there to talk about?"

George snapped his fingers. "The Queen. The Kraktens are planning to move her, take her body back to Austra. The Intelligence Officer is planning to attack them and grab the body to stop them. He thinks, if they can take the Queen's body, they can force the army into the woods."

"Will they return it after the army does so?"

"I don't know him. I don't think I can answer that question."

Tanglwyst smiled at Gomez as he refilled her cup. "Thank you, Gomez. What was his name?"

"Battlebutt or something. It was a ridiculous last name. I figured he must have been joking."

"Did he answer to Aethelraed?"

"Is that the General?"

Tanglwyst nodded.

George shook his head. "The General was injured and was confined to bed. I think the Intelligence Officer was in charge."

Tanglwyst exchanged a look with her brother.

Myrgen shook his head. "Uncle 'Raed would never truck with someone without honor. If they say they'll return her, they'll do it."

Tanglwyst didn't refute it but did not look convinced.

Alexander squeezed her hand, then looked at the group. "So, Tanglwyst and I will use the amulet of Giles to go to Patras and get Emmy and the Queen Mother ready to travel to Austra, then take them there."

Myrgen reached into a satchel at his hip. "Here are two letters, one for the Seneschal, one for Catherine, from Sovereigna. They explain her wishes."

Alexander took them. "Thank you. This will help considerably."

"Also, there is a bottle we need from her vanity. It's an extract of essence. We have the formula for it and it's something Emmy will need later. Sovereigna is making a batch of it as we speak in Summerland."

Alexander processed that. "I truly want to talk to you about this afterlife. I may want to convert. How long before she's finished with the potion? Will we need it to transport Emmy?"

Myrgen thought for a moment. "That might not be a bad idea. The Wisp Summons is irreversible. Once she enters it, she can't escape and will have to die. The essence potion is what kept Sovereigna from falling to it. But if we give it to Emmy, we won't need the one from Austra and can proceed with our plan to break the Karma spell."

Lucifer tapped the table absently with a wing feather. "Will there be enough essence from this 'Emmy'?"

"I have no idea. She's not quite three years old. It will either be quite weak or crazy potent."

Tanglwyst watched the feather Lucifer was playing with. "Expect weak. Because of Alistair."

"True."

Alexander took a deep breath. "Okay. So, Myrgen, you're going with Lucifer and meeting with Gloriana so we can find a way to communicate with her. Gwen will act as messenger."

Myrgen nodded. "Yes."

"What are the Saints doing?"

Clara glanced at Giles. "You and George need to find that other amulet. The corrupted one. We can't let anyone get their hands on it."

Giles agreed.

"Brigit and I will stay here and help with getting the refugees settled. There's still a lot to do here. Things are being provided to us but most of the inhabitants are a little frightened of them. We saw parents giving their children ship rations so they wouldn't eat the tainted food here."

"Oh honestly. For the days when people *appreciated* magic."

Brigit scowled at him. "Giles, this Covenant was put in the middle of *nowhere* so you wouldn't be bothered by average people. There's always been a mistrust of magic. Besides, you put people off. It's part of the Gift, you said."

"Well, yes."

Clara looked at Brigit, her eyes wide. "That's the *Gift*? I thought he was just an ass."

"Oh, he's both. Make no mistake."

"Where do you want me, Sire?"

Alexander looked at his best friend. "Gomez, you're going home."

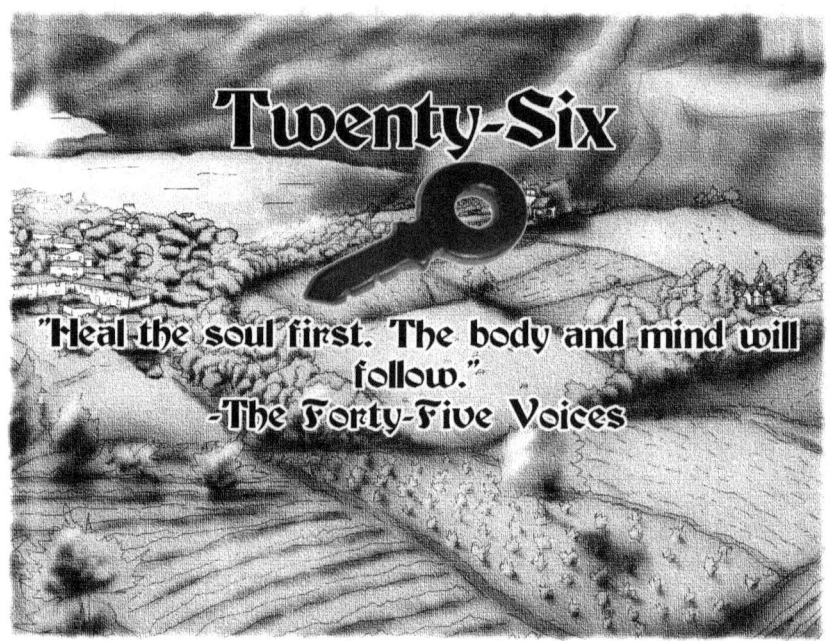

Twenty-Six

"Heal the soul first. The body and mind will follow."
-The Forty-Five Voices

Alexander turned to Tanglwyst as the others stood and prepared to be on their tasks. "How long will it take you to get ready?"

"I was thinking... I should stay here. Help Clara and Brigit get everyone else informed."

"I... I'm really not comfortable with that. These people killed you."

"Yes, but you fetched me away from all that." She smiled a strained smile and Alexander noticed her skin was pale.

"My Lady..."

Her eyes closed and she swayed a little. Alexander grabbed her arm and caught her. Myrgen saw the activity and rushed over.

"Damn. Is there someplace she can lie down?"

Alexander looked at Myrgen. "What's the matter with her?"

"She miscarried last night."

Alexander's heart sank. "I've got this."

He held Tanglwyst and touched Myrgen and they disappeared. They appeared in his room. Myrgen looked around.

"Is this her bedroom in St. Giles?"

Alexander picked her up and carried her to the bed. "Not really. It's just everything I can remember. Why didn't she say something?"

"About the miscarriage? When would she have said it? We went into the meeting a minute after she got here. I suggested we get on with it because I could see her starting to falter."

"Whose…?"

"Nicolai. She was not heartbroken to lose it but apparently, being dead has adverse effects upon being pregnant."

"It probably would have been stillborn had she carried it. The soul situation, coupled with the time dead…"

Myrgen nodded. "I had the idea that maybe the Land could take responsibility for the ensoulment of babies but then the Giver returned and I was assured that the Giver's presence would be enough. Then she was taken from the world again and now, I don't know what to think."

She opened her eyes and looked around. "What happened?"

"You stood up too fast. That's all."

Myrgen scowled at Alexander. "Your blood loss took its toll. You need to rest."

She lay her head back. "You told him."

"Yes. It was silly to try and dismiss it. He's a healer. He can help you through this. And if he's going to rely on you so heavily that he'll chase your tiny soul through the afterlife, I figure keeping him in the dark is a bad idea."

Alexander smiled. "Yeah. I'm not a turnip."

"What?" She lifted her head to look at him. Her lips were upset but her eyes were laughing.

"It's something Madeline said to me last night."

"*Madeline* did? I see. Well, fine, but I'm not a turnip either. And neither are these people. Their homes have been destroyed. They need to know what we are going to do about it."

"What do you propose, My Lady?"

"We have Captain Nesbit here. And Helen Might, who ran my household from the vineyards. There are more community leaders here too."

"And your town's best stayed behind to help. The Wise Wench…"

Tanglwyst looked away. "Was her body found?"

"Not that I know of. But I don't know who has checked. I will speak to Gomez and see what he has heard. I need to fill the human contingent in on what happened in the meeting."

Myrgen nodded. "Aethelraed too. He's a brilliant strategist and he tends to focus upon winning. We need to keep him informed or he just might take thing into his own hands."

Tanglwyst snorted. "Indeed. My holdings are gone and my land there still occupied, from what I can tell. I had Preston leave for Patras so he could be with his husband, right before we sailed off. He has the business contracts. All I brought with me was some letters of credit I could use in case we needed them in the south."

Alexander squeezed her hand. "So, your money is gone now."

She laughed. "Clearly you know nothing of finance. No. I just didn't want the army to have the letters of credit."

He smiled. "You against supporting the troops?"

Her smile went away. "I'm against civil seizure and imminent domain. The army did not build my home or office, work my fields, or make my trade agreements and they'll do nothing to get those losses back to me after they steal them. At least Sovereigna offered to rebuild my holdings, which, even if they never do, is more than the Mervol army will offer."

Alexander's brow furrowed and he felt chastised. "I was kidding, My Lady. I meant no offense."

"You act like I don't know that. I do. I would just not make light of such a practice. It's identical to Charles deciding his life and desires outranked your life's pursuit when he abdicated. Or when Catherine threw her tantrum and a hundred thousand Emilianites were murdered, including my nephew. I'm pretty sure your family has moved on with their lives and dealt with a few minor inconveniences since then, but a lot of people *died* thanks to your royal privilege and dismissing the weight of these decisions."

"I see."

"I realize to you, there have been some benefits in your case, but there are none for my holdings, nor my family here. Everything that told their stories is gone. Letters, portraits, clothes, books, items their children and grandchildren made them are all *gone*. I've already had my home in Patras turned into a barracks without my consent, my home and vineyards destroyed, and my flagship sank in service to this war. My office is likely to be commandeered by the officer George spoke of, especially with the church destroyed. Not a silver of that will be compensated. The army won't even sweep up after they decide to move out."

Alexander sat on the bed. "I had no idea you felt like this."

"Our father served with Aethelraed in the last three Emilianite wars. He used to bring home gifts for me and our mother, plus little weapons and outfits for the boys. It wasn't until I was a widow that I discovered these were 'spoils of war', and they belonged to Emilianite and Augustinian families before they were appropriated through 'civil forfeiture'. I spent my first year as owner of the Trading Company *returning* those given to me. It's how I made my connections and investments all over the world."

A snicker came from the door. They all turned to see Gomez standing there. "Forgive me, My Lady. What you do is honorable and the right thing to do. I am often amazed by your actions and words. They are not what I thought."

"Then why are you laughing?"

"I am marveling at the amazing messes His Majesty seems to get himself into with you."

Alexander looked upset and embarrassed. "I don't 'get myself into these'."

"I beg your pardon but *you do.* You fight tooth and fist to get into these. I mean you *work* for these and she puts you in a headlock *every time.* You chose this, brother. And you keep choosing it."

"Hey, nothing worth having comes easily."

Tanglwyst arched an eyebrow. "Says the guy with the magic traveling amulet."

Alexander snorted at their collective smirks. "I am glad you're here, Gomez. Do you remember everyone that stayed behind instead of being evacuated?"

"Rowena, Monique, the blacksmiths, the alchemist, woodcarver, Ace the smith's apprentice."

"Do you know if any of them are alright?"

Gomez glanced at the hallway. "Yeah. They seem to be okay."

Delighted calls and screams rang through the Great Hall and Alexander went to find out what was going on. People were flooding into the Great Hall and gathering around a group of people who were standing, dusty and tired, in the middle of the room. He walked over to them and opened his arms to welcome them.

Rowena hugged him, a little surprised by the gesture. The smiths and others likewise were eager to join their families.

Alexander greeted Monique with a hug as well. "Where did you come from?"

Monique smiled. "An escape tunnel I didn't even know existed. Came right here from St. Giles."

Giles grinned. "Oh yeah! I forgot about those! Before I got the amulet working, we built tunnels between here and Cliffport and Serenity."

"Why?"

"Trade. Cattle exchanges and wagons and stuff. Paper. Lots of that."

"Wait, you can drive *cattle* through it?"

"All year. Serenity is a temperate climate and grew food all year. With no winter, and magic to enhance it, we had crops growing constantly. We never had to worry about the weather that way. It was essential because we lost some fields to that necromancer."

Alexander smiled and stepped back to let other townsfolk greet their friends. He walked over to Myrgen, who was standing with his arms folded.

"That's good luck."

Myrgen looked at them all smiling. "Yeah. I wonder what Catriona just went through to do that."

Gomez walked over and took Myrgen's place as he returned to check on Tanglwyst.

Alexander glanced at his friend. "I'm glad they're okay."

"Me too. Look, we need to figure out what we're going to tell everyone here. You are planning on leaving and heading to Patras, then probably back here to get the Lady, since she's both been to Austra *and* used that amulet. I wanted to say that you need to go from *Patras* to Austra, not to here first. If the amulet doesn't work on Fae people, the Princess will be left behind."

"Why wouldn't it work on her?"

Gomez looked at him, concerned. "Elizabeth."

Alexander held up his hand. "That was different. That amulet was corrupted."

"How many Fae have you tested it on?"

Alexander rubbed his eyes. "Yeah, I see what you mean. Maybe I should…"

Gomez stepped between him and the gathering of people when Alexander's eyes settled upon Monique. "I think that would be extraordinarily bad judgment, Sir. Those are community leaders, which is exactly what Tanglwyst was saying we needed here. I don't think it will be wise to test on any of them."

"You think they *all* are part Fae?"

"I think they all are likely Land Worshippers. The Blacksmith works ores, the alchemist works herbs, the jeweler works precious metals, and we already know about the tavern owner. And if they *are* part Fae as well, we just doomed them to never set foot in Mervolingia again."

Alexander looked at Gomez. "We're… *not* in Mervolingia anymore."

Gomez nodded as the realization fell across Alexander's face. "Exactly. We are inside the borders of the Black Forest, which means we have brought refugees to *Krakte*. And we didn't tell anyone, including the refugees."

"I didn't even realize. We're refugees too then."

Gomez pointed to the meeting room. "I was studying those maps in there, which are very interesting since they show the expanded Black Forest taking up all of York now. Something I noticed was that the Covenants may be in the middle of a country, but they are sovereign territories, beholden to no king or Church. There seems to be a doctrine in case there is a war or something. They take no sides and do not aid any parties in these so Giles helping us is actually breaking some sort of code of theirs."

"I really appreciate that. I hope he doesn't get in trouble."

Gomez arched an eyebrow. "From *who?* As far as I know, he's the last mage."

"He and Raven."

"Right. Except Raven isn't available now. And Giles was part of a rebellion in Heaven, so he may just be feeling like that is the continuation of that."

"Well, we have to get ready. I'm leaving Tanglwyst behind for now. She needs to rest. She had a miscarriage last night."

Gomez put his hand on Alexander's shoulder. "Is… Are you…?"

"No, Nicolai's. Myrgen said she was not upset to lose the child. However, being around Emmy right now could be… challenging."

"I'll let everyone know we're going."

Alexander went to Tanglwyst. Myrgen was hugging her and kissing her forehead. He stood and patted Alexander's shoulder on his way by. Alexander sat on the bed.

"What was that?"

"We were talking about the presents father brought us. He has no idea what's happened to his things now that he's doing all this. He doesn't really care though."

"He's changed since all this started."

"That's the thing. He really hasn't. He's always been protective of me and the people he loves. This isn't out of the ordinary for him at all."

"I see. Well, I was likewise coming in to bid you goodbye. I need to get to Emmy and get her to Austra. And I'm not sure using the amulet is a good idea. Gomez said the trip might hurt her."

"Ask Giles. Maybe he knows."

"Maybe. Anyway, this is your room now. I'll have Giles make another one for me when I return."

"I don't want to kick you out of your room."

"You're not, you're not. I just don't want to assume a place here with you."

She smiled and took his hand, kissing it. "Thank you."

He smiled. "May I?"

She nodded, perplexed.

He leaned down and kissed her. She melted into him and he into her. It was sweet and powerful and he realized he had almost lost her. His eyes were wet when he pulled away.

"Be careful out there, please."

He hugged her. "I will. Please rest. I'll need you when I head to Austra."

Raymond opened his eyes. He looked at Fenn. "Did you say something?"

A knock came at the door. "Raymond?"

"Oh!"

He got up and opened the door that he had sealed against the wind. Giles stepped in, shaking the snow off him.

"I was just thinking about you and your donkey. I know where you two can go where she'll be comfortable and you will be safe. You ready?"

"Uh." Raymond looked around. "Yeah. It's not like I keep a lot of things with me."

Giles touched Raymond's shoulder and Fenn's head. When they reappeared, they were surrounded by golden fields of wheat. In the near distance was a farmhouse and a little farther away was a small village. The sun was warm and inviting.

"Where are we?"

"Serenity. It's a special place where the outside world won't find you."

"Is that supposed to be a threat?"

Giles blinked. "No, no. I just- We have a lot of things that need doing here and I'll be bringing others here too. I thought you and Fenn might like it."

Raymond looked around. "I see what you mean. Well, enough dawdling. I'd better get to work."

"I also wanted to let you know that the Giver is with Karma and the Bringer."

"Oh. Well, that's probably a good idea. Thank you for telling me."

Giles smiled and disappeared.

Twenty-Seven

"A good head and a good heart are a
formidable combination."
-The Forty-Five Voices

Giles went up to Clara and Brigit. "I moved Raymond. He's safe now and his donkey will be alright."

Brigit looked around, nodding. "Good. Monique and the others arriving managed to gather most of the populace in this room. It might be a great time to talk to the people about going to the other Covenant."

Brigit stood on a chair and several people looked at her.

"Everyone, I would like to have your attention, please."

She waited for everyone to quiet down.

"I think most of us have heard what His Majesty showed Madeline about your homes."

Murmurs and nods punctuated the room.

"We have a few things to offer but first, we want to answer your questions about where we go from here. Please, raise your hand and stand when we point to you so everyone can hear your question. I'm sure it will be the same as someone else's."

"When can we go home?"

Brigit looked for the speaker, who did neither of the things she requested. She looked at Giles.

He came over to the table she was on and stood on a chair too.

"What do you envision when you think of going home? Familiarity, right? Safety, consistency, right? You think of a warm hearth and happy people on the streets."

Nods and approval.

"We do that all the time. But that's not the reality of it."

A woman at the back stood. "It's still what we want. Even if our homes are destroyed, we want to rebuild them."

Madeline's husband stood. "Out of what? Wood, from the Black Forest? We can't harvest that. Ever. We can only go so far south, past Aislyn's house, before we can't harvest there either."

"We should be allowed to make that decision for ourselves."

Nods again.

"Okay. Who wants to go to Cliffport? I'll take everyone right now on scouting missions. I have three places to show you. Cliffport, which you know as St. Giles. Serenity, which has farms and fields and a tavern. And here. So, if you would like to go to look at what your choices are, please join me up here in an hour. Anyone who wants to come, may. Please be advised that Cliffport is a war zone so I would not let your children go there to see it in case they are shot and killed by a flaming Fae arrow."

He got down off the chair and Brigit just stared at him.

"Really?"

She got down and turned him to face her.

He shrugged. "His Majesty was right. People need to make informed choices. When he took that woman to Cliffport, it showed her what the danger was and how she and her entire family would have been dead by now if they had stayed. But only showing her worked. He could have *told* her about it but it does not disrupt the fantasy of what these people envision as 'home'."

Clara sighed. "Because home isn't a place. It's an emotion."

Giles pointed to her. "Exactly. What they want is safety and warmth and they won't get that with a Fae army there on the premises."

"I have a question."

They turned to face the man and small child.

Giles looked at him. "Yes sir?"

213

"You seem to have magic. And someone said you created the fire that walls off the Fae army from the rest of the country. Why don't you just move all the Fae into the woods? Then they can't hurt us anymore and we can go home."

"Why should I do that?"

A few more people came over to them.

The man glanced at them, then back at Giles. "I don't understand the question."

"Why should I do that? Why should I shove these Fae into a wood that they can never leave just so you can go home?"

"You kind of answered the question. So, we can go home."

"Why should *you* going home take precedence over, say, me removing the barrier altogether?"

"Because we…"

A man stepped forward. "Because you're a saint. The Patron Saint invoked against monsters. We worship Heaven. You owe it to us to answer our prayers."

"So, I work for *you* now?"

"Yes. You have to do what we say."

Giles frowned. "So, you're telling me I'm your slave? Because *you* worship Heaven?"

Mumbling around the man made him falter on his strong stance.

"I brought you here with a snap of my fingers and you think *I'm your slave?*"

Now the group was stepping back from the man.

"What makes you think I can't put you anywhere I want to?"

The man mustered his resolve. "Because I say so, as a believer. You can't hurt us."

"Do you have a family here?"

"Yeah. Why?"

"Do they want to get rid of you? Is that why you were sent up here to be belligerent?"

"What? No!"

Giles leaned in. "Are you *sure?*"

"You can't hurt me. You're a saint and I would stop worshipping you, which means you…"

Giles looked at him, curious. "Yes? I what?"

"You…"

214

"What *exactly* do you think we got from you in Heaven? Do you think we ate your prayers as sustenance? That was where we got our power to answer your prayers?"

The man got confused. The rest of the people around him likewise exchanged looks of bewilderment.

A woman cocked her head. "Then what *did* you do up there? Where do we go when we die?"

"You become small beads of gray light."

Clara, Brigit, and Giles looked at George, and the rest of the room turned to face him.

"Not *sentient* beads of gray light, either. There's not some beautiful paradise or mansion or mingling with the Saints. Being a Saint is a blessing and a curse. Once a year, on our feast day, we could not turn off your begging for help. But the rest of the year, we could. If a Saint heard your prayer and answered it on a day that *wasn't* their feast day, it was because they were spending time listening to you. Clara did it all the time.

"Our only job up there, the only thing that mattered, was taking this liquid essence from an urn and using an Angel's feather to put a single drop into the body of a newborn baby that had been named. But the urn ran dry, and I know why. Because each bead is only this big, and the drops were easily twice this size."

He held up a soul.

The other Saints reacted with horror. The people saw their response and got worried.

"George, why do you have that?"

"Because, Clara, I could see these people making a decision that people made around you before. They were going to try and hurt you. You said we can't leave them in the dark anymore. I agree."

He turned to the people. "This is a soul. This is a dead person. See the color? This is probably this person's last run at the world because it's very dark. But they were more good than evil, so they get one more shot. If they don't become a better person, then they go to Hell when they die. And everything they ever were is destroyed."

"They burn, and suffer, don't they?"

"Sort of. They burn, but they don't suffer."

Now everyone turned to see Lucifer. His wings were out. The people dropped to their knees and covered their eyes.

"Since we're telling the truth and all."

Clara squeezed George's hand and Lucifer brought his wings back in. It took a few minutes for people to come to grips with the fact there was an angel in their midst. Eventually, they got their wits about them and their curiosity won out.

Lucifer and George spent the next hour answering questions about Heaven and the afterlife. Finally, people turned back to Giles.

"So, you want to show us some different places, right?"

Giles smiled and held out his hands. "Gather 'round, all who are going on the tour."

Monique leaned over to Brigit as Lucifer put away his wings. "This might get us some converts, huh?"

Brigit looked at her, surprised.

Monique smiled. "Land worshippers can tell other Land worshippers."

Brigit inched closer to Monique. "How?"

"A distinct *lack* of concern about the afterlife. You see these people? They have a fear of dying. The reason every one of us that stayed in town did so was because we know our fates. We don't fear dying like these people do. They think they will burn. What kind of place tortures souls? And why would anyone risk that by choosing that afterlife?"

Brigit looked around at the people who were leaving with Giles. "Having served up there for hundreds of years, I can attest that the ones who went to Hell were the lucky ones. I don't want to be a Saint. Being cast out was the best thing for me. Unlike Giles, I never studied magic so I don't have that. But I remember *painting* and *sculpting*. I want to do those again. I want to be creative again."

"I will run an inn in Summerland. I just know it. It is the joy of my life to do that. To help people transition into their new world and life. To give them comfort in their challenges, and support in their grief. To celebrate their victories and life experiences. I *loved* that. I would live forever in Summerland doing that."

"Giles said there's a tavern in Serenity. Something about 'good neighbors' making the bread. It was *really* good bread too."

"Oh, that sounds like something I want to look at."

Brigit's brow furrowed. "Will *I* go to Summerland?"

"That's up to the Land, dear. But if you worship it and follow its teachings, I believe so."

"Where do you hear its teachings?"

"Directly from it. Like, what is your instinct when Giles was talking there?"

Brigit lowered her voice. "That the people had *no* idea what they were talking about. And I felt very scared for the Krakten army. These people don't care about them. The army was here for a reason. And these people don't care at all about what that reason is. And according to that one man in the meeting, they need to rescue the Princess from a Fae thing so she doesn't die?"

Monique nodded. "People that are born in a Fae place or with Fae blood need to be around it. It's why so many of us will open inns. Fae inhabit places like that and you can add features to attract or repel them. But people with Fae blood will always stay at a Fae-friendly inn to make sure the Wisp Summons does not occur. See, humans change, but Fae die if they do. So, since humans are *constantly* growing or changing, the Fae part is in danger. It lashes out in an attempt to stop the changes and the danger. That is very bad for anyone nearby.

"But if they are near a Fae place or at an inn, or a place of Land worship, then they can draw energy from that place and it settles the Fae. It feels strong enough to not be lost and there is balance."

"As a healer, this is fascinating."

"Well, Fae humans need healers that understand their needs and difficulties. Honestly, that may be why the Land picked you."

Brigit smiled. "Picked me? That's got a good feeling to it. Do Fae ever choose to worship Heaven?"

"I don't know. I believe Elizabeth, the former Queen may have converted. I remember hearing she was Coronated in the See in Patras. I can't imagine how uncomfortable that must have been."

Brigit frowned. "The Essence. She probably removed her Fae essence to withstand it. Excuse me. I need to see if Alexander has left."

Alexander and Gomez stepped out of a doorway and Brigit ran up to them.

"Good, you're still here."

Alexander jerked his thumb over his shoulder at the door across from the room. "Yeah. Tanglwyst felt uncomfortable taking my room so we got Giles to tell us how to create her own and moved her. She's resting right now. Will you please check on her while I'm gone? She has wine and other things for helping her get her blood strong again."

"She lost a lot of blood recently?"

"Miscarriage."

"Oh Alexander. I'm so sorry."

"Not mine. We haven't done that at this time. It was from a previous incident. What did you need?"

"That essence stuff her brother mentioned. I think Elizabeth probably had some."

Gomez looked at Alexander. "At the palace?"

"The nature of the Fae blood indicates she had to have a way to distill it out of the blood. Otherwise, she never could have gone to the Church for her Coronation. It would have induced that Wisp Summons."

Alexander rolled his eyes. "Yeah, that went on for hours. The reception afterwards was in there."

Gomez sighed. "Her dresser would have been cleared off and all her things disposed of months ago."

"Maybe a staff member kept it"

"I doubt they would admit that. Stealing a traitorous queen's items?"

"Alex…"

They turned to see Tanglwyst starting to get out of bed. Alexander moved quickly to her side.

"You need to rest."

She waved him off. "I will if you ever leave. But first, there was a laboratory behind Elizabeth's wardrobe. It has a false back. You have to close the door for it to open. The essence might be in there."

He kissed her forehead. "Thank you. Now rest."

"Shoo."

He smiled and they left, closing the door this time.

Twenty-Eight

"Use a memory to coax a new companion."
-The Forty-Five Voices

Alexander and Gomez appeared in the catacombs at the crossroads. It took a moment for their eyes to adjust and even then, there wasn't enough light to make out more than a few irregularities.

"Be careful and follow me. I can get us to my room."

Gomez put a hand on Alexander's back and they moved slowly forward. He found a wall and the stairs going up and felt like he was able to move with more certainty now. He followed the wall up the stairs and to the right. When he found the dead end, he shifted to the left-hand wall and found the catch that released the door.

A small amount of light now aided them and he closed the catacomb door behind them. Several small votive candles burned in his prayer nave.

"You always leave candles burning?"

Alexander shook his head. "Probably the staff. They tend to make the rooms up like someone is expected to be in them."

They went into his room and Alexander closed the door. "Looks like we made it without anyone noticing."

"Was that important?"

Alexander smiled. "I like surprising the sycophants."

Gomez buttoned his roughed-up coat. "Well, as much as I really want to stay and reconnect with the torturing of nobility, I have a family that has forgotten what I look like."

They hugged and Alexander let his best friend leave his side.

He looked around the room and was hit with a flood of memories. He remembered that Catriona was in Karma's Hand that moment and that their journey would be fraught with pain. If this would free Alistair's lips, he needed to endure it.

He locked the door and let them come. They flowed like ghosts around the room.

When he had walked into the prayer nave, following Heracles, and discovered her.

He touched her down-turned face, raising it to look into his eyes. "Is something wrong?"

"I'm not certain I'm up to stepping into full light," Catriona took a step back into the darkness. "Not here. Not with you."

Alexander leaned back against the wall by the doorway. "I know exactly how you feel. We'll wait until you're ready."

"And if I never am?" Catriona stepped away, pretending to examine the votives.

"Then they will find my bones leaning against this wall in a hundred years."

In the middle of the room, when she had said the problem with Nicolai and her would soon be dealt with.

"What do you mean, 'dealt with'?" Alexander searched Catriona's eyes. When she looked away, unable to keep eye contact, his own eyes narrowed in understanding. "You're leaving him, aren't you?" Catriona tried to move away from him but he held her tight. "You are. By the Saints, you're leaving him." He took her in his arms and kissed her hair. "Thank you, Heaven."

"Don't move me in just yet, Alex. I'm not free yet. I may never be. If he wants to, Nicolai can decide to call me an adulteress, and he would be right. If I'm caught, it would be the obligation of your brother to put me to death, by your own laws. I'm just thankful he doesn't know it was with you."

"I could have him killed."

She put her head against his chest, letting him encompass her with his arms. "That isn't funny."

"Maybe I wasn't trying to be."

On the bed, with her sitting on top of him, her dark hair cascading down. She had just told him about Elizabeth's plan.

"I don't mean to burden you further, Alexander. What can I do to help?"

"Honestly? Stay here with me a while. Let me enjoy one measure of peace."

"Don't you need to stop her?"

"I will, but I have a little while. Interrupting the Ritual requires precise timing. And now is not that time."

Catriona climbed off him and sat beside him. "I can do that."

He tried to let the memories go, let them fade away. He went to the hearth to start a fire and saw the burn in the rug.

Alexander went to the hearth and stoked the fire to a strong blaze. An ember spit itself onto the hearth and bounced to the rug behind him. Catriona stepped in absently and delivered it back onto the hearth, mindful of crushing it into the fibers of the rug where it could smolder and ignite. Suddenly, Alexander stood and turned and the two found themselves within a breath of each other.

She started to step back but he grabbed her hips and kissed her. The force of his sudden passion caught her off guard and she gave in, folding into him like a flag when the wind stops. Her hands had gone to his chest, and they slid gently, then eagerly up to his neck, her hand slipping into his hair as she let her need for him take over.

The kiss finally ended, the passion surging around the room like a rampaging ghost, leaving them both breathing heavily. She swallowed.

He looked into her eyes. "Stay with me. Please."
"Tonight?"
"Forever."
"I can't."
"Then tonight will do."

He hadn't become the man he was yet. He wouldn't until after Charles was discovered. He missed the person he was in her arms, at that moment. That time before all of this.

But then he had changed, by magic so insidious, he wondered if it was manufactured by Karma.

He hefted the griffin decanter and checked the goblet on the fireplace mantle beside it. It was dusty and he wiped it out with his sleeve. The decanter was full and he poured some brandy and put it back on the mantle. He had always kept it above the table because Heracles had a very long tail.

Claws at the door drew his attention and he opened it. He was all but knocked to the ground by the large wolfhound. A keeper ran up behind him a minute later.

"Sire! You're home."

Heracles was licking Alexander's face too much to speak but he kept getting a mouthful of dog tongue from laughing.

"Yes- *ptt*- Yes, I just- *ptt*- Down, boy!"

The keeper pulled the dog off the King and Alexander got to his feet. He went to the bed and sat down and Heracles bolted over to him, dragging the keeper like he was a small cloth.

"I'll take it from here." He took Heracles' collar and made him sit. Then stroked his ears. "How was he?"

"He stays on your bed. I have to remove him in the afternoon so the staff can clean in here. At first, he wouldn't let them in."

"Where are my griffin pillows?"

"Those... are being remade. I'm sorry, Sire."

He frowned at Heracles. "Why did you harm the pillows, boy? I've left before for a long time."

"You've always brought him to the kennels before. And the loss of the King and Queen also seemed to make the palace strange to him."

"Oh, I'm so sorry, Heracles. I'll take you with me from now on."

"Will you be leaving again soon, Sire?"

222

Alexander looked at the keeper. "I'm afraid I must. Where is the Queen Mother?"

"Preparing for court, Your Majesty. There has been a lot of business."

"Yeah. I expected there would be. I'll see her in a minute."

The keeper bowed and left. Alexander got up and Heracles jumped onto the bed and lay down, watching his master.

Alexander went to his wardrobe. There were several beautiful outfits befitting a king and he looked at his current clothing, worn and stained from the trials of the last few weeks. A knock came at the door and he opened it.

Catherine hugged him. "How are you?"

He returned the hug. "Not too good. I have a lot to tell you."

He reached into his doublet and pulled out two letters. He handed her the one marked Catherine.

She took it. "This is from Sovereigna."

"It's more than that. I'll talk to you about all that when you're ready."

She opened it and read it. Alexander focused upon the clothes to give her a little privacy. He pulled out a blue set with gold trim. "I took a bath last night. That should be good enough, right?"

"Of course."

He took the clothes into the prayer nave and got undressed. He put on the clean clothes and was annoyed that he forgot the order things went on in.

"I need a different style. These just don't work for me anymore."

"I can have designer get you some renderings. I have someone working on clothes for me for your Coronation."

She sounds distracted. She's still reading but she's still attending to me too. Amazing.

Eventually he was able to come back out. His clothes were a little loose, which actually made him happy. He was worried he put on weight with the amulet being his primary source of exercise. Then he realized he had barely eaten in two weeks.

He looked at his mother. She was staring at the letter, her eyes dry. She looked up.

"You've lost weight."

"It's been stressful lately."

"Yes. I imagine so. When did she give this to you?"

"This is a much longer conversation than it seems at first. Do you feel you have time?"

"Yes."

Alexander gestured to the hearth chairs and told her everything.

Two hours later, she understood what they all wanted to do.

"And she's alright, somehow?"

"According to Myrgen."

"Well, keep *that* name in your head. There has been plenty of strife because of him, and Dominic. Emmy has been my constant companion as I've handled the financial issues we've had come up. And I have just the nobles for you to assign the task you want for the army."

She stroked the writing on the letter. "She wrote this from beyond the grave. This is… I am astonished. And you went to Heaven to retrieve Tanglwyst."

"I did not think to reach out to Sovereigna. Do you want me to?"

Catherine shook her head. "No, but I'll send something back to her. We'll figure out a way to communicate. We always do. So, we need to get Emmy to Austra and she wants me to stay with her. Darling, that means we must handle your Coronation before she leaves, since she won't be able to attend otherwise."

"We *could* but I have given that some thought. At the Haunted Covenant, or Serenity, we can have her attend. Or I can have her watch from the forest."

"That would be very cruel. She would want to go to you. She loves you."

"I don't know that I can be ready before she needs to be there. I'm not willing to risk her life for my Coronation."

"How is Tanglwyst?"

"She's recovering. She miscarried last night."

Catherine looked at her son. "Nicolai?"

He blinked, stunned. "You're the first person who hasn't assumed it was mine."

"She was pregnant when I met her. You had not slept with her then. I assume that hasn't changed."

"How did you know?"

"I could sense it. She had been wearing those clothes since her escape and there was not a single stain of blood on them. Women of her age don't have that luxury."

He closed his eyes and ran his fingers through his hair. "By the Saints, I never noticed."

"No. Men and women have been taught that it's a shameful thing. It disgusts men to think there might be something non-sexual about a woman."

"I have learned so much from her, and you, these last few weeks. Hope I can do right by you both, and Emmy. Oh, has anyone cleaned out Elizabeth's room?"

"I imagine so. Why?"

"There's a possibility that she has essence extraction there. If so, we can give it to Emmy and that will buy us some time."

Catherine glanced through the note. "Sovereigna does mention it here. She's making some where she is. Can that be brought out?"

"Apparently. I had no idea there would be this much back and forth between people who have died."

She smiled. "We should head down."

"Indeed. Anything I should know?"

"You'll pick it up as you go along. I'm sure of it."

Myrgen entered Sovereignlumin and went to the Winter door. He opened it and tried to shout but it didn't work. The wind gusted his words back into his throat. He closed the door and looked at the stairs heading up. He looked around and saw the room was empty. A small note lay on the bier.

Lie here.

He looked around and climbed onto the bier and lie down. The lid came down and he fell instantly asleep.

He opened his eyes to find James and Gwen looking over him. James had lifted the lid.

"Why do people do that?"

Myrgen looked at James. "There was a note. It said to."

"It's essentially a glass-covered coffin. Why would someone want to nap in there?"

Myrgen gestured to Gwen. "Ask your sister. It was in her handwriting."

James looked around the room. "Who are you pointing at?"

"Gwen. She's right... Oh no. You can't see her. She's standing right next to you.

James looked where Myrgen had gestured before. "Here?"

"Yeah. You can't see her because you haven't died."

"Neither have you."

Myrgen glanced down. "Actually..."

"Honestly?"

"Couple times now."

"Huh. So, is she still right here?"

Myrgen raised James hand. "That's her face."

"What, like did you just put my hand in her *face?*"

"No, no! Just your fingertips."

"This is where her nose would be, isn't it? You put my fingers in her nose!"

"No! I'm- she's – "

Then Gwen couldn't hold it anymore and started laughing.

"By the Fae, you're *awful!*"

James smirked. "I know. So, what brings you here, Myrgen?"

Myrgen rolled his eyes, then got back to business. "We had that meeting and here's what we figured out."

He explained everything they talked about and answered questions as best he could. James made some mulled wine as they spoke and the room became pleasantly cozy. He mentioned the voluntary torpor idea Catriona had suggested.

James shook his head. "Yeah, I checked into that. If she goes into torpor, that speeds up the process for Lucifer's demise. But that's not the important part. She's the only Fae lord upright at the moment. If she goes down, Heaven will destroy every Fae in the world."

"The Papal City is encased in thorns."

"And what do you think is maintaining them? It's the presence of an active Fae Lord. If she falls, the thorns fall, there's nothing to stop the slaughter of Fae kind. Giles already destroyed nearly every magical beast in the north before being killed by a Fae curse. Not to mention that the Fae can't escape the Black Forest, which has spread, by the way."

"We know."

"But you know who can come and go at will? Human church armies. We already overheard the Mervol General talking about grabbing Sovereigna's body so they can force the Fae to leave, then kill them in the woods."

Myrgen sighed, closing his eyes. "Dammit. I was really hoping he wouldn't try that. Look, I'll take care of that one. I also need to get something from Gloriana. Or someone. I need someone who can produce a powerful illusion. I can supply the essence for it. I just don't have the ability to cast it."

"Well, make that your second priority, then. We need to stop that damn thing before it takes Gloriana out."

"I need to stop by Persephone to see Raven after we finish here. Is there a better way to reach you?"

"Yeah." He patted around on his outfit, then went to his coat and pulled out a palm sized shard. "This is part of Gloriana's pillar. She trimmed some off in case I needed it. I can get another one, if necessary."

Myrgen put it in his satchel. "Gwen, do you need anything?"

"I'm good."

"Then I'm off."

Myrgen headed out the door.

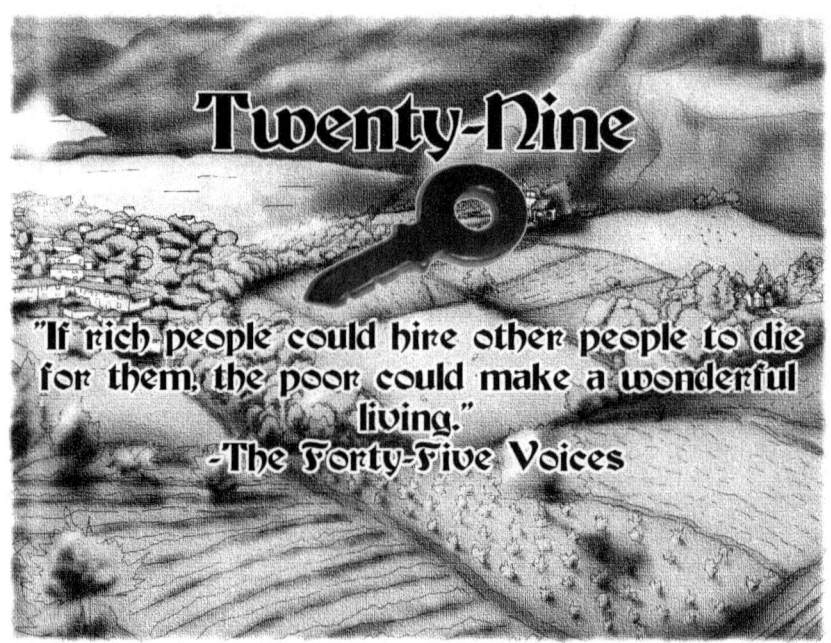

Twenty-Nine

"If rich people could hire other people to die for them, the poor could make a wonderful living."
-The Forty-Five Voices

Raymond tapped Giles on the shoulder. "New neighbors?"
Giles nodded. "They are looking around. How's your donkey?"
"Fine. Where's Jude?"
Giles frowned. "I… don't know. Where did you see him last?"
"With the Giver. She left with him."
"How long ago?"
"Yesterday? Day before?"
"The Giver was taken by Karma, at the trap."
"Was Jude with her?"
"I will be right back."

Giles disappeared and arrived at Persephone. He went down to the trap. Raven seemed to be asleep but he looked up as Giles came to the cave opening.

"You're awake. I had a question. Did Jude come here with the Giver?"

Raven frowned. "No. Just the Giver."

"Damn. He's missing."

Giles thought for a minute, then went to the Giver place where Lauriel had drowned him. He saw Jude sleeping on the Giver's bed and touched his shoulder to wake him. There was no response.

Giles disappeared with Jude back to Raymond. Once there, Jude started awake.

"Where am I?"

Giles knelt beside him. "You're in Serenity. It's a Covenant that we established centuries ago."

Jude sat up and shaded his eyes with his hand. "The snow is gone. Did we win?"

"Uh no. We haven't yet. But there's a lot to tell you."

Giles explained all that had happened and the plans for the world.

Jude stroked his beard. "The Giver was very interested in finding more souls that had fallen. She wanted to create like she did when she landed. She said she's never been allowed to be creative before."

"Been allowed? Strange. Allowed by whom? Who is telling the Giver and Bringer what they are *allowed* to do?"

Monique came over to Giles. "That inn, who built it?"

"Um, a Fae fellow we met a long time ago. Ember is what we called him."

Monique blinked. *"Embertwist?"*

"Yeah, that was the guy. He was here for a long time too. I made sure he didn't make any deals with people that killed them or took away their free will or impregnated them with anything without their consent."

She arched an eyebrow, frowning. *"How?"*

"I just made him promise. I gave him the land for it and told him he could build an inn there."

"You gave him the Land? In exchange for what?"

"For not doing anything sketchy with it. That stuff I just said."

"No, that was in exchange for the Inn itself. What did he give you for the *land*?"

"Oh. Nothing, I think. He admired our little Covenant and I told him he could have that land there to build on."

Monique closed her eyes. "You gave a Fae something without making a bargain for it?"

"I thought he would like it. He did too."

"How long was he here?"

"As long as I was at least. He wanted the deed to tie to my lifespan… Wait. Was that a bad thing?"

Monique rolled her eyes. "If people end up staying here and that trade tunnel goes back into effect, I'll run this Inn. But you will make *no* deals with *any* Fae. Period. Ever. You stupid… Ugh!"

She walked off. Giles looked at the other Saints. "What was that about?"

Myrgen stepped into the opening of the Karma trap and hesitated. He doubted he was more powerful than Raven, Lucifer and Gloriana combined, but he still wasn't sure. Raven looked at him.

"I'm getting all kinds of visitors today. Giles was just here."

"Oh. He didn't stay?"

"No. Just asked about Jude and then left. I don't think it's a good idea for you to come in here."

"Yeah, I feel the same way."

"Is there anyone who can come here that isn't a huge risk?"

Myrgen thought. "Brigit is turning to the Land. I can ask her."

"Yeah. She's a good choice."

"I'll send her along. I don't want to leave this without someone to hold onto it."

Raven nodded and went back to sleep. Myrgen looked around.

I gotta get me one of those amulets.

He looked at the letter to Raven. "Hey, you still around?"

Raven opened his eyes again. "What is it?"

"Where's Lauriel?"

"Right here. Why?"

Lauriel came out from behind Raven and stretched out a yawn. Myrgen smiled. "Glad to see the voice of reason is attending you."

"He didn't like the plan I had for getting the Giver into the trap so he stayed behind, in case I needed help. Once I was in here, there was no one to go get."

Myrgen ruffled Lauriel's head fur. "Thank you."

Lauriel pushed into the head rubbings.

Myrgen reached into the satchel. "I have a message from Merrick. Unfortunately, he's moved on so he can't answer any follow up questions."

He started to open it and Lauriel stopped him.

Raven panicked as well. "Whoa! Hey, that's a sealed letter from a Fae servant. If you open it and it's not for you, you'll die."

"Yeah, I know. But the letter doesn't erase once it's opened and you can't do it. If I get Brigit in here, she can't open it either. I have to get to Summerland anyway and this is the fastest way."

Lauriel looked skeptical but it didn't stop Myrgen.

"See you, buddy. You take care of him."

He opened the letter.

A few minutes later, he was just outside the garden wall of the mansion.

Huh. That's handy. I must have thought ahead. Nice to know I can skip the walk.

He walked in and checked the study. It was empty.

"Lucifer?"

"Down here."

Myrgen walked down the stairs to the Hell level. "Is Brigit still at the Covenant?"

"Hm. Not sure. Giles was taking people to the other place to show it off. Whatcha need?"

"Raven needs some help. I was going to talk to her. What are those?"

"I tried to reach out with the Pillar in the meeting room but it was black. So, I brought it back here to see if anyone had any ideas. Saint Teresa suggested bringing them down here, since the souls get purified here. It worked!"

He held up the large chunk for Myrgen to see. It glowed like the pile behind him.

"I have these too. I gave you one, but I recalled it when the big one didn't work right."

"I have a shard from Gloriana's. Apparently, we can shave them off. I almost left it with Raven but..."

"Karma probably watched its own trap? Yeah, I had the same thought. I was going to even use it to communicate with Alistair but I didn't think it would work."

"We need a way to make sure no one can tell what's going on in there."

Lucifer rubbed his chin. "You know, there's something obscuring the Haunted Covenant. It's tricky to find the place if you don't know where it is. I thought maybe that was why the Pillar didn't work there, at first. I wanted to try this before asking about it."

"You think that will protect Raven?"

Lucifer shrugged. "No idea. But it's worth it to try."

"Can you ask Giles? I don't have one of those teleporting amulets."

"Can't you travel through the Land?"

"Ordinarily, yes. But the Black Forest is divine. It stops Land Magic."

"Ah. Yeah, I'll bet it does. I'd take you there myself but I go through Heaven and, well…"

Myrgen nodded and looked at the Pillar near a pile of souls. "Heard anything from her yet?"

"No. I've got it near me all the time, just in case. I'll let you know if she reaches out. Sorry about his attempt to hurt you by having her in bed."

"I doubt he would go so far as to rape her, but then again, he did that to the Midwinter Queen so who knows?"

"I think he would have to be the violent kind of rape to take it from Catriona. He used mistaken identity rape on Gloriana, which was non-violent. I don't think he has it in him to be violent with her. Regardless, different type of wrong is still wrong."

"Yeah."

"I can see this is not a great subject. Where are you off to now?"

"I was going to go back to Cliffport to see if Giles was there to get me back to the Covenant. But I'm not sure what to do next. Alexander has no doubt given Catherine her letter from Sovereigna. He'll take the other to the Seneschal. I'm in a waiting game now. I figured I'd talk to Sovereigna on the way by and see if there's anything else she needs or has. I just feel…"

"Lost?"

"A little bit."

"Well, I tried to build an urn out of those soul beads. They do *not* adhere to each other at all. Even if you lick them."

"How did you *make* Heaven then?"

232

"The Air Dragons helped. They connect to the Dream Dragons and 'dreams are of the Giver', apparently. So, we thought of what we wanted and they used the urn stuff to create that dream."

"Dreams are Giver?"

"Yeah, and creativity is Bringer. No idea who came up with *that* idea."

"Anika and Tib told me to paint. Maybe I should."

Lucifer let him make the decision without interference.

"Okay, I'm heading to Summerland. If you see Brigit before I do, please ask her about Raven."

"Will do."

Alexander walked into the King's office and threw a goblet into the fire. It shattered. Catherine looked at it.

"You're not going to last a minute if you can't handle *that*."

Alexander waved his hands around, frustrated. "How? How do you do it, Mother? The Rocheforts *insist* that the Tersans give up the rights to harvest the forest, while refusing to give up the rights to harvest forest to Ariel and Robert so they can rebuild their city. How can these people be so – "

"Corrupt?"

"Yes!"

"I daresay that's my doing. I let so many of them curry favor with me when I was holding the throne for your brother."

"Were they *ever* good people?"

Catherine shrugged. "No. But you let it get to you so badly. Alex, you have to find a way to get through it."

"I just kept stabbing myself in the palms because I knew I couldn't say anything. If this isn't helping Catriona, I don't know how long I can keep it up."

"Is there any way to find out?"

"Not unless she contacts someone or Alistair does. We may not know until something breaks." He poured himself a goblet of wine and offered some to his mother.

She waved it off. "I have checked on Elizabeth's things. No one found anything of import in her room."

"I'll go check it myself. Tanglwyst told me what to look for. What are you going to do now?"

"What I always do after court. I'll play with Emmy, then take a bath. It always helps."

"That sounds glorious. I'll join you for the Emmy part but then I think I'll go for a bath in my own room."

She arched an eyebrow, bowed, and left.

He drank the wine and went to Emmy's.

An hour of stuffed dolls and sword fights later, he went to Elizabeth's room. He closed the door and looked around. Evening had moved into twilight so there was no light in the room. He lit a candle in her prayer nave and opened the wardrobe. It was empty and he stepped inside and closed the door. He felt the back and found a catch that opened into a dusty room.

He held the tiny candle aloft until he found a lantern to light. Once that was going, he was able to inspect the place. Alembics and bottles were everywhere, along with several small chests. He opened those and saw herbs and flowers plus one with desiccated corpses of small animals and insects. He saw a larger chest and worried what could be in it. When he got closer, he smelled old decomposition and decided to leave that chest alone.

On a table were several completed potions and some recipe books. He read them over until he found what he was looking for. He read through the ingredients list and found he didn't recognize many of the items. The instructions were even stranger and he gave up on understanding it. Instead, he took the book and bottles in a small basket, then grabbed the lantern and left the room.

He sent a message to his mother to meet him in the King's chamber tomorrow and returned to his room. Heracles was on the bed and he smiled at his companion.

"Ready to go someplace new?"

He touched Heracles and they arrived at the hallway outside his room at the Covenant. He concentrated and opened his door. His room from the Palace stood before him, with one minor change. He now had his own privy and bath. Heracles was distracted by the activity in the

Great Hall and Alexander took him into the bedroom to set down the items, then they went to join the others for dinner.

Brigit saw him and smiled. "Well, hello Handsome! Where did you pick up a stray like Alexander?"

Alexander ruffled Heracles' ears. "This is my dog, Heracles. He and I smelled some very good food out here and felt we needed to investigate. I also have some things I need you to have a look at, if you don't mind."

"Of course. Sit down."

"I will in a moment. How is Tangl?"

"She ate a mostly bloody steak at lunch and several root vegetables I requested for her. She's been sleeping other than that."

"Can I go check on her?"

"Well, I would leave Heracles with me. Having him jump on the bed might not go over well."

"Heracles, sit. Wait."

The dog sat and watched his master, then sniffed around at the empty plates. Brigit put one on the floor for him.

Alexander knocked on the door and creaked it open a small amount. There was a fire in the hearth and the room was warm. Tanglwyst stirred and turned to face the door.

"Alexander, what time is it?"

"Apparently dinnertime. Are you hungry?"

She yawned and nodded. "I think I'll eat something. I feel a bit better than I did earlier. I do need something though. In that top desk drawer, the one on the side, there should be a wooden box of herbs. Can you make that into a tea for me?"

He walked over to the generic desk and found the box of herbs. "This place came well stocked?"

"Sort of. I told Giles I needed to return to St… to Cliffport and get something out of my room there. Giles told me to just concentrate on what I needed and then go in my room where I expect it to be. It worked."

"What are these?"

"An herbal mixture a client of mine makes to help with miscarriage recovery. It's a very popular trade item we sell and it is nothing to pirates. Even when we've been raided, they always leave those."

"Who buys them?"

"Midwives."

"I knew it as soon as I asked it. I got my first healer training with a midwife."

"I remember you telling me that. You changed clothes."

He poured water over the leaves. "Had to. Held court today. I think I know why Charles abdicated."

"That bad, huh?"

"These people are so blatantly corrupt. I want to execute them after every sentence, go get their souls, bring them back, and execute them again after the next one."

"That's a lot of effort for people you want dead."

"And it would be a waste to look for them in Heaven. They will never make it there. They are on their *last* tour of the world."

"Does knowing that make it better?"

He brought the tea over to her. "No. Because suffering never purified anything, and these people are causing a lot of suffering. Rochefort's relatives still claim he was falsely accused."

"But, those children. The damage he did to them."

"Do not get me started. I'll burn them all but I will say they are in the running for the failure with the Fae army."

"Is it better to do it that way?" She took a sip of the tea.

"I think so. It's complicated, but the more I can make it look like evil is winning down here, the more I hope Catriona can get out of Alistair up there. That's really how I'm getting through this. Otherwise, every selfish liar would be met with a headsman's axe."

She smiled.

He looked at her, nervous. "Why are you smiling?"

"I've missed that person I met last winter. I was worried he was gone for good."

"Being back at the Palace reminded me of several things. Sitting court is different with this new perspective. Are you hungry?"

"Yes. Give me a few minutes and I'll come out."

"I can bring you something."

"Brigit has me on a strict diet. Maybe you can send her in?"

"Sure. I need to have her look at some things."

He got up and left the room. He went to his patron Saint and was surprised at the large stack of plates on the floor. "What's all this?"

"The kids have been bringing them by. Several people were unable to bring their pets and I had no answers about where they are now."

"Well, cats will undoubtedly be fine but I haven't seen a single dog in Cliffport."

"Where could they have gone?"

"Possibly into the woods. Down by the docks. I have no idea, to be honest."

"That's actually unsettling. If they are in the woods, they are hopefully traveling in packs for safety."

"I should ask Aethelraed. Maybe he's seen them. If he has, I'll bring them here. Anyway, two things. I have some herbs and recipes I need you to examine. Second, Tangl says you have her on a specific diet for her convalescence?"

"Yes. Do you want to take it to her?

"That would be great. I'll get the herbs and things."

Brigit left Heracles and Alexander went and got the basket. He set it on the table and scrubbed Heracles' shoulders until she returned.

"This was in Elizabeth's laboratory. Maybe you can make sense of it. I didn't understand the terminology."

Brigit nodded and pulled out the book. He took the food to Tanglwyst's room and knocked, waiting for her confirmation to open the door. She was sitting by the fire in a robe.

"I got tired of being in bed. Where's yours?"

He set the plate on the table next to her tea. "I'm actually going to bathe and get the stink of court off me before I spend time around humans. But I brought a friend with me if you feel like walking around."

"Maybe tomorrow. I got up but I can feel I'm not quite ready yet to be out and about."

He gave her a kiss on the top of her head. "I'll leave you to it, then. Good night, My Lady."

Thirty

"Despise not death, but welcome it, for
nature wills it like all else."
-The Forty-Five Voices

Myrgen walked to Summerland and went to Elizabeth's keep. He heard glass tinkling in the clear night air. He went into the laboratory and found Sovereigna putting a cork in a bottle, then sealing it with wax.

He knocked on the open door after she put it down. She jumped a little, putting her hand to her chest.

"Sorry. I was in my own thoughts."

"That's why I didn't knock when you were holding a pan of hot wax. How is it going in here?"

"I have made a few potions to see if I understood what I was looking at. These three are successes."

She gestured to a set of bottles with wax seals and paper labels.

"Are any of them the Essence Extractor?"

She held up a red one. "When this is consumed, it will empty into a second bottle. The second will be blue. It trades at a one-to-one ratio."

"How much will Emmy need this first time?"

"How big is she?"

Myrgen put his hand at his hip.

"She will need about one-third of the bottle. That should stem the problem for now."

He took it and put it in his satchel. "I'll make sure it gets to them. Anything else?"

"Just a few experiments. This one is a healing remedy for poison. This is quite common for alchemists since we often have to taste our concoctions and that's not always safe. This last one is a memory enhancer. We used it for investigations. Here."

She held out a pouch with three sections.

"This should keep them from clanking against each other and risking them spilling."

"Oh."

He took the bottle out of his satchel and put the three in the holder. There was a tie to go around the neck of the bottle in each slot. He utilized them and then shook them a little to test the ties.

"Thank you very much for this. Do you need anything?"

Sovereigna glanced at his satchel. "Did you deliver the letter to Catherine?"

"I did not, but I gave it to Alexander and he left for Patras around noon. I'm sure she has it by now."

"Yes, I believe he would make sure she got it as soon as he could. He and she made up, you know."

"Really? He hated her for, well, for an incident that happened several years ago, under Charles."

"She saved him from my wrath less than a tenday ago." She cast her eyes down at the memory and fought the tears that threatened.

"Your Majesty, do you need me to stay?"

"Would you mind?"

He smiled. "Not at all. I need to catch you up anyway."

He sat with her as she worked on a few more things. One was a powder that helped a horse run fast. Another was a wayfinder powder. By the time he had her caught up, he had been outfitted with several new items.

"I'm starting to need a bigger satchel."

She laughed. "I'll keep working on this. It brings me joy. I have to translate all of these before I can go on."

"That may take years."

"I know. That's my point. I keep thinking, maybe, if I wait around…"

"You won't be alone?"

"One can hope. When we were together, after Alexander and Tanglwyst left us that night, I *think* I felt her turn to us. It's possible she'll come here when she passes on."

Myrgen smiled. "I never knew. Catherine didn't seem happy, to be sure, but she gave birth to several children."

"As we all know, having sex and giving birth do not denote sexual preference. Especially amongst royals."

"I'm so sorry that you had to go through that, but glad you found your other half."

"So am I, Hunter. It's late though. I think I shall retire and take the rest of this up tomorrow."

"Then I shall leave you to it." He bowed and left the area.

He stepped outside the garden and looked at his home with Catriona. He didn't actually *need* to sleep and he didn't want to go there and be alone. He turned to the forest and went to the Cabin on the Cliffs. Again, not to sleep but as a back door into the world. It was after midnight and he hoped most of the patrols were not around. The snows had stopped and the night was clear but there was no moon. This would aid him getting to town but he wasn't sure where to go from there.

He knelt outside the door and touched the ground. The trees here were not connected to the Black Forest and he could feel the rock beneath him, the shapes it took that actually filtered the runoff from the rains and privies until it got to the sea.

Then he noticed the tunnel.

It went under the town, starting at the Wise Wench. And it was *huge*.

He made his way to the Tanglwyst Trading Company building and hid from a patrol that walked by. They were carrying lanterns, which stopped them from seeing past that light. It made them visible but prevented them from seeing anything.

These aren't guards. Guards would not hold the light in front of them. These are soldiers. Probably folks who've never been in an unlit street before.

The snowfall had tracks all through it and the streets had been cleared of it. He watched them go by and slipped over to the burnt-out husk of the tavern. The cellar door was open and he went inside. Shelves that were untouched by the fire stood next to each other. Most of the shelves had been cleared out and he saw several large circles where mead or ale barrels had been. He knelt on the floor and felt for the tunnel.

Over behind a massive wine keg that went all the way to the ceiling was a small opening about the size of a human. He slipped between the keg and the wall and suddenly there was no wall. From the outside of the room, it would have looked like the shadow from the wine keg. He could see the cellar just barely and smiled at the cleverness of the hiding place.

He turned around and walked about a quarter mile away from the keg when he heard a noise. He touched the wall and read it. A torch was a few feet ahead and he realized he had not used a flint and steel since his first death in Zara. He remembered Catriona calling the lava to heat the valley and wondered if he could do likewise.

Please, Land, light my way.

A small glow began under his hand and a tiny vein of lava, like the walls of Ashstone, formed and shot down the tunnel. As the light rose, he saw several pairs of red eyes gathered in the tunnel and as the light came up, they began to growl.

Tanglwyst woke up and turned over in her bed to face the fireplace. She saw someone in the chair, asleep and it took her a minute to recognize that the thing on the floor was a large dog. She propped herself up on her elbow and the dog lifted its head.

"Heracles?"

The dog's tail started thumping against the chair and Alexander started awake. He stretched and looked over at her.

"I'm sorry. I didn't mean to wake you."

Alexander rubbed his neck. "It's quite alright. I wasn't planning on sleeping here."

She smiled. "Liar."

He got up and stretched his back. "Okay, I'll admit I *was* lying when I said that but I am not right now."

She sat up. "Do you want to lie down?"

"Yes. Simple answer, yes. But before I do, do you need anything?"

"No. But you don't have to leave. You can sleep here."

"Oh, that would not work. Here, I'll show you."

He walked over to her bed and lie down in it. Seconds later, Heracles jumped onto the bed and placed himself firmly between them. He stretched the whole length of the bed.

"I see."

"It gets worse. Just wait."

After a few minutes, the dog settled in and turned on his side. He put his feet firmly on Tanglwyst's body and pushed. She fell out of bed, almost hitting her head on the table next to it. Alexander got up and rushed over to her but she was laughing and waved him off. Heracles paid no mind to them at all and continued to take over the whole bed.

She looked at the animal. "Foul beast."

"Why do you think I came in here and slept in the chair?"

He helped her to her feet and touched her hair. "Are you alright?"

"No harm done. Those herbs make a huge difference. It's how I was able to function during the meeting. Could you refill my kettle, please?"

"Of course."

He left and she used the privy while he was gone. She was still bleeding, but the color was starting to taper to brown. That was a good sign. She could tell she would still need to limit her activities, but she now felt like she could do some.

He came back a few minutes later and hung the kettle on the fireplace hook. She went to prepare the tea and found the mixture tied into bundles in cheesecloth.

"Did you do this?"

"Yes. Catriona showed me how."

"I didn't think to do it, for some reason. I guess I must have been quite out of it."

"Are they a good size?"

"Yes. In fact…" She popped two of them into the kettle and let the water infuse and brew them as it heated.

"That would horrify someone from York."

"I know. But none of them are here. You don't have to stay up. It's too early for someone who has to endure court tomorrow."

"It is but I like the company and I need my strength for these creatures."

"Tell me what happened?"

Alexander laid out the entire dispute about the rebuilding of St. Marguerite and the harvesting of the forests. "The Rocheforts are demanding reparations from the Crown for the 'senseless murder' of their representative in St. Andrew. They do not consider me a viable source of the information because there were reports of me in St. Andrew and St. Marguerite the same day so it was *clearly* someone masquerading as me and who made the accusation. Since I should be offended someone upheld the will of an imposter, the Crown is ultimately responsible for the incident and owes them one hundred thousand ducats."

"One hundred thousand ducats?"

"Yes."

"What did Catherine say?"

"Unfortunately, she didn't expect me back unannounced so when I decided to show up, I screwed up her strategy. She had told them no decision would be made until I returned to make it. If I don't rule in their favor, they'll say the ruling is unfair and cite that I'm not yet King. In the meantime, people in St. Marguerite are stacked several families to a house, most of which are scarred by the fire. Those with no families are on the streets. Morgan Wolf has opened his resort for as many as possible, but the damage was extensive."

"Didn't you say you saw her before court?"

"Yes, but I gave her Sovereigna's letter, the one Myrgen gave me. She was preoccupied, plus I told her everything we learned. I think she just forgot about that. Moreover, with Myrgen and Dominic gone, there's no one running the treasury so they have been standing outside the doors demanding to go in and get what's their due."

"You need a lawyer."

He nodded. "And a chancellor."

Tanglwyst narrowed her eyes. "Isn't there a Pillar-thing in the meeting room?"

"Yeah. What are you thinking?"

"C'mon. I have an idea."

They left the room, Heracles lifting his head to watch them go, then flipping off the bed to follow. They entered the meeting room and she went to the Pillar.

"Can you get it working?"

Alexander looked at her and smiled. "Yeah. Hang on."

He pulled a small bright bead from a small pouch and put it in his mouth. His Power of Sovereignty came on and he touched the Pillar.

"Who are we calling?"

"Lucifer."

The Pillar cleared and showed Lucifer on a beautiful chair.

"Alexander? What can I do for you?"

Tanglwyst leaned in. "Actually, it's for me. Can you reach Myrgen?"

"Yes, but I need you to get Giles for me."

"Uh, okay. Right now?"

"Yes. He is trying to reach Giles right now."

Alexander nodded. "I'll be right back."

Tanglwyst watched him leave, then looked at Lucifer. "What's happening?"

"He found a bunch of animals in a tunnel. He can't feel the tunnel past a certain point so he believes it goes into the Black Forest."

"Monique and a bunch of people came from Cliffport through a tunnel. Is that it?"

"Probably. I mean, how many can there be?"

Brigit and Alexander came in.

"Ah Brigit. Myrgen wants to talk to you too. Where is Giles?"

"He went to Serenity."

"Got it. Hang on." Lucifer concentrated and the Pillar went white. A few minutes later, Giles teleported into the meeting room.

"Hey all, what's the matter?"

The Pillar came back up and Lucifer was in it again. "Myrgen found a bunch of animals, several hurt, in a tunnel under Cliffport. Do you know where that is?"

"Uh, yeah, yeah. Where?"

"Near the edge of the Black Forest, but not in it yet, he says."

"Alright. I'll be right there."

He disappeared.

"He'll take them to the pool. Come on."

Alexander led them to the healing pool. They arrived as about twenty dogs and cats were swimming to the edges. Myrgen was holding one that started to move and splash as it was lowered into the water. After a few seconds, it was active again and started swimming for the edge.

Dogs shook, spraying water all over cats who ran off and cleaned themselves.

Tanglwyst got in the pool and took a puppy off Giles' hands. "What happened to them?"

Giles shook his head. "I can't say. I don't speak dog, but some of them are pretty traumatized. There were several that didn't make it."

Myrgen wiped his face. "I sent them to Summerland. They'll like it there."

Several of the animals came back to the pool and started drinking. Tanglwyst stroked the puppy's fur but it didn't seem to be getting better.

"Giles?"

He looked at the puppy. "I think this one is too far gone."

Myrgen came over to it. He took it from her. "I can't send him home from here. The divine power cut us off."

Alexander waded to him. "I can take you. Hang on."

They disappeared.

Tanglwyst watched the animals drinking and looking healthier. "Is there enough healing for them all?"

"Yeah, there should be. Animals are simpler than people. It should be alright." He looked at her. "You're looking better too."

She looked at the water, then at Giles. "Oh no. I wasn't... I didn't mean to take the healing myself."

"Well, the pool is very indiscriminate. It only notices if you're hurt, not if you want to be healed."

"We need to get these guys some food. Is that possible?"

"Of course."

They headed up the stairs to the kitchens.

Alexander teleported Myrgen to the Cabin on the Cliffs. Myrgen looked around, then set the dog on the ground and waited for it to breathe its last. He petted it and reassured it the entire time. When it passed, he waited and then sent it into the ground. In its place, a small bush sprang up in the soil.

"What's that?"

Myrgen smiled. "Dogwood. What else?"

Alexander stood up. "They were all in some tunnel?"

"Yeah, it's in the Wise Wench cellar. I don't want to show it to the troops though. Not until I know what happened to these animals."

"I agree. Let's head into town. Maybe someone can tell us."

They walked into the village and Alexander asked for General Aethelraed. They were brought before the Guards Barracks. The soldier went in and came out a few minutes later with a stranger.

"I'm Josephus Manglebottom. I'm in charge here."

Myrgen looked past him. "Where's General Aethelraed?"

"He's resting. I'm the officer on duty. What can I do for you?"

"This is His Majesty, Alexander Angloume. Maybe you've heard of him?"

The officer looked at Alexander and his eyes went wide. "I'm sorry, Sire. I did not realize you were back. Please, come this way."

He led them to the City Guard Office, which was lit with lamps and had a fire going.

"Now, Sire, what can I do for you?"

"You can tell me what's wrong with Aethelraed."

"He suffered an injury a few days ago. He's awake and giving orders during the day but he needs his rest."

Myrgen pointed to the man. "Manglebottom. That's who George meant."

Alexander looked at Myrgen and nodded. "Yeah, that must be him. My companion and I found several dogs and cats recently."

"Oh? Where, Sire? We can get rid of them for you."

"Get... get *rid* of them?"

"Yes. The General gave orders that any animals found be slaughtered for food for the men. The granary blew up in the attack that put the barrier up and the General needed to make sure his men were fed."

Myrgen's eyes were a slow, low heat of rage. "How many men are here?"

"We have twenty-five men in town."

"There are months' worth of supplies for a very busy tavern inside that building, they have been picked over in fact. Where are *those* supplies?"

"They were sent back to the army down the road. We have been getting food stores from the houses and when we have found animals, they have been butchered and prepared by the cook."

"Butchered? Who is doing the butchering?"

"There's a young man whose family has a butcher shop in Patras."

Alexander swallowed. "*How* young?"

"Plenty old enough, Sire. Thirteen. He wanted to join the army and we couldn't put him in battle. We found out what his family did and put him to work."

"Why did he join the army at such a young age?"

"He said he didn't want to take over the family business."

Alexander stared at the man and Myrgen started pacing.

"And you carried this order out?" Alexander was stiff as a board.

"I suggested the boy. He had no other value. Don't be squeamish, Sire. We haven't told the men what it is."

Alexander blinked, then looked at the man's eyes. "Open your shirt."

The officer frowned but obeyed. His neck was bare.

"You aren't wearing an amulet."

"What? No. I wear no jewelry in the field."

Myrgen looked at the man, then at Alexander. Myrgen grabbed the man by the shirt and threw him in the street. Josephus stumbled but kept his feet.

"What is the meaning of this, sir? Who are you?"

"You're telling me that you aren't like this because of an amulet. This is just you all the time?"

Myrgen shook his head.

"Yeah, you're done."

A column of lava spewed from the ground around the man, destroying him.

Thirty-One

"Fear gives intelligence even to fools."
-The Forty-Five Voices

Alistair looked at the spout of lava that jumped up around the Mervol officer. "I can't tell if that's a good thing or a bad thing."

Catriona picked up a piece of flat bread and put curried chicken on it. "Well, how would that be a good thing?"

"That guy deserved it."

"That extreme?"

"Yeah. I would have done that if I could have. He traumatized that child, murdered people's pets, and fed them to soldiers without telling them what the food was. That guy was a problem."

"Alright, now, how is that a bad thing?"

"Cuz killing. Never a good thing to murder someone. He was also a high-ranking officer in the Mervol army and the head of their intelligence. So, the plots and spies he had out there doing things will be returning and not have someone to report to that understands the missions. Also, it was *Myrgen* who did it and the King watched, helpless. That will let his enemies call him weak. The repercussions from this can be very far reaching. And Myrgen calling upon the Land like he's entitled to? He's not *you*. The Land might take exception to being summoned like that."

"That sounds like a lot of bad. Does it equal the amount of good?"

Alistair pursed his lips and thought about it. He looked at her. "No. I don't think it does."

She put a black stone in a dish. "It looks like you need to add some balance."

"I agree. So, my beloved, here you go. Do you miss *earthquakes*?"

She blinked slowly. "Interesting."

Alistair frowned, his visage showing his agitation. "I hate this."

She closed her eyes. "I know."

He got up and left the room. She watched as the gout of lava started to fall back to the ground and Myrgen dismissed it. There wasn't even a corpse to recover.

Endure, my love. I'm learning.

Alistair went to the Giver and sat on the bed beside her. Uriel did not seem to be coming out of his downward spiral.

"How is he?"

She didn't look at Alistair. "Not better, but he's declining slower."

"That's good, right?"

"I suppose. Thank you for giving us sanctuary. I don't understand why the Bringer wanted me in a trap that could do this to someone."

"I have no idea. Did she say anything to you about it?"

"No. Only that man who took Uriel's place did. And you. You knew he was trying to trick me."

"I've known Raven for a very long time. It's his fault all the bad things in my life happened. I wouldn't be here if it wasn't for him."

"He really hurt you?" She put her hand on his.

"Yes. A man we both knew was killed, a great man. Raven used Fae magic to change my appearance so I could pretend to be that man. And everything fell apart from there."

"Why did he want you to be the great man?"

"Because the man was a king at a time when the country was in terror. Raven thought it would stabilize the country."

"Did it?"

"Yes, but not before I did a lot of damage to some very powerful people."

"I'm so sorry you've been betrayed."

"I… I wasn't *betrayed*. I just… I was put in an impossible situation that was made worse by my presence. And it still is, right now."

"What do you want, then?"

Alistair looked at her. "I want to not be Karma."

"Then let go. Leave."

He felt his soul flicker, like it was about to let go of all of this.

Then he remembered the trap.

"No. I can't."

She looked at Uriel again, then let go of Alistair's hand and stood up. "I'm going to lie down for a while."

"I understand. Let me know if you need anything,"

Alistair looked at Uriel. "I don't know when, but I'm pretty sure I'm going to have to kill you."

Uriel did not move and Alistair got up and left him.

Myrgen let the molten rock flow into the ground from whence it came and waited for the response. It was just before dawn, and the light had been very bright. But despite this, no one came from the barracks, no one came up from the street, no one came from the buildings.

After a minute, he looked at Alexander. "Why did you come with me?"

"I wanted to see what happened to people and creatures that the Land accepts. You were crying, yet you said they go to a great place."

"I was crying because this creature so young was hurt. He will be happy in Summerland. But here, his life was cut short by brutality. I can't abide that."

"We should find that child, the one doing the butchering."

Myrgen nodded. "I've been here a lot. The store is this way."

They walked towards the docks and near the harbor, stores and streets were cut from the living rock. They heard barking and ran to the store. Inside, dogs and cats were tied up making lots of noise, but the young man was not. He had tied a rope to the rafter and hung himself.

Alexander gathered the animals and took them to the Haunted Covenant, while Myrgen took the lad down and laid him on the ground. He tried to send him into the ground but the earth rejected him.

Alexander returned and looked at them both. "What's wrong?"

"He's a product of Heaven. I can't commit him."

"What do you want to do?"

"I *want* to return him to his family, but I don't have any way to do that."

Alexander looked at him. "I think I have an idea."

They went to the Covenant and arrived in the crypts. Alexander motioned to the door. "Open that, would you?"

Myrgen did, and Alexander took the boy into the room. The village was quiet and slumbering so Alexander just left him in there.

"I'll check on him later."

"That place looked almost like Summerland."

"It did?"

Myrgen went back in the room. He walked down a street, looking at the houses. He came back to Alexander, nodding.

"Yeah, I think that it may be connected. I'll have to look around. That would be great for me because it would give me a way back here."

"Well, good luck. Also, Tanglwyst seemed to think I needed to talk to you about some things going on in Patras."

"Let's go talk then."

Tanglwyst, Giles, Brigit, Alexander, and Myrgen all ate breakfast in the meeting room. The Great Hall was so noisy from everyone celebrating their pets' return, it was impossible to talk and be heard. George and Clara came in an hour after everyone else.

Giles smiled. "Just in time to listen but not eat."

George went to the sideboards. "I'll eat and not listen. How's that?"

"Good enough."

Alexander stood. "George, I fear I may have to have you at Cliffport after all. Last night, the commanding officer on duty was executed. We need you to step in to help the General."

"Executed for what?"

"Looting and destroying property. Also torture of a Mervol soldier and murder."

George tore a piece of bread apart. "Good riddance."

"Thank you. I'll take you there before I have to return to Patras."

He sat down and Myrgen stood. "I gave the letter from Merrick to Raven, the one about the spell. He's going to need some help deciphering it though."

Giles shrugged. "Well, I'm pretty sure that's me then."

Brigit looked at him askance. "You sure? He was quite angry at you when last you saw him."

"No, last time I saw him, I just asked about Jude. He seemed fine with me. Besides, I'm the only other mage in the world. He has to work with me."

Myrgen reached into his satchel and pulled out a shard. "Well, we want to make sure you have a way for us to contact you though. Lucifer gave me these. They are part of the Saint Pillar, which I believe you'd understand. However, it's possible they are unattuned since all connection has been burned away. They were in Hell and, with the 'crossed thread' thing, I have no idea if they have an affiliation or not."

He slid it across the table and it rested between them. Brigit picked it up. She concentrated and it showed Myrgen. Giles looked shocked.

"I'm sorry, Giles, but I was never going back there."

He sighed. "Yeah, I think I always knew that. I don't think I will either, but I'm fine going to the village in the crypt."

Alexander and Myrgen glanced at each other then back at the others.

Myrgen gestured to the shard. "Can you see Raven in that?"

She concentrated again and Raven's room appeared.

"Good. Alright then. Giles, do you need a shard to attune?"

Giles looked at the shard Brigit held. "I'm suddenly not sure which individuals it would show. I think I'm aligned with Heaven but I *was* kicked out."

"But your magic is still divine."

"Right. Okay. How many of those do you have?"

Myrgen looked in the satchel. "Four."

Giles caught another shard and focused. It showed Heaven and he smiled. "Okay. So, we have a Giver shard and a Bringer shard. We're ready to go. You ready, Brigit?"

She looked at her clothes and nodded. "I think so."

He looked at the rest of the group. "In listening to the people out there, Serenity is going to be getting some new residents. Turns out the people here want to go where there's land and sun and community. Having their pets home with them seemed to make a difference."

Clara picked up a piece of cheese from George's plate. "It's possible they didn't realize what was missing until it was returned. Now that their families are whole again, they no longer feel tied to their destroyed city."

Tanglwyst focused on her water and didn't look at Alexander or Myrgen when they looked at her.

"Regardless, the Haunted Covenant should be back to being haunted by dinnertime. No more of these pesky humans around."

Alexander folded his hands. "Is there a healing pool in Serenity?"

"No. There's a tunnel back here if we need the pool, though."

"Well, at least it will get time to be restored then."

Giles stood and touched Brigit's shoulder and the two disappeared.

Tanglwyst got up. "Well, if everyone is clearing out of here, I should go make sure I haven't left anything. If you'll excuse me."

Alexander stood. "I'll be right over to help."

She glanced at him and left.

Myrgen picked up the plates and took them over to the sideboard. "Alexander, do you remember everything we talked about?"

"Yes. I think so. If I need your help, I'll take a moment and reach out to you."

"Sounds good."

"Hey, before you go, I wanted to talk to you in private."

Clara and George were talking quietly, not paying any attention to them.

Myrgen crossed his arms. "Okay. Here or elsewhere?"

"Over there, please."

They walked to the far corner of the room and Myrgen put his back partially to the room.

"What can I do for you?"

"I want to marry your sister."

"Okay. What does she think of that?"

Alexander looked nervous. "I think she might be receptive."

"Then what do you need me for?"

"I'm... asking for your permission, and your blessing."

Myrgen laughed. "Okay then, no. You have neither."

Alexander closed his eyes. "Because of what happened in Caratia?"

Myrgen's brow furrowed. "What? No."

"Patras? Rouen?"

"Alexander, I have lived a thousand lifetimes since then. I barely remembered Elizabeth until I saw her in the Afterlife. And I got *there that time* because an old family friend beheaded me for treason. No, the reason I'm expressly forbidding it is because you are clearly under the impression *I can.* Which means you think there is anyone in this world or the next, or the *other* next, that has a say in her decision.

"She's a grown woman, widowed twice. Even the Law says she's autonomous. I think I'd deny it because I don't want her married to an idiot who practices archaic ownership rituals."

Alexander smiled. "I will take that reprimand to heart. I do apologize. I guess I'm just grasping at normalcy."

"I let go of that after my lady returned in a pool of lava. It changes a person, you know?"

"I really should have abandoned it myself when this all started eight years ago, when you kidnapped Catriona."

"Four months."

Alexander frowned. "What?"

"It's only been four months."

Alexander shook his head. "Wait... that can't be right. Are you sure?"

Myrgen smirked and patted Alexander on the shoulder. "I'm right there with you. Looks like George and Clara are ready to go."

"Thanks for talking to me."

"You bet."

Thirty-Two

"Anger can either fuel cruelty against another
person's greatness, or greatness against
another person's cruelty."
-The Forty-Five Voices

Alexander knocked on Tanglwyst's door and entered when bidden. "Finding everything?"

She shrugged. "I guess I just wanted to have some time to myself. All of St...*Cliffport* is leaving the area. Some of them permanently. I'm sure Monique and Rowena can never leave this place again."

"Fae blood?"

"Yeah, though maybe they can. I've never noticed them needing to extract their Fae essence."

"If they are around Fae, they don't need to take it. They were obviously around Fae."

"I suppose that's true. And from what I overheard, they will be around them in Serenity too. I just won't see them ever again."

"You can't relocate to Serenity with them?"

"I can't do business with people in a separate dimension."

Alexander frowned. "Why not? From the looks of things, that might be necessary. They'll be the only ones growing food."

"Access. I don't have access by any means to the place."

"There's a tunnel. One you can drive cattle through."

"With an opening barely large enough for a person to squeeze through. How do you get a whole *cow* through it? And remember, that town is occupied now. Military chest-puffing with another army, which, from what I can tell, doesn't even know they are *doing* it."

"I have a question for you. Are you upset about the lost trade, the lost village, or that you've lost your favorite place?"

"*Places.* Plural. I've lost my home in Patras, my home in Cliffport, and my home on the sea. If something happens to my offices, I'll be literally homeless. Right now, the only thing of value in my office is the building itself. The access to the port and shipping trade is gone. That's on top of having several contracts I need to fulfill that I can't anymore."

Alexander went over to her and hugged her. She accepted it.

"Is this a time where you need to find solutions, or just talk to release the frustration and anger so you can get to your own solution without interference?"

She looked at him. "That was incredibly insightful."

"I have been told I have a gift for saying the right thing."

She thought about it while continuing to hug him. "I'm not sure. I *definitely* feel the need to rage against the night, but I also don't see even the twinkle of a solution right now. I may need to sleep on it."

"I tried to give you time to rest but you decided to get up and wade through a healing pool."

She raised her head. "Yeah, that really did happen. It certainly helped me. I feel better than I have in years, since you healed me at the Drum and Nightingale three years ago."

"Tendays. That was three or four tendays ago."

"How...? No, you're right. Is it just that every hour brings something new?"

He kissed the top of her head. "Yes. I feel like a year has passed every time I sleep all night."

"Has word even gotten to York about your brother's death yet? Or Yndia? Or Mande?"

"It's definitely gotten to Mande. Cipriano offered his daughter to me. She's twelve."

"Wow. Horrible, but sadly not uncommon. Since women die in childbirth regularly, the rich men just purchase a new one and carry on, especially in Mande."

He looked down at her. "You good now?"

She nodded. "Thanks."

He stepped back. "I was hoping to talk to you. We have a lot of things coming up and I needed to know how to progress with them."

"Alright. Talk away. It might help my processing of my own issues." She sat on the bed.

"I love you. And I want to know where we stand."

She touched his hand and he took a knee before her. "I love you too. I really do. That's actually been something I'm warring with during all this. Slowly, being around you has removed nearly every option I have for *not* being your wife. It's almost like you *planned* it." Her eyes narrowed, though they had humor behind them.

"You've discovered my insidious plot. All of this has just been to convince you to marry me."

"So, you moved Giver and Bringer to woo little ol' me?"

"Had to release one from captivity to do it, remember?"

"Ah yes. My, you must really want me."

"I do."

She looked at the ceiling, her eyes narrowing. "To have such power over all the world in my hands."

"Hey, what other man can do that? I can point out several people from court just yesterday that can't."

"Ugh. Mentioning court is *not* a way to get me to join you."

He sat on the floor. "I remember a certain tea party where you told me you loved court."

"There were times when it was wonderful. When people were rewarded for their service. Those times were great. But the sycophants took that away. I saw so much backstabbing and ugliness there when I was staying with Elizabeth."

"That might have been a product of the previous influence of the Quill and Ink. I haven't used it since you gave me back the Power so it's possible court will be different now."

"You were there yesterday. Was it different?"

He looked at his hands folded in his lap. He sighed and shook his head. "No. It was just as bad. In fact, it was worse. I used to dodge them.

Gomez actually protected me from them. But I did it because I thought myself above it all. I knew I was going to sneak out and be gone for months pursuing something I loved. I never felt chained to it like Charles did. Now, I see what he meant."

"How did your mother manage it? She stayed rich throughout your father's reign, infidelities and all. I can name seven women off the top of my head who have lost a lot of their fortunes killing off unfaithful spouses."

"Oh, she handled it herself, the business part, I mean. I think it helped her feel like she had a place in the world. I remember her always writing letters and making business decisions for her holdings. She showed me those when I was younger."

Tanglwyst thought about this. "What do you *want* to do instead?"

Alexander leaned back on his hands. "Oh, let's see. I really liked healing those people in St. Andrew. I want to go to St. Marguerite and claim that forest as my own so I can use it to rebuild. I want to take Giles with us and use his magic to do that a lot quicker. I want to help the people in those cities to ride out these problems."

He frowned.

"What is it?"

"There are people in Marguerite that are stacked in the remaining houses that are homeless due to the fire. I want to see about bringing them to Serenity. I know it won't solve things permanently, but it will help while we get this all sorted out."

"Have you been to Serenity yet?"

"No. You?"

"No."

He reached out his hand. "Help me up. I want to see if we can take others there."

She pulled him to his feet and they left her room.

Giles and Brigit appeared in the storeroom at Persephone. He pointed to the tunnel. "It's this way."

"Raven warned us off this place once, remember?"

"Yeah. Now we know why."

They followed the vine-covered tunnel to the trap room. Lauriel came from behind Raven to growl at Giles. He walked over to Brigit and sat, tail sweeping a clean spot on the floor.

Raven lifted his head. "I'm seeing more people today than I did for years. Except when I was a cat, because tavern."

Brigit crouched to rub Lauriel's ears. "That's why they say if you're ever lost, stay put."

"I'll remember that next time I get lost."

Giles folded his arms across his chest. "We have a question. There was a Yokotaman woman at your Covenant before."

"Yes, Snow."

"Do you know her country's belief on where souls come from?"

Brigit looked at Giles, confused.

Raven frowned. "Uh, yeah. The entire culture is based upon ancestor worship and the air dragons. They govern the country. It was odd because they never seemed to move on. I have no idea where new souls come from but I decided, since it was from monsters, it must be the Land."

Brigit stood. "Monsters come from the Land?"

Giles flashed a glance over his shoulder at her. "Yeah. It's why my divine magic was so effective."

She blinked. "You are so *blissfully unaware* of your surroundings at all times, aren't you?"

Lauriel rolled his eyes. Raven shook his head and looked away from the man.

Giles realized his misstep. "I'm sorry."

Brigit snorted. "Yeah, well, you have your answer to that random question. Feel free to leave now."

"I was actually going to stay and help you, Raven. Myrgen said he brought you a letter from Merrick?"

"Yeah, but I can't read it."

Giles got a condescending look on his face. "Too complicated?"

"Too *wet.* Lauriel tried to hold it up for me and slobbered some details."

"Oh."

"Besides, this magic is a little too modern for you. It was written *this* century."

Brigit snorted a laugh.

Giles frowned but remained silent.

Brigit looked at Raven. "We also have a couple of shards so we can communicate with the others."

She pulled out the shards and Raven nodded to them. "Is that going to draw from Heaven if you use it?"

"Yes."

"Well, we need to not use those to contact them unless it's an emergency. I don't want to drain their resources."

Giles raised a finger. "I can power it. With my magic."

Raven arched an eyebrow. "What resource do you use that isn't powered either by Heaven or the Land?"

"Well, magic is its *own* resource."

"Man, you really *are* out of date. We learned in 1198 that magic grows from the Land unless its divine. It's been in the basic teachings of Magic Theory since then. That's why Fae do it so easily while the Church has to do it through ritual. Land creatures are naturally attuned and Divine creatures have to have a gift for it to work. Then that gift must be trained. You'd know that if you could read a current text book."

"Well, you weren't smart enough to preserve any through non-magical printing, were you?"

"No. *The Church* destroyed all magic *in your name.* Then some Archangel destroyed the last living mage before he could transfer them."

"Michael is dead."

Giles and Raven looked at Brigit.

"I thought you should know."

"That just means everyone was hurt for no reason."

"Not quite. Catriona killed him and returned his power to the Giver. So, there's that."

Raven looked at her, grimacing a little at the effort. "Thanks for telling me."

Giles folded his arms. "I would have told him."

Raven rolled his eyes. "Oh for- "

Brigit turned on Giles. *"It's not about you! None of this regards you at all! You are NOT the center of the universe, Giles! Your bloody opinion DOESN'T MATTER!* There are *literally* hundreds of thousands of people in this world who can do whatever you think makes you so *Stone bleeding ESSENTIAL.*

"You have *one job* in this world: Relocation of vulnerable families. *One* that can be performed by a *toddler* or this *dog* with a simple tool that a human king is currently wearing. *One!* Your ego has blinded you to people's suffering so much, I would have *you* into his trap but you don't have any *friends* that would help you *survive it!"*

She waved her hands dismissively, looking away from him. "You know what? Get out. Go back to being alone in your conch shell with the memories of your dead family. The living out here are trying to save the world. Go. This is a Land Place now. Get out."

Giles started to open his mouth and then he disappeared.

Brigit stopped, looking around. "What happened?"

"Oh Brigit, I could kiss you. You just declared this a Land place. *And it worked!* That means this area hasn't been claimed for holy ground to either side before now."

"What will that mean?"

"Well, a couple of things. First there's the boost to the region which shuts out the influence of the forest, which then boosts the fuel of the Fae. That's very important. Oh! And Catriona will like it for the picture things. Oh! And also, we can visit other places! But we need to not say anything about it to the, you know, because he will know it."

Brigit frowned. She looked at Lauriel. "You can't actually explain that, can you?"

Lauriel harrumphed.

"Okay, try again?"

Raven opened his mouth, then closed it and frowned. "I don't think it will make a difference. It's part of my nature to be confusing."

"Wait. Is... Is that why Lauriel was so vital to you? The Wisp Summons? Because you're half Fae."

"Yes. Someone finally figured it out! *Yes!* If he had died, I would not have had a way for the Summons to not explode me. And I would not be a very good person to have go on a killing spree."

Brigit sat on the ground, stunned by the revelation and the ramifications of the discovery. "No. If you have similar abilities to Giles, no. You going homicidal would be devastating."

Raven was bouncing in his manacles. "Exactly!"

"So... So, my declaration of this as Land means this is holy ground for the Bringer now?"

Lauriel nodded. Raven laughed. "Yes!"

"Which means things *not* of the Bringer can't be here if we don't want them here."

"Yes!"

She looked up at Raven in delight. *"Or LOOK here!"*

"Yes!"

"I just cut off the creator of the spell from watching this place!"

Lauriel licked her face joyfully and she hugged him.

"Now we can work on the spell and not risk giving away what we're doing. It's probably best not to mention the, you know, trap creator, though. They hear when their names are called."

Brigit straightened, nodding. "Like praying. Got it. Okay. So, what, what do we do now?"

"We work on that spell."

Brigit deflated. "I sent away the only other mage in the world."

"True, but you have made this a Fae sanctuary and Fae are naturally magical. And *you* are here and that's immensely better."

"Me? How?"

"You don't slobber."

Brigit laughed. "Here. Let me look at this thing. I might be able to figure it out."

"How?"

"I was an artist before I was a saint. And frankly, lamp black is *very* difficult to get out. The page below will be stained. All I have to do is clean it. And I'm *very* good at cleaning scrolls. Is there a desk and a few supplies around this place?"

"Lauriel, get the lady her supplies!"

Lauriel barked.

"Oh. That's true. Brigit, follow Lauriel. He'll take you to the best place possible. Merrick's old lab."

Lauriel created some stairs so she could get out and they left with a wave and a smile.

Thirty-Three

"Giving birth should be your greatest joy, not your greatest fear."
-The Forty-Five Voices

Giles popped into the half-empty Great Hall as Tanglwyst and Alexander were looking around.

"Ah, there you are. Can you take Tangl and I to Serenity? We would like to see if it can handle a few more people."

"Uh, yeah. Sure."

He put his hands on their shoulders and they arrived in a sunny, warm location. People were already walking in and out of elaborate houses shaped like conch shells, soft pink blending into pale orange, then into white.

Tanglwyst looked around shocked. "Who *built* this?"

"A troll, actually. Brigit threw me out of Persephone."

They both looked at him. Alexander furrowed his brow in confusion. "How?"

"She said, 'Get out. This is a Land place now.' Screamed it, actually. Next thing I knew, I was talking to you two."

Alexander and Tanglwyst exchanged a look. She nodded to Alexander. He nodded back.

"It's a good thing she did that. If she declared it a Land place, isn't that like you declaring the Haunted Covenant a holy place? It becomes a domain, right?"

"Yeah. I just… I keep messing things up with her. I just don't know how to talk to her."

"Uh, well, what do you keep saying?"

"Giles, while you and Alexander talk about this, I'm going to look around so I can see about bringing my office here. Is that okay?"

"Huh? Oh, sure. There are offices over there in that building for the city. You can set up in there, if you like."

"Thank you."

"Well, like today, I was just telling Raven how I was his only option and…"

Tanglwyst walked quickly out of earshot. She went into the municipal offices and saw the remains of what might have been a scuffle. Rowena was looking around as well.

"Hello!" The jewelry maker walked up to Tanglwyst and they exchanged a hug.

"How are you doing?"

"It's been interesting, I'll admit." Rowena tossed her long, brown hair over her back. She had a lone white stripe framing her face.

"It looks like there was a battle or something."

"Yeah. But it was *so* long ago, there's no trace. I can tell something was on these shelves, but no idea what. Lovely architecture, isn't it?"

Tanglwyst smiled. "Yeah. It really is."

"Did you see the town square?"

"This isn't it?"

"No. There are a lot of stores in there. I'll show you."

They walked out the front door and around the road which spiraled into the center of town. The City Hall was across from the Tavern which then fed into more and more houses, all again shaped like conch shells.

"Have you looked in the houses?"

Rowena nodded. "They are interesting. Inside is pretty normal. The bedrooms are upstairs, living areas downstairs. But the shell reflects the light of either the sunrise or the sunset into the bedrooms, depending upon which side of the street you are on. And casts this beautiful, warm glow inside. I can only imagine how my jewelry is going to shine in here."

She gestured to a medium-sized building. They entered and Tanglwyst marveled at the abalone shelves and display cases. Each shelf shone in the ample light coming in the window.

"This is beautiful."

"Come see the work area."

Rowena took her in the back.

"This is just like your set up in St. Giles."

"Well, my set up wasn't unique. Worktable, stove, drawers, pegs. Honestly, this could be a butcher shop as easily as a jewelry store. I do like the storage room though. And there's a bedroom upstairs with its own privy. I was a little unsure about that but I ended up trying it."

"And?"

"It's a miracle of modern architecture."

"Do all the shops look like this?"

"Yeah. Almost identical."

"Hm. Do you think it will work for you?"

Rowena glanced around. "Yeah. I mean, I know our homes are destroyed. I don't want to work in a place where some corrupted priest built a weapon that murdered a hundred Fae. I couldn't walk in there after he did that. I'm just glad I wasn't there when it happened because he would have killed me."

"Where were you?"

"Honestly? Looking for the Prince. He asked me to build him something. I didn't get the chance to, but I drew up a design."

She opened a drawer in the workroom and pulled out a ring design.

"That's beautiful."

"He asked for an overlapping design of Saints Giles and Michael in silver. I think he was trying to put something on you that would protect you from Fae magic."

"Oh. I wouldn't worry about that now. I'm not concerned about that."

"He also didn't realize I was part Fae or a Land Worshipper. I was never going to make this for him. He was expecting *real* silver and I can't do that. It's only my considerable human parts that enable me to even touch silver at all. But since he was trying to protect himself or you or whomever from the Queen, I knew the real thing would matter. I wasn't about to risk their life by not using the right stuff.

"Oh, speaking of which, I saw that your ship was lost."

"Saw it?"

"Yeah. I went outside to get an idea where we might be and saw the entire center of your ship in the front yard. I knew it was yours by the banisters."

"I never went outside. I think I believed seeing it would make it real."

"You've lost a lot over all this. I heard you were put under house arrest. That Gomez fellow suggested maybe he should seize your office for the Crown."

"I'm glad he didn't try."

"Me too."

"I have to get back out on the sea. I have your ores to pick up."

"Hey, I won't need those for a while. Monique says there are Fae in the tavern that keep the food stocked. We don't need money here right now. We'll be fine."

"Alexander and I are going to go around the country getting people who are suffering from the weather and bringing them to the two Covenants. I think the city folk will appreciate the Haunted Covenant, while the country folks who know how to harvest and grow things can come here. What do you think?"

"Well, keep in mind that people living here won't be paying taxes to the Crown of Mervolingia."

"That's true." Tanglwyst looked at the buildings outside. "I'm going to rescue Alexander now. He's giving relationship advice to Giles."

"The Stones help us all."

She went back to the area where she left the men and saw they were gone. She started to get angry when she saw Monique standing in the doorway of the tavern, cleaning a cup. Tanglwyst walked over to her and saw Alexander and Giles drinking ales and toasting friends. Alexander looked up and saw her, then stood.

"The Lady has returned. As promised, I must depart. You keep practicing."

"I shall. Thank you, Your Majesty."

Alexander bustled past Monique and slipped her a small gold ring with a ruby on it. "For your trouble."

266

She looked at it and arched her eyebrow. "You expect him to be *this* much trouble?"

"I'm not taking anything for granted. You ready to go, My Lady?"

"Sure. Where to?"

"Did you see anything here you... wanted?"

"Honestly, I don't know. I'll have to give it some thought."

He turned to her and took both of her hands. "Tell me where you want to go and I will take you there."

She looked around. "I need to go back to the Haunt."

"'Haunt'"?

"Yes. That's what I saw Giles write down."

"Your room?"

"The Great Hall."

They returned there. She looked around. Jude was talking to some people who were waiting for Giles to return. She saw Captain Nesbit and waved to him.

"I need to talk to the Captain. Will you speak to Jude?"

"What do I need to talk to him about?"

"He's the Patron Saint of Hopeless Cases. You have a Coronation problem."

Alexander nodded and walked off. Tanglwyst went to her friend and sat on the table near him.

"My Lady. You look as sad and displaced as I feel."

"We have contracts to fulfill. Any idea how we'll do it?"

He shook his head. "Without a ship to get the dirt, we can't."

"I've been thinking about that. Did Giles *really* remove the whole middle of the ship?"

"You still haven't been up to see it?"

"I've been..."

"Afraid?"

"Seeing her like that would... break my heart. I know it."

"What are you going to do?"

She looked at the stairs. "I guess I'm going to break my heart."

He stood and offered his arm. She looked at Alexander and he watched her, concerned. She eased his concern with a smile and went upstairs.

The landing above was nothing like she expected. She didn't know what she thought it would be like but she never expected it to be a cellar.

The place was in disrepair and looked scary and unsettling. She was glad she wasn't alone.

They went up the cellar stairs to the kitchen of an inn. The place had furnishings covered in white cloths. These moved in the wind that howled through the cracks in the walls. A light dusting of snow revealed the holes in the floor so they were able to avoid twisting an ankle. The shutters clattered against glassless windows.

By the time they stepped outside, she was happy to be in the open cold.

"That place is unsettling."

"It's called the Haunt. See?" He pointed to a sign hanging on creaking iron chains. The sign proclaimed it *The Haunt Tavern.*

"That's a tavern?"

"Apparently."

Then she saw the hulk of the ship, covered in snow. It had fallen on its side, the Crow's Nest only ten feet above the ground. Her flag was draped in snow and stiff from ice.

She pulled her doublet around her tighter and walked over to it. The deck was miraculously intact. The shards of dome were still attached to the railings on the sides and her quarters were not there but she could see two officer quarters were still mostly there. The beds were secured to the deck by frames but in swivels, like a hammock, so they were dangling suspended, waiting for their masters to take a nap.

She saw the rest of it was stripped bare. Worse, half her secret passages were laid bare. The shipwrights who built it were no longer around, having built her twins and then retired on the money she spent. She touched the wood and it was still strong. The cuts were clean.

This practically looks salvageable.

She wasn't sure but she still felt like it had its spirit. It *knew* her.

The wind howled through the area and she climbed into the tilted ship to get out of it. She walked on the wall and jumped across an open door.

The Captain followed her. They got to a spot that was sheltered but still had light coming in.

"Can you feel that?" She still had to raise her voice a bit but at least she could hear herself.

"What?"

"The ship is still alive. It's just been amputated."

268

"What are you thinking?"

"We know a shipwright."

David's eyes widened. "That we do. That we do. But how would we get it there?"

"We might have to bring in Giles for it. Are you okay with that?"

David thought about it, then nodded. "I think I am."

Alexander watched Tanglwyst and Captain Nesbit go upstairs and felt a little pang of jealousy. He shoved that aside and looked at Jude again.

"I'm sorry, what?"

"Your Coronation. What needs to be done?"

"Yes. Well, I need to have new clothes, which means being near a clothier consistently so I can be fitted. So that's a challenge. There needs to be a time for confession and absolution so I go in pure to the throne, no sins. I need to make sure the arrangements for the ball, feast, etc. are being handled. I think my mother is already on top of that.

"The army has to be recalled so I need to get this situation in Cliffport sewn up. You know, I'm surprised at how easily I'm calling it Cliffport now."

"Oh, that's because the church was destroyed."

"What?"

"Yeah. The Church implanted holy stones in the rafters to rework the magic in the area after the Soulless War. I got credited with that idea so I have a strong handle on that process."

"Did you inspire it?"

"No. Not even a little bit."

"Huh. Alright. Anyway, under normal circumstances, I'd be assigned a wife, bishop, and household. Later, I'd be shoved into a crown, shoved into a marriage, and shoved into a woman, all with as many people as possible looking on."

"Okay, that sounds like a nightmare."

"I've watched it happen twice. My first brother did so when I was four, so I didn't have to watch too much of it. I was sixteen when Charles finally went through it all. Mother felt he needed to be a king before he became a husband and father. He actually defied her on both accounts."

"And what about you?"

"All I really care about is making sure my people are safe. I have a lot of things to fix from when I was under the influence of an evil amulet. And some evil ink. There's been a lot of evil dark stuff in my life…"

He stopped, thinking.

"What is it?"

"I think I just realized what that ink in my brother's room is. Excuse me a moment."

Alexander disappeared and arrived in the King's bedroom. Nina and Catherine were there, along with Emmy. He marched over to the desk.

"Mother, which is the Quill and Ink?"

She frowned. "I…" She looked at the three identical bottles.

He put all three on a tray with the golden quill he had used to write Nicolai's Writ of Destruction, then took them to the long table. He turned his back to the table and threw all three bottles and the quill into the fire.

All three shattered but the one on the left *screamed*. The quill was destroyed in an instant.

Nina and Catherine ran over, Catherine picking up Emmy and shielding her from the fire. The ink burned quick and he exhaled as he watched it.

"What was *that*?" Catherine's voice displayed her horror as easily as her face did.

"It's a sound I've heard before. When Tanglwyst burned the amulet that corrupted me."

Catherine handed Emmy to Nina. "It's the same thing?"

"Yes. And every time someone used it, their eyes swirled like ink, *that* ink, in water. Because it can't abide fire."

"Where did it come from?"

He looked back at the fire. "That I don't know. But I suspect the Church."

Nina gasped. "I beg your pardon, Your Majesties. The *Church*? I'm sure you're wrong."

Catherine shook her head. "No. He's right. The Church built several gifts for the ruling monarchs in the world, to try and control them. For Mande, it's the custom jewel in the Royal Crown. For us, it was this Quill

270

and Ink for decrees. For York, it's the Scepter of State. They are required to be used at all the Coronation ceremonies.

"By the Church."

"I can't believe it."

Catherine turned to her. "You can't? You can't believe a Church that ordered the Inquisition would do something like this?"

"The… that was to destroy heretics and mages."

"The Pure Birth Requirement is the work of the Inquisition, Nina. Surely you knew that."

Nina tore her eyes away from the fireplace. "It was?"

Alexander looked back and forth between the women. "Pure Birth Requirement?"

"If a child is born and it is suspected it has any kind of spiritual connection *other* than to Heaven, it is to be killed on the spot by the mother. If she will not, then she will be killed as well after watching the child die."

"At birth?" It was Alexander's turn to be horrified.

Nina looked away, unable to meet the King's eyes. "Yes. So, if a child is born in a tavern, or a wood, or pond, it is to be killed at once. Because the soul is not of Heaven and is unclean. It will become a monster if this is not done."

Catherine's voice was cold and flat. "The Inquisition murdered thousands of women and children, burnt every inn and tavern, and set fire to the woods where they could. It's where much of our farmland came from in Mervolingia. Every tree we have except the woods around St. Teresa are new growth from the destruction of the woods. They were harvested for use in rebuilding the cities. The rest of the woods were left to rot along the Caratian border."

"And this is still practiced?" Alexander ran his fingers through his hair, incredulous.

"Yes."

"How often?"

"Your children will be spared if you are Coronated, Alex. It is assumed all children born in the Palace are on holy ground."

"You think I care about my hypothetical children? This is *barbaric*! How can this still be going on?"

"There's a way to get away from it." Nina finally met Alexander's eyes.

He dropped his hands onto the table. "Speak. Please."

"I have never used it. But I know women who have. There is an underground. But I don't know how to get in touch with it. I've never had to. Both my daughters were born in the Church birthing halls."

"We can't let this happen anymore. Mother, what can we do?"

Nina blinked. "Sire?"

"I can't have this happen. No woman should ever have to go through that."

"It was one of the founding principles of the Emilianite church, my son. That's why it was so popular so quickly."

"But Emilianite souls still come from Heaven."

Catherine nodded.

"Sire, how did you *get here*?"

Alexander looked at Nina. "Saint Giles walks the earth right now. He made an amulet that takes me places. He will join me, if you need him to. In fact, I need to discuss this with you. Nina, are you free at the moment?"

"No, I'm really not and I need to go right now."

She ran for the door with Emmy.

Thirty-Four

"The most dangerous people are the liars who believe they are telling the truth."
-The Forty-Five Voices

Catherine grabbed Alexander. "Run. Don't use the amulet. She's afraid."

Alexander ran after Nina. The Captain stopped at the hall a moment, looking panicked.

"Nina, what's wrong?"

She took off down the hallway and ran into Elizabeth's bedroom. She locked the door behind her. Alexander pounded on the door. Catherine turned to a guard. "Bring the Chatelaine. We need this door opened."

The other guard outside the door came up to him. "Should I break it down, Your Majesty?"

"A solid oak door? No. We couldn't do that. Not in time. Keep talking to her."

Alexander ran back to the King's bedroom and went into the secret passage. This one was a straight shot outside, unlike Elizabeth's. If she took the secret passage, she would be in the catacombs, which were dangerous if you didn't know them.

Once in the passage, out of sight or everyone else, he pulled out the Bringer shard. He may have grown up here, but only one person knew these tunnels.

"Myrgen."

Myrgen's face appeared in the shard. "Need help already, Alexander?"

"Yes, but not about that. Where are you?"

"Outside the Haunted Covenant, looking at Tangl's ship with her."

Tanglwyst's face moved next to his. "Alexander? You left so suddenly. What's wrong?"

"I have a problem. I'm in the King's secret passage. Nina just grabbed Emmy and ran off with her."

"What? Why?"

"I don't know. But I don't know the catacombs."

Myrgen nodded. "Right. Not like I do. Have you been to the crashed ship?"

"Just think of going here." She turned the shard to show the *Sulocco's* Crow's Nest.

Alexander envisioned the Nest. He appeared in it and fell out into the snow immediately. Tanglwyst and Myrgen ran over to him.

Tanglwyst crouched beside him. "Are you alright?"

"No. My pride is broken."

Myrgen offered a hand to help him up.

Alexander winced. "Yeah, I'm gonna need to fix that. Hang on."

He disappeared, then reappeared about ten seconds later with wet pant legs. He looked at Tanglwyst. "You coming?"

"No. Go."

Myrgen and Alexander disappeared.

Nina locked the door and set Emmy down to look around.

There's an escape passage in here. I know it. All the royal rooms have one.

She looked at the prayer nave and started moving votives, looking for the catch. She heard Alexander talking to someone, then it was quiet. She tucked her hair behind her left ear. She didn't know how long she had. Alexander had appeared out of nowhere and made *ink scream*. How long had he been dealing with dark magic? She remembered the guards saying he had cut Elizabeth down without so much as a blink. Then she was told how he had fought Nicolai in Rouen.

Apparently, he has been like this for a while. That must be what he was doing every summer.

She had been told about the evils of magic since she was a child. Her time in the Church seminary had been one lesson on witches and mages after another, how they sold the world to monsters who consumed people's souls. The tapestries on the walls and carvings on the backs of the pews were always at eye level for children so they could learn about the horrors of wizards and fantastic beasts. When she heard the Kraktens were part monster, she never believed them. Then she saw the drawings in different books and had nightmares for a month.

If he found her, he might kill her. He'd have to. She knew his secret.

Catherine was speaking now, but Nina focused. None of the votives moved anything so she started feeling the wall that was the most likely to have a passage behind it. After a moment, she found a stone that clicked. The passage opened but it was black as midnight in there.

She grabbed Emmy and a votive and stepped into the catacombs.

"Night night?"

Nina glanced down at Emmy. "No dear. Not night time. We're going *exploring*. We're looking for… kitties."

"Kitties!"

"Yes. But they're black kitties so they're very hard to see. Can you help me keep an eye out for them?"

"Kitties!"

"Kitties!" Nina smiled and moved quickly down the passage.

She found wide stairs down and saw a lump on a wall. She held the votive up to it and saw it was a torch. She lit it quickly, allowing her to assess her surroundings. She almost took it from the sconce but that would give away her position in the dark. Better to leave it and use the votive to light their way.

She heard someone talking, then silence and realized she didn't have any more time to waste. She tucked her hair behind her ear again, then focused, trying to hear any indicators of where to go.

"Kitty?"

Nina looked at Emmy, who was touching a wall stone. The wall gave way to a passage and Nina hurried to it. She looked around, and took Emmy's hand to lead her inside, closing the passage behind her. She checked the hallway, noting in the dim light that it formed a T. She looked left and right but didn't see anything in the low light.

This is an escape passage. This has to have an escape.

She turned right and walked down the hallway. It ended in a closed door. She opened it and was surprised to smell something akin to perfume, but old. Had the door not been closed, it would have long since faded but the bed here smelled like a woman.

She saw no passage out except where she came in so she backtracked and took the other passage. She didn't go very far before she noticed something moving down the hall. She pushed Emmy behind her and proceeded forward, her knife drawn.

A bloody shift, snagged on several boards blocking off another passage, moved in a slight, chilly breeze from the other side of the boards. They were not a solid blockade, but more haphazard, like they only wanted to discourage people from entering, not block off the passage completely. A small piece of cloth lay on the ground on the other side. Nina listened for noises of pursuit and heard none. She lowered the votive to inspect the boards. They were old and already cracked. She could see footprints in the dirt on the other side.

Someone's been through here. Two people. Recently. There's a way out through here.

She took the shift and wrapped it around the center of a cracked board. Then she moved Emmy back.

"Watch out, honey."

She kicked the board where the shift was. It cracked more but the fabric muffled the sound so it didn't carry. She smiled. She kicked at it a few more times until the board gave way. She heard voices behind her and stopped to see if they were coming in. They faded away. She kicked again to make sure the board was broken and then she grabbed the shift and pulled it away.

The opening was small, so she held the fragments of the board back.

"Emmy, go through there. Can you climb through there, honey?"

"Why?"

"There's a kitty over there."

"Kitty!"

Emmy crawled in through the hole and Nina saw it was probably big enough for her as well, but would be too big for Alexander.

He's using magic though. He's a heretic. He needs to be stopped before he corrupts Emmy. If I can get us out of here, I can get us to the Bishop. I can stop him. I can save Emmy's soul, and the kingdom.

Emmy plopped through on the other side and started to toddle off into the dark.

"Emmy, don't wander off." Nina whispered her command and Emmy obeyed, at least for the moment.

Nina bent over and wriggled into the opening. It was tight. The boards scraped her skin through the shift and her uniform, but nothing ripped. However, the uniform was a problem.

She pulled herself out and started taking off the doublet, listening the whole time. She got the doublet off and threw it into the hole, then climbed through. Then she heard the sound of stone on stone and things grew brighter. She reached down and grabbed the votive, and saw light coming down the hallway.

"Nina! Emmy!"

Alexander's voice carried through the stone passages. She arranged the shift as it had been, then put the votive under her coat and moved to the side of the broken boards, several steps away.

"Emmy?"

That's Myrgen. Has Alexander fallen in with the traitor now too? I thought Myrgen was executed by Aethelraed? I saw the message myself.

She heard them come down the passage.

"This is where Tanglwyst was held, and down there was where we put Tib, er Alan."

"Emmy!"

Emmy was a little way away in the dark, too far for Nina's comfort but she couldn't do anything about it right then. They couldn't get through the boards and Emmy was looking at something else.

"Emmy!"

"Awex?"

The torchlight shone through the boards. "Emmy, honey? Where's Nina?"

"Nina."

"I can't see you, honey. Come here."

"Nina."

"Alexander, that's the burnt-out church, where Catriona and I escaped from. I know how to get there. It's dangerous. There are rotted boards everywhere."

"Go. I'll keep her here. Nina? Where are you? Why did you take Emmy?"

Nina looked around in the illuminated area. She saw little footsteps leading off into the dark.

Why isn't Emmy afraid of the dark, like my girls?

She moved carefully, quietly, away from Alexander. Emmy was moving up ahead.

"Kitty?"

Nina suddenly realized what Emmy was chasing was probably not a cat, but a rat or worse.

"Emmy. Leave the kitty. Emmy."

Her whisper sounded loud in her ears and she looked back. Alexander started pulling on the boards, the torch on her side of the barricade, lying on the ground. She realized she only had a few moments before he broke through.

"Emmy, where are you?"

"Nina?"

"Emmy?" She pulled out the votive and saw Emmy standing near a dark hole in the floor. Nina's heart thumped with fear.

"Emmy, come here."

Emmy turned and Nina saw her back towards the hole. She was smiling, like she was playing a game.

"Emmy, come here, right now."

Emmy stopped, just as her heel would have gone into the hole. Nina rushed over to her and grabbed her. She picked her up, dropping the votive and her doublet. The votive fell over and spilled wax onto the doublet, but the wick burned brighter, casting a small amount of light. Nina looked around and stepped away from the hole.

Suddenly, Alexander was right in front of her. She screamed and stepped back.

278

The floor gave way and Alexander reached out, grabbing for Emmy. *Don't let him touch her!*

Nina twisted away, stopping him from grabbing them as Alexander teleported away. Nina fell through the floor, realizing Emmy was now beneath her. She landed on her and felt several little bones break. Something speared through her chest and suddenly, she couldn't breathe.

Sovereigna heard a noise and looked up at the window. She had just gotten dressed and walked over to it, smiling at the sunshine on her face. A little girl with red hair was in the town square. No one else was around her.

Sovereigna went down to see her, looking to see if anyone else was going to greet the child. She was far too young to be here.

"Hello, sweetie. What's your name?"

"Emmy."

"Where did you come from, Emmy?"

"Night night."

Sovereigna knelt beside her and looked into her daughter's eyes. Her blood ran cold.

"Who's your momma, child?"

"Momma?" The child looked around. "Nina? Awex?"

Awex? Alex?

"Alexander?" Her eyes displayed the panic she felt.

"Awex!"

By the Fae. No.

Sovereigna picked up the child and closed her eyes as the tears came.

Alistair felt a surge and looked at the Giver. "Who do you love?"

The Giver cocked her head. "Love?"

He looked at Uriel, then back at her. "No. You wouldn't. You've been gone too long. I need Catriona."

He turned away from the Giver and ran over to Catriona, sitting among the pillows. He fell to his knees and kissed her.

"Remember that? Do you remember loving me?"

She pushed him back. "Yes. Of course."

"And them. You remembered them." He gestured to the incense house attendants.

"Alistair, what's wrong?"

"You have people you love. Your family, your crew. You are tied to this world. You have *connected* to this world. Please. Hold onto that. Hold onto how many people you love."

"Alistair, they've moved on. Drake, Anika, Tib. They've moved on. They're gone."

"Octavius."

"He's with Estelle. The *Enigma* is dead."

"No. No… You… you need to love something. Something you want to preserve. You are Caratia's protector."

"I am the Land's Protector. I am its people's protector."

"Then *protect* them."

"What has happened?"

"Protect them!"

And suddenly, she was back in her meditation chamber.

Thirty-Five

"In politics, if you want something said, ask a man. If you want something done, ask a woman."
-The Forty-Five Voices

"General?"

Aethelraed opened his eyes. "Yes, soldier?"

"See? I told you I saw him move. Sir, we can't find Commander Manglebottom."

Aethelraed frowned and sat up. "What?"

"And the golden knight is back."

The soldier speaking nodded to the window. Aethelraed stood up and looked outside. He heard a terrible howling.

"What's that sound?"

"It just started. It's coming from the valley."

Aethelraed opened the door and walked outside. "Can I help you?"

"I'm Saint George of Canterbury. This is Saint Clara, Patron Saint of Barren Women."

"You really don't need to introduce me like that. This man isn't a barren woman. Clara is fine."

"A pleasure, My Lady. Please come inside. Quickly. We've had some trouble from the Fae army firing on people."

He hustled them into the barracks and closed the door.

"Gentlemen, please watch for any activity."

"Yes sir."

"Now, what can I do for you?"

George motioned to some chairs and the three of them sat. "There have been several developments that we need to talk to you about. They concern your army's actions, going forward."

Aethelraed stayed silent but his eyes kept flicking to activities on the street. The buildings just beyond the town square had not been destroyed and two archers lay on the roof he could see. They were talking and agitated.

"Excuse me a moment sir." He stood and went to his soldier, whose shirt was bulky from the bandages under it.

"What is going on there? Can you tell?"

"No. The best vantage point in the city is next to that building the archers are on. It's got a window that faces the battlefield."

"Then the soldiers inside should have intel. Where is the next in line for that position?"

"Here? No one."

Aethelraed sighed. He looked at the Saints. "My Lady, as a saint, are you immortal?"

"I… yes, we believe so."

"Then we need to continue this discussion from a different place. I need to know what is happening."

He opened the door and the three left the building, following the injured soldier. He ran to the building next to the Tanglwyst Trading Company. The soldier opened the door. He led them up to the second floor and to a room with an east-facing window. A tower shield with a small viewing slot had been put against it. Two soldiers were present, one sitting at a desk, writing on paper.

"Now they are reaching into the fissures."

The soldier at the desk turned to the newcomers and stood. "General."

The soldier at the window turned, dropping a slot guard on the shield. "Please don't cross in front of the window. They're deadly shots."

Aethelraed looked at the floor and tower shield and saw blood splatter surrounding the slot. The soldier was holding a mirror.

Clara's eyes went wide at the implied horror. She looked at George, who stepped protectively in front of her.

Aethelraed turned to the soldier at the desk. "Is that a report?"

"Yes. The Krakten army just started screaming and wailing a couple minutes ago. We've been watching their activities. They are… confusing, and horrific. Sir, we think they might be preparing to attack."

He handed Aethelraed the mirror and opened the slot in the shield.

George stepped closer. "Please. Allow me. I can't be killed."

Aethelraed handed George the mirror and moved out of the way. George shifted Clara behind him, out of the line of fire, and frowned, assessing.

"They are four very large ogres reaching into a steaming fissure. The heat doesn't seem to be injuring them. They are adding the hot mud to a pile. Another group of these are… it looks like they are taking the mud away…"

"Where?"

"I can't see, General. Not from this limited vantage. Hang on."

George moved the tower shield to the side and looked around. A heavy thud hit him in the visor, knocking him back. Several more hit the room, splashing mud so hot, it started to burn the floor. George flung the mud on his visor aside.

"They are making an arsenal."

Aethelraed and the soldier moved the tower shield back in place but it was hit a second after it was placed. The slot was opened and the mirror employed while George removed his helmet, which was starting to steam. They watched the tower shield wood get a little darker on this side.

"The mud is on fire."

Aethelraed looked at the mud on the floor. There was no flame, but it was definitely scoring the wood.

George dropped his helmet as it started to turn red from the heat. "What *is* this stuff?"

"I don't know." The floor started to smoke and he glanced at the window as another clod hit the shield. "Get out. Everyone, get out now!"

They all got outside as little wisps of smoke started to rise from the opposite side of the building.

Clara's eyes fell on the building next door and the sign above the door.

The Tanglwyst Trading Company.

She saw that the mud clods were focusing upon this house in front of them and that the clods would splatter, coating everything nearby. Spots on the ground where the mud hit the remaining grass had blacked freckles. She glanced at the office next door and noticed something.

The wood isn't burning.

"George, we need to get Giles and Tanglwyst here."

"Why Tanglwyst?"

"Call it a hunch. I think she can help. Something is *definitely wrong*."

Aethelraed moved them all towards the guard office as fast as he could across the open area. Once inside, the soldiers stood watch by the front door.

"I'm sorry to have put you in that danger. I didn't expect that."

"General, this is why we need to talk. There is a lot you don't know right now."

Clara looked at George. "We can talk about that in a minute. Use a shard. See if you can reach Giles."

He pulled out a shard and focused. "Giles."

Giles appeared a few moments. "George. Yes?"

"Something is happening with the Fae army. Can you come here?"

"Yeah. Hang on. Where are you?"

"The City Guard Office in Cliffport."

"Will do."

Clara turned the shard her way. "Bring Tanglwyst."

"Okay."

The shard went dark.

Aethelraed looked at the soldiers, then back at the Saints, motioning them to sit by the fireplace. "You might need to watch yourself. Such might be viewed as witchcraft by less informed folks, and Alexander has already got them talking about such things."

George straightened, glancing at the soldiers but not lowering his voice. "Your King has seen Heaven with his own eyes. The Saints still in place are working to continue our task and support the human race. But we are going to have a fight on our hands on multiple fronts if we don't step in the right places in the next few hours. He needs to be Coronated, which means he'll need the army back in place in Patras."

"I can't leave this area while a hostile force inhabits that valley."

"I know. So, either Clara and I can stay here and take care of the protection of the area, or she and I can attend his Majesty."

"How would the two of you defend this area?"

"I'm Saint George of Canterbury."

Clara leaned forward. "Sir, what happens to them if they come through that fire?"

"Well, it burned the King. I imagine it will do worse to them."

"And the only way to go out of there traps them forever in the woods?"

Aethelraed folded his arms across his chest. "Yes, that's the belief."

"Then there's nothing they can do that doesn't imprison or destroy them. You aren't needed here. But Alexander needs you there."

Aethelraed frowned. "My lady, I agree with you about the situation here. But my presence at the Coronation would damn him, not Crown him. I do not swear my loyalty to the King automatically. I have to judge his worthiness. At this time, I have seen no leadership from him at all. This is a military situation that should be uppermost in his agenda and he has popped in and disappeared over and over. Allegedly, there was a peace treaty reached but no one got the chance to write it down? Just a message saying an agreement was made and would be put to pen the next morning. That was days ago.

"Now the Queen he made that agreement with is dead and I was just told my Intelligence Officer is missing. I am now caught up on things that have nothing to do with this conflict. Now I need to be brought up to speed on things that *center* on this conflict. Is he available for that or not?"

George and Clara looked at each other. Aethelraed stood.

"Then thank you very much for your update, but I need to focus upon my own responsibilities. I have an officer to find."

"He might be at the blind in the woods."

Aethelraed arched an eyebrow at George. "What blind?"

"What was that?"

Giles shook his head. "I have no idea."

Tanglwyst frowned. "Hand me the other shard."

"Wait." The shard they were holding lit up.

Lucifer's face filled the shard. "Catriona's back. Just arrived."

"I knew it. Can you have her contact us on the Bringer shard?"

"Yes."

The other shard glowed and Tanglwyst looked at it. "Are you alright?"

"Alistair sent me back, just now. He said I needed to protect my people. What's wrong?"

Tanglwyst swallowed. "I think something's happened to Emmy."

"Oh no. Where is Alexander?"

"I don't know. I think he went to Patras. But there was an awful screaming noise coming from the village when we just talked to George and Clara."

Catriona exhaled. "I understand."

"We're meeting George and Clara in Cliffport at the City Guard Office. Can you get there?"

"Yes, but it will take me a few minutes to get there. Can you keep them occupied?"

"I can try. See you there. And dress for the occasion." The shard went dark and she looked at Giles. "Let's go."

"And your ship?"

She looked back at the hulk. "She isn't going anywhere without me."

Giles put a hand on her shoulder and they disappeared.

Tanglwyst and Giles arrived at the Guards' Office. Aethelraed bowed in greeting. He hugged Tanglwyst.

"So good to see you, my dear. Why are you out here?"

Giles smiled. "We believe we have a solution."

Aethelraed turned to Giles. "I was speaking to the Lady. Please sit down."

Clara smiled.

"Thank you."

Tanglwyst let the howling fill the room. It was amplified by the lack of a wall in the jail cell. The sound echoed around the room.

"What do you propose?"

Giles almost spoke but Aethelraed put his hand up right in front of his face.

She turned to the window. "Her."

Everyone looked.

Aethelraed frowned. "Wait. She's… she's dead."

"Please. You don't have what it takes to kill her."

Tanglwyst went for the door. Aethelraed grabbed her arm. "My Lady, please. That woman is dangerous. She fought and killed an Archangel."

"Then I'm pretty sure I'd rather she was on our side." She pulled from Aethelraed's hold and stepped outside. The two soldiers watched her go, then looked at the General.

"We should be with her, Sir."

Aethelraed looked at the men, then nodded. "Indeed we should."

They all followed her outside.

Tanglwyst bowed to Catriona as the soldiers and General joined her outside. The soldiers stepped protectively in front of her, drawing their weapons. Tanglwyst tried not to hold it against them, but she had really wanted the chance to talk to Catriona without a watchdog. Any comment that indicated they were in touch with "the enemy" could go very badly for Alexander. Catriona looked at her as she strode closer, and Tanglwyst felt herself be read by the Caratian warrior.

The Bringer of Death was wearing a Caratian long coat, boots, gloves, and her hair was untethered. She looked just like she always did before a trip at sea, minus the hair. She looked at the soldiers and Tanglwyst saw her read them too, and watched them react to the penetrating gaze. She swept over Aethelraed as well, but he did not seem to respond.

"General."

"My Lady. We meet again."

Catriona said nothing.

Tanglwyst straightened, exhaling. "My apologies for the loss of your messenger."

"My condolences on the loss of your brother. So now we know how the *men* will act."

The soldiers bristled, taking a step forward. Aethelraed put a hand on Tanglwyst's shoulder. The wailing was setting all their bodies on edge except Catriona's, who was relaxed and still poised to attack.

"What do you plan to do here now, Ma'am?" Aethelraed's voice was steady, though Tanglwyst could feel the tension in his hand.

All around the town, soldiers and guards were showing up in the square in answer to the wailing screams. They saw Catriona in the center and a few of them recognized her. Suddenly, a large ball of steaming mud flew into the barrier. It disrupted it, causing the blue fire to sputter out all along the battlefield. The soldiers and guards threw their hands up to cover their heads but the mud completely missed Catriona and the group with Tanglwyst completely. Fae warriors screamed their war cries and charged the openings.

The soldiers and guards moved forward and Aethelraed pointed a sword at Catriona's throat. "Call them off."

Arrows from the rooftops fired as the mud balls smashed against the cobblestones. Several were pelted off their perches. The holder of the Blue Bow put an arrow at Catriona's feet from behind. Tanglwyst pushed Aethelraed aside and stepped forward. She looked at the soldiers.

"Enough!"

The men stepped back, startled. They looked at the women, then back at the rushing hordes almost to the extinguished barrier.

Tanglwyst looked at Catriona. "We could really use your help."

Catriona lifted her head. Her eyes turned to jade green and a black stone sword filled with golden flecks rose slowly from the ground. Tanglwyst glanced at the street behind Catriona, at the archer with the Blue Bow trained on the Death Bringer's back.

He fired at her head.

She turned and knocked the arrow aside. It disintegrated on the ground. She looked at the man wielding the holy bow. He drew the arrow again and fired. She knocked it aside. Aethelraed thrust his sword forward and it shattered on the armor that was suddenly on her body. Bits of metal flew off in every direction, cutting the faces of the men surrounding them.

Stone armor, translucent black with gold flecks covered her, elaborate carvings catching the light. The men were fighting to give their attention to the swarming monsters and the one immediately before them in human form.

The archer looked at Aethelraed. He held up his hand and watched Catriona.

She nodded to Tanglwyst and leapt into the air, a giant pillar of stone pushing her from the ground. She gave a roar and Tanglwyst heard it carry across the valley. Another pillar rose to meet her in the center of the battlefield and she landed on it solidly. The thunder from it sent a shockwave out that knocked everyone but Tanglwyst off their feet. Several people scrambled on the roofs, clinging to the edges before dropping down.

The fissures around her closed, making the steamy air clear in a few moments, giving everyone time to get to their feet. The soldiers and guards looked up at Tanglwyst and she knelt and helped Aethelraed and the others nearby to their feet.

"Why didn't it knock you down?" The note-taking soldier looked in her eyes as she lifted him up.

"She didn't want it to." She looked at the others around her. "You need to know what's going on here. That army answers only to a female of the royal line. Up until a few days ago, that person was Sovereigna. But your archer killed her. That army has managed to stave off a frenzy for all this time, but they can't leave and they have no leader. That wailing you were hearing was the last of their resolve."

"What is she going to do?"

"What no one else can."

Tanglwyst could see the army and valley through the ashen remains of the Wise Wench. The people on the other side of the valley seemed to be paying attention, as well as the Krakten army.

When the steam disappeared, the army along the road had scrambled. Swords were drawn and the Mervols prepared for battle. But the Krakten army paid them no heed. A few soldiers pressed the attack on the edges and the Kraktens ignored them.

The Mervol army started to advance and a line of identical soldiers, in armor like hers, sprung from the ground to stop them. A few Mervols down the street attacked them, their swords clanging and giving off sparks against the armor. The stone soldiers did nothing. The Mervols stopped after a couple swings. The ones near Tanglwyst looked at the General.

The General kept his eye on Catriona. The howling silenced. Catriona surveyed the Fae.

"I have heard your call. I am here."

Tanglwyst saw the Fae take a knee and the wave swept through the encampment. The platform she was on lowered back into the ground and the army stood. Several large officers and half-ogres in sashes came up to her.

The General stiffened. "Soldier."

One of the soldiers from the barracks looked at him. "Yes sir?"

"Keep an eye on things here. Report any changes."

"Yes sir."

He bowed to Tanglwyst. "Whenever you're ready, my Lady."

"Thank you. I'll be along in a minute."

Aethelraed went into the Guard Office.

Clara, George and Giles came over to her. She glanced at them, then motioned them forward towards the other army and away from the Mervol soldiers.

"That was smart." Clara looked at Catriona getting reports from the ranking members.

"I'm glad it worked."

Giles looked at them both. "What happened?"

"I figured that the Krakten matrilineal started somewhere. It only made sense that it began with the Death Bringer, since all things Land go through her. And since we know she can have children, I played a gamble."

Giles looked at the stone soldiers. "What are those?"

George folded his arms. "The Caratian army, I imagine."

"Huh? Caratia didn't have an army when you walked the world."

"I have heard soldiers pray about them. Pray for help, for strategy, for mercy. But I have never seen one."

"Then how do you know these are them?"

"Because I recognize *nothing* about them. Clara, I will go see what the General is planning. Don't stay out here too long. Tanglwyst is not one of us. She will freeze."

Clara nodded.

"Come on, Giles."

Giles cast one last look at Catriona and then went with George.

Tanglwyst saw Catriona look her way. Tanglwyst pointed to her office. Catriona acknowledged it and continued with her conversation.

"Do you want to go with them or come with me?"

Clara snorted. "Oh, I won't be in that ego-infested man box."

Tanglwyst watched Catriona a few more moments and walked to her office.

It took about an hour for Catriona to join them. Tanglwyst poured tea for her and set it on the table.

"Everything okay now?"

"Yes. I see why Alistair said I needed to protect the world."

"Is it in danger?"

"Apparently. But the Krakten army has calmed. There is a processional preparing to take the Queen home."

"Are they staying in the valley?"

"No. They will all leave. There's no reason to stay with the Princess gone."

"What will you do?"

"I don't know. Once inside the forest, my connection with the Land is muted."

"Because it's divine."

Clara got a thoughtful look on her face. "Giles built the place. He can probably navigate it just fine. Move the forest aside to give access to the Land."

Catriona nodded. "That's probably true. I plan to escort the Queen back to Austra. But after that, I'm not sure what to do."

"Won't the country require your rule?"

"I am the Land's protector, not its ruler."

Tanglwyst smirked. "That's not what I saw."

Catriona smiled. "Well, the tricky part is finding another capable of serving as Queen."

There was a moment of silent thought between them.

"Catherine should go with you. Without Emmy… She'll be alone."

"Isn't she needed in Patras?"

"I think she'll take the option. If I take her place."

Catriona studied her. "I see."

"I mean, he clearly can't do it alone."

Catriona smiled and shook her head. "No. He'll be lost without you. And I can say he has sincere affection for you. He is committed."

Clara sat back in her chair, toying with her cup. "Well, first we have to get him through the Trials to the throne. After that, we can set about helping the kingdom heal."

Tanglwyst looked at her, narrowing her eyes in contemplation. "Actually, I think that needs to happen in reverse order. He doesn't deserve the kingdom if he doesn't help it first. By the way, I'm sorry for the loss of your ship, Catriona."

"The same for you. I read in him that you lost it rescuing your friends."

"Well, don't count that beast out just yet. Her heart is still there. I'll rebuild her. I'll need Giles' help though. Just to transport it. Then you're welcome to him."

Clara's eyes widen in annoyance. "With his ability, he *can* irritate multiple people in faraway places almost simultaneously. I'm sure he can get your ship to a dry dock, you through the Black Forest, and still piss off Brigit at Persephone."

Tanglwyst shrugged. "Alexander mentioned bringing him to St. Marguerite to help repair things or simply move the population to Serenity."

Catriona nodded, picking up her tea. "That is a good idea, but it will take an awful lot of direct discussion for that to happen."

"If he gets the Power of Sovereignty back, he can make a declaration and get people to gather in certain places to make the trip. Most displaced people can't afford to just walk to Serenity, but they can gather at the local church easily enough."

"I'll try not to keep him. What will you do after you get your ship to dry dock?"

"Head to Patras. We have a Coronation to pull off."

Thirty-Six

"Use the stones from the field to form a path to the river."
-The Forty-Five Voices

"The women are heading off to another building. I thought they were going to come in here?" Giles looked back at the men.

Aethelraed handed an ale to George. "They are probably tired of your rudeness."

"My…?"

George handed Giles the ale. "Come on, old boy. You know you're difficult to be around in large doses."

"How did I get married then?"

"If I recall correctly, she killed you, right?"

Aethelraed smiled. "I can see it."

He handed George a second ale and poured a third.

"I don't know why people dwell on that part. She was bewitched to do that, we believe."

George arched an eyebrow. "We?"

Aethelraed sat down. "The woman outside. Who is she?"

"Well, that's a long story, I think." George joined him.

"She was here earlier, claiming to be the Dûcesa of Caratia. She fought the angel that Alexander brought to the Church. That's her handiwork there."

Giles glanced at him, humbled. "Yeah. We heard that from Alexander."

George eyed the General. "You worried?"

"Yes. She knocked aside the arrow that killed a Fae Lieutenant."

"You also killed her companion."

"In my defense, he is a traitor."

"Is he still?"

Aethelraed smiled, nodding. "I see your point. I don't know what the law says about dealing with traitors after they have been beheaded. It's probably never come up. But it is invariably going to matter to the public who was not here to witness it. They'll still see him as a traitor and Alexander cannot pardon him and still keep his enemies at bay."

"How many enemies does he have?"

"There are always those who challenge the succession. It's part of the process. I will challenge his ability to command the army. Another noble will challenge his governing of his resources. Someone else will challenge him physically. That person will try to assassinate him. If they succeed, they are promoted in the court. If they fail, they are executed for treason. The King can choose to pardon that person, but they don't have to.

"But those are *assigned* villains. There are always those who seek power and if any of *those* decide to campaign against him, he is not likely to see that blade coming."

Giles came and sat down with the others. "You think that will be more or less likely at this stage?"

"More. He has not had a presence in this battle and now an outsider who attacked a clear creature of Heaven has just claimed the army of Krakte in full view of his soldiers and officers. He will need to oppose her to win their loyalty.

"That is, unless he's smarter than he's shown so far." Aethelraed took a drink.

Giles glanced at George. "You have our attention."

"And that is how you cast Amanuensis."

Brigit looked from Raven to Lauriel. "That was the longest, most convoluted lesson I have ever heard."

Raven frowned. "You asked."

"Did I? I can't remember now."

She looked at her work. She had not understood the words in the document at all, but the ink had stained the parchment darker than the slobber and ink had.

"There is clearly something special about your drool, Lauriel. I have dropped scrolls in a fountain and never lost a letter. I should bottle it and sell it as a correctional fluid. I'd be rich overnight.

"Okay, so I think I have all of this page done too. Does this make sense?"

She held up the third page of the letter as close as she could to his face.

He looked it over. "Yes. All that makes sense."

"Do you understand what he was saying?"

"Oh, I'm not trying to yet."

She blinked. "What?"

"I'm making sure the letters and symbols are correct. Otherwise, I'll jump to conclusions that might be wrong. That's why I'm having you clean them out of order."

She started to protest, but Lauriel put his paw on her knee. She looked at him instead and nodded. "You're right, Lauriel. That actually *is* pretty smart."

"I'm sorry you couldn't get into the Fae realm."

She stood and stretched, finally getting up from the stone desk Lauriel had made for her. There were shelves and easels on the wall across from Raven, also made from the stone, and they had set up a nice little office.

"I was actually thinking about that. If Fae can't leave the Black Forest, but Lauriel can leave here and go to Sovereignlumin, can the Fae use this place to leave the Black Forest?"

Raven blinked, then looked at Lauriel. The Fae wolf jumped up the stairs and ran into the tunnel.

"Take Brigit with you!"

Brigit left with the animal. The wake of her excitement sent the pages on her desk fluttering to the floor. The words were too small to read from his vantage, but that was when he saw it. It wasn't the words. It was *the way* the words were laid out that was getting his attention. They formed a pattern, a *diagram*. He looked at the finished pages, then overlapped them in his mind. In the order they were in the missive, the patterns formed a warning, but rearranged in reverse order and the symbols now represented *hostage*. That was not the expected outcome for something that was a warning going forward.

He rearranged them again, even pages first, and the symbols said *life*. Odds first said *death*.

He heard footsteps running and Lauriel and Brigit burst into the room. He had a flower in his mouth that Raven recognized from Caratia.

"It worked! Lauriel can leave!"

"Fantastic!"

She danced around with the Fae wolf, knocking the papers around. A few landed face up, some face down.

The symbols in that order made his blood run cold.

"Do that again, will you?"

"Huh?"

"Throw the papers in the air."

"What? Why?"

"Because it will be fun."

She shrugged and smiled as she did as he asked. Different pages landed upside down, but the message did not change.

Free us.

Giles looked at the others. "And that would work?"

"Oh yes."

George stood and walked to the window. "Do we tell her?"

Aethelraed sat back, sighing. "That's my current dilemma. Is it interference if I do?"

"I feel like we should talk to her about it. We may be misreading this whole thing. I mean, we recently got everyone who was involved in this mess in the same room and we all knew what to do and where to go from there. After that, this just feels like we aren't communicating and we really need to."

Giles nodded. "I know what you mean. I'll broach the subject with her."

The protests were stopped before they were uttered when Giles put his hand up.

"I know, I know. But she wants me to help with her ship and I can. Once that gets under way, we'll have time. I know how to repair it, but it will have to regenerate and that takes time. I think she'll be receptive."

"If you screw this up…"

"I won't, George. I won't. But, maybe I can talk to Alexander at the same time. That would probably be best."

Aethelraed lifted his cup in a toast. "*That* I can drink to."

The door opened and Clara and Tanglwyst came into the room.

Tanglwyst closed the door behind them. "Catriona has returned to the army. A couple of your soldiers looked like they were going to give her trouble but they apparently thought better of it."

"Which ones?"

"The archers on the roof, specifically the one with the Anna's bow."

"I need to take that back. I don't like it in the hands of a stranger." Giles walked outside and waved his hand. He walked back in with the bow.

Aethelraed looked at him a moment, then at Tanglwyst. "My Lady, Giles said you were having him repair your ship?"

"Yes. It was damaged recently. He said we could fix that and still be of use for the season. That will stop my crew from being out of work, which matters to their families."

Aethelraed smiled, nodding. "You're very responsible, My Lady."

"They are my responsibility."

George set his cup on the floor. "Clara, I was thinking of returning to Heaven. Do you want to come with me?"

"Actually, I need to join Jude and make sure the people in Serenity are settling in."

"Ah. Yes, that makes more sense. Giles can see to it you get there, right?"

"We have to return to the Haunt anyway, right, my Lady?"

Tanglwyst nodded. She looked at Aethelraed. "Catriona doesn't harbor any bad feelings towards you but does recommend you not kill any messengers she sends your way anymore. They might have important information."

"I'll be nice."

"Thank you. Giles, let's get to work. We have a lot to do."

The people leaving with Giles disappeared. Aethelraed motioned to George.

"Good luck."

"Thank you."

George departed as well.

Clara went up to Jude and started talking to him. Giles and Tanglwyst went upstairs to the *Sulocco*.

"So, I have a spell that will effectively regenerate lost appendages, but for inanimate objects. However, this will take a while."

"How long?"

"Possibly overnight."

She grinned. "Giles, that's *hardly* a long time. She would be in dry dock for the season under other circumstances."

"Oh, well it's forever for a mage."

She grinned. "Yeah, I can see that. Okay then, let's get to it?"

"Sure. But while that happens, I would like to talk to you about something with Alexander."

"Um, no."

Giles faltered. "Er, no?"

"There is no place for you to talk to me about Alexander. If you have a concern about him, speak to him. If you have a concern about me, speak to me. But do not speak to him about me or me about him."

"But- "

"No. Now, if you are about to make the repair of my ship contingent upon you speaking to me about Alexander…"

"Wait, yeah! I- "

"No. You won't."

"Look, I'm the mage here."

She turned to him. "Do you have *any* idea how incredibly much I have done *without* having a mage in my life?"

298

Giles started to speak but stopped.

She pointed to his mouth. "What you just did there was the right thing to do. Remember that move. Use it often."

He rolled his eyes. "Yes ma'am."

"So, if that is all, we can now walk away from my ship and I will mourn it. But I'll not be held hostage over your help. If you do not freely give it, then I honestly should not be using it. And if you require payment, tell me now so I know the cost."

"No, no. Please, that's not what I meant. I just… He needs…"

"No. He doesn't."

"Aethelraed said- "

"He's wrong."

"I think that you- "

"No, I'm not."

"Let me finish a sentence!"

"Is that sentence going to have me somehow sitting a throne near Alexander?"

"Um…"

"Then I do not deserve that sentencing. I have not done *anything that* wrong."

Giles gritted his teeth and lips together, then threw some magic at the ship and stormed off. Tanglwyst watched as the edges of the surfaces started glowing and getting a little bigger. She smiled and gave him a few minutes to get ahead, then went back inside as well.

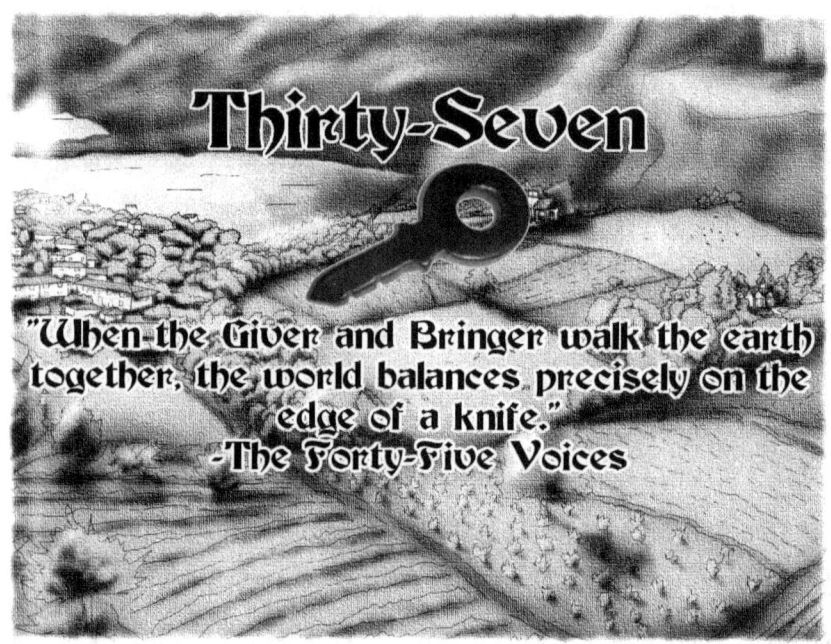

Thirty-Seven

"When the Giver and Bringer walk the earth
together, the world balances precisely on the
edge of a knife."
-The Forty-Five Voices

Alexander teleported down to Nina and Emmy.

"Myrgen! Help!"

Myrgen appeared at the edge of the hole. "Oh no. Are they...?"

Alexander moved them both up to Myrgen, then all of them to the healing pool. He moved Nina off of Emmy and lifted the child so her face was out of the water.

"She's not moving. She's not breathing."

Alexander bounced her tiny body. "Give it a moment."

Myrgen watched the child but nothing changed.

Alexander closed his eyes. He lifted her to his chest.

Nina groaned and got on her knees. "Where am I?"

Neither man looked at her. Myrgen put his hand on Alexander's shoulder.

"Hey. I have an idea. I'm going to try what you did for my sister."

Alexander looked at him. "Can you... Wait, she was raised Augustinian. Won't she be in Heaven?"

"She's part Fae. In fact, she's one-quarter Fae. She'll be in Summerland."

"Should I go check, just in case?"

"How would you find her? With Tangl, you had a connection."

"I…" Alexander shook his head. "No, you're right. I couldn't find her even if I knew what to look for."

"Give me a chance."

"How?"

"That room with the village. I said before -"

"That you thought it connected! Right! Go. Hurry. Please."

Myrgen slogged through the pool and went into the crypt.

Alexander turned and saw Nina looking at them. She stepped back, her knife drawn.

"She's dead, Nina. You can't hurt her more than you already have."

"Where am I?"

"You're in a series of inhabited caves in the Black Forest."

"How did I get here?"

Alexander walked past her. "I brought you here."

She stabbed him in the back with her knife. He screamed and fell to a knee. She drew back the knife and stood ready to defend herself. Alexander felt the wound heal up and he kept walking to the crypts. Her heard her dagger drop into the water.

"Who are you? What are you?"

He climbed out of the water. "I am a man who is holding his dead niece in his arms, hoping his friend can bring back her soul in order to save the world."

Nina waded out of the pool and he heard her running up the stairs. He was surprised that he wasn't angry at her, like he had been with Madeline. He didn't feel the need to correct her point of view or show her the error of her ways. They were working on the problem. He would stay by Emmy and wait for the pool to replenish.

Nina ran up the stairs and ran down the hallway. There were several men in rooms that watched her run past and they came out as she went by. She more found stairs and ran up them as well. She ended up in a huge room with several fireplaces and tables, and several more people eating and talking.

A man with a beard stopped her.

"Hey, what's wrong? Are you alright?"

"I'm... I don't know where I am. The king..."

"Alexander?"

"Yes. He's... he..."

"He's here? He's back?"

"Yes."

"Can you take me to him? Please. He left so suddenly."

Nina tried to figure out where to run. The man seemed to understand this and took her hand.

"Or not. Do you want to look around?"

"I..." She closed her eyes and took several deep breaths. Once she had her heart under control, she opened them again. "Yes. Yes, thank you."

She saw the stairs on the other end of the room and fought the urge to run up and continue until she ended up someplace she'd been before.

If I need to...

"I'm Jude. Are you hungry?"

She looked at him. "You're who?"

"Jude."

"Like the Saint?"

He smiled. "Yes. Just like the Saint. You seem very scared. Why are you scared?"

"Because I...killed the Princess."

"You... *killed* the Princess? Princess who?"

"Marie-Elizabeth. The Heir to the Mervol throne."

Jude paled. "Why?"

"I was saving her."

Jude folded his hands. "Tell me what happened."

"Alexander showed up out of nowhere. He was suddenly there. I was looking right at the place where he appeared. He grabbed the ink and quill on the desk and threw them in the fire.

"The ink screamed."

Jude frowned, confused, but didn't interrupt.

"It *screamed*... I... He looked like that was what he *thought* would happen. Then the Queen Mother said there were all these other things around the world that were also corrupted and that *the Church* was what did this! Then they started talking heresy and blasphemy. He was going to convert, I know it. He was already talking about magic and witchcraft.

"I grabbed Emmy and ran. And there were all these tunnels. And then there were boards and we went through and there was a hole..."

She started crying. The stress of everything overwhelmed her and she laid her head on her arms on the table. The tears flowed and flowed. Jude rubbed her hair and let her. After a while, she felt drained and she lifted her head.

Jude looked at her eyes. "Why don't you lie down? You don't have to sleep if you don't want to. But it might help."

He stood up and offered his hand to her. She looked at his hand and suddenly, he was *right*. She was asleep, that was almost certainly it. This was a nightmare.

"Yes. Yes. I need to lie down."

"This way."

He took her to an area with several doors, just off the hall. He gestured to the door and let her open it. Her hand touched the door and she knew it. It was *her* door, to *her* room. The room was the one Tanglwyst stayed in and she realized the smell in the catacombs belonged to that woman.

That's why it was so familiar.

Jude stayed outside the door. "Do you need anything?"

She looked at him. "No. No, thank you."

She smoothed out the bed and laid down on top of the covers.

Jude smiled and pointed to the Great Hall. "I'll be right out here if you need me."

She closed her eyes and let herself go to sleep.

Myrgen entered the room with the village and found it bustling. A young boy was helping a woman with a cart full of fish, and Myrgen realized he knew the boy. It was the butcher. He was smiling and talking about fishing with the woman. He went up to them and bowed.

"I'm looking for Summerland. Do you know where it is?"

The woman smiled. "I have no idea where that is."

Myrgen sighed. "I could have sworn I knew the feel of this place."

He walked past the houses and went for the edge of town. There were some trees and he looked for some sort of landmark. He saw nothing. He went to the trees and climbed one. The countryside was not noteworthy, woods and little else to give him any idea.

I need a landmark. Something.

He climbed down and knelt on the ground. He thought of it rising above the woods and when he looked up, he saw he was above the woods and saw something that made his heart leap.

Sovereignlumin.

He moved the pillar of stone he was on and rode it like Raven's earth sled. Once there, he turned towards the mansion. He dropped it down into the ground and he ran into the mansion.

Lucifer looked out of the study. "Myrgen! I was trying to reach you just now. Catriona's back."

He stopped. "Back? How?"

"Alistair released her."

"That's because Emmy died. Speaking of which, I need to bring her through here. May I?"

Lucifer waved him away. "I'll take care of it. Go."

Myrgen ran out of the mansion, leapt over the garden wall and ran into town.

"Emmy! Emmy!"

He moved around the fountain, shouting her name.

"Myrgen!"

Sovereigna was standing in the garden, the little girl by her side. Myrgen ran over to them.

"Emmy, you're okay?"

"Yes. Gamma."

Sovereigna smiled. "We've been playing here. Look. She's harvested so many things for me."

She pointed to the basket Myrgen had filled before. The roots were attached to the plants in some cases and only a few petals from other. It was utter chaos.

"It looks wonderful. Sovereigna, I'm going to try and take her back."

She took a deep breath. "I was hoping you would." She bent over and picked Emmy up. "As much fun as it is to have you with me, I have to let you go with Myrgen. Will you, honey?"

304

Emmy grabbed onto Sovereigna's neck and gave her a big hug. "Do you want to come with us?"

"No. I have things to do here. But I do have something for you."

She rifled around the basket and pulled out a bottle of red fluid. "It's the essence remover. I was able to get another bottle ready. In case you need to get someone else out."

He hugged her, then reached out for Emmy. "Wanna go see Alexander?"

"Awex?"

"Yes, honey. Alex."

She reached out for Myrgen's hand and wriggled so she got away. They headed towards the mansion on the hill.

"I love you, Emmy."

She turned and waved at her grandmother.

Alexander heard a noise behind him and turned around. Myrgen was standing at the door of the room.

"Did you find her?"

Myrgen nodded. "How do we do this?"

Alexander picked up Emmy's body and held her against his chest, like she was asleep on his shoulder.

Myrgen understood. He picked up Emmy and walked her around until she laid her head on his shoulder. Once she was comfortable and seemed to be asleep, they interacted and Myrgen handed Emmy's spirit to Alexander, superimposing her into her body. Myrgen put his hand on her back and smiled.

Go back. It's not time for you yet.

Emmy opened her eyes and started having trouble breathing. Alexander panicked and ran to the pool. He put her in the water and several very frightening moments later, she was breathing okay and starting to go back to sleep again.

"She's back. I can feel her heartbeat."

Myrgen bowed his head and released all his tension.

Alexander smiled. "Thank you. Thank you."

He stood and climbed out of the pool. He walked up the stairs and into the Great Hall. Jude saw him and Alexander nodded to the hallway with his room from last night. Jude opened the door that had replaced the hallway. Alexander set her on his bed, dripping wet clothes and all, and let her sleep. He lay down next to her, not caring he was soaked too.

Jude started to close the door and Alexander lifted his head. "Leave it open, please. And can someone contact my mother and let her know that Emmy is alright?"

"Of course."

Alexander put his arm across Emmy and fell asleep.

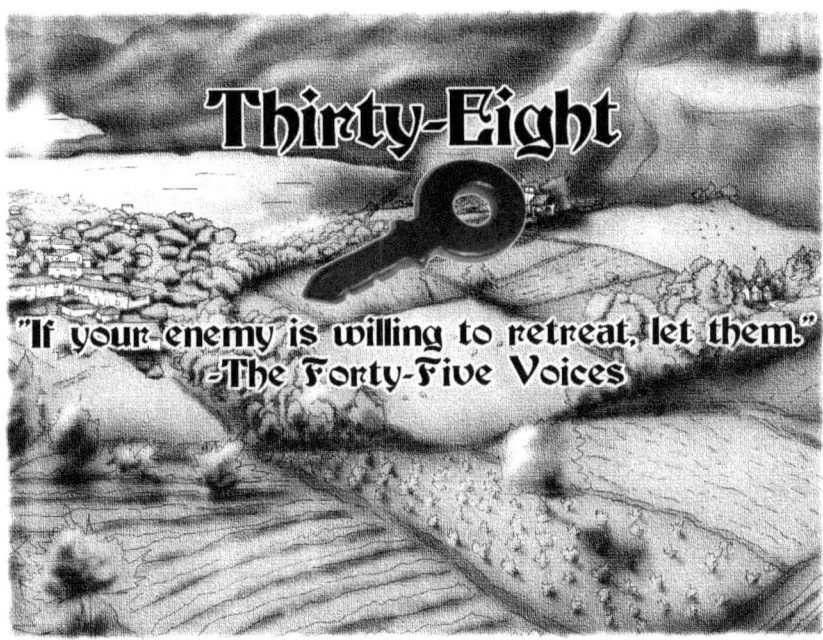

Thirty-Eight

"If your enemy is willing to retreat, let them."
-The Forty-Five Voices

Alexander rolled over and fell off the bed. Heracles rolled onto his back and Emmy put her arm across the dog's chest. Neither of them woke up. He heard a snort and looked up. Tanglwyst was smirking in the doorway. He got up and walked over to her.

"Is this your doing?"

She raised her hands in protest. "Hey, *you* left the door open."

"I knew he was around and so were you. I didn't want her to wake up because Heracles wanted in."

"Maybe you *are* smart enough to be king after all." She kissed him.

He looked in the Great Hall and gestured towards it. She shook her head and opened the door across from his, pulling him into her room.

He closed the door and then, she was kissing him. His mind went away from the events of the day and the need for her encompassed him entirely. He locked the door and started unbuttoning her doublet. She let him, enthusiastically getting him out of his own clothes. Shoes became an issue and they ended up with a string of clothing in bizarre pairings marking their path to the bed.

With slightly fewer garments to remove, he pulled the covers back on the bed just in time for her to push him down and start kissing his chest. They scrambled onto the bed, Alexander almost not caring about the idea of being on the floor but still trying to remember courtesy. It was almost too difficult to think of anything but being with her.

When she put her mouth on his rigid penis, he stopped thinking altogether and just went with it all.

Myrgen walked up to Giles. "You look upset."

"Oh, your sister just… She won't let me advise her on what to do with Alexander."

"With *Alexander*? *You* want to advise *my sister* on *Alexander*?"

"There is a role for her to play and-"

"Oh, no you didn't. A 'role' for her to 'play'? You do not get to decide who is a 'player' in this. This isn't a stage production."

"No, it's far more important and I need her to make sure he gets Coronated."

"Oh, he'll be coronated alright. I think that's happening right now, in fact."

"What?"

"Look, if you want to help him, help me. We need to get to Patras and to the Queen. I just told Tanglwyst everything that happened and Jude said Nina was put to bed in the Professors Wing. So, let's let the rest of the populace get some sleep and get Catherine her update."

"I haven't been to Patras."

Myrgen frowned. "Oh. Well, what was it called back then?"

"There was a central location called Moot."

"Okay, let's go there."

Giles took him to the place he remembered. The streets were busy and filthy, the snow brown and yellow and black where it wasn't simply walked into slush. Homeless people were sitting in small areas with shelter, where buildings came together or trash was piled up. Myrgen looked around for a landmark.

"We're in Patras."

"Well, that's lucky."

Myrgen saw some city guards walk by the end of the alley. Myrgen turned to the people huddled together near a tiny fire. There were three small children, one coughing badly. None of them had the proper clothing to survive in this weather.

"Giles."

He looked at the children. Myrgen walked over to them and knelt down. They were too cold to even feel fear.

"Do you have someplace they can go?"

"Of course I do."

Giles disappeared with them.

Myrgen put the small fire out and waited. Giles returned a few minutes later.

"I took them to the Haunt first, to heal them, then to Serenity to Monique. She should be able to help them get settled."

"Thank you. Now I know where we are and where we need to go." He pointed to a spire barely visible in the alleyway.

Giles nodded. He disappeared and reappeared a few moments later. "There's a garden, a stable, a-"

"The garden. Please."

Giles took them to the garden. Myrgen went to the bush that hid the passage to the catacombs.

"This way."

Giles followed him and when they were in the dark, Giles lit the torches in the catacombs.

"Thanks. I think she'll either be in her room, or in court. I can access her room. Court will be trickier."

They went through the tunnels to a wall and Myrgen took a deep breath before opening it into a prayer nave. He crept into the room in case she was not alone. She was there, with four other people. He waited until she looked his way, then let her see him before ducking back into the dark.

She cleared her throat. "Ladies, excuse me a moment. I need to pray."

The women curtsied and left. Catherine stood and walked to the prayer nave.

"Myrgen, isn't it?"

"Your Majesty. I have news of Emmy. She's alive."

Catherine closed her eyes and sighed. "And Nina?"

"She's also resting. We have her at the covenant. Alexander is nearby."

"Do we know why she did it?"

"Yes. She told Saint Jude that she believed the King was speaking heresy and blasphemy, like he was converting to Emil. Also, that he was a witch"

Catherine looked away. "That's what I feared. She lost her entire family to Emilianites as a child. There were no orphanages in her town so she went to the nearby church. As a ward of the Church, she was indoctrinated against magic by the priest who mentored her in the seminary where she was raised. She left the Church when she fell in love and had two young daughters. She told me they were killed in the Massacre by Emilianites on Saint Michael's Day.

"She saw the event as a sign to become a guard."

"That was barely three years ago. How did she get this far in her advancement?"

"By being better than every man out there. She was set to take Nicolai's job when Alexander put him in that spot instead. I think she's always resented him for that."

Myrgen glanced at the floor, not sure what to say.

"I understand you also lost family three years ago. I wanted to tell you I am truly sorry for that."

"Charles needed to be better than he was. He needed to stand up to you."

"He did. But he couldn't. There was an inkwell that the Church gave the Crown, along with a Golden Quill. It was supposed to channel the Power of Sovereignty to make a decree stand with all for whom it effects. Except it was corrupt. What it truly did was set your entire reign based upon the first decree you wrote as Sovereign. For Henri, it was that Diane be his consort and afforded equal status to me. For Francois, it was that his brothers and sister be given the freedom to do as they chose. For Charles, his first decree was to say I never needed to bow to him. I know what he was trying to do. But the Ink corrupted it. After that, he could not stop himself, and neither could I from taking advantage."

"That's why Alexander didn't stop you from bowing when he killed Elizabeth."

310

Catherine flicked a hard gaze of shock at him. "How did you…?"

"Catriona and I were in the crypts. We saw the entire thing, from the moment Elizabeth took the last steps of the fake ritual."

"Were you two together by then?"

"No. But not long after that."

"I would like very much to meet her."

He glanced over his shoulder. "Well, it turns out that I have a person that can help with that. She kind of needs to meet you too. We need to take Emmy to Austra and she will need you there to help her rule. Right now, Catriona has control of the Krakten army. But it needs to be Emmy's, not hers."

"I need to be here for Alexander's Coronation. So does Emmy, as his heir."

Myrgen reached into his satchel. "Here is something Sovereigna made for her. It will take her essence so she can return and here's another bottle to get her through to the Coronation. Do you want to come and get her now?"

"How?"

Giles stepped forward.

They arrived in the Haunted Covenant. Catherine looked around. "Where are we?"

"About ten miles north of Cliffport."

Myrgen leaned over to Catherine. "That's St. Giles."

She looked at Giles. "That's within the Black Forest. Emmy is one-quarter Fae."

Giles put his hand to his chest. "Yes. But I *made* the Black Forest. I know how to get around it, and out of it."

"May I see her then?"

Jude gestured to the hallway and to the door on the left. It was open and Emmy turned over, very much awake.

"Gamma?"

She got up and Heracles flipped over and jumped off the bed. They walked over to Catherine. She picked Emmy up.

"Oh, she's wet."

Giles snapped his fingers.

"Oh, never mind."

Emmy started to fuss and Heracles jumped on Catherine, almost knocking her over.

Catherine bounced Emmy on her hip. "On second thought, perhaps now is not the best time to try this young lady's patience."

Myrgen gestured to Giles. "Giles has been to your room now. He can pick you up when you're ready."

"I appreciate it. Thank you."

"I'll take you all to your respective places then." Giles took them to the Palace.

Catherine bowed. "Thank you. I hope I'll see you soon then, gentlemen."

Myrgen took them back into the catacombs, then looked at Giles. "Can we arrive someplace other than right in the town square?"

"Why? My wife's bow is no longer with them."

"Spoken like someone who has only died once."

Giles acknowledged that and they arrived in the woods behind Cliffport. They didn't get a breath of new air in their lungs before they were stopped by low, sinister voices.

"I overheard the woman saying they can't use her magic in the forest. We can take the queen's body and use it for leverage."

"Leverage for what?"

"Sacrifices. We make them deliver their army to us. Then we use this amulet to sludge them and kill all of the Fae. We need an arsenal of that stuff so no Fae ever dares attack a human."

"Filthy monsters. Thank the Saints Giles is among us now. He'll kill them all."

"In Saint Giles' name."

Giles looked at Myrgen, his expression simultaneously offended and contrite.

Myrgen held up his hand, dismissing the issue, then pulled out the Bringer shard and envisioned Catriona. When she responded, he gave her his *Read Me* expression.

She did and then turned to see him waving to her. He pointed to the men, then to several other positions where he could see archers waiting in ambush. She nodded.

"What's she looking over here for?" The first archer's whisper carried like an actor's.

"Take her out."

"That will give away our ambush. We have to wait."

She turned to face the men and several fireballs of lava flew from the ground and landed on them. The trees could not burn, and neither could the brush or kindling on the ground. But the men, they could burn, and did.

Giles watched as the amulet on the one man's neck came in contact with the lava. The darkness within screamed as it died. "I think that's the last of those amulets."

"That feels like something that should be checked on. Will you please ask my sister to do so? I recommend a note under the door."

"I'll do that. You have the Giver shard as well?"

"We do. Thank you."

"I'll check on you. Let me know before you head out with the Queen."

"Alright."

Myrgen headed off past the burning bodies and over to his beloved.

Giles disappeared.

Myrgen walked up to Catriona, who was standing with a Royal Guard.

"Good aim, my love."

She smiled, bowing. "They had an amulet?"

"I think it's the one George borrowed, the one the priest made. Giles thinks that should be the last of them. With the angels who were supporting their making now gone, they should not come up again."

She turned to the guard in the sash. "Herr Gerhart, may I present Myrgen de Sablonierres."

"Welcome, Hunter. I was telling the Bringer we will be ready to transport the Queen home tomorrow."

"I should like to go with you."

"We would like that as well. Until tomorrow."

Catriona and Myrgen both bowed.

"Where are we going to be tonight then, My Lady?"

She glanced at the humans now running to the forest. "I can't leave here. Time to send the soldiers into the woods as well. I was truly hoping that wouldn't be necessary."

The soldiers of the Land turned towards the woods and started marching. At the foot of the valley where they parted, more soldiers came out of the ground to fill in for the vacating infantry. The humans were startled and the soldier on watch ran to the Guard Office to report.

"Aethelraed's not going to be happy about this."

Catriona snorted. "Do you think he sent the archers to take the Queen's body?"

"No. That feels like Manglebottom's work. We don't have to worry about archers anymore, now that Giles has the bow again. Those men in the ambush had the same number of arrows in their quivers. They divided them evenly, which means they are in short supply. How long will the ores be unworkable?"

"Indefinitely."

"What about nails?"

"Can be forged into weapons."

"Can you stop that?"

"Maybe."

She knelt down and touched the earth. "I have forbidden the working of weapons by anyone other than a Land smith. I can affect anything coming out of the ground going forward, but not anything that has already been drawn. So, they can dismantle houses for the nails to make steel."

He shook his head. "I wish that was unlikely. But warmongers only want to war. If that's what it takes to get their weapons, that's what they'll do."

"I know. Come, let's tour the army. Perhaps we can find some hope in their faces."

Thirty-Nine

"The most reliable religious figures are
people who don't consider themselves
religious."
-The Forty-Five Voices

"So, I have to ask. What did I do to deserve that? Because whatever
it was, I need to assign a staff member at the palace to have it recur every
hour."

Tanglwyst laughed. "I saw you with Emmy, and Heracles. And you
were too damned sexy to hold back."

"So, your weakness is children and dogs?"

"No, my love. *Yours* is. And seeing you be that comfortable in your
own skin was incredibly attractive. And, it made me think that's how you
might be with your own children."

He intertwined his fingers in hers. "That feels like maybe the recent
pregnancy talking."

"Undoubtedly. But it's also very true. I have wanted to be intimate
with you before, it's true, but not for the right reasons. I honestly knew I
was pregnant because I had not bled for a while. I tried to get you to
make love to me before in the hopes the child could have you in its life,

with Nicolai gone. But that would have been *very* wrong. *That* was the pregnancy talking. And when you declined, I knew it was the right thing to do."

"I would have, you know. I wouldn't have cared that it didn't carry my blood. It carried yours. That would have been enough."

Tanglwyst shook her head. "Fine. I'll have sex with you again."

Alexander laughed but did not interfere.

Giles wrote the note and folded it. He sent the missive off on its merry, which followed the air currents across the hall of sailors and under the door of the Lady. Then he walked over to Captain Nesbit.

"The ship should be finished by tomorrow."

A sailor standing beside him arched an eyebrow. "Excuse me?"

Giles looked at him. "The ship is being rebuilt. Upstairs. It should be ready by tomorrow."

"Captain?"

David sighed and dismissed him.

He ran to some of the others and mentioned something, then bounced to another table and did it again. Then he ran up the stairs and several other crewmen and women followed.

David looked at them. "Well, you sure know how to clear a room."

"What did I say?"

"That their livelihood wasn't in limbo after tomorrow."

"Was that an issue?"

"Most of these men have sailed on the *Sulocco* for seven years. They have a routine and expectations. Being on land with no purpose was very hard on them. In another week, they would have started deserting the company."

"They are welcome to stay."

"I believe they know that. But some of them have families and the question of being rudderless or being rudderless with their families was going to cause some hard decisions. Now, they won't have to."

"How do you know the way to the Storm King's Island?"

"Pure luck. We were coming south from Glarren when we were blown towards the island by a sudden storm. We ended up on the island.

The ship was intact. We harvested supplies from the island, made repairs while Tanglwyst and I explored with a few folks, then determined there was a way through after coming across a giant map. In fact, not dissimilar to the one in that meeting room of yours. Anyway, the cartographer determined there was a way through and, if we did it right, we could go back and forth. Been doing it ever since."

"Why though?"

"That feels like a question for the Lady."

"What? Why?"

"Because that's a business discussion, and it isn't my business."

"Captain! Have you seen this?"

"On my way, son." Captain Nesbit bowed to Giles and followed the sailor up the stairs.

Tanglwyst kissed Alexander. "Water?"

"Here, let me."

He sat up and took a moment.

"What's wrong?"

"My legs are unstable."

She laughed again.

He got up and wobbled over to the pitcher near the chairs. There were two goblets, both already filled with water. "Wow. This place…"

He brought them over and they drank.

She gestured towards the pitcher. "I don't even know why they have that thing. The goblets just refill."

Alexander looked at his. "You're right. Hey, I'll be right back."

He set the full (again) goblet on the table by the bed and went to the privy.

She saw the note near the door and got up. "So, is this the part where I ask for clarification on what we are now?"

"Well, I had a question about that. You seem uncomfortable about Queen. Do you want to be Consort? You have the responsibility of Queen, the respect, but you can leave when you want. If I ever marry, you could leave altogether or stay on as an advisor. The offer for Queen still stands though. I don't want you to think otherwise."

"You still think I'm right for a part like that after what we just did?"

He came out of the privy and handed her a towel, then got a robe for each of them. "How would this change that? I made you a virgin, my Love. It was only right I take that off your hands."

She laughed. "That's right, you *did*! You monster."

He put the robe around her shoulders and took the towel back. "I love your laugh. And your snore."

"I spent years developing both just to impress you. I just make it appear effortless."

"The sign of a true master."

She tied the robe and he did likewise to his own, then fetched his water. She sat by the fireplace, the note in her lap.

"Honestly, I just want to make sure you don't make a mistake, especially if there might be a better choice out there. Like maybe the ruler of Caratia."

He knelt before her. "I am always going to love Catriona. She's simultaneously my first love, my first loss, and first utter failure. She was the first woman I ever made love to. But we have both *really* moved on from anything we had together. And she and Myrgen are *right* for each other. I will happily have them both at my Coronation, my wedding, and the Presentation of my Heirs when my children are born. I will ask them to be their spiritual parents, in fact, guiding my children's souls, because, honestly, *who better*? They have become allies to me and my people."

He took her hand. "You are the woman I love. I need you, I want you, and I will face challenges with more confidence with you by my side than alone. But understand, I *will* face those challenges regardless. This whole thing has been a sobering and humbling experience. I used to think, in my heart of hearts, that if I wanted a thing, that was the same as deserving it. It enabled me to put the effort in to earn it, but I always believed it was then going to be mine. Even when I was being my most benevolent, I still made sure there was something for me.

"But seeing Myrgen risk and lose *everything* he had earned because he saw Elizabeth being attacked really gave *my* life choices perspective. And every time he succeeded and was rewarded for it made me angrier because I realized my own selfish desires were dooming me. He even saved *my* life by making sure Elizabeth got that fake ritual. The man has died *twice* and let me tell you, he *really* didn't have to. He had the power to end all of us with the wave of his hand. I saw it.

318

"You were the first person to ever really tell me no. You were the first person to tell me I had made some *very* bad life choices and you did not hold back. And if I *never* get to call you wife, or Your Majesty, if I never wake beside you again, or make love to you, I will still have your guidance if you'll give it to me. If that means no strings, no legal ties, then there will be none."

His eyes sparkled. "Oh, but if you do, My Lady, if you do let me do those things, we will make a difference to every person in this Kingdom. I swear it."

She watched his eyes, her own very wet from the emotional outpouring. "I have no words more eloquent that what you just said. That's going to be the worst part about being with you."

He snickered, casting his eyes down. "I'll try to rein it in."

"Oh don't you *dare.*"

He touched the note. "What's this?"

"Something from Giles. It was slid under the door. Don't worry. If there's one thing I've learned about this place and that man is that he likely didn't do it himself. Apparently, 'mage' is another word for 'lazy'."

"What's it say?"

"That Myrgen destroyed the amulet the priest made, but that we need to make sure no others are out there. He says we need to ask the Church."

"Like Heaven? He's a *Saint*. Isn't that *his* area?"

She tapped the note to her lips. "I think we need to get dressed. I want to talk to my grandfather. But before we do, I am thinking about what you have offered. I'm just doing my *damnedest* not to answer when under the sway of your talents. I can't have you thinking you can just talk me into things. It has to at least appear like it's my idea."

"I'll accept that."

Alexander went across to his own room to prepare himself for a meeting with the Pope. Tanglwyst cleaned up and did likewise, opting for a Toledan surcote so she could wear her regular clothes beneath it but still look presentable. The Covenant's wardrobe made it appropriately white and gold. When the knock came at her door, she opened it to Alexander in gold and blue.

"You let the room pick for you too, huh?"

He held out his arms and looked at his outfit. "I guess this is what I think I should wear to talk to your grandfather."

"And this is what I should wear to talk to the Pope."

"Ah. What would it have chosen for you if you were asking about your grandfather?"

She waved her hand up and down his body. "Apparently, blue and gold."

They walked through the nearly empty Great Hall to the Meeting Room. Giles watched them go but instead of following them into their meeting, he allowed himself to be dragged upstairs. Both of them were silently grateful. They sat down with the great map behind them and held hands.

"I'm quite nervous."

She smiled. "Don't be. I was researching these before, remember? I just hope he's okay."

Pope Gregory glanced at his mirror as it shimmered to life. He saw his granddaughter's face for a moment, then willed it dormant.

"And how long have they been here?"

The gruff Cardinal frowned at the four people kneeling before His Holiness. "Weeks, it appears. *This girl* claims they came here by magic, but this man insists he is a messenger for the Crown of Mervolingia."

"And the other two?"

Henri bowed his head. "Just visitors on the day the thorns rose, Your Holiness."

"Pilgrims, actually." Ce'Nedra took Henri's hand. "My husband was cured by King Alexander and we made a pilgrimage to the Holy City."

Gregory looked him over. "What was your ailment, my son?"

"I lost an arm in a battle with a child killer." Henri nodded to Sylvaine. "Her husband, to be exact."

"And the King restored your arm?"

"Yes sir."

Gregory looked at the Cardinal. "Is this why they are in my chambers, Your Excellency?"

"Hardly. They must be *lying*, Your Holiness. No *man*, much less an un-ordained monarch, could possibly have done this."

The mirror awoke again and Gregory got up and walked away from it, putting the group between him and the mirror. The group shifted to face him.

"So, you're telling me that these people, who have nothing to gain from lying, told you a tale of the future King's miracles, and your punishment is to give them a private audience with me?"

Tanglwyst waved at Gregory, then Alexander's face moved into the mirror. Gregory gave a blink and inclined his head slowly.

"And where is the King of Miracles now, Your Excellency?"

"I... of course..."

"You don't know. But I do. He was touring the country in search of a Queen among his people."

Alexander pointed to Tanglwyst, then clasped his hands pleading. She rolled her eyes. He crossed his fingers and looked hopeful. Tanglwyst moved him aside and pointed at the map behind them to the Mervol border.

"However, the sudden growth of the Black Forest and other incidences in the north have him dealing with more international matters."

Tanglwyst and Alexander pantomimed sword fighting and archery with him dying.

"There appears to be a war."

They pointed to Krakte.

"With Krakte. That means the Fae forces are involved."

They nodded. He pointed to Krakte, then to Tanglwyst, then put his hands on the side of his head with his fingers up, like a crown.

"The Krakten Queen..."

Alexander nodded. Then he collapsed, head lolling to the side, tongue out and eyes closed.

"...is dead. This has caused quite an upheaval in the kingdom. With the Black Forest extended past even *our* borders, anyone within cannot leave, at least none of the Fae natured persuasion."

Ce'Nedra's face sank. "Who killed the queen?"

Alexander looked ashamed, rubbing his face. Tanglwyst put her hand on his shoulder and pointed to Mervolingia.

"Mervolingia."

Henri looked at Ce'Nedra, then back at the Pope. "Was it Alexander who did it?"

Alexander shook his head, then drew a bow.

"No. It was a Mervol soldier. An archer. But His Majesty is making it right as we speak."

Tanglwyst and Alexander both nodded.

"That is a very kingly act for someone not yet ordained, Quentin."

Jude walked behind Alexander and Tanglwyst. He looked at the Pope and waved.

"And it appears Saint Jude is watching over our young king in his time of need. Since he is my personal Patron Saint, I find this very comforting."

They both turned to see Jude behind them, then turned back to Gregory.

The Cardinal seemed quite out of his depth. "Well, I suppose that's a very good sign then?"

"And this man, Henri, who says the King healed his arm after it was wounded-"

"Severed, sir. Removed with an axe." Henri squeezed Ce'Nedra's hand.

"*Removed* even. You find this unlikely?"

Alexander looked at Tanglwyst, then nodded.

"My Lady Ce'Nedra, was it? How many people did Alexander cure?"

"Dozens, Your Holiness. Every raped and maimed child tortured by Lord Rochefort. Every person who lost an eye or a limb at the mill or on a fishing boat. Even people who had sepsis, or were sick with tumors. He cured them all."

Gregory looked at the mirror and Alexander nodded. Tanglwyst hugged him as he looked upset by the incidents.

"And this took place when?"

"Second week of the season, Your Holiness."

"So, months ago. Why do I have no reports of this? Did no one see fit to inform the Papal City of such a miracle?"

Henri spread his hands. "I sent a bird for the priest in St. Andrew myself, sir. The next day. And several letters from grateful townsfolk right after Lady Tanglwyst left."

"She was there too?"

322

"She and Gwen Douglas helped when pilgrims swarmed the town after the King left."

Alexander nodded, smiling at Tanglwyst. He kissed her hand. Gregory stroked his beard to hide a smile.

Quentin straightened up, getting stiff backed again. "Perhaps the letters never got here before the thorns arose."

"But my granddaughter managed to make it here, spend four days investigating the library, and go back home in that time?"

"I..."

"Henri, how many letters did you send for the villagers."

"At least one a day. Around thirty-two. And three birds."

Felix the Messenger looked at Henri. "I have one of them, Your Holiness. Or at least I did. The Cardinal took it. It's in his cassock right now."

Gregory looked at Quentin. "Boy, find it then."

Felix stood and reached not the Cardinal's cassock.

Henri saw the opened letter to the Crown. "I sent that to the Mervol Royal Palace. It was unopened until that man took it from us."

"There's blood on this."

Felix glanced at the others. "Yes sir. I'm sorry. It's mine."

Alexander was furious. He leaned in to watch the scene. He looked at Gregory.

"Your Majesty, may I read this missive meant for you?"

"You may, Your Holiness."

Everyone turned at the sound of Alexander's voice. The Cardinal's eyes grew wide with horror.

"Your Majesty, it is a follow-up report to 'the other letters', stating there have been a few more child disappearances and that Lord Rochefort is no longer leaving witnesses.'"

Henri frowned. "That was sent in the day Duncan stopped him. Right before close of business."

Alexander's face dropped in regret. "I never got to thank him for that."

Tanglwyst squeezed his hand.

"Felix, was that letter sealed when it was in your possession?"

"Of course, Sire. You never know when Krakten sealing wax has been used. We never open letters addressed to specific people."

"Did the Cardinal open it?"

"Yes, Sire. We all saw him."

Sylvaine, Ce'Nedra, and Henri all nodded.

"I believed it was contraband, Your Holiness. And dangerous. I am well within my right to do so."

"Quentin, why are you acting like this? I've never known you to be corrupt or extreme."

Henri glared at the man. "It's the amulet."

Alexander and Tanglwyst tensed. "What amulet?"

"The one he's wearing right now."

Cardinal Quentin disappeared, leaving everyone coughing and waving away the stench.

Gregory looked around. "Where did he go?"

"Anywhere he's already been."

Tanglwyst leaned on the table. "Except he panicked. He's probably in the amulet's room. It takes you there automatically if you get too afraid."

Henri got to his feet. "That room was destroyed. He's in the basement!"

The four of them bolted from the room. Gregory saw the guards look at them. "Follow them and arrest Cardinal Quentin."

The guards drew their weapons and ran off. Gregory closed the door and touched the panels. A glow came up around the room.

"That should keep him out of here, at least."

"The amulets are divine, but have an infernal component."

"I could tell, my boy. That's why I set that ward. The brimstone gave it away. Excellent timing, by the way. You made me look positively omniscient."

"We didn't realize you had a communication crystal."

"Well, on my side, it's a divine magic mirror. It was made to communicate between the Papal City and the Archbishoprics. A hold over from the days when Sir Richard walked the world."

"We don't have Sir Richard but we have Saint George." Jude was perky, which seemed a bit out of place, given the circumstances.

"So, the Saints are walking the world again, I see."

"It's a long story, but yes." Alexander looked at Jude, then back at Gregory.

"And now you want to marry my granddaughter? I thought she was accused of treason and regicide."

324

"My brother faked his own death so he could run off with his mistress. But he *was* being poisoned. By the Queen. Tanglwyst and her brother Myrgen were wrongly accused."

Tanglwyst sighed and closed her mouth.

"Not quite the whole story, my dear?"

"No. But in the end, it's close enough."

Gregory smiled. "Well then, this is good news."

"And now for the bad."

They told him everything.

Forty

"When you must walk through the land of
the enemy, do so with respect."
-The Forty-Five Voices

"What do you want to do now?"

Tanglwyst stretched. "I kind of want to check on the ship."

They got up and all three went outside. The *Sulocco* was not yet complete but the sailors had gotten to work on it. Stone supports on both sides cradled it upright and slightly off the ground.

Giles was standing there as the sailors cheered and climbed aboard.

Alexander smiled at the celebrating. "What happened?"

Jude crossed his arms. "I heard creaking and thought someone needed to know. So, I told the Captain and they got Giles out here."

Tanglwyst looked at Giles. "You didn't add brace supports when I told you about the necessity of them? I said the ship will break itself if left on its side."

"I figured you were a businesswoman. You didn't know anything about ship making."

"Are you bleeding kidding me? I've been sailing and building these ships, designing the interiors, for *twelve years*!"

"Yes, but just putting flowers and sheets and furnishings and -"

"No! *I* drew up the interior plans. I worked with a master shipwright to figure it out."

"So, a man did the real work?"

Alexander leaned over to her. "Should I?"

"He's not worth it."

Giles rolled his eyes. "Wow. Someone's on her -"

She hit him in the mouth and stormed off.

"It's actually not a curse with you, is it?" Alexander shook his head. "You're just this big of an entitled jerk, aren't you?"

Giles spit out some blood. "I... No. I really am cursed. I did this to my wife until she killed me. It resets whenever a woman enacts violence upon me or I get killed. Now I'll have about a week before it gets strong again.

"This repair will be done by morning. The crew is getting things loaded for the trip. We move it all tomorrow and get everyone under way."

Jude patted Giles on the back. "You're hopeless."

Alexander snorted and went back inside.

The next morning, the sky cleared. Tanglwyst and Alexander looked at each other.

"That's not good."

Alexander shook his head. "That it isn't."

"Is Heracles back home then?"

Alexander nodded. "I was going to bring him with us but I don't know what we'll be dealing with in the Black Forest and I wanted him with Emmy. He seemed okay with that."

"Good. You'll see him soon."

They climbed on to the ship and found the crew bustling already. Captain Nesbit came over to them as they came on board. Alexander stood at the rail.

"Permission to come aboard, sir?"

"Granted. Thank you."

"I wouldn't want to be cursed while here."

Tanglwyst smiled at Alexander, then looked to David. "The sky is clear. That's not good. It means Gloriana is conserving her strength."

"We thought the same. The hull is almost closed. We figure after breakfast, she will be whole and we can get her in the water."

Alexander looked at the ship. "Can he take the whole thing? He didn't before."

"He had a circle drawn around the center of the ship at the time. That's what he used to move it. See how the supports have grown in the night?"

Tanglwyst looked over the railing. "Oh, I see it. That wasn't here when I left last night."

"He did it afterwards."

"Yeah, Alexander told me about the curse. I think I can help him with that."

Alexander smiled. "You're just going to hurt him every day, aren't you?"

"Every. Damned. Day."

Giles came up to the railing and started to walk onto the ship. Tanglwyst punched him in the throat.

"It's polite to ask to permission to come aboard."

Giles gasped and reeled, falling to the level below.

The sailors looked over the edge and when he groaned and moved, everyone went back to work.

"I love you." Alexander kissed her.

"You should."

An hour later, Giles was on his feet again. Alexander handed her the amulet and she and Giles teleported away. When they returned, Giles raised his hands and the entire ship was gone.

She handed the amulet back.

"Where did you take him?"

"The Storm King's Island. We have a pick up to do there."

"There's something on that island that you trade for?"

"Yes. And it is very beneficial to both parties."

He arched an eyebrow. "Will that ever be something I can know about?"

"I don't know."

He waited but she seemed to have nothing further to say. "You still going to Cliffport?"

"As much as we need to get ready for Coronation, we also have a lot to finish up here."

"We?"

She turned to face him. "If you'll have me."

He picked her up and kissed her. "C'mon. Let's get this done."

Nina got up and walked out into the Great Hall. She looked around, confused. She saw Jude.

"Where am I?"

"You are in the Haunted Covenant. About a day's walk north of St. Giles."

"How did I get here?"

"You were hurt. You were brought here to heal."

She looked around the empty Hall. "Where are the others?"

"They had places to go."

Her eyes went wide and she put her hand to her mouth. "Where's Emmy?"

"With her grandmother. She went home."

"No!"

Jude drew back. "Excuse me?"

"I have to get her out of there! She's in danger. He'll kill her, sacrifice her to get power."

"Why do you think that?"

Nina tried to calm herself. She brushed her hair behind her ear and took a deep, steadying breath. "He appeared out of nowhere. He made ink *scream*. He's changed. He's abandoned the throne to go all over the world. He's trucking with traitors and who knows what else?"

He'll kill her…

"Nina, I need you to answer me. Where did the black mark on your ear come from?"

Nina felt her left ear.

"And how did you know I meant that ear?"

"Because… that's…"

"That's where you hear the voices?"

She looked at him.

No.

"Voice. Just the one. It sounds like my own."

Jude patted her arm. "I was worried that might be it, that something was whispering. Will you come with me for a moment?"

Nina followed him into the meeting room. He went to the Bringer shard and tried to activate it.

"Darn, it isn't working. I was afraid that would happen. And you've already been in the healing spot."

He tapped his finger against his chin. "I remember hearing that holy ground can help with this. I guess we can't get more holy than Heaven!"

He touched Nina's hand and all of a sudden, her entire vision was overwhelmed with light. She heard people talking and felt woozy. The voice in her head went silent and Nina touched her ear.

"It's gone!"

Then her body was consumed by harsh silence and she felt her life compressing. The weight on her soul was crushing and she relived every sin she ever committed. The feeling of fear consumed her as Alexander reached out to the little Princess and she knew, she *knew* if he got his hands upon her, she would be damned. She twisted away from Alexander and in so doing, she felt the child's body protected from the monster that was her uncle. She felt peace. When Emmy's body hit first and crumpled beneath her, she felt horror and sadness at the loss of the sweet girl, but justified and vindicated mercy of her death saving her soul.

She started to fall, tiny and unrepentant, and she felt this sensation of rolling and rolling. Then she was in a dark place, the sound of fire crackling nearby. She felt as if she was being hung, and the rope broke before her neck did, that sense of accepting death, but then relief of getting another heartbeat to live. She felt the realization that she was not at home, nor at the castle, and that she needed to get back.

She knew the truth about Alexander now. She needed to stop him.

Jude exhaled and smiled. "I was hoping it would be that simple. There was a lot of divine energy up there, so I hoped it would do the trick. But there was so much, it could kill you. That was the Afterlife."

"I need to get back to Patras."

"Yes, about that. You will probably need to walk. I can go up to Heaven and back but going elsewhere would require us to spend more time in Heaven and you'd die."

"Oh."

"But don't worry. I'll stay with you. I kind of know where to go."

He pointed at the map. "See this purple line? That's a tunnel highway that goes to Cliffport, what you call St. Giles. Then we just head down the road back to Patras."

She nodded, thinking. "What's that purple line?"

"That one goes to Serenity."

"What's Serenity?"

"A very nice community. You might even like it there. It could be quicker too, since that's where Giles went. He can get you home in the same way Alexander got you here."

"Through witchcraft?"

"My Lady, he's Saint Giles the Monster Killer. Are you telling me you think Saint Giles is a witch?"

"I…"

"Let me ask you something. What *exactly* is a 'witch'?"

"It's a woman who casts spells on people to turn their souls over to Hell."

"And how did you hear about 'witches'?"

"The Church told us about them. The Inquisition hunted them down and saved us all."

"I see. And how are they different from the mages who saved the world from the Soulless?"

"The mages caused it all. Magic was the reason everything was destroyed."

"Were you there?"

She frowned at him. "What? Of course not."

"Well, I was in Heaven when all that happened, and my experience was quite different. Come on. I'll talk to you about it while we walk. Since magic seems to be a problem for you, we'll head to Cliffport. Get dressed for cold weather and we'll eat and be on our way."

Alexander and Tanglwyst arrived in Cliffport. She looked at the damage again and sighed. "On second thought, I think I need to go to Austra with Myrgen and Catriona."

He took her hand. "Are you sure?"

"Alex, I'm a fugitive."

"I made a decree."

"And how many people do you think you lost because of it? It's probably why you have more enemies at court than you used to."

"I have more enemies at court because I don't want to marry their daughters. They can't control me so they don't like me."

"How will you handle that?"

He sighed and looked at the line of Caratian soldiers. "I'm not sure. If I were honest, the people I would discuss this with will be leaving today. Myrgen is a master at politics and Catriona understands people and their motivations. And having them as allies could make a huge difference in dealing with the potential uprising of nobility. Besides, I need to be able to go to Emmy regularly."

She looked at him. "Then come with us."

"Really?"

"It will be on foot. Can you handle walking?"

Alexander got an indignant look on his face. "Are *your* boots good enough for that?"

She smiled. "Alright then. This can also test us as a couple. This kind of trip will either break us up or make us stronger."

They walked up to the Caratian soldiers and bowed. "I'm here to take the Queen to Austra."

The soldiers parted for her but stopped Alexander from entering.

"He's with me."

The soldiers did not change their stance.

She looked around and saw Myrgen helping load a wrapped body onto a litter. She waved to him and he came over when he was finished.

He gave her a quick hug. "You ready to go?"

"Sort of. I brought something with me but the soldiers won't let it through."

He looked and Alexander waved.

The soldiers moved aside.

"Thank you."

Myrgen gave Alexander a hug as well, which both surprised and was welcomed by the King. "Are you coming too?"

"Yes. We just talked about it. Tangl doesn't feel safe returning to Patras and she knew Sovereigna. We want to help." Alexander looked into the woods and saw a long line of Caratian soldiers going north. "Is that an escort?"

"No. Protection. Some Mervol soldiers were going to steal the Queen's body, hold it for ransom to get the Krakten army to leave, then destroy it when they were no longer capable of doing anything about it. Catriona destroyed the amulet the soldier was wearing, along with the soldier."

"We told Grandpa everything. He says we have his support, as much as he can give from his prison."

Alexander glanced at her. "Now we just have to convince the kingdom your sister is not dangerous."

"I understand. It was so familiar and natural to be there, but I've already been beheaded once. Our inner circle of cohorts isn't enough to let me walk the streets yet without hiding my face from the guards."

"Speaking of which, thank you for helping with Emmy and my mother."

"Gladly. C'mon. We're just about to head out."

Catriona was directing the army, who had packed up the entire valley. The area was picked clean.

Tanglwyst marveled at it. "This looks ready to replant."

Catriona gestured to the army. "They planted it yesterday. I even found enough of your parent root grapes to sow the field. It will be a lower yield than you're used to, but they will be restored in a couple years."

"Provided the Mervol army doesn't destroy it all."

"The Royal guard said that Sovereigna declared peace and that they were going to stay behind and rebuild. Then she was killed and the treaty, which was not yet drawn up, was broken. Several soldiers and officers were interested in staying behind to carry out her final orders. I'll leave that up to you to decide."

Tanglwyst looked at the half-Fae milling about, their fur coats thick for the trip back to Krakte. The valley was clear of snow but no warmer than the rest of the area.

"All of these people have families. I'll not use their labor when they could be reunited with their loved ones. Besides, there's no way to build anything. All the wood is on the other side of the Mervol army."

Catriona smiled. "Who said anything about using *wood*?"

Myrgen and Catriona led them to the head of the processional, just behind the litter with Sovereigna upon it, and they went into the woods.

Tanglwyst looked behind them as they left the valley. "The Caratian army isn't coming too?"

Catriona shook her head. "The Land has taken that valley. The Heaven worshippers have no place walking there."

Tanglwyst looked at Alexander. "So, that place is not Mervol territory anymore?"

Myrgen looked at them. "No. Technically, it's Krakten. They took it, so unless they return it, it will be disputed area. Since Caratia is an ally of Krakte in war, we'll hold it for them."

Alexander glanced at the soldiers lining the forest. "Is there something I can do about that?"

"Not until you're Coronated."

Alexander exchanged a look with Tanglwyst. She took his arm. "You sure you still want to be here instead of getting things done at home?"

He looked around. "I'll head to Patras when we stop for lunch or the night. Mother and I can talk about the arrangements."

She turned to Myrgen. "Where is Giles?"

"He went home, I think. He said he was going to get his laboratory operational. He has a Bringer shard to find us when he's ready."

Alexander leaned over to Tanglwyst. "How far away *is* Austra?"

"When there were roads, about two days travel by carriage from Patras. I'm not as worried about the lack of roads as I am about the things that were in the Black Forest whenever we rode past them. Now we're walking through them and I'm not sure we're ready."

Alexander fingered the amulet and Tanglwyst didn't blame him.

Forty-One

"One never knows an ally or an enemy on sight."
-The Forty-Five Voices

When they saw a tower in the distance near the end of the second day of travel, Catriona pointed it out to Herr Gerhart.

"What's that?"

"I fear I don't know, Bringer. It was not visible from the road when we came this way."

Myrgen kept his eye on it. "What are you thinking?"

"That you and I should check it out."

Myrgen sighed. "Sometimes, I bleeding *hate* being immortal."

Tanglwyst gestured to Alexander. "We'll go too."

Myrgen glanced at them both. "You sure? You're not immortal."

Alexander shrugged. "Yeah, but if something happens, you'll come fetch us, right?"

Gerhart stopped the processional.

They walked towards the tower, everyone cautious. The daylight filtered through the trees, but the cloud cover made everything dreary.

Alexander put a hand on Myrgen's shoulder. "Why did she end the Caratian Army escort an hour ago? With the diffused light from the clouds, enemies could be anywhere in this place."

Catriona glanced at him. "Because the Caratian army isn't infinite. I need to protect that valley and to bring them any farther would have opened up the valley for Mervol occupation."

"Yes, but that all just for show, right?"

"It's all for *your* show, Alex. You're the one who needs the threat to remain in order to stop your enemies at court. Without the occupation, there's nothing to stop them from staging a coup."

Alexander looked around. "I understand that. It just… I feel like we're walking into a trap."

Someone was sitting near the base and they relaxed when they saw it was Giles.

"Ah, there you are. I figured you'd be by here sooner or later."

"What are you doing here, Giles?" Myrgen helped him to his feet.

"Just here to be on hand. This place is a refuge for some very dangerous creatures and I had planned to join you but you left before I got back. I came to the closest point I could remember."

Alexander flicked a glance into the shadowy parts of the surroundings. "What kinds of creatures?"

"Like there is a hive of mind-control bees around here. They used to be in this tower but they're gone now. And there's an outcry of marpies about an hour north."

Catriona looked up at the tower. "Well, Myrgen and I met the bees right when the snows started. They fled east, to Persephone."

"Wait. Raven was there by then. Though not necessarily in the trap, now that I think about it. That must have been what all those marbles on the ground were. I thought they were seed pods."

"Marbles?"

"The place was covered in them. Probably killed by the cold."

Catriona swore. "We were hoping to protect them. They were sentient."

"Yeah, I remember. They also would have mind controlled the inhabitants of that town you mentioned. It's probably better that they were destroyed."

"How much farther is Austra, do you know?"

Giles shook his head. "No idea. There wasn't a corresponding city up here. Just a bunch of hunting camps. And wymmicks."

Alexander smiled. "Really? Wymmicks?"

Myrgen looked uncomfortable at the idea. "What are those?"

"Lion centaurs, upper half human, lower half lion. Fierce warriors, that fight with bows and wielding swords while covered in armor."

Tanglwyst looked at him. "How do you know that?"

"Mother *loves* fairy tales. Stories of fantastic creatures were always my favorites."

Myrgen put his hands on his hips and glared at Giles. "And you took over a *day* to let us know we were in potential danger?"

Giles shrugged. "I had no idea where you were."

Tanglwyst looked nervously around the darkened woods. "Maybe we should scout ahead. The army can protect Her Majesty, but I'd like to head off any challenges so her progress isn't slowed."

"I'll see if I can find the village you are looking for."

"Capital city."

"Capital city. Right."

He disappeared, then reappeared instantly. "Oh.... That's right... the Forest has a ceiling..."

Then he passed out. Catriona dropped beside him and checked to make sure his neck wasn't broken. She found a lump forming on the top of his head. "Well, whatever he hit, it knocked him out."

Tanglwyst watched him go down. "I wonder if that ceiling was female."

Alexander crossed his arms, also watching Giles drop. "You already hit him this week, remember?"

"Oh. Right." She looked at Myrgen and Catriona. "We were going to scout ahead?"

Catriona looked up at the couple. "We can't just leave him here."

Alexander crouched down. "I've got this."

He disappeared and reappeared a few seconds later with wet shoes and pant legs. "He'll be fine now."

Tanglwyst smiled. "You need to learn that spell that dries your clothes."

"I agree."

Suddenly, a woman-lion warrior shimmered into view.

"Are you alright, My Lady?"

Tanglwyst bowed. "I'm fine, Kandhar. Are you alone?"

"No."

Several other wymmicks dropped their camouflage.

"Good. We have a question for the Governance."

"Understood. Thank you for removing the Mage."

"I'm glad he removed himself. I didn't want him anywhere near you."

"Tangl dear?" Myrgen said what the others were clearly thinking.

She looked at the others. "Kandhar, this is my future extended family. Family, this is Kandhar, Protector of the Jeweled City."

"This way please."

Myrgen leaned over to her, his voice a harsh whisper. "*This* is why you suggested we scout ahead?"

"Actually, I have been expecting Giles to show up for a while. I couldn't let them reveal themselves until he was handled."

Myrgen turned to Catriona. "You knew this, didn't you?"

She feigned surprise. "How could I have *possibly* known about this?"

"Uh-huh."

"I could tell she was looking for something but I wasn't going to read her to find it. That would be rude."

Alexander leaned over to Tanglwyst. *"You know wymmicks?"*

She smiled at him and didn't reply. Myrgen wagged his finger at her. "Oh no you don't. You explain right now."

"Several years ago, when I was out returning spoils of war, we were sailing down from Glarren with a load of wool and sheep. A storm blew in and we anchored for the night partway between the Storm King's island and the cliffs. That night, we saw lights at the base of them, near the water line. The next morning, we took a boat over to the area and found a cave.

"We went in and there were these magnificent creatures."

Kandhar smiled, gesturing to Tanglwyst. "It was quite a surprise to us too. I had never seen a human before. I was as fascinated as she was."

Tanglwyst grinned at her friend. "We talked and I managed somehow to not offend them. We learned that they had a ton of old rocks and stones that were worthless to them so they would throw them into the ocean when they were done with them. That's what they were doing the night before.

"We asked if they had anything to trade and they just had these rocks which were useless for planting. Turns out, the rocks were uncut gemstones. So, we traded the sheep and wool we were carrying, and a couple sailors to get them set up for shepherding, for the gemstones. We asked about setting up a regular visit but the things they needed most they couldn't get. When we asked what it was, they pointed to the Island and said they needed soil for farming from that island. Plus, there were herbs that helped with 'misbirths' that were only found on that island. Unfortunately, due to the nature of the forest, they couldn't get it themselves.

"We volunteered to bring back Mervol soil but they said that the island soil was the only kind they could use. But they had a way to navigate the storms so we could get there. They gave us a compass that would steer the ship through the maelstroms."

Alexander pointed to Tanglwyst. "That's why you weren't afraid to take the refugees there."

"Exactly. I knew we could get there unscathed. The compass was calibrated to pass the Maelstroms, but it wasn't set to handle the extra storm that arrived out of nowhere. Anyway, we brought back a hold full of dirt and herbs and plants and a ton of other things, including household furnishings from the Giant's house that is there. We usually make a trip out here to start the season and return to the Jeweled City with a hold of dirt and plants which grow like weeds over there."

"Why don't you just gather the herbs yourself? Cut out the middleman."

Kandhar shook her head. "The plants she wants are a hybrid. Yes, they mingle over on the island, but we can separate the traits we want through selective breeding. Supplementing with the original strain strengthens the herbs we grow. We add them into the rows and let them cross-pollinate. Unfortunately, the hybrid is a black widow and drains the original strain. That's why they don't grow naturally on the island, despite both parents being there. They don't grow near each other. And all it costs us is a bunch of useless rocks we were dumping onto the ocean."

Alexander smirked at Tanglwyst. "Which is hidden somewhere, right? That's why you weren't worried about expenses per se, but more about getting people their homes and families back."

"Pretty much. I have money when I need it. I have stashes all over. But the people I trust are not as plentiful. The stones are still uncut so they aren't as valuable as cut ones would be, but that works out just fine for me."

Myrgen shook his head, smiling. "That's how you built up your business so quickly. I had no idea how you could get that far, that fast with just seventeen ships twelve years ago."

"Kandhar and her people have been very good to us."

Kandhar looked over her shoulder at them. "Don't make us out to be *too* altruistic. We are tricking this stupid human woman into taking garbage rocks in exchange for precious soil, livestock, and food. Plus, she travels to the dangerous island to do it."

Tanglwyst laughed. "I'm not very smart."

Alexander looked at Kandhar. "You don't use the stones to build houses?"

"Oh, we do. These are the leftovers that we give her. This way."

Kandhar touched a small stone and it split apart to reveal a large, wide stairway going underground. They went down, following the wymmicks, until it opened into a cavern. It spread out for a mile, glittering houses made entirely of sapphire, ruby, emerald, topaz, and amethyst. A larger building in the center combined the gemstones into a beautiful array. A large globe of glowing white-gold hung above it, slowly being covered by a pale blue cover.

Kandhar pointed to it. "The globe acts as a sun and moon reflector, so things sleep during the night and are nourished by the sun during the day."

Tanglwyst pointed to the city. "Stores line a pair of long avenues that intersect, quartering the city. They start at the central building."

Alexander looked the town over. "Do the different sections mean something? Maybe segregating species or professions?"

Kandhar shook her head. "No. Everyone just moved into whatever home they chose. The Great Architect built what he wanted on a whim. People moved in much later. The avenues just provide access. Every home has a garden plot and in the center of each section is another area for growing more food. Around the entire thing is a fenced field where the livestock roam and thrive."

"What's that center building?" Catriona nudged her chin towards it.

Kandhar smiled. "It has many uses. The first is as a place of learning. Magic and science are taught there. The next floor up is our governing offices. The third floor is the mining factory. We take the stones mined by the tunnel systems and transfer them into more reasonable sizes so things can be manufactured. We used to dump the final waste stones, fragments too small to be of use, into the sea but now, we set those aside for when the *Sulocco* visits."

"Speaking of which, it should be here any time now. I sent it directly to the Island. I'm sorry we fell behind."

"We saw that the ceiling is shedding snow. It was not the time for it. We wondered if that played a part."

Myrgen looked up. "Wait, is that the root system of the Black Forest?"

"It is impenetrable and cannot change. It makes it very strong. We mined away everything that was not the forest, originally thinking to create a hole for the sunlight to come in. When that didn't happen, we discovered things like rain and snow *did*."

Alexander gestured to the city. "Is every house inhabited?"

"Oh, no. Our Grand Architect just builds what comes into his head. About one-eighth of the houses stand empty. He has focused his attention to the tunnel for the last several years."

She gestured to the great hole in one side of the cavern wall. Lights glowed all along it as it traveled well into the distance. Two side walkways carried wymmicks and other creatures as well as humans into the tunnel and two center ones carried stones and personnel out, all moving on their own.

Tanglwyst peered over at it. "How is the tunnel coming?"

"We broke through a few months ago. Trade has been much easier."

"I'm so glad. Will you be taking the garbage rocks to them now?"

"No more than we have been all along. They care more about ores than stones anyway. Steel production is up and we have several new mechanical components since the year started."

Catriona gestured to the ceiling of roots. "Has the Black Forest expanding had an impact?"

"It has, but the depth of that is yet to be seen."

Alexander's eyes showed concern. "Have they attacked the human settlements?"

Kandhar looked shocked. "Attacked? Hardly. They have rejoiced. When a half-Fae child comes to learn at the Shimmering College, they can never return to the outside world. This means only full humans can bring messages or visit. The Expansion has allowed long separated family members to reunite. It is a glorious time! That's why the city is so empty right now. They are in Austra for the party."

Myrgen stopped. "Wait, is that why we're down here? To see if the army can come through?"

Tanglwyst nodded. "I didn't want to just bring them in without permission. Marching an army through a territory without warning could be seen as an invasion."

They got on a walkway that moved on its own and it took them in a large open door of the second story in the center building. They walked through elaborately sculpted halls into a main chamber. Inside were a plethora of silken-clad mythical creatures, doing various tasks. Kandhar went up to a group of these standing together.

"Your Governances, may I present the Death Bringer and Hunter."

Kandhar and the rest of the wymmicks parted, leaving the party standing alone. Catriona and Myrgen looked at each other and stepped forward, bowing.

"Your Governances. We bring before you the King of Mervolingia, on a diplomatic mission to Austra. We are returning the Queen of Krakte to her people and ask permission to bring her army through here."

The wymmicks' Governance bowed. "We are honored to meet you, Your Majesty. She is of course granted access for her people. Why does she not ask this herself?"

Alexander took a knee before them. "I regret to inform you that she died on the field of battle."

The Governance muttered in horror and sorrow. "What happened?"

"It is my fault. The Angels desired war amongst humankind. They sought to make it happen by any means possible and used my people and hers to do so. They have succeeded more than they have failed, I'm afraid."

Catriona put her hand on Alexander's shoulder. "The army bearing her body was behind us. May we send for them so she will not be in the cold?"

The wymmick put a fist to her chest and bowed. "Of course. We will fetch them immediately. Our scouts saw them on the way to the Mervol border. We hoped to hear they were victorious."

"They were. They defeated the will of Heaven, thanks to the Death Bringer's arrival." Alexander gestured to Catriona.

"This is a tale we wish to hear, but we will send a scribe with you to record it. Until then, please, eat with us and raise a glass to her greatness and bravery. Tomorrow, we will make our way to the capital city and aid in her presentation.

"Rise, Your Majesty. Thank you for escorting her back, and for accepting this burden upon your soul."

"My kingdom, my responsibility."

Tanglwyst stood by his side as they all went to the dining hall for dinner.

The next morning, everyone headed out to the tunnel. The scribe assigned to the task was a stout, indigo-haired half-Fae who took down not just the tale of the battle, but of everything leading up to that moment. She got everyone's perspective individually to better understand the narrative, with a different book recording each member's tale. The information about Heaven was especially interesting to her, as well as that of Summerland. She spent as much time listening to the different stories as she did asking questions. The friends countered and added to each story, asking questions of their own, until they arrived in Austra.

Before they emerged from the tunnel, the Governances took the four aside.

"We have these for you. Please wear them."

Each was presented with a brooch. Tanglwyst put hers on immediately. Her clothes transformed into an emerald green gown with silver trim and white lining. The sleeves and bodice were cut to reveal the white silk beneath and it all defied gravity.

Alexander put his on and was covered head to toe in blue and gold of a similar style. Upon his head sat a gold crown with the crest of Mervolingia in the center.

Myrgen donned his and was covered in greens and browns, with amber embroidery that ran through his clothes like veins in a leaf. On his back was the Granite Bow and at his hip was the White Granite Sword.

Catriona's was black with flecks of gold that moved around it like lights through a prism. Her sword was her Stâpâna's emblem, the pommel shining in the accents. Pinned to her shoulder were three green and silver braids and a cloak with the arms of Krakte cascaded down her back in a military fashion.

All signs of fatigue and travel had been removed. Hair was decorated with matching gems and jewelry decorated every wrist, ear, and neck.

Alexander offered his arm to Tanglwyst and escorted her to the processional. Myrgen and Catriona followed suit.

The doors to the city were opened and the processional went to the castle. People were cheering and dancing in the streets. Music poured from several mead houses and inns and every manner of human-Fae mixture was talking and greeting each other like old, long lost friends.

Many saw the processional but few understood what it was. The soldiers re-entered the city like a parade. Musicians fell in with the army to celebrate their return. Dancers carried silk streamers alongside the Queen's body, which the Governance had draped in green silk organza.

Krakten Main was an ornate place that was clearly the inspiration of every fairy tale castle. Tall spires crowned the corners and silk banners flew from every peak. Krakten banners cascaded down the walls by the portcullis. The merriment continued right up to the gates of the palace itself. A line of people was coming and going, all dressed in their finest. Two liveried half-elves stood by the open doors.

One bowed to the group. "Names?"

Everyone deferred to Myrgen, and he stepped forward. "I am Myrgen de Sablonierres, Hunter companion to the Death Bringer. I present the Death Bringer, The King of Mervolingia, and, um… Lady Tanglwyst de Holloway. We are escorting home the Queen Sovereigna."

The other herald stopped a group of party-goers from entering and came over to the form being carried on the litter. He waved the guards over as the onlookers started to pile up, gesturing the group to follow them inside.

Fae, half-Fae, and human alike all mingled in the shining hall below. No musicians were present, yet music cascaded around the room like confetti.

The second herald ran inside and up to a dais with two sizable thrones. A large human man with skin nearly as black as moonless night sat next to an empty one, smiling happily at the merry makers. The Herald bowed and spoke to the man, who stood and pulled a lever beside his throne. The music stopped and he grinned, spreading his arms wide to the assembled populace.

"My great friends! Our Queen returns!"

The people cheered and turned to face the doors. They spread apart, letting the processional make its way across the floor. Cheers were replaced with heart-wrenching cries as her draped form passed. People knelt and in seconds the whole room was quiet. Catriona, Myrgen, Alexander, and Tanglwyst took up positions at the four corners of the litter as the King came down to her.

The drape upon her was translucent but clearly the man hoped it was not her, as did many of the people watching. He pulled the drape away to reveal it was indeed his Queen, and the room deteriorated into cries and loud wails in recognition.

"What happened?"

Alexander cleared his throat, his own emotion showing in his voice. "Heaven conspired against her and killed her, along with the Voice of Command, Bartolemaus Johner. She had negotiated peace with Mervolingia and received justice for her daughter Elizabeth before she fell. I have brought her here to honor that peace accord"

"Is the assassin dead?"

"Yes. And the Angels that were behind it."

"Who killed the assassin?"

There was a small rumbling and an eagle archer stepped forward. "I did."

"Then I bestow upon you great accolades from the throne of Krakte. We will address his tomorrow."

The eagle archer took a knee. "Sire, if I may."

The king cocked his head. "Speak."

"Sire, this is Myrgen de Sablonierres, former Chancellor to Queen Elizabeth and the Hunter to the Death Bringer here. He and the Death Bringer stopped an attempt to steal and harm her body. They then accompanied her to this place, to be certain nothing would happen to her."

The King of Krakte looked at the assembled companions. "I am most honored at your presence. Thank you beyond all thanks for bringing her home to me. This is the first time laying eyes upon my beloved in this room. We have never been able to occupy it together."

He looked at Catriona's attire and bowed deep. "Death Bringer, it has been far too long since I have heard your name. And now you lead our army."

"Only until your throne lifts up a new Queen. We know Sovereigna's heir and wish to bring her here. The daughter of Elizabeth and granddaughter of Sovereigna."

"Why did you not bring her with the Queen?"

Alexander bowed. "That is my fault, Your Majesty. I need her in Patras for my own Coronation."

The King turned a baleful eye upon Alexander and Tanglwyst felt the pit of her stomach fall to the floor.

"Who are you that speaks out of turn?"

"I am Alexander Angloume, Heir to the Mervol Throne."

The attendees gasped, and a few swords were drawn from their scabbards. The King held up his hand for silence.

"You travel with the Death Bringer. Is this your desire, to feel her embrace?"

Alexander flicked an uncomfortable glance at Tanglwyst over the phrasing. "Not anymore, Your Majesty. She has a lover already."

The King's eyebrow arched and he looked at Catriona, who was visibly fighting a smile. Myrgen likewise was flattening his lips to hide his laughter.

Tanglwyst snorted.

The King looked over the companions and broke into a laugh, which cut through the tension. The rest of the room varied between thinking it was incredibly inappropriate, and incredibly funny.

"Well, Sovereigna always loved to laugh and did so frequently in this place, I'm told. Come, join us as friends this night. Tell the tale of her to us. I am King Rhyzard Dudek, Die Elegante Lösung. You are my guests."

Forty-Two

"Good or ill luck is all in the interpretation."
-The Forty-Five Voices

Alistair looked at the situation with the Krakten forces and closed his eyes. He knew giving them safe passage would cause problems later but for now, his friends were safe. He wanted to lie down, to sleep, but something told him to stay on his feet. Besides, there was a nearly dead angel in his bed and he didn't feel like sharing.

He felt out of balance in part because he could not see the trap anymore and therefore, felt cut off from his only real purpose in the world. He stumbled to the pillows and lay down.

His eyes closed and he felt himself drift.

He was at sea again, and he got up, anxious to feel the wind in his hair and the ocean brine in his nostrils. James was talking to the Quartermaster and he came over to Alistair.

"We have a problem, Uncle. We are missing a sword."

"What? How?"

"We don't know. It's not in any of the containers or anyone's bunk or sea chest."

He caught a glint down in his room and walked towards it. A shadow passed and he drew his sword, prepared for the worst. He entered his room and something jumped him, slicing at his sword arm. He raised the sword a little too late and caught half the blow with his shoulder. He pushed the attacker back and swung at them. The attacker turned into the blow, rolling down Alistair's arm to punch him in the gut.

Alistair doubled over, dropping his sword. The attacker kicked him back and swung at Alistair's head. He put up his hands and the blade cut right through them all. Blood spurted out, covering his chest and face. The assailant walked over and slipped in the blood, falling next to Alistair. The sword went spinning into the shadows.

Alistair flipped over onto the assailant and brought his elbow down hard into their throat. They tried to breathe but Alistair leaned on their throat with his forearm, strangling them. He heard feet running to him and he held up his hands to the assistants. They arrived in the door as he noticed his hands were intact.

He started awake and saw he was leaning on Uriel's throat. He leapt off the bed, confused. His hands were fine but Uriel looked like he was no longer breathing. He lifted the Angel and tried to get him to breathe.

"*Lucifer!*"

The door to his dimension flew open and Lucifer looked around. "Alistair!"

"Help! Help him!"

Lucifer rushed to the bed and saw Alistair looming over Uriel. "What happened?"

"I was dreaming… I was being attacked… Lucifer, what do I do?"

Lucifer gave Uriel a soul bead and a few seconds later, he coughed a breath. Alistair collapsed on the floor and Lucifer knelt beside him.

"Thank you."

"You alright now?"

Alistair looked at Lucifer. "I almost lost him. I need to get him out of here. He's not safe here anymore."

"I can take him. I'll make him a room. Or he can go back to Heaven. They are cleaning the place up there. He'll be okay."

"Yes. Yes. Please. Get him somewhere."

Lucifer picked up his cousin and carried him out of the bedroom. He saw the Giver asleep in another room, one without a door. He looked at Alistair.

"What about her?"

"Let her sleep. I'll tell her when she wakes up."

"Why don't you come with me, okay? We'll eat something and wait for Uriel to wake up."

Alistair looked at the Giver. "I…"

"She'll be fine. If you want to make sure she doesn't leave, seal the door back up."

"I tried to kill you."

"Yeah, but you failed. I have petit fours and brandy. C'mon."

Alistair went downstairs and closed the door.

Raven looked at the symbols again. "Brigit, Lauriel, we need to talk."

They turned to him. Brigit tool a deep breath and braced herself. "Okay, hit me."

"So, when Merrick made the spell notes, he wrote more than just the words. He did symbols in the words too."

Brigit held up her hand and thought about what he just said. "Okay, I think I can understand that. Keep going."

"Oh. Hey, that's smart! Take it in little chunks so you can eat them!"

"Digest them, but it's all the same. Continue."

"Okay, so the symbols are not close ones but far ones."

"Okay. Wait. Like, you can't see them up close but you can from a distance?"

"Yes!"

"Hang on." She set the pages on the floor and climbed the stairs to the mouth of the cave. She looked at the pages. "I'm not sure I see it."

"Put more distance between you."

Brigit tried to go farther back but she still couldn't see the symbols. "Maybe I can't see it because I don't have the gift."

"But you're an artist. You can find patterns, right?"

"Hm. Let me see. Now that I know I'm looking for a pattern… Hey, Lauriel, can you join me and raise us up to his eye level?"

Lauriel put himself on a pillar and when Brigit got back in the room, did the same to her. She looked at the pages.

"Okay, tell me what you're seeing, Raven. Where do my eyes need to go?"

He described the shape and at first, she didn't see it. But then Lauriel drew the shape with his paw and she saw it.

"Is that it?"

"Yes!"

"I want to copy this down. Get me back on the floor, Lauriel."

He did and she got her sketch book. She got back up on the pedestal and Lauriel elevated it. She used the perspective to pencil it in, and Raven confirmed that was the shape.

She continued, with his and Lauriel's help, to recreate the symbols. It took a while, but she managed it. She got all the way through before she noticed Raven wasn't talking anymore. She checked him, and he had fallen asleep. She looked at Lauriel and he lowered their plinths to the ground. Lauriel laid down on the floor.

Brigit looked at the symbols and flipped through them, trying to see the pattern Raven mentioned. She didn't have the gift, so none of it made sense to her. Still, it was soothing to look at them. She spent time writing the words and symbols together. Her mind wandered and she felt herself go into her Holy Trance, a mental state where she made art to the exclusion of all else.

When she snapped out of it, the book was closed and she felt tired. She took the book to a room she had gotten Lauriel's help to renovate. It was in one of the fallen towers and had all kinds of interesting shelves and debris from three centuries ago. She had wanted to know what they were like and what they did, these mages of Persephone, but all that knowledge was gone now.

She put the book under her pillow and laid down on the bed Lauriel had found for her. In a few minutes, she fell into a deep, dreamless sleep.

Giles woke up in the forest, cold and alone. His head hurt and he teleported to the Healing pool, just to be sure there was no permanent damage. It was dark, and he could see the outline of the Storm King's island in the moonlight. He remembered how full the Covenant had felt the last several days and how much he had missed the company of other mages.

Magic was back in the world now, though. Perhaps, the gift would start to show up again. He truly hoped so, since the only other mage that existed did not like him.

He went to Persephone and listened to the quiet. No one seemed to be stirring. Maybe Brigit had gone to bed.

He walked down the hall to the trap room and saw the pages Merrick had done in a stack near the opening, on what looked like a stone desk. He reached down to retrieve them, then stopped as he noticed Lauriel watching him, Fae eyes glittering with distrust. The animal growled, tensed, and leapt.

Giles grabbed the papers and reappeared in his sanctuary in Serenity.

I'm just going to copy them so I can study it too. If I can come up with something Raven didn't see, I can offer it as a peace gesture. I have a few days before I start being difficult. Then, I'll just find Tanglwyst and ask her to hit me again to correct it.

He put pages on a table and gave the command to copy them. Within minutes, exact copies of the pages were created. He took his copies and read through the spell.

Raven's assessment had merit, but Giles realized he had learned a lot just being around the younger mage. He may not have studied magic hypothesis with the new breakthroughs but Giles was able to make a few leaps of faith which had paid off. When he was done with the third go through of the spell, he figured he had the gist of it.

The spell was one of dormancy. Anything touched by the spell would go dormant and stay that way until the spell was broken. But the power supply for this spell was beyond worldly. In fact, it *was* the world. The spell was designed to use the world to feed the spell. But where was the spell *going?* What was so big, it needed to draw from the world and Heaven to put it to sleep?

He found a small symbol embedded in the paper. He looked at the others and found this as well. But they weren't the same symbols. It wasn't a watermark.

It was another spell.

He studied it, and cast a magnification spell, using the copying spell again to get the full information. He studied it for a few minutes.

I know this. It's a memory spell. But it's got a component I don't have here in the lab.

It needed a soul.

Some souls fell out of Heaven, near here.

He went to the map from before he died and cast a locator spell based upon loose soul stuff in the world. A few places lit up. Near a hunting camp to the north was a bright light, like several pieces together. But that was too far away. They fell to the world near the ring of stones.

He cast the magnify spell again and looked closer at the map near Serenity. He found a small, singular soul in a tree branch. He focused upon this item and retrieved it. He put the soul in a pestle and crushed it with a mortar until it was liquid. Then he used it to fuel the memory spell.

Earthquakes, volcanoes, and tidal waves dominated his sight. Destruction everywhere. Nothing lived, because anything that tried was destroyed. Then he looked up and saw titans so huge, the world was like a bath toy for a child to them. They moved the parts of the world to suit their whims and laughed, two of them, at each other's creations.

But then they disappeared, and everything got quiet. Plants bloomed, animals and monsters bred and populated. Humans evolved and grew. Magic and Fae taught them how to interact with the world. They built and grew and learned.

Then the world shifted and there was a moment when the great sky creatures were in view. But only for that moment. Then, the world settled and the inhabitants fixed what was broken and buried what was dead. This happened over and over until the creatures that lived in the world prayed for the suffering to stop. They didn't want it to end, just to stop being destructive.

Giles remembered the earthquakes, the sudden volcanoes that created islands in the sea. There was a vein of fire čaro under Caratia and one of the Headmasters at the Estate kept it secret. Giles and his companions had their families. He had created Serenity because it gave him peace of mind that if the world got destroyed around it, Serenity would still exist. No volcano or tidal wave or earthquake could destroy what was not there.

He watched as the world settled into a rhythm, and humanity grew and changed. But now, it was at war with the very creatures that helped them become human.

He had played such a role in that, he could credit himself with the destruction of over a hundred species. But still the world was stable. It would not pull itself apart and people could be changed. Lucifer had souls, pure ones. They could get the world on the right track again.

So long as there was a world.

When he came out of the memory, the pages were scattered on the floor. He stood and was about to pick them up when he noticed a pattern in the writing. He stood up, then stood on the table to get a better perspective.

He moved the pages around, reading the pleas from something greater than all of them.

Free us. Free us, please.

Giles looked at the pages for a very long time. Then he got down off the table and gathered them up, both what he wrote and the originals.

Then he lit a brazier and burned the spell.

Appendices

Appendix A: Characters of the Saintlands

Aggie- Innkeeper of the Fair Winds Inn and Tavern in St Marguerite. Husband of Flora, brother-in-law of Martin.

Aislyn Cortright- Nubian woman in St. Giles.

Alan Moriarity: Catriona's son. After his Naming Ceremony, Victor Tiberius Morstadora.

Albreda Wulftorhüter- Noblewoman of Krakte. Her and her husband Reinmar are inventors.

Alexander Angloume (ANG-loo-may): King of Mervolingia, Alexander succeeded the Throne after Charles. Alexander is also the Duke of Anjou, the family lands of the Angloume house.

Alistair MacGlarren: In service to Gloriana, the Midwinter Queen, Alistair is also the bloodline heir to the throne of York. The original Black Sparrow, he retired from this position after succeeding in learning about Tanglwyst's pirate operations. He stopped when Catriona, his former lover, found out. Alistair is also the father of James and Gwen. Since his death at the hands of Duncan McVryce, he has been serving Karma in the afterlife.

Allen Hobbs- Royal Patrolman for the Bordeaux Highway between St. Giles and Cliffbase.

Anika Zapolya- Dûcesa of Caratia. Holder of the Heartstone.

Antoinette: Cook in the mornings at the Patras Royal Palace.

Archbishop Alonzo de Patrone: Archbishop of Patras.

Artemisia: Mythical name of the Moon and mother of the Sea Goddess Calista.

Bartolemaus Johner- The Voice of Command (Lieutenant to Corrigan Starshadow).

Black Sparrow: Notorious pirate who attacked the Tanglwyst Trading Company. Taken out by Catriona Moriarity.

Brigit- Patron Saint of Healers. Alexander's personal patron saint.

Bringer- Short for Death Bringer. An entity of Power that has been missing for centuries. Counterpart to Giver.

Calpurnia Allegheri (cal-PUR-nee-uh AL-uh-GAIR-ee) the Autumnal Sovereign - Fae Lord of Autumn. Currently asleep in the tower of Sovereignlumin.

Catriona Moriarity (CAT-tree-OH-nah MORE-ee-AR-it-tee): Stâpâna of Caratia. The Stâpâna is the Protector of the Land's People in the country of Caratia, the second highest rank in the country. The Stâpâna is chosen through a secret ritual known only to those in Caratia. Lover of Myrgen.

Cecelia de Firenze- Simultaneously the proprietor of the Brew Ha House in guardianship of the Caratian Pass to York, and the head of the kitchens at the Royal Palace of Patras, respectively.

Ce'Nedra van Oppal- Innkeeper of the Black Cat and Anchor Inn in St. Andrew.

Cipriano- Annibal Cipriano Malatesta, King of Mande.

Charles Maximillian IX: Former King of Mervolingia, ruler and instigator of the St. Michael's Day Massacre.

Clara of Weltonshire- Patron Saint of Barren Women. Hero of the Soulless War, her holy footsteps blessed the soil where she walked. This soil was gathered by Raven Grasshair to corral the Last Child so that he could be captured and banished by Calpurnia. Although Heaven accepted her as the new Patron Saint of Barren Women (displacing Raymond non Nonattus after his ejection from Heaven), the Papal Council never acknowledged her.

Corrigan Starshadow the Midsummer King- Fae Lord of Summer.

Diane de Poitiers- Mistress to King Henry II. Murdered Henry in a jealous rage and then committed suicide due to being fed Cyprian Herb by him.

Dominic D'Medici (DOM-uh-nik dee MED-ee-chee): Fiancé of Gwen. As Acting Chancellor of Mervolingia, he is in charge of all funding and expenses for the entire kingdom.

Don- A general title of noble station. In Augustinian countries, it means Lord.

Drake Zapolya: Dûce of Caratia. The ruler of Caratia can be either male or female and is chosen directly by the Land through a ritual involving several trials and finally culminating in a ceremony in the town square of Zara.

Duncan McVryce: A notable member of the Back Streets of Patras, Duncan has played a role in several events involving members of the Royal family, the Augustinian church and Tanglwyst's interests.

Ealusaid (EL-uh-SASH)- Proprietress of the Benevolent Friar on the road to the Papal City.

The *Enigma*- Catriona's ship, it houses a Fae spirit named Estelle, that is the daughter of Corrigan, the Midsummer King. Estelle is wife to Octavius.

Entivia "Boots" Malatesta- Horse in the Stable of Assassins owned by Giovanni Sangiardo.

Embertwist Apocraphix the Vernal Monarch- Fae Lord of Spring.

Estelle Starshadow- Daughter of Corrigan and wife of Octavius.

Father Benjamin: A priest in service to Marco Giovanni, he was killed helping Catriona escape her captivity in the breeding pens of the Giovanni estate.

Felix Benivieni - Official messenger for the Royal Palace in Patras. Childhood sweetheart of Sylvaine Rochefort.

Flora- Innkeeper of the Fair Winds Inn and Tavern in St. Marguerite. Wife of Aggie and sister of Martin.

Fuccochio, Benivito (foo-KAH-chee-o)- Clothing designer in Florentine, Mande. Known for his fairness and incredible designs, his patrons are catalogued by the royalty and nobility of Mande.

Gabriel- Archangel. Patron Saint of Autumn.

Gillian Malatesta- Princess of Mande and daughter of Cipriano.

Giver- An entity of power being held captive in Heaven. Counterpart to Bringer.

Gloriana Talnig the Midwinter Queen- Fae Lord of Winter.

Gomez de Santander: Head of Alexander's personal guard, Gomez began as a guard at the Giovanni estate.

Gweneviere "Gwen" Douglas (GWEN-eh-veer DUG-lus): Handmaiden of Catriona, Gwen has the distinction of being her most trusted companion. Daughter of Alistair and Gloriana, twin of James.

Hamish Ó Caoindealbháin (HAY-mish oh CAY-lin)- Chief Ferryman for the Office of the Ferrymen in Kilgarren, York.

Helen Brightwater- Chatelaine for the Sanctuary Vineyards, held by the Tanglwyst Trading Company. Wife of Matthew Brightwater.

Henri de Porthos (OHN-ree dee POR-thos)- Chief Bookkeeper for St. Andrew. Beloved of Ce'Nedra.

Isabella D'Medici- Lawyer for the Tanglwyst Trading Company and cousin to Dominic D'Medici. Wife of Othon of Burwick.

James Douglas- Captain of the *Crimson Veil.* Brother of Gwen.

Jess Beck- Goatherd in Caratia. Husband of Rae.

Johannes- Bo'sun on the *Enigma.*

Karma- Entity of Balance. Worshipped by default in Yndia.

King Henry II: Father of Francois I, Charles, Alexander and Margaret, husband of Catherine, Deceased.

Kyri de Holloway- Daughter of Tanglwyst. Lives in Pardua, Mande, in the Storm Catch. Proprietress of the Storm's Catch Inn and Tavern.

Last Child- The last child left from the original children resurrected before the Soulless War. These children were returned by the Land to walk the earth, but their souls were already returned to Heaven with their deaths. As a result, they searched the world, draining life and destroying souls in their attempts to get one of their own. The Last Child hid away in Clara's basement and escaped because he convinced Mephistopheles to turn against Lucifer and serve him instead. Mephistopheles took him through the ground, thereby destroying all the farmland in York.

Lauriel- Fae wolf. Caretaker and responsible party for Raven Grasshair.

Lawrence of Cleves- Keeper of the Watch on the *Enigma.*

Lucifer- Archangel. Caretaker of Hell.

Marco Giovanni: Mandian Count and head of the Apolodorus family, Giovanni almost married his cousin to secure a large financial conglomerate but murdered his son and then committed suicide the tenday before his wedding, leaving the Apolodorus fortune to his oldest child. Father of Dominic.

Marica the Gold Wife- First creation of a mage entirely by magic, the blacksmith Hephas used a life spell to animate a metal statue he forged. The Land granted this and infused the Gold Wife with the ability to work earth magic. Unfortunately, Hephas only wanted her to speak to him, but he worded the spell poorly for the sake of rhyming. As a result, only one person at a time can understand her.

Martin- Proprietor of the Fair Winds Inn and Tavern in St. Marguerite, along with Flora and Aggie.

Matthias Lovas (muh-THI-us LO-vahs)- Stable Keeper of Ashstone in Zara, Caratia. Killed in the Second Mandian Invasion protecting Victor Tiberius Morstadora.

Merrick Blackburn- Mage at Persephone and hero of Soulless War. Beloved of Calpurnia, he watches over her as she recovers from the spell she cast to capture the Last Child.

Michael- Archangel. Patron Saint of Summer. Lost in the Soulless War.

Michael - Myrgen's Nubian Slave. A very large man who is fiercely loyal to Myrgen.

Michelyne- The Third Dûcesa, her name was only discovered after she died and was asked what her name was by the inhabitants of Summerland.

Miguel (MIH-gel)- Anika's cat from before she became Dûcesa.

Monique Delorme- Proprietress of the Wise Wench Tavern in St. Giles, and author of the Wise Wench Tavern Book.

Morgan Wolf - Vicar in St. Marguerite, and Myrgen and Tanglwyst's brother.

Myrgen "the Grey" de Sablonierres (MUR-gun dee SAB-yon-air): Former Chancellor to Mervolingia, he was accused of the regicide of King Charles. Wandering the world in search of his path, he is Catriona's lover.

Nicolai Moriarity - Husband of Catriona Moriarity and father of Tib. A guard in the Patras Palace. Dead by poison.

Nigel - King Charles's Castellan before Myrgen.

Nina Richelieu – Guard in of the Royal Palace at Patras, she is Gomez' second in command.

Octavius - First mate of the *Enigma* under Captain Catriona Moriarity, husband to Estelle.

Osondrea- Scribe for the Sanctuary Vineyards belonging to the Tanglwyst Trading Company.

Othon of Burwick- Former personal bodyguard of Tanglwyst. Husband to Isabella D'Medici.

Persephone- Covenant tower of Mages in York that was the war effort against the Last Child in the Soulless War. Also seen as the name of the entity that was the source of magic under the Covenant.

Pope Gregory - Head of the Augustinian Church.

Preston Cowley- Manager of the St. Giles Home Office for the Tanglwyst Trading Company. Married to Steve.

Princess Isabelle - A Mandian Princess of marrying age

Princess Marie-Elizabeth - The daughter of Elizabeth and Charles.

Queen Elizabeth of Krakte - Queen of Mervolingia, married to Charles Maximillian IX. Mother of Marie-Elizabeth. A school friend of Tanglwyst's along with Adriana Cappelletti.

Queen Elizabeth of York- Queen of York, and friend of Alexander.

Queen-Mother Catherine D'Medici - Mother of Charles and Alexander. Married to Henry II.

Rae Beck- Goatherd in Zara, Caratia.

Raphael- Archangel. Patron Saint of Winter.

Raven Grasshair- Mage from the Covenant at Persephone, son of Corrigan, in sworn service for Calpurnia. Ward of Lauriel.

Raymond non Nonattus- Patron Saint of Barren Women, expunged. Cast from Heaven after granting babies to a dozen Glarren women after they converted to the Augustinian faith. The women rejected the faith and returned to worshiping Fae once their children were born.

Reinmar Wulftorhüter- Krakten inventor and husband of Albreda.

Richard of Kent, Sir- Noble knight in service to the Covenant at Persephone. He and Raven went on a quest to get Clara's name in the Saintly Record. This quest failed but exposed the corruption in the Papacy. His death at the hand of Inquisitors sparked the Emilianite movement.

Rowena of Avalon- Jeweler in St. Giles.

Sinister Glove of Embertwist- Lieutenant to Embertwist.

Slade Stormchest- Stâpân to the First Dûcesa. Died protecting her from the Last Child right before it was banished into the void by Calpurnia's spell. The Last Child touched him instead of her and was then taken by the spell as he turned into a soulless.

Sovereigna Shwartzwald- Queen of Krakte, Elizabeth's mother, Marie Elizabeth's maternal grandmother.

Sovereignlumen the Eternal- Father of all Fae and beloved of Magic.

Svein (Sven)- Proprietor of the Benevolent Friar and husband to Ealusaid.

Sylvaine Rochefort- Widow of the Lord Rochefort who terrorized the families of St. Andrew. Childhood sweetheart of Felix.

Symonne- Proprietress of the Drum and Nightingale Inn and Messenger Service, guardian of the Caratian Pass to Mervolingia. Wife to Tomas.

Tanglwyst de Holloway (TANG-gul-wist dee HALL-oh-way): Owner of the Tanglwyst Trading Company and Catriona's secret partner. Sister of Myrgen and Morgan Wolf.

Thessius- Glarren member of Catriona's crew on the *Enigma*. Former First Mate to Ramirez on the *Crimson Veil*. Quartermaster on the *Enigma*.

Thomas the Diminutive- former Stâpân of Caratia, only one of two members of this order to resign the post without dying.

Tomas- Proprietor of the Drum and Nightingale Inn and Messenger Service, guardian of the Caratian Pass to Mervolingia. Husband to Symonne.

Trimelda Daniels- Dreamwalker for the Fang and Claw. Caretaker for Clara's Way and Clara's Bed. Clara's Bed is the monument to the Soulless War that is held in trust by the Crown of York. Couples who are seeking to get pregnant went here to conceive. As such, this became a royal honeymoon spot for post-coronation copulation.

Tristram Wulfschlager - Captain of the *Righteous*, one of Catriona's ships.

Tulio d'Or- Bandit king that holds the Contested Forest.

Uriel- Archangel. Parton Saint of Spring.

Urien Atreides - Husband of Tanglwyst de Holloway, a Latian Merchant who owns The Atreides Trading Company, which along with the Tanglwyst Trading Company controls 73% of the Mervol - Mandian trade.

Ûr- Caratian form of noble address

Wilgefortis- The wife of Raven Grasshair, she was also the Baroness of Canterbury in York and the Seneschal of Persephone during the Soulless War.

William- Navigator on the *Enigma*

Xannu (ZAN-noo)- Proprietress of the Open Lotus Incense and Bath House in Rouen.

Zachary Crow- Stable hand for the Benevolent Friar and adopted son of Svein and Ealusaid.

Appendix B: The Augustinian Calendar

The world of the Saintlands has four seasons, and those are the purview of the Fae Lords. Embertwist Apocraphix, the Vernal Monarch, rules over spring, Corrigan Starshadow, the Midsummer King, rules summer, Calpurnia Allegheri, the Autumnal Sovereign, reigns over fall and Gloriana Talnig, the Midwinter Queen, rules winter.

The combat these lords, the Church originally invoked the Archangels against them. These were sufficient but as Heaven gave the Church the Saints, these former humans were invoked in addition, adding to the strength of the protections against Fae trickery. The saints were originally celebrated upon the day of their ascension and delivery by Heaven into the Rolls.

However, 300 years ago, the Church, in the aftermath of a great war, decided to write down a formal calendar, honoring saints for their purviews instead of their date of ascension. This was to battle non-church beliefs, unify the masses and establish lines of Church control.

Pope Richard I told the cardinals to which he assigned this task to begin the year prior to the apex of Gloriana's control, so as to get ahead of the rise of her power. The Cardinals discussed it and Cardinal Cosimo of Pardua offered up Genevieve, invoked against disasters, to start the year. Richard approved and the calendar was begun.

Genevary became the first month and the months were divided into 31 day sets with tenday weeks. In the center of the month, the 16th, is the Devotional Day, where all work stops for a day to pray and invoke the saints of the month. This strengthened the divinity in the realm, repelling anything not Heaven related. Although the new calendar reorganized the role of Saints during the year, many days are still known by the saint who ascended upon that day, though the Archangel's days were established during the Augustinian Calendar.

Months

1st: Named after Saint Genevieve, **Genevary** 16 honors Sebald, Martin of Tours, and Raphael the Archangel. Genevieve is invoked against disasters, which abound in the Saintlands during the winter. Sebald once burned icicles in a poor woman's home to produce heat. Martin of Tours cut his cloak in half to give to a naked beggar. Raphael brings the heat of the sun and dawn to battle freezing cold.

2nd: Named after Saint Vitus, **Vitusary** 16 honors Medard, Catald, and Barbara. Vitus is invoked against storms but is also the Patron saint of dancers so balls abound in Vitusary. Medard is invoked against bad weather because he sheltered the beautiful queen Angelica, granddaughter of Saint Marie Angelica, when she fled the intrigues of the Mervol court during a storm. Medard gave his own tent so she would be safe and dry. An eagle sheltered him from the weather, creating an umbrella for him as he rested. Catald cured the ill and is invoked against plagues, which often abound from bad weather. Barbara was saved when lightning struck her attackers during a siege.

3rd: Named after Saint Florien, **Florias** 16 honors Vincent, Jude, & John of Nepomuk (bridges & flooding). Florien is invoked against floods, a common problem in the Saintlands the third month. Saint Vincent Ferrer is the patron saint of builders, often put to work during this time. Jude helps the hopeless. John of Nepomuk strengthens bridges during floods to save the towns.

4th: Named after Saint Elmo, **Elmos** 16 invokes Fiacre (gardeners), Phocas (market gardeners), and Uriel the Archangel. Elmos starts the sailing season, so Saint Elmo, patron saint of sailors marks this month. Fiacre and Phocas bring the first harvests from winter, began indoors or in warmer climes to feed the masses while Uriel protects the people from the lies and trickery of thieves.

5th: Named after Saint Walburga, **Walpurgisnacht** 16 invokes Valentine, Rose of Lima, & Theodore of Sykon (reconciling the unhappily married). Walpurgisnacht 1 allows the young and amorous to pursue each other unhindered and as such, this month marks the beginnings of many marriages. Valentine honors true love. Rose of Lima honors florists and flower growers. Theodore, known for his counseling skills, reconciles the unhappily married, reminding them of the way they felt their first month of marriage.

6th: Named after Saint Wilgefortis, **Vilgfort** 16 honors Felicity (women wanting sons), Monica (wives), & Marie Angelica (nun who married). Felicity is invoked by women wanting sons, usually royals, due to her miracle of delivering sons whenever she was a woman's midwife. Monica honors wives as she was Heaven's example of a perfect wife and Marie Angelica was a nun who married for the sake of the world. A vision held that Marie Angelica would have a daughter who would alter the church and though she was a nun, she was persuaded to leave her vows to fulfill this vision. Her daughter, Tanglwyst Angelica, inherited a powerful shipping company which was destined for the hands of a corrupt Church. Her sacrifice honors all women who must abandon their own dreams for the sake of a greater good.

7th: Named after Saint Maurice, **Maur** 16 honors Elizabeth (war), Clara (savior in the Soulless War) and Michael the Archangel. This is the season of war, and thus, the people invoke Saint Maurice to keep their soldiers safe while away from home while Elizabeth is invoked to find peaceful resolutions to wars. Clara was a woman whose role in the Soulless War enabled the plague to be destroyed through the spreading of soil she had walked upon, preventing the plague from crossing it. Michael fought the creatures of Hell to preserve the faithful during the great wars.

8th: Named after Saint Francis, **Franco** 16 honors Hubert (hunters), Andrew, and Sebastian. Saint Francis honors all animals and those who tend them. Hubert honors the hunters. Andrew the fishermen and Sebastian protects archers.

9th: Named after Saint Thomas Aquinas, **Aquin** 16 honors Ivo, Augustine, and Albert. The season of scholarly pursuits, Aquin honors those who devote themselves to study. Ivo honors lawyers. Augustine honors theologians and his ideals of Heaven are the basis for the Augustinian Church. Albert honors scientists and herbalists.

10th: Named after Saint Benedict, **Benedine** 16 honors Gabriel the Archangel, Giles, & Margaret. As this is a time of darkness descending upon the land and things turning cold, people were often creating tales of ghosts and fear. Those who had died in the wars of the summer or in the professions of the year were often "seen" wandering the desolate places during this month. To counter these tales of fancy, the church brought in their strongest saints against fear and superstition. Saint Benedict fought his greatest fear, being homeless, and opened his home as a shelter. As such, he is their patron saint. Giles protects against night terrors. Margaret defends against those being attacked by devils, enabling their escape. Gabriel the Archangel heralds Heaven's will, driving away doubt and fear.

11th: Named after Saint Ferdinand, **Ferdin** 16 honors All Saints (Fer 1), Eloi, and Anne. To celebrate the survival of the month of fear, All Saints Day was noted as the first Church holiday. It also honors those responsible for the greatest achievements of humanity: Ferdinand for Engineers, Eloi for jewelry and metal smithing and Anne for pregnancy.

12th: Named after Saint Brigit, **Brig** 16 honors Cosmas & Damian, Raymond, and Roch. A most notable saint, Brigit was one of the first saints ascended to Heaven after giving her life to heal others. Her blood created a fountain by which those who were ill or damaged could be restored. This fountain is in the center of the Papal Palace in the Papal City. Cosmos and Damian are conjoined twins who became doctors. Raymond honors midwives. Roch is invoked against epidemics.

Weekdays

Day 1: Honorasday: named from Honoratus, for bakers.

Day 2: Bernaday: Named after Saint Bernadette, shepherds.

Day 3: Rufinasday: Named after Saint Rufina, potters.

Day 4: Simproniday: Named after Four Crowned Martyrs, stonemasons.

Day 5: Julianusday: Named after Saint Julian, boatmen.

Day 6: Vincentsday: Named after Saint Vincent Ferrer, builders.

Day 7: Wencesday: Named after Saint Wenceslas, brewers.

Day 8: Genesday: Named after Saint Genesius, Actors & Comedians.

Day 9: Columbasday: Named after Saint Columba, poets.

Day 10: Dismasday: Named after Saint Dismas, undertakers.

Appendix C: Religions

Augustinian (AHG-us-TIN-ee-uhn)

The Augustinians believe God made the world and made Heaven. God set up the ability for Man to ascend to Heaven body and soul by doing good works. If a human is good enough and helps enough people, they can become a Saint. Each Saint in the Augustinian Rolls was once a human and their name appears in the Heavenly Roster when they ascend. The Heavenly Roster is a book kept in the Papal City on the Official Altar in the center of the Cathedral under constant guard.

In the 1300s, the Church stopped acknowledging new names in the Roster after The War of the Soulless which they blamed upon the heathen religions. The reason cited for this denial was the War made it difficult to believe all the reports of ascended Saints. At the time, it was unknown by the populace about the Heavenly Roster but after the declaration and an investigation by nobles outside the church, this information was revealed to the public. Regardless, once the Pope responsible passed away and the scandal was uncovered, the new Pope acknowledged the updated Rolls and the new Saints were canonized.

The main Tenant of Faith in the Augustinian religion is the Saints are the world's connection to Heaven. It is only by praying to the Saints that one can communicate with Heaven. It is against the Laws of the Church to pray directly to God, bypassing his appointed representatives, to make requests, though one can offer praise unto Heaven without invoking a particular Saint. However, if one prays to a particular saint for guidance or assistance and they receive it, it is against the laws of the Church to not acknowledge the Saint who answered the prayer.

Emilianite (uh-MEEL-ee-uhn-ITE)

After the War of the Soulless and the Scandal of the Unacknowledged Saints, a group of followers broke away from the Church. Citing corruption in the dictations of the papacy, it was determined that apparently the Church could communicate directly to

Heaven without the help of the Saints since they refused to acknowledge the Saints received in the Rolls. They called these Saints "the Abandoned Children" and called themselves Emilianites, after Emilio, the patron Saint of abandoned children.

The Emilianites believe that man cannot be trusted with the will or intent of Heaven through a conduit, for that can be hidden or destroyed. Instead, they believe man can be more assured of correct information if he prays directly to Heaven. If Heaven wants the Emilianites to pray to a Saint, they will communicate that Saint's name to all the Faithful. Until that happens, the Emilianites will pray directly to Heaven. Since the Scandal of the Unacknowledged, no Emilianite has ever noted a Saint's name being given to them. As such, they continue to offer prayers only to Heaven.

Land Worship

The Maker split in two, creating the Heavens and the Land. Both are sentient and great entities unto themselves. Heaven holds the Well of Souls and deals with all things ethereal such as dreams and thoughts, ideas and concepts. The Land deals with all things physical, be it body, plant or liquid. If it can be held, it is the purview of the Land.

When the body dies, the Land takes it into itself and dissolves the flesh, leaving the soul. The soul is filtered and cleansed of the sins of its life and when all the sin is gone, the soul that is left is returned to the Well of Souls. The Land interacts with the people on a daily basis, feeding them, clothing them, healing them. They trust the Land and count on its gifts for life.

Calista's Call

Oceanus, Father of Waters, was alone and lonely. He wandered across the world without drive or direction. Sometimes, to relieve his boredom, he would slice through a mountain or sink an island he made but, in the end, he was aimless and alone. Then, one night, he heard a stirring song. It beckoned him from across the Land and he fell upon a beach, kneeling before the singer. A beautiful maiden of silver hair and glowing pale skin sat naked on the beach, her voice filling the night. He crept up behind her and she saw him and screamed, then grabbed her clothes and fled to the sky.

Every night, he went to the beach to fall upon the shore, begging her to return. He brought her gifts from the sea and faraway lands, creatures and stones, wood and plants. Eventually she peeked from behind the curtain of night and slowly emerged, a little more each night, until she fell in love with Oceanus and they made love upon the beach. They created a daughter of rich blue skin like her father and glowing white hair like her mother. They called her Calista and the salt from their tears of joy at the sight of her soaked her, making her touch turn water into salt water.

Calista watches the sea and keeps her secrets and those of her followers. She is a fickle goddess though, and prone to fits of fury that can seem unprovoked. When she is happy or dealing with honorable people, her hair is the white of sea foam. Mermaids gather the honored dead and if a sailor is a good follower, Calista recognizes them and grants them the ability to live underwater as merfolk in her cities. Her dolphins and sea mammals guide ships through treacherous areas and are always signs of her pleasure.

But she has her primal side as well and when dealing with the dishonorable, she sends her teeth to rend them. Her hair turns bloody red and her sharks and sirens call the evildoers to their destruction. If there is an argument in ship at sea and sharks arrive on the scene, it means someone in the fight is lying. If a criminal is sentenced to death at seas, the sharks will take him, but if the criminal is remorseful, they take him to the depths where he becomes a Marked One and serves Calista for as long as they breathed air. Sirens call the unjust to the sharks' maws so if one hears a siren's call, the heavier the sins on their soul, the harder it is to resist them.

If a body is rendered with fire at death, Calista will know them not and shall cast their spirit out of her mouth to walk the earth forever.

The Ancient Ones

Sovereignlumen was a good king. He loved Magic so much, that he mated with her, and fathered the Fae. The Fae were everywhere. They were the merfolk in the sea and the harpies in the air. They were the pixies and dryads in the trees and the white-furred talking animals in the snows. All the magical creatures, great and small, frolicked in the love of their mother and father. The Fae loved humans and played with them, guiding them to good places and punishing the lazy or wicked with their games and tricks.

But then a sickness came, one that threatened all the magical creatures. Dark men captured the Fae, torturing them to find the sources of Elemental magic. Sovereignlumen roared and rode to war against these dark men and felled them. In the battle, he was mortally wounded and returned home to die. He gave to his four eldest his power, divided as to their gifts.

To his youngest son Embertwist Apocraphix, he gave the powers of Spring. The Vernal Monarch is the quintessential thief and like a thief, it comes in the night, stealing the cold of winter and revealing the living things beneath her skirt. To his oldest son, Corrigan Starshadow, he gave the powers of Summer. As the Midsummer King, his paladin nature marches forthright towards the good and just.

To his oldest daughter, Calpurnia Allegheri, he gave the powers of Autumn. Calpurnia so resembled his beloved Magic, she channels the gifts of change and harvest during her reign as the Autumnal Sovereign. To his youngest daughter, Corrigan's twin, he gave the power of Winter. Gloriana Talnig, the Midwinter Queen, uses the cold to stop disease and preserve and heal, but also to punish the wicked and delay the unjust. The children split and went to different parts of the world to preserve their realms from the followers of the Dark Men, but each season, they return to Sovereignlumin, the great Tower That Watches All to transfer the power of the seasons.

Karma

Karma is all about balance. For each act, there is an equal and opposite reaction in a person's life. As they get closer to the end of their life thread, they can find themselves bound by the threads they have thrown. Negative acts cause sticky threads, positive acts throw stabilizing threads. If a soul has cast more sticky threads than stabilizing, they can be caught up in the negative and it will strangle them. Thus, are many of the symbolic gods of Karma multi-limbed creatures.

The Primordial Egg

The Primordial Egg twitched and cracked and from the shell, four Dragons emerged. They opened their mouths and breathed forth the world. The Earth Dragon formed land and grass, ore and metal, wood and dale. The Water Dragon formed oceans and rivers, lakes and streams, snow and ice. The Fire Dragon breathed the sun and stars to warm the world. And the Air Dragon gave life and the moon. As all things came from magic, all creatures upon the world were magical, and all things communicated with one another in the combined tongue of the elements.

But then, a threat loomed on the face of all and it tried to conquer the magic in the world. It's flashing sword and violent means crushed all but its own belief, slaying the dragons in the world. The Elemental Dragons Rose against it, but to destroy the threat meant to destroy all they loved as well. Instead, they seized their followers and sealed them away in special places. The Earth Dragon hid the giants and Dwarves in the mountains. The Fire Dragon hid her faithful in the ash and lava. The Water Dragon took her children and gave them the ability to breathe water. And the Air Dragon took his children to the sky, to the place between life and death.

At first, they spoke aloud to one another, but monsters found their hiding places, so the Dragons broke the world and spoke only in secret languages so none could find their whereabouts. The Earth Dragon spoke through entrails and omens, the Water Dragon through storms. Fire claimed its own hypnotic power and Air spoke through the dead. Together, they all keep the legends and the magic safe, making certain that only those who wish to keep magic in the world can find them.

Fang and Claw

The practice of having an animal choose to join with a person's soul to guide them is standard practice in the followers of Fang and Claw. They also believe in the consuming a part of the animal allows for that animal's superior quality to enter the consumer.

As a rite of passage, warriors of the tribes will hunt a dangerous animal with which to partner. Shaman may not be led by a dangerous animal, but by a wise one such as Snake or Owl. And those who become the Seers find themselves in the company of spiders.

Appendix D: Countries

Caratia (CUH-ray-SHEE-uh)
    Capital City: Zara
    Native tongue: Caratian (CUH-ray-SHEE-uhn)
    Dominant Religion: Land Worship

Glarren (GLARE-uhn)
    Capital City: Kilmory (kill-MORE-ee)
    Native tongue: Glarren
    Dominant Religion: The Ancient Ones

Krakte (KRAHK-tuh)
    Capital City: Austra
    Native tongue: Krakten
    Dominant Religion: Augustinian, Emilianite, the Ancient Ones

Latia (LAH-tee-uh)
    Capital City: Cheryb (SHARE-eeb)
    Native tongue: Latian (LAH-tee-uhn)
    Dominant Religion: Calista's Call

Mande (MAHND)
    Capital City: Vincenza
    Other Cities: Pardua, Florentine, Calais, Aquila, Balona, Trieste, Naplles, Genoa
    Native tongue: Mandian (MAHN-dee-uhn)
    Dominant Religion: Augustinian

Mervolingia (MER-vole-LIN-jee-uh)
    Capital City: Patras
    Other Cities: Rouen (ROO-en), St. Giles, St. Andrew, St. Marguerite
    Native tongue: Mervol (MER-vol)
    Dominant Religion: Augustinian, Emilianite

Nubia (NOO-bee-uh)
  Capital City: Leeus Brul (lee-OOS bruul)
  Native Tongue: Fangspek
  Dominant Religion: Fang and Claw

The Papal City (PAY-puhl)
  Capital City: None
  Native tongue: Mervol
  Dominant Religion: Augustinian Church Seat

Toledo (toe-LEED-dough)
  Capital City: Tuscan
  Native tongue: Toledan
  Dominant Religion: Land Worship

York (YORK)
  Capital City: Landen
  Other cities: Canterbury, Kent, Oxford, Cambridge
  Native Tongue: Yorkish
  Dominant Religion: Emilianite

Yndia (YIN-dee-uh)
  Capital City: Yantap (YAN-tap)
  Native tongue: Yndian
  Dominant Religion: Karma

Yokotama (YO-ko-TAH-mah)
  Capital City: Kūki doragon
  Native Tongue: Yokotaman
  Dominant Religion: Dance of the Air Dragons

About the Author

Tonya Adolfson has been a member of the Society for Creative Anachronism since 1988 and has met thousands of people with very interesting personas. Many of these people have made it into these books and she is grateful to them for enriching her life.

Tonya lives in Boise, Idaho with her husband, two children, two housemates, four cats and three dogs and yet, strangely, the house is actually pretty clean.